BINOCULAR VISION

BINOCULAR VISION

New & selected stories

EDITH PEARLMAN

PUSHKIN PRESS
LONDON

Pushkin Press
71-75 Shelton Street
London WC2H 9JQ

Original text © Edith Pearlman 2011

First published in the US by Lookout Books in 2011
This edition first published in the UK by Pushkin Press in 2013

ISBN 978 1 908968 1 11

Book design by Claire Bateman and Rachel Jenkins
for The Publishing Laboratory

Proudly printed and bound in Great Britain
by TJ International, Padstow, Cornwall
on Munken Premium White 90gsm

www.pushkinpress.com

for JOSEPH

CONTENTS

INTRODUCTION

TO THAT GREAT LIST of human mysteries which includes the construction of the pyramids and the persistent use of Styrofoam as a packing material let me add this one: why isn't Edith Pearlman famous? Of course by not having the level of recognition her work so clearly deserves, she gives those of us who love her the smug satisfaction of being in the know. Say the words *Edith Pearlman* to certain enlightened readers and you are instantly acknowledged as an insider, a person who understands and appreciates that which is beautiful. Still, I think that *Binocular Vision: New & Selected Stories* should be the book with which Edith Pearlman casts off her secret-handshake status and takes up her rightful position as a national treasure. Put her stories beside those of John Updike and Alice Munro. That's where they belong.

I first read Edith Pearlman when I was the guest editor for *Best American Short Stories*, in 2006. Somehow two of my favorite stories in the more than one hundred I was given to choose from—"On Junius Bridge" and "Self-Reliance"—were by the same writer, a writer I'd never heard of. How was this possible? Katrina Kenison, who was then the series editor, told me that finding new Edith Pearlman stories year after year was one of the greatest pleasures of her job. After a ridiculous amount of consideration, I decided to include "Self-Reliance" in the collection, only because taking two stories by the same author simply isn't done. From there I went straight to her backlist: *How to Fall*, *Love Among the Greats*, and *Vaquita*. My transcendent love for Edith Pearlman was sealed.

But even when love is sealed, it can still grow. When *Best American Short Stories 2006* was published, there was a party for the book in Cambridge, Massachusetts, and for that party three actors were hired to do readings of three of the stories from the collection. It was going to be my job to do the introductions, except that two days before the event, one of the actors fell through. I was told it would be up to me to read "Self-Reliance."

While I am no stranger to giving public readings, there's a big difference between reading your own work and performing someone else's work alongside two professional actors. And so I locked myself in my hotel room and, sitting in the middle of the bed, I practiced. It is not a long story and I easily read it aloud twenty times before I was sure I had it. I am here to tell you: There are very few things that hold up to being read twenty times aloud, and very, very few things that improve with every pass, but the more I subjected "Self-Reliance" to repetition, the more it bloomed. I felt like a junior watchmaker taking apart a Vacheron Constantin. I knew the story was good when I first read it, but when I had read it twenty times I could see that it was flawless. Every word in every sentence was indispensable, every observation subtle and complex. The rhythm of the language carried the reader forward as much as the plot. Every time I thought I had mastered all of the nuances, the story offered up another part of itself to me, something quiet and undemanding that had been standing back and waiting for me to find it. This is not to say that the stories in this book need to be read repeatedly in order to be fully comprehended. It's to say that there is such richness in them, such depth of spirit, that they are capable of taking you as far as you are willing to go.

It is without a trace of vanity that I tell you I brought the house down that night. Edith Pearlman herself was in the audience, which made me feel like I had the lead in *Uncle Vanya* on a night that Chekhov was in attendance. My only challenge was to keep from interrupting myself as I read. So often I wanted to stop and say to the audience, "Did you hear that? Do you understand how good this is?"

A year later, I was asked to give a reading at my public library in Nashville for adult story hour (grown-ups who come together at lunch to hear grown-up fiction) and I had the chance to read "Self-Reliance" again. A repeat performance! The considerable crowd went wild. They wanted to know how they had they never heard of Edith Pearlman before. I told them I understood their confusion. I had used less than half of my allotted hour and so I suggested a discussion of the story.

"No," someone called out. "We want another Pearlman story."

"Read another story," the audience cried.

So I picked up one of her books (it was a library, after all) and started to read aloud. And even though I wasn't prepared, the brilliance of the work carried me through. It turned out to be the second-best reading I have ever given.

When I was asked to write this introduction, an invitation I leapt at, I sat down to read the manuscript with a pen in my hand. I thought it would be a good idea to underline some of the best sentences so I could quote them along the way, but I could quickly see the ridiculousness of that idea. I was underlining the entire book. Okay, I thought, just put a check by your favorite stories so you can be sure to mention them, but by the time I'd finished reading the book, every one of them was checked. Every story.

What you have in your hands now is a treasure, a book you could take to a desert island knowing that every time you got to the end you could simply turn to the front cover and start it all again. It is not a collection of bus crashes, junkies, and despair. Despair is much easier to write about than self-reliance. These stories are an exercise in imagination and compassion, a trip around the world, an example of what happens when talent meets discipline and a stunning intelligence. This collection offers a look at an artist at the height of her powers. Once you have read it, I hope you will go forth and spread the news. Edith Pearlman has been a secret much too long.

ANN PATCHETT
Author of *Run* and *Bel Canto*
Nashville, July 2010

SELECTED STORIES

Inbound

ON THE SUBWAY Sophie recited the list of stations like a poem. Then she read the names from the bottom up. Saying something backward made it easy to remember, sealed it in.

When the family got off at the Harvard Square station she frowned at a platform sign. "Outbound?" she asked her mother.

Joanna was bending over Lily's stroller, adjusting the child's harness. So Ken answered. "Outbound in this case means away from the center of the city," he said. "There are two sets of tracks, coextensive." He paused. Coextensive? Sophie had learned to read at three; her vocabulary at seven was prodigious; still . . . "They coextend," he tried. "One set of tracks carries trains outbound and the other carries them . . . ?"

"Inbound," Sophie said. "Then when we go back to the hotel we'll go inbound. But why aren't the inbound tracks next to these ones? Yesterday, under the aquarium . . ."

Ken inhaled deeply; for a moment Sophie regretted getting him started. "This Harvard Square station used to be the terminus," he told her, "the last stop. When the engineers enlarged the system they ran up against the sewers, so they had to separate inbound and outbound vertically." He had invented this explanation, or maybe he'd heard it somewhere. "Inbound is one level below us." That much he was sure of.

The family walked down a shallow ramp to the concourse. Sophie led the way. Her straight blond hair half covered the multi-colored hump of her new backpack, a birthday gift from her parents. During their early-married travels Ken and Joanna had worn explorers' rucksacks to out-of-the-way places. After Sophie was born they traveled only to France, always with their little girl. This venture from the northern plains, across half the country, was the first family excursion since Lily's birth two years ago. "An excursion is a loop," Joanna had lightly explained to Sophie. "We start from home, we end up at home."

Ken, pushing the heavy stroller and its calm passenger, kept pace with Sophie. Joanna was at his heels, swinging the diaper bag and her scuffed brown pocketbook.

On the concourse Sophie paused. "The stairs are at the left," Ken said. Sophie started toward them, her parents like friendly bears behind her. Other people on the way out pushed through unresisting turnstiles, but because of the large stroller Ken and Joanna and Sophie and Lily had to use the gate near the token vendor's booth. The stairway to the street was broad enough to climb together. Ken and Joanna lifted the stroller between them. All four, blinking, reached the white light of Harvard Square at the same time. Lily, startled and amused by the hawkers, made her familiar gurgle.

"Mama," she said to Ken.

"Dada, darling," he returned.

"Dada."

"Sophie, Sophie, Sophie," said Sophie, dancing in front of the stroller.

"Mama," Lily said.

She was not yet able to say her sister's name, though sometimes, on the living room floor, when Sophie was helping her pick up a toy, Lily would raise her odd eyes and gaze at the older girl with brief interest.

She had Down's syndrome. At two she was small, fair, and unfretful, though Ken and Joanna knew—there was little about Down's that they did not now know—that the condition was no guarantee of placidity. Lily was just beginning to crawl, and her muscle tone was improving; the doctor was pleased. In the padded stroller she could sit more or less erect.

"Lily clarifies life," Sophie had heard her father say to one of his friends. Sophie didn't agree. Clarity you could get by putting on glasses; or you could skim foam off warm butter—her mother had shown her how—leaving a thin yellow liquid that couldn't even hold crackers together. Lily didn't clarify; she softened things and made them sticky. Sophie and each parent had been separate individuals before Lily came. Now all four melted together like gumdrops left on a windowsill.

Even today, walking through the gates of the university that looked like the college where her parents taught, but redder, older, heavier; leaving behind shoppers in Harvard Square; feeling a thudding below their feet as another subway hurtled outbound or inbound; selecting one path within a web of walks in a yard surrounded by buildings . . . even today, in this uncrowded campus, they moved as a cluster.

"Massachusetts Hall," Ken pointed out. "The oldest building in the university. That's the statue of John Harvard over there. And dormitories new since our time—would you like to live here someday, Sophie?"

"I don't know."

Clumped around the stroller they entered another quadrangle. There was a church on one side and, on the opposite side, a stone staircase as wide as three buildings. The stairs rose toward a colonnade. "That's the fifth-biggest library in the world," her father told her.

"What's the . . . sixth?"

He smiled. "The Bibliothèque Nationale in Paris. You were there."

Paris? Sophie recalled stained glass. They'd had to climb narrow, winding stairs to reach a second floor. Her mother, soon to give birth, had breathed hard. Blue light from the windows poured upon them—upon her tall, thin father, her tall, bulging mother, her invisible sister, herself. She recalled the Metro, too, as smelly as day camp.

"The Bibliothèque?" her father said again. "Remember?"

"No."

"Ken," said Joanna.

They drifted toward the fifth-biggest library. Joanna and Ken carried the stroller up the stone stairs. Sophie, in a spasm of impatience, ran to the top, ran down, flew up again. She hid behind a pillar. They didn't notice. She welcomed them at the entrance.

Inside, an old man sat at a desk inspecting backpacks. The family crossed a marble hallway and climbed marble stairs that ended in a nave of computer terminals. At last Lily began to whimper. They pushed the stroller into an area of card catalogs. Joanna picked Lily up. "We'll go into a big reading room," she crooned into a lobeless ear. "We'll look out a window."

Sophie watched them walk away—her mother so narrow in the familiar black coat. "Where are the books?" she asked her father.

"My little scholar," he said, and took her hand.

The entrance to the cave of books was just a door. An ordinary, freckled boy who looked like her high school cousin casually guarded the way. Her father fished in every pocket for the card that would admit them; finally he found it.

"Children—," began the boy.

"Ten minutes," Ken promised. Sophie had heard this tone reassuring a woman who had slipped on the ice in front of their house; her father had used it also to soothe their cat when she was dying of cancer. "We're in town from Minnesota. I want her to see this treasure. *Five* minutes." The boy shrugged.

Sophie followed her father through the door. Her heart, already low, dropped farther, as when some playground kid shoved her. Upright books were jammed shoulder to shoulder within high metal cases, no room to breathe, book after book, shelf above shelf, case following case with only narrow aisles between. Too many books! Too many even if the print were large. This was FLOOR 4 EAST, said painted letters on the wall.

They walked up and down the aisles until they reached the end of 4 East. Then they turned; 4 East became 4 South. Behind a grille stood an aisle of little offices, all with their doors closed. Sophie wondered what her mother was doing. Section 4 West came next. It was just like 4 East, books, books, books; a tiny elevator hunched among them. "Where does that go?" she whispered.

"Up to five and six," he whispered back. "Down to three and two and one and A and B—"

"Are the five minutes up?"

"—and C and D."

This time it was Sophie who led the way—easier than she'd anticipated: you just hugged the perimeter. There was even an EXIT sign. The freckled boy outside nodded at them.

Her mother waited next to the stroller. Lily was sitting in it again, sucking on a bottle. Sophie kissed Lily seven times.

"Was she impressed?" she heard her mother ask.

"Awed," her father said.

She gave Lily a ride, moving among card drawers on wooden legs. Ken and Joanna watched their children appear and disappear.

"Those silent stacks," he said. "The elevator, where I first kissed you—I'd forgotten it." He kissed her again, lightly, on the elegant cheekbone that neither girl had inherited.

She kept her face raised, as if seeking sunlight. Then: "Let's try the museum," she said.

"Sophie will like the Renoirs," Ken agreed.

But at the museum Sophie found the *Seated Bather* spacey. Her father directed her gaze toward a painting of ballerinas haphazardly practicing. What was the point of that? Only one work caught her interest: substantial angels with dense overlapping feathers and bare feet reflected in the sand. "So you like Burne-Jones," he rumbled.

They were soon back on the street again, talking about lunch. Ken and Joanna decided on a favorite restaurant, hoping it still existed. They headed in its direction on a sidewalk next to the backs of buildings. "The library's rear door," Ken said, pointing. Sophie averted her gaze. They crossed the street at the traffic light.

That is, three of them did. Sophie, her head still awkwardly turned, got caught on the curb as the light flashed DON'T WALK. Her parents lumbered away. Other people bore down upon her, blocking her view. By the time the crowd rushed past, the cars on the street had begun to roll again, and she was forced to stand still.

That was all right. Standing still was what she was supposed to do when she became separated from a parent. "If both of us run around, you see, the chances are that we'll never be in the same place at the same time," her mother had explained.

"Like atoms," Sophie said.

"I guess so . . . But if one of us stays put, the moving one will eventually cross the still one's path."

It made sense. Sophie had imagined that, in such an event, she would turn cool, a lizard under a leaf.

Instead she turned hot, even feverish. She sang "Go Tell Aunt Rhody" under her breath. The sign changed to WALK. She sang "Rhody" backward. Her mother would soon cross her path. But her mother could not leave the stroller. The sign changed back to DON'T WALK. Her father, then. He would stride across the street, two leaps would do it, he would scoop her up, he would put her on his shoulder, though she was much too big for such a perch. She would ride there for blocks and blocks; the restaurant would have a peaked roof and a lot of panes in the windows; they always chose restaurants like that.

JOANNA HAD MANEUVERED the stroller rightward, had taken a step or two, had turned back for Sophie, not seen her, looked right, twice, and then left, down a pedestrian walkway, and spotted amid a crowd of kids around a mime the fair hair and multicolored backpack of her daughter. Her heart bobbled like a balloon.

"Where's Sophie?" Ken said at her shoulder.

She pointed confidently and pushed the stroller close to the slanted window of a bakery. She'd lift Lily out and all three would have a good view of the mime—he was deftly climbing an invisible ladder—and of the delighted children, particularly Sophie in her new backpack and her old turquoise jacket, only that kid's jacket was green and she was taller than Sophie and her hair was yellower than Sophie's, much yellower. Only an unnatural parent could mistake that common candle flame for her dear daughter's pale incandescence.

SOPHIE, TELLING HERSELF to stand still, was jostled from behind. She turned to object, but the jostler had disappeared. The sign changed to WALK. Without forethought, though not unwillingly, she leaped into the street.

Sweaty, gasping, she fetched up on the opposite curb. She did not see her family. She saw strollers here and there, but none of them were Lily's; they were the fold-up kind for regular kids. She saw a wheelchair. *That* wasn't relevant, she scolded herself, brushing her nose with the back of her hand. Lily would walk someday. A jester with a painted white face seemed to wave. She ignored him. She drifted toward the center of the square. Earlier she had noticed a newsstand . . . a kiosk, her father had said.

The newsstand turned out to be a bright little house of magazines and newspapers and maps. A man wearing earmuffs sat at a cash register. The place shook slightly every few minutes: the subway was underneath.

There Sophie waited, alone and unknown and free.

By now her parents would have retraced their steps. They had already crossed her empty path.

She felt most comfortable near the far wall. Foreign newspapers overlapped one another. There were French papers. She recognized *Le Monde* from that trip to Paris. *The World*; her father, if he were here, would request the translation. There were newspapers from other parts of Europe, too—she could tell that their words were Spanish or Italian, though she did not know the meanings. In some papers even the alphabets were mysterious. Letters curved like Aladdin's lamp, or had dots and dashes underneath them like a second code. Characters she had seen in Chinese restaurants stood straight up, little houses, each with a family of its own. Lily might learn to read, her mother had said. Not soon, but someday. Until that day, all pages would look like these, confusing her, making her feel more left out. Still, in a few years' time she would be walking. She would stand close to Sophie. Maybe too close. What does it mean? she would whisper. What does it mean? she would whine, and pull at Sophie's sleeve.

The man with the earmuffs gave Sophie an inquisitive look. She turned to study a newspaper. Each word was many letters long, and each letter was a combination of thick and thin lines. She knew all at once that this was German. Her father played Bach on his harpsichord, from a facsimile of an old manuscript; the title and the directions were in German. If Sophie stayed in this pretty little house for the rest of her life she could probably learn one or two of the languages whose alphabet was familiar. Here was how she would do it: she would read the English papers thoroughly and then, knowing the news by heart, she would figure out the words' partners in the other papers.

JOANNA AND KEN were behaving sensibly. Joanna was waiting near the mime, who was now walking an imaginary tightrope. He stopped, alarm on his painted face. He was pretending to lose his balance. His stiffened body canted slowly sideways in discrete jerks like a minute hand until at ten past the hour he collapsed into himself and in a wink became a man hanging from a tightrope, left arm upward and unnaturally long, right one waving desperately, legs splayed.

Ken had gone looking for Sophie. He would follow their route backward to the museum, into the museum, from the Burne-Jones camp-counselor angels to the Degas and the Renoir. He would return to the library if necessary; Joanna imagined his tense interrogation of the man who inspected backpacks. The mime was collecting a thicker crowd; she had to crane her head to watch him. Sophie would enjoy this outdoor show once Ken found her, if she had not been snatched into a car, if she were not to end her life as a photograph on a milk carton. Joanna must not think that way, not not not; she must imagine normal outcomes like normal mothers, like mothers of normal children. The girl has wandered off, ruining our day because of some rush of curiosity, hyperintuitive they call her, *I* call her inconsiderate, doesn't she know enough to make things easier, not harder, don't we have it hard enough already with little Miss Misfit here, oh, my sweet Lily, my sweet Sophie, my darling daughters; and so I'll gaze at Lily dozing and think of Sophie when she was an infant and slept on her side in her crib with arms extended forward and legs too; she looked like a bison on a cave. I remember, I remember . . . *She* probably remembers, she with the genius IQ who can sing songs backward. Ken loves to show off her memory and her queer talents, his prize onion. The mime's pedaling to safety; he's earned that applause. Haven't I got coins for his hat? But I can't leave the stroller, we can't leave each other, any of us. Of course Sophie will remember to stand still as soon as she realizes she's lost. Where would she go? She doesn't know this town. She's seen only the museum, she didn't like it, and the library, she hated it; Ken was hurt. She liked the subway. All kids like the underground: sewers, buried treasure, zombies. All kids like trains. They want to be headed somewhere, inbound, outbound . . .

Ken's face was putty.

"The library?" she needlessly asked.

"No," he panted.

"Come," Joanna said. "I know where she'll go."

SOPHIE, WRIGGLING ONE ARM out of the backpack, decided to start with the French newspapers. She was to study French next year anyway, with the rest of the special class. But she was pretty sure that she wouldn't soar with the new subject. She was tied to her first language, hers and Lily's. Still, she'd learn the rules. She'd listen and sometimes talk. Now, staring at *Le Monde*, pretending that the man with earmuffs had gone home, she let her eyes cross slightly, the way she wasn't supposed to, and she melted into the spaces between the paragraphs until she entered a room beyond the newsprint, a paneled room lit by candles, walled in leather volumes, the way she had wanted the fifth-biggest library to look. Though more books had been written than she could ever read—she had realized that as soon as she saw Section 4 East—she would manage to read a whole lot of them, in golden dens like the one she was seeing. She would read as many as her parents had read. She would grow as large as her parents had grown. Like them she would study and get married and laugh and drink wine and hug people.

Steadied by this vision, she let herself look further. Her life would be lived in the world, not in this paper house. She foresaw that. She foresaw also that as she became strong her parents would dare to weaken. They too might tug at her clothing, not meaning to annoy.

Lily would never leave her. "She will always be different, darling," her mother had said. At the time Sophie had thought that her mother meant we will always be different. Now she added a new gloss: I will always be different.

She felt her cheek tingle, as if it had been licked by the sad, dry tongue of a cat. At full growth Lily's head would be almost level with Sophie's shoulder. Lily would learn some things. Mostly she would learn Sophie. They would know each other forward and backward. They would run side by side like subway tracks, inbound and outbound. Coextensive.

She had to return to her family now; she had to complete the excursion. She shoved her free arm into the strap and settled the backpack on her shoulders. She walked past the man in earmuffs without saying good-bye.

KEN AND JOANNA bumped the stroller down the subway stairs. Ordinarily they would have joined the line at the token vendor's booth to be admitted through his gate. Instead Joanna inserted a token and hurried through the turnstile. Ken handed her their little girl across the device. He pressed his own token into the slot and turned around and lifted the stroller above his head and burst through the stile buttocks first. They put Lily back into the stroller and rushed toward the ramps.

"Outbound?" said Ken.

"She knows better."

On the ramp they had to arc around an old woman who had paused mid-journey with her trash bag on her left and her collapsible cart on her right. "That's okay," she called.

The inbound train had just left. The platform held five people who had missed it: three students, one bearded man, and a tall black woman—an islander, Joanna could tell; her regality proclaimed her origins, that magazine under her arm was probably in French.

Sᴏᴘʜɪᴇ ᴡᴀsɴ'ᴛ ꜰᴀʀ ʙᴇʜɪɴᴅ ᴛʜᴇᴍ. She had found the subway entrance as soon as she left the little house. While her father was bearing the empty stroller backward through the turnstile, she was beginning her descent from the street. While her mother was choosing inbound, Sophie was thinking about joining the line of token buyers, of promising to pay later. She decided not to risk conversation with the man in the booth. By the time her parents reached the inbound platform she was slipping underneath the turnstile. She started down the ramp.

She saw them before she reached the bottom. Her mother sat on a bench, holding Lily in her lap. Her father, standing, bent over them both. They looked like everyday people, but Sophie wasn't fooled—her mother's knees were knocked together under her coat and her feet were far apart, their ankles bent inward so wearily that the anklebones almost touched the floor. Without seeing her father's face, she knew he was close to tears. An old woman with a cart leaned against the wall. As Sophie appeared the woman said, "Now your reunion," in a conversational tone, though rather loud.

Ken turned and unbent: a basketball replay in slow motion.

Joanna took relief like an injection; pain was killed and feeling as well. She saw that the child had undergone some unsettling experience, but Joanna had no sympathy to offer now. Perhaps this once Sophie would be given the blessing of forgetfulness.

And indeed Sophie moved forward with a light tread, as if she had not just witnessed the future unrolling.

Lily attended slackly. But then she raised her mittened hand.

"Phie!"

Day of Awe

He was the last Jew in a cursed land.

A ruined country, a country of tricksters. Rich haciendas hid within the folds of mountains. Guns lay under crates of bananas. Even the green parrots practiced deception. They rested in trees, not making a sound; suddenly they rose as one, appearing and departing at the same time, leaving the observer abandoned.

The only Jew!

In truth, there was a second Jew: his son, Lex. They faced each other across the kitchen table. Lex seemed to pity the plight of his father: that on the eve of Yom Kippur there was no corner in the city where a Jew could pray for forgiveness with nine others.

"They all fled to Miami after the revolution," Lex said. "Taking their money with them."

Robert winced.

Lex said, "We'll find you a minyan, Bob." He looked at his father with compassion.

But was it really compassion? Or was it the practiced understanding of a professional social worker? Just as he had adjusted to his son's use of his first name, Robert had reconciled himself to Lex's womanish vocation. But he had not become accustomed to the nods, the murmured assents. He himself was an investment consultant.

"We've gone through the guidebooks," Lex reviewed. "Shall we hunt down a Shapiro in the telephone book? A Katz?"

Father and son laughed. Their own name was Katz.

The little boy looked from one to the other.

He was a thin child despite a seemingly insatiable appetite. His name, Jaime, printed in Lex's hand, adorned the crayoned scribbles taped to the refrigerator.

There they sat, in front of those unambitious efforts, in the scarred kitchen of a small house on a muddy street in the capital city of a Jewless country. Robert was still wearing his pajamas. Far away in Beverly Hills, the drawings of Robert's granddaughter, Lex's niece, also decorated a refrigerator. *Maureen Mulloy*, the signature read. Maureen Mulloy printed her washerwoman's name herself. The Mulloys' Mexican housekeeper hung up the artwork. Who else could do it?—Maureen's parents practiced law twelve hours a day.

Jaime. It was pronounced "Hymie." Robert speared a slice of papaya from the breakfast platter.

Lex was reading the telephone book. "No Shapiros, Bob. No Katzes, either. I'm not even listed—my phone belongs to the organization."

Robert ate a slice of pineapple.

"I'm going to call the embassy," Lex said.

"Ex," said Jaime, slapping Lex's arm. "Tengo hambre."

"Qué quiero?" Robert attempted. "I mean, qué *quieres* . . ." Lex had already risen. He and Jaime stood side by side, composedly surveying the contents of the refrigerator, a slight young man and a very slight child. "Qué quieres," Robert repeated, softly. His hesitant spoken Spanish was getting him nowhere with the boy. Why had he spent a month listening to those damned language tapes? Why had he come here, anyway?

Five days ago he had descended the aluminum steps of the airliner and stepped onto the tarmac, already blistering at two in the afternoon. He was used to hokey airports. He wasn't used to the absence of jet lag, though—he seldom journeyed from north to south. The sun had stood still on his behalf. No need to nap, no need even to eat, though on the ride from the airport Jaime insisted on stopping for a tamale. "Ex, Ex!" he shouted, pointing to the stall. Lex pulled over. Robert smiled at Lex, indulgent parent communing with indulgent parent. But Lex ignored the smile. His attentiveness toward this soon-to-be-adopted son was meant to be approved, not joined.

The boy dropped consonants, confusing Robert. That first

afternoon, Robert looked at a picture book with him. *Vaca*, cow, became *aca*; *caballo*, horse, *callo*. Little Maureen would become Een, he supposed, if the cousins—could he really call them that?—ever met. They might not meet for a long time. The family was scattered: Robert and Betsy in Massachusetts, their daughter Mulloy née Katz out in California, Lex here in Central America two years already, God knew how much longer.

"I'll stay until the adoption is final," Lex said late that night, after Jaime had finally gone to bed. "That's another six months. Afterwards . . ." He shrugged his thin shoulders. "I won't go to Chicago, that's for sure. I don't want to be in the same city as Ron." Ron was his ex-lover. "Perhaps Jaime and I will come back to Boston."

Robert nodded. "There's a bilingual program in the schools."

"Spare us." Lex rolled his eyes. "We'll continue to talk Spanish at home," he went on. "Jaime will pick up English at school, in playgrounds—as immigrant children have done for generations."

He can hardly speak his own language, Robert didn't say. *He can't count. He doesn't know colors.* "How old is he? Seven, you wrote? He's . . . small."

"We use the evidence of bones and teeth," said Lex. "Central Americans are smaller than North Americans, and those with a lot of Indian blood, like Jaime, are the shortest. I'll invent a birth date when I apply for his passport. I'm going to say he's five. He's about three emotionally—a deprived three. No one ever sent him to school. When I first met him at the local orphanage a year ago he didn't talk at all. He's matured considerably since being with me."

Robert felt weary, as if jet lag had claimed him after all.

And so he had gone to bed, in the narrow room off the kitchen. His window faced an inner courtyard just big enough for a clothesline, a sink, and a single tree that bore hard citrus fruits. There the parrots hid.

After Sunday, Robert was on his own for a few days. Lex was working, and Jaime attended day care. Robert awoke each morning to the sounds of the two at their breakfast. He figured out most of what they were saying. Jaime repeated the breakfast menu, the few chores, the routine of the day care center. Then he repeated them again, and again. Between repetitions Robert heard the rustle of the newspaper and the slur of rubber wheels along a linoleum floor. Jaime was playing with his small toy car. He supplied the motor with his own throat. "Oom!" Twenty-five years earlier, Robert and Betsy had shared the *Globe* while, at their feet, two charming toddlers rummaged in a pile of Legos. Jaime wasn't ready for Legos, Lex had explained. He wasn't ready even for the starter set Robert had brought as a gift. Jaime didn't get the idea of construction. He had probably never seen toys before the orphanage found him— maybe he'd played with a couple of spoons, or filled an old shoe with dirt. Maureen, Robert remembered with satisfaction and guilt, could already erect elaborate towers.

Before leaving for work, Lex always knocked on Robert's half-open door.

"Entra!" Robert practiced.

Lex would then say something about the day ahead. Would Robert like to visit the university? Lex could give him a library pass. If he wandered into the outdoor market, would he please pick up a pineapple? Jaime, still on the floor with his murmuring car, poked his head between Lex's knees and then raised it, his little golden face between the denimed legs solemn, or perhaps only uncomprehending.

When they were gone Robert heaved himself out of bed. He boiled bottled water for tea and ate three plain crackers. Despite this abstemious caution he invariably passed several loose stools and a quantity of brownish water. "Nothing to worry about as long as there's no blood," Lex had told him after the first episode, the second night of the stay. Lex's voice had been reassuring but his lips were prissy; and Robert, standing outside the bathroom with his belt unbuckled, raised a defiant chin like a child who had soiled his pants.

But the morning diarrhea always left him feeling better, as if he had explosively asserted himself in these austere surroundings. He next read the front page of the newspaper, using the dictionary often. Then he took a shower in cold water and shaved in cold water and got dressed. He stuffed his fanny pack with map, dictionary, currency, and flask. He wore it frontwards: a tummy pack. After putting on sunglasses and a canvas cap, he left the house.

He had arrived on a Saturday; by the end of Wednesday, the day before, he had tramped all over the city. He had wandered into the barrios. He refused Chiclets and Valium peddled by street vendors. He stumbled upon a small archaeological museum tended by some devoted women. There he learned that the great-beaked toucan was considered an incarnation of the devil.

And he stared at the windowless edifice within which members of the National Assembly, according to the new popular insult, farted their disagreements. He traveled by bus to two hot, dusty towns. Both had museums of martyrs. Back in the capital, he had spent late Wednesday afternoon at the huge outdoor market. Pickpockets roamed the place, he had heard. He kept his fingers lightly on his canvas pack.

He bought Betsy a necklace of black coral. Though he loved and admired her, he missed her very little. Her absence this trip had not been a matter of dissension—they had farted no disagreements. There were reasons for her not coming: Lex himself had been home recently; his house here had only a single guest bed; and this not altogether regular situation—a young man becoming a father to a young boy—seemed to demand the presence of an unaccompanied older man, *the* older man, the grandfather.

Grandfather! To a child whose whole being seemed at odds with itself—the eyes soft, even tender; the mouth, with its widely spaced teeth, slack; the body taut, subject to occasional spasms. Yet he would become part of the family, a Katz. Jaime Katz. What would Robert's grandfather, a rather sallow person himself, have made of such a development? He recalled Zayde Chaim shawled in silk on the Days of Awe . . . and it was at that moment, standing in the market, his hand on his canvas belly, that he remembered what day it was. The day before the day before Yom Kippur. In twenty-six hours, Kol Nidre would be sung.

Now, on Thursday morning, the embassy answered Lex's inquiry: to its knowledge there was no community of Jews in the city, in the country. Lex hung up. "They have one Jewish staff member. She goes home to Texas for the holidays."

"We've struck out."

"I'm sorry," Lex said, and stood up. "I have to go to work. About tonight . . . I had forgotten Yom Kippur . . . a few people from the organization are supposed to come for dinner."

"Let them come," Robert said. "I'm not such a worshipper, you know. I don't fast. At your bar mitzvah I had to retool my Hebrew, and even then it wasn't so hot."

"Jaime?" Lex called into the bedroom. "Rápido, por favor." He turned again to his father. "You worked over those syllables like a diamond cutter. Betsy used the transliteration."

"She'd never studied Hebrew."

"But you were heroic. For my sake." He bowed his head.

"I wish I could do it again with my high school Spanish," said Robert, hot with embarrassment.

Lex raised his head. "For his sake," he said, indicating with what seemed to Robert a faggy lift of one shoulder the child in the bedroom. A vat of lava bubbled in Robert's intestines; he managed to contain it. How reckless he'd been to eat that fruit. Jaime was taking his sweet time putting on his backpack. The shabbiest barrio kid in this mess of a country had a backpack. "Vámonos!" Lex said at last.

Jaime came running. Lex went outside to warm up the Jeep. Jaime turned in the doorway and waved a silent good-bye to Robert—he had yet to call him by name. Farewell here was signified by a beckoning gesture. The motion startled Robert every time; it startled him now. He took a step forward, as if the child were really summoning him. Then he halted, hissing. This place! An invitation to come closer was made in an equally ass-backward manner: wrist limp, you wagged the back of your hand at the person you wanted, as if shaking him off.

Was the child laughing at him? No, it was only one of those wet smiles. Robert dutifully mimicked Jaime's come-hither movement. He felt like a cop directing traffic. He felt like a dirty old man. Jaime grinned and banged out. Robert bolted for the bathroom.

HE SPENT YOM KIPPUR EVE with a gaggle of gentiles. They weren't bad, Lex's fellow workers. A high-minded couple in their sixties, slack of belly, gray of hair, giving their final years to just causes. A pretty young nurse. A second, older nurse, freckled and tough. Some others. They ate rice and beans, expertly seasoned by Lex. Jaime played on the floor. Occasionally he whined for Lex's attention. Lex would finish what he'd been saying, then he'd turn his eyes to the boy and listen to the high voice repeating short, insistent phrases, and reply with a "sí" or a "no" or some grave explanation.

The adults talked of the torments of the country, the centuries of cruelty as one generation mistreated the next. "The church has a lot to answer for," said a fierce Canadian woman. "Those first missionary schools—they taught us how to inflict pain." He wondered what she meant by "us"; then he remembered that she was a Native American, a member of an indigenous people. He had met her earlier in the week when she'd dropped by. With her untidy hair and glasses and dissatisfied mouth she'd reminded him of his cousin from the Bronx. He'd met the churchy couple earlier also, at an evening lecture on cooperatives that Lex had taken him to. But this was the first social gathering Robert had attended, and he realized belatedly, when it was almost over, that it was a party in his honor.

Early the next morning they packed up the Jeep. They were to spend the weekend visiting orphanages in the mountains—Robert, Lex, Jaime, and Janet—the freckled nurse, not the pretty one.

Janet did the driving. She knew how to handle a Jeep. She drove fast on the two-lane highway, passing whenever she could. When they were stopped by a pair of very young men in fatigues, each holding a tommy gun, she answered their questions with such authority that Robert expected the teenage soldiers to stick out their tongues for her inspection. Instead they waved the Jeep on. Robert jounced along in the front seat. In the back Lex showed Jaime how the big bricks of Legos fit together. Jaime watched indifferently, his fingers around his toy car.

They stopped late in the morning in a lush little town. There were coffee estates nearby, Janet said. In the courtyard of a restaurant, parrots watched from fronds. Jaime ran toward a cat he knew and settled down in a corner of the courtyard. The proprietress-cook brought the child a dish of pasta before welcoming the others in perfect English. She had a large, curved nose and a wide smile. "She's Chilean," Janet said when the woman had returned to the kitchen. "Her corn lasagna is terrific. She's been active in revolutionary politics." Robert understood: arms smuggling.

Two graceful waiters with angelic faces served them. Robert knew not to take their androgyny seriously. "Girlish on the outside, tough guys within," Lex had said about similar men. "Not gay." Robert did not ask whether Lex had enjoyed a native lover. Some years ago he had ascertained that his son practiced safe sex; he and Betsy wanted to know nothing further.

The corn lasagna was indeed delicious. Jaime shared his pasta with the cat. Robert would have liked to linger over coffee, to walk around this town and visit its museum of martyrs; to return at the cocktail hour and enjoy an aperitif with the South American adventuress while the parrots dozed. Instead he paid the bill and shook her hand and bid good-bye to the birds with the proper summoning gesture.

In an hour they had left the highway and were climbing. Farms gave way to trees, boulders, scrub. Janet expertly circled craters in the road. Bracing himself against the plunges of the Jeep made Robert weary—or perhaps it was the lunchtime glass of Chilean wine. He leaned against the headrest, closed his eyes . . . and was awakened by something creeping along the side of his neck. He slapped the creature. It was a small hand.

"Sorry, Jaime. Excúlpame. Hey!" for the child had slapped him back.

"Jaime." Lex's voice was as authoritative as Janet's. Some low, rapid Spanish followed. Then came a tap on the shoulder and a presentation across that shoulder, in front of his face, of three Lego bricks imperfectly joined.

"Asa," Jaime said.

Casa. House. "Bueno," Robert said, mustering enthusiasm. He turned to meet those attractive eyes, that odd mouth. Lex smiled primly.

Just before two o'clock they reached the town where they were to spend the night. Robert carefully got out.

"You need a back rub," noticed Janet.

The town square was a bare knoll. A church faced the square. Its stucco walls seemed to be unraveling. The one-storied inn sagged toward its own courtyard. Robert was shown to a rear bedroom. From his window he could see oxen.

Janet and Lex invited him to walk to the orphanage with them. "Thanks, no," he said. "I'll sit in the courtyard and read." And write another postcard to little Maureen.

But as soon as they had tramped off, he felt forlorn. He would not stay; he would follow his son.

They had told him that the orphanage lay two miles out of town, on the straight road west. He walked fast, at first. Within five minutes he had caught sight of them, and soon he was passing the low stone huts that they had just passed, each with its open door revealing a single room, the same room—a couple of cane rockers, a table.

The same expressionless woman stood in each doorway. Children played in the mud. Had Jaime been born in such a home? More likely he had sprung from a shack like those Robert was passing now—tin and slats, the latrine in back made decent by a curtain.

Lex and Janet walked together in the middle of the road. Jaime darted from one side to the other. Janet was taller than Lex. Her light brown hair humped over her backpack and draggled, khaki on khaki.

At the end of the road a crowd of small boys waited behind a gate—just a couple of horizontal logs—a not entirely successful attempt to keep out nearby animals. Jaime scrambled between the logs. Lex and Janet vaulted them.

Robert climbed over the top log, his bones creaking. He heard, as if in the distance, the sound of crying. Perhaps it was his own old-man's wail.

HE HAD LANDED amid the boys. Boys, boys everywhere. Boys: grimy triangular faces under black bangs. Boys: wearing clothing that a decade ago and a continent away had been high style—rugby shirts, jams. Boys: none seeming above ten years old, though he knew better. Perhaps some were twelve. Boys: waiting for guns and cholera.

"Bob!" Janet cried. Lex smiled a welcome.

They made immediate use of him, sending him to listen to the complaints of the orphanage director, a fiery young man with a thin mustache. Robert, sitting down, surrounded by boys, riffling through his dictionary every few words, managed to make out that the problem was money, both cash and credit. Supplies were low. The last cook had made off with the radio. Robert wrote down everything the fellow said and then got hustled away to umpire a three-inning softball game. The boys were not adroit. Then Lex arranged an obstacle race. Robert was assigned to hold an inflated clown's hand in front of his chest. This hand had come out of Janet's backpack; she'd blown it up in three exhalations, her freckles enlarging and then diminishing on her cheeks. Each obstacle racer had to slap the hand; some kids slapped Robert by mistake. Their teeth were as white as Chiclets.

Soon they were corralled into a grim refectory. "Cerca me!" some pleaded. He sat down next to a little beige fellow with reddish hair.

All the boys were given crayons and paper. The stuff might have been gold. They drew for half an hour, in blissful silence. Meanwhile Janet examined some inflamed ears—she had an otoscope in her backpack, too. Lex talked with a scowling child in the director's meager office. The child looked less angry after the session.

Robert praised the artwork. He helped the artists print their signatures. The red-haired runt was Miguel O'Reilly. Miguelito was particular about the slant of the apostrophe in his name.

These outcasts—did they know how deprived they were? Lex had told him about them: some abandoned at the gate as infants, some starved and abused before they arrived as toddlers, some rescued from prostitution, or at least reprieved from it. Jaime had served for a while as the mascot of a street gang.

To the boys Robert must seem a patriarch. They were respectful of his Spanish—the stunted vocabulary, the lisp of remote conquerors. They were respectful of his gray hairs, too. In their country a man of his age should already be dead.

The light was reddening, the shadows were lengthening, the parrots would presently lift themselves without a sound from their trees. The afternoon would soon end. Somewhere, elsewhere, maybe in Miami, a congregation was praying together, was feeling united, singular, almost safe.

A child with a birthmark asked to inspect his watch, looked at it gravely, then returned it with a smile. Two others insisted on showing him their dormitory. He peered under the iron cots; he was supposed to laugh at something there, though all he could see was dust. Perhaps a mouse had recently scampered.

He sat down heavily on a cot, startling the children. He drew them close, one against each knee. They waited for his wisdom. "Avinu malkeinu," he muttered.

A bell rang: dinner. They stiffened. He let them go.

Oh the thin, hard, greedy boyness of them, undersized nomads fixed for a few years in a patch of land at the end of nowhere. Cow shit in the yard. Beans for dinner on the good days.

Jaime had entered all the play. He'd had a very good time.

They walked back to the inn in the dusk. Some of the huts were little stores, Robert now noticed. Dim bulbs shone on canned goods and medicines. Televisions flickered in the remote interiors, illuminating hammocks. How misleading to call this world the third. It was the nether.

Lex had packed a cooler of sandwiches and Cokes that morning. "Jaime can't manage a second restaurant in one day," he now explained to his father.

"What was the first?" Robert wondered. Then he remembered, as if from a rich tapestry seen long ago, the smile of the Chilean woman and the knowing supervision of her lime parrots.

"I have enough food for us all," Lex said.

Janet shook her head. "I'm going to take your father to the café."

The café, behind the inn, was an open kitchen and three tables. A couple of men dined together at one of the other tables. No menu: today's offering was chicken in a spicy sauce. Robert hoped his stomach could manage it. He bought a bottle of rotgut wine.

"L'chaim," Janet said.

He raised his eyebrows.

"My great-grandfather's name was Isaac Fink," she said. "He was a peddler who wandered into Minnesota by mistake, and stayed. The family is Lutheran to its backbones. Still . . ."

"Still, you are somewhat Jewish," he said politely. "Skoal."

They spoke of Lex's talent and of Jaime's eagerness. They spoke of the children they'd seen that afternoon, and of Janet's work. She planned to spend another few years here. "Then a master's in public health, I think." Her face grew flushed. "I was serious about giving you a back rub."

And perhaps this part-Jew would be willing also to inspect his tongue and massage his weary abdomen. He had assumed she was lesbian. She probably was lesbian. One could be something of everything here. "Thanks, but no," he said. "It's Yom Kippur night."

"Oh, I see," was her bewildered response.

In bed alone he found himself wondering whether the handsome Chilean chef might also be a little bit Jewish. And that native Canadian woman from last night's party—such an expert kvetch. He and Lex should have searched harder for eight more Jews. In a room behind a tailor shop in some town lived a pious old man, too poor to have fled to Miami. In one of the squalid barrios a half-Jewish half-doctor dealt in abortifacient herbs. Atop a donkey, yarmulke concealed by a sombrero, a wanderer sold tin pans.

The entire population could be Jewish, Jaime included: people descended from Indians who feared the toucan—what was a toucan but a bird with a schnoz?—and from haughty Marranos who prayed to Yahweh in the basements of basements.

THE NEXT MORNING found him at last master of his bowels. He packed his overnight case and walked across the square to the crumbling church. Inside, though Christ on the wooden cross was naked, plaster saints wore velvet robes. The townspeople, too, seemed dressed up. He spotted one of the men he'd seen in the café last night. Today the man was sporting the yellow jacket of a gaucho.

Robert sat near the back and listened to the Mass. The sermon began. He did not attempt to understand it, though the Spanish was slow and simple, and the subject was *misericordia*, mercy. *Rachamim*. He thought about Lex, now packing the Jeep for the day's trip to more orphanages. Lex was settling the bill, too. "This trip's on me," he'd said, refusing Robert's money. An admirable, disappointing fellow. *May you, too, have a son like mine*, Robert thought—the old curse, the old blessing.

A small hand fell on his arm. He twisted his head and saw Jaime. The child danced away, then turned and stood in the open double doorway. Behind him was the treeless square; behind that was the inn, some other houses, the rising hills.

"Ob," Jaime hissed. "Ob!" and he flapped his hand as if warding off a nuisance. Get lost, he seemed to say. Come here, he meant to say. Robert knew the difference now.

Ob. *Ab. Abba*, father, Abraham. *The father of a multitude of nations have I made thee.* Have you? Through whom? Through Maureen Mulloy, a half mick? Through Jaime Katz, an indigenous person?

A multitude of nations: what a vainglorious idea. No wonder we are always in trouble. How about a few good-enough places? he said silently to the priest, to the Christ, to the God rustling in his ear. How about a people that takes care of its children, even those springing from unexalted seed . . .

"Ob!"

Robert rose. He followed his grandson out of the dark, merciful church and into the harsh light.

Settlers

ONE EARLY SUNDAY MORNING Peter Loy stood waiting
for the bus downtown. It was October, and the wind was strong
enough to ruffle the curbside litter and to make Peter's coat flap
about his knees, open and closed, open and closed. He wouldn't
have been sorry if the wind had removed the coat altogether, like
a disapproving valet. It had been a mistake, this long glen-plaid
garment with a capelet, suitable for some theatrical undergraduate,
not for an ex-schoolteacher of sixty-odd years. He had thought that
with his height and thinness and longish hair he'd look like Sher-
lock Holmes when wearing it. Instead he looked like a dowager.

It didn't matter; this was not a neighborhood that could afford
to frown on oddities. Brighton Avenue, where he now stood, was a
shabby main street. Congdon Street, where he lived, was home to
an assortment of students, foreigners, and old people. A young couple with matching briefcases had recently bought one of the peel-
ing houses in the hope that the street would turn chic; they spent
all their free time gamely stripping paint from the interiors. On
weekday mornings white-haired women in bathrobes stared from
apartment windows while their middle-aged daughters straggled
off to work, and then kept on staring. The immobility of the stay-
at-home mothers suggested that their daughters had locked them
in, but often at noontime Peter would see one of them moving toward the corner. Her steps would lighten as she neared Brighton
Avenue. Here was life! Fresh fish, fish-and-chips, Fishberg the opti-
cian . . . Also on Congdon Street was a three-storied frame building

with huge pillars and sagging porches—a vaguely Southern edifice. Inside lived an entire village of Cambodians.

Peter had moved to this seedy section of Boston three years earlier, upon his retirement from the private boys' academy where he'd taught English. His plain apartment here pleased him far more than his aunt's town house in Back Bay. He had dragged out several decades in that town house, first as his aunt's pampered guest and then as her legatee. He had sold it for a good price to the young self-made millionaire next door, Geronimus Barron. No one had hurried Peter out after the sale, though he was eager enough to leave; but within a month of his departure, Barron had knocked down the wall between the houses, gutted entire floors, and installed solar panels and skylights. The magnificent place that resulted was featured in *Architectural Digest* and the *New York Times*. The lovely tiled fireplace in his own bedroom, Peter noted with pride, remained untouched.

The bus came. The few passengers aboard already looked fatigued. Peter, his own heart light under his silly coat, began the weekly journey.

"How's the research?" Meg Wren was asking him a few hours later.

Jack and the three children were playing with a soccer ball in the field in back of the house. The field sloped gently toward the woods. A mile away was the Sudbury River. Peter couldn't see the river now, from the kitchen, but he could glimpse it from the third-floor guest room where he stayed whenever he spent the night.

"I'm having trouble placing Mrs. Jellyby," Peter said.

"Mrs. Jellyby?" Meg repeated, wrinkling her long brow.

Peter waited. Her blue gaze was intelligent, but he was not sure exactly how well read she was. She had been born and raised in Wisconsin and had come east after college, almost fifteen years ago, and had quickly married one of his former students. They'd met at church. "*Bleak House*?" Meg said.

"*Bleak House*," Peter commended. "Mrs. Jellyby is the crackpot who spends all her time collecting money for the natives of Borrioboola-Gha. Her own ragged children keep tumbling down the stairs. Their house is filthy and falling apart. 'Never have a mission,' her poor husband warns the heroine. These days we would applaud Mrs. Jellyby's selflessness. We'd be glad to know that she cares about Africa—funny how some things never change."

"'Ye have the poor always with you'?"

"Yes, and they're always the same poor. Mrs. Jellyby carries her ardor to excess and neglects the need nearest her. Not a very Christian form of charity."

Peter paused. He had been lecturing to Meg, taking advantage of her daughterly attention. In years spent among self-important high school teachers and garrulous old ladies, he had accustomed himself to the listener's role. Now he had found someone who listened as attentively as he did. It was as if she had inherited the talent from him—or, since that was impossible, had caught it. And this house of hers—so old, and so fresh—it too seemed to want to hear what he had to say. "Mrs. Jellyby's philanthropy isn't very Jewish, either," he went on. "You could make a case that her charity is in Maimonides' seventh degree—she doesn't know the names of the people she's relieving and they've certainly never heard of her. But Dickens meant her to be a figure of fun, and he keeps arguing with me. He says that Maimonides was talking about charity closer to home, and that Mrs. Jellyby doesn't qualify at all . . . I do get a bit carried away, don't I?"

Meg was silent. Of all the silences he had ever experienced, Meg's was his favorite. It was not disappointed, like his mother's; not bored, like those of the women he had courted; not embarrassed, like that of the search committee that had failed to award him the headmastership; not sleepy, like students in late-afternoon remedial classes; and not terrifying, like his mute aunt after her stroke.

"I think you're enjoying this task," she said after a while.

"Carrot scraping?" he said, smiling. He had been scraping carrots for her while they—he—talked.

"Thinking about Dickens and Maimonides," she said. "Finding Maimonides' eight levels of charity in the novels of Dickens," she carefully amended. "It does sound . . . nice. I knew you were interested in Dickens. But I didn't know you were interested in Judaism."

"I'm not interested in Judaism. Only in Jews. They're so complicated . . ."

"Mmm," she responded, noncommittally.

"Always have been." At Harvard just after the war he had noticed that his brightest classmates were the Jewish boys. They were at home with Swift's grotesques and Jane Austen's ingenues. Mastering Middle English was a snap after Hebrew. Shakespeare's tales were just another set of Midrashim. Every exchange with one of those students had left Peter admiring and envious. He wondered what encounters Meg had thus far endured—dinner-party debate? Lordly attempts at seduction? . . . And here was her husband, open-faced, steady as the junior high school principal he was. He walked in grinning, his arm outstretched.

The three children bounded in behind Jack: two boys and a little girl. The younger boy's hair matched the pumpkin on the windowsill. Meg said that his coloring came from her side of the family, though her own smooth hair was brown. The children greeted Peter lightly, as if a week had not gone by since they last saw him; as if he hadn't spent more than an hour on bus, trolley, and little train; as if he lived there always. Someday he must really live there, Meg had said more than once. The third-floor room was just the place to retire from his retirement.

AFTER LUNCH the three adults drank hot cider under an apple tree and talked about the children.

"They're lazy," Jack said. "I tried to teach Ned chess the other day. Too difficult, he said. Checkers is good enough for him."

Meg said, "It's good enough for a lot of people."

"Oh, Meg. We send them to private schools. We shore up this old house for them." He wasn't complaining, Peter noticed; he was proud.

"You spend two hours a day commuting," Meg added.

"I do. So they've got to," Jack said.

"Got to what?" she said, laughing.

"Play chess." And he laughed, too. "What do you think, Peter?"

"What do I think about what?" Peter hedged.

"About our three hooligans. About the worth of private education. About the country life." Jack breathed deeply. Generations of farmers and ministers expressed themselves in that pleased inhalation. The house had always been in his family; some ancestor had built it. A century ago he would have farmed the land with his sons and a few hired hands. They would have made a genteel go of it. The boys would have gone to Harvard as a matter of course. Now he had to weary himself every day as a schoolmaster, and his children would have to compete for college places against the grandchildren of longshoremen and Pullman porters. To strengthen them for the fight, Meg drove them to their Cambridge school every morning and home again in the late afternoon. In the interval she worked as a programmer, also in Cambridge.

Peter said, "I think the house is its own reward."

The stone wall in the garden was reddened by the afternoon sun. The kitchen windows gleamed like water. Roses bloomed with a soft fire—there would be one or two still glowing as late as Thanksgiving, Peter remembered—and zinnias and asters flourished along the path to the door. It was a house to come home to. That the young Wrens were inside watching television seemed not hopeless, just sad. Meg's modesty and Jack's busyness perhaps did not perfectly serve their offspring.

"Children tend toward the mean," Peter suggested.

"The mean and nasty," Jack said.

"The mean between Jack and me?" Meg said, doubtfully.

"The mean of their own generation," said Peter, smiling.

"Is that unavoidable?" she said, not smiling.

He didn't like to drive, didn't own a car, but if he lived here he could drive the kids to school and back, and Meg could work at home. She was a valued programmer; her company would allow her that privilege. These days any arrangement was possible. And eventually his aunt's legacy, unexhausted, would go to the children.

In the mornings the young of Congdon Street went off to school, the bigger ones shepherding the smaller. Even the smallest had pilgrim backpacks. Some mothers walked along behind, not interfering, just watchful. Peter wondered if the women took turns as monitors. The daytime danger was from traffic. Peter, too, kept an eye on the children from his window. Sometimes, out early to buy the paper, he found himself in their midst; a little crowd of small Asians and Central Americans would divide briefly for his sake and then reunite behind him. He felt like a maypole. The children wore every shade of corduroy. How were they faring in the Land of Opportunity? he wondered. The manager of the Cambodian building, N. Gordon, was being brought to court because of his failure to maintain the building properly. The failure was not his fault, his lawyer had countered. The place was overcrowded; these people kept subletting to one another.

Peter went out every day. He now recognized some of the slow-moving white-haired women, and smiled at them. He used the main library downtown. He read a book about Dickens and Sabbatarians and another about Dickens and Jews. Sometimes he met a former colleague or student for lunch. He went to afternoon movies and sat in the back row with his long legs on the seat in front of him. He went to friends' houses for dinner, or fixed himself healthful meals at home.

THE WRENS gave an annual afternoon party on the Sunday after the Game. Meg did the work herself, with some assistance from the family and from Peter. She baked cheddar cheese puffs. She twisted salami into flutes and arranged crudités around a bowl of yogurt. Peter remembered his aunt's cook's zealously constructed trifles, each layer less edible than the one before. Meg's canapés were at least tasty.

That morning Peter stood at the kitchen counter, spreading fish paste onto little squares of pumpernickel and admiring the view out the window. A stand of spruces made him think of Christmas. Beside him, Meg sliced cucumbers. They were both wearing jeans; both had a birch-tree litheness. He might have been her older brother.

The crowd at the party was, as always, varied—local gentry, old friends, coworkers, a pair of ancient female cousins of Jack's. Also there was a group of parents from the children's school, including two notables, both Jews: a psychologist who was also a TV commentator, and Geronimus Barron, Peter's former neighbor. Their wives were not particularly attractive, just assured. A generation ago, Peter reflected, Jewish wives had been well dressed and cultivated and full of leisure. Now they were all practicing medicine. You couldn't keep up with people like that.

He was popular at this party. People remembered him from year to year. A friend of Meg's whose husband was leaving her had once wept on his shoulder in the pantry. That couple seemed to have reconciled, he noticed. The Wrens' dentist fancied himself a devotee of Dickens, although Peter was under the impression that he had read only *Oliver Twist*. The cousins made much of him. "We'd like to talk to you more often than once in a blue moon."

"Would be lovely," he said.

"We'll have to get Peggy to arrange it." Peggy?

"Happy families are *not* alike," someone was saying.

"More to be pitied than censored. She snoops to conquer." Who was that punster? Oh, the TV psychologist . . . And somehow Geronimus Barron was at his side. How long had he been standing there?

"It's nice to see you again, Mr. Loy."

"Peter," Peter corrected. "I didn't hear you come up, Geronimus. You were as quiet as a tiger."

"Is that what a corporate takeover feels like?" asked one of the cousins.

"I don't know," Geronimus said. He had a habit of answering as precisely as possible whatever question had been posed. This gave him an obedient air. "I don't want to take you over, Mr. Loy—Peter— but I wish you were part of my staff. Margaret says that you're the last of the lucid thinkers."

Margaret? Geronimus, hands in pockets, smiled a courteous refusal to the teenager passing a tray of wine. The cousins, as if to make amends for so abstemious a guest, took two glasses each. How old was this quiet tycoon? Peter wondered. Forty? You could put him naked and empty-handed on a desert island, and in five years he'd be chief minister to the native king. Maimonides had risen to court physician in record time . . . "What else does Margaret say?"

"Peggy never talks much," said one cousin.

"Still waters run deep," said the other.

"She and I serve together on the scholarship committee," Geronimus said, and the talk turned to minority recruitment. Peter had just received the latest bulletin from the boarding school he himself had attended. The school had recently invited two South Bronx boys to study there, and two unhappier faces had never before been immortalized on high-quality vellum. Entrapment, Peter called it. Geronimus listened.

THE NEXT MORNING Meg said that she would drop the children at school before leaving Peter at Harvard Square. Peter was pleased to be part of this family ritual. A curved line of automobiles humped forward slowly. Only one car at a time was allowed to disburden itself. The students getting out of the cars had the ragamuffin look of the rich. Meg wore a ski sweater and did not look rich, just wholesome. "Think of Jack's long drive every day," she was saying as they left the school grounds. "It's no wonder he can't finish his doctorate—he spends all his time on the highway. Sometimes I think we should splurge on a chauffeur. It would give Jack two more hours a day to work on his thesis. He could sit in the backseat with a laptop. Is that mad?"

"On the contrary. It's innovative. It's the sort of solution Geronimus Barron would think up."

"Is it? Jack won't hear of it."

"Give him time." He glanced at her worried profile. "Jack is flexible," he said. But that was a lie. Jack was rigid. He, Peter, was the flexible one. His was a flexibility achieved late in life, after unhappiness and disappointment, and he was proud of it. Postponed achievements were perhaps the best. Maimonides had married for the first time in late middle age, and had even sired a son . . . Meg turned toward him with a warm, even a marital, smile. "I wish I could take you all the way to your apartment, but I have an early conference."

"I have to go to Widener," he lied again.

She pulled up near one of the Yard gates. Peter opened the door.

"My dear," he said.

"*My* dear," she said, charmingly. She waited for him to get out and slam the door. Then she drove away.

ONE NIGHT IN DECEMBER there was a fire in the Cambodian building. Some woman had created a makeshift barbecue on her kitchen floor because the stove no longer worked or the gas had been shut off. Not much damage resulted, and nobody was forced to relocate, but for an hour all of the building's inhabitants stood in the street like the little band of refugees they were. When the firemen announced that it was safe to reenter the building, they filed in. Peter, watching from his window, would have liked to invite some of them for a cup of tea, but which ones? He wished Meg were beside him in her quilted robe.

IT WAS THE FRIDAY NIGHT before Christmas. Weak electric candles burned in some windows, and the hopeful young couple with the matching briefcases had installed a tree in their living room, but they were in Stowe, at the mountain resort, and the tree's lights were out. The rest of the street was unfestive. Peter's apartment, the exception, was glowing—he loved Friday nights; even though he no longer had a job he still felt an end-of-the-week release— but the shivering presence of Jack Wren was robbing his place of warmth. The man had stayed late at school to make sure everything was in order before vacation, like a proper principal, and then he had driven straight into Boston with all the Friday-night traffic, straight to Peter. He had arrived at seven o'clock. It was now after eight. Peter kept idiotically offering him food. Jack kept refusing. He would go home soon, he kept saying. He and Meg had not separated yet. They had not told the children. They were still man and wife. Meg was expecting him. "It's unbelievable," he said.

Not to mention unseemly, Peter thought. Also untrustworthy. And what was Geronimus Barron planning to do about his own wife? But he knew the answer to that question. Mrs. Barron—properly, Dr. Barron—was a distinguished immunologist; plenty of scientists were no doubt eager to keep her company. Geronimus, too, seemed to like her. Theirs had been a good marriage, Peter realized. They would part as friends.

But what about the Wren children? he asked himself, rattled. How would they fare on the inevitable vacation when they were forced to share a villa or a yacht—or, more likely, a tent and a latrine—with the overachieving Barron kids? Well, maybe the Barron children, too, tended toward the mean. Jews were subject to the same Mendelian laws as everybody else, Peter reasoned. Jews were . . .

Jack said, "They take our jobs, our money, our positions at schools. They take over our towns. Now they are taking our women."

"Not our houses," Peter murmured. "Not all our houses."

"Meg never liked our house."

"No, Jack. Maybe she says that now, but—"

"She always said it." Jack pressed his nose against the window like one of his sons. "She would have preferred to live in some split-level in the boonies and send the kids to public school. Now I wish we'd done that. She wouldn't have met any Geronimus Barron at the Nothingsville PTA."

Peter had to agree. Which proved, he supposed, that Meg and Geronimus had been destined for each other. She had once told him that she wasn't meant to be gentry; that she wasn't aristocratic, just simple; and that, despite her ease with computers, she wasn't particularly bright. Nor was she ambitious. They had been alone under the apple tree with her sleeping daughter. When he opened his mouth to argue with this unexpected and certainly inaccurate disclosure, she put her finger over his lips. "Just an ordinary prairie girl," she whispered. He remembered now the blinding beauty of her pale, freckled face and her blue eyes, and he understood that what she felt for Geronimus was a prairie love, irresistible as the wind.

He moved to Jack's side and put an arm around the younger man. In the supportive embrace, Jack held himself straighter.

"You'll never get over her," Peter said, "but the rage will ease, and the sorrow."

"Yes," Jack said. Peter wondered without much interest who would marry Jack. Some nice woman. She would appreciate the house but would not realize that its furnishings included a retired teacher with a bee in his bonnet about Dickens and Maimonides. Peter would be invited to visit perhaps once a year. As for Geronimus and Meg, they would live in a penthouse overlooking the redeveloped harbor. A caterer would take charge of their hors d'oeuvres. He hoped they would keep him on their party list.

Along the sidewalk below hurried a large man and a tarty-looking woman. On the other side of the street two young men walked, arguing. Though they had left their bookbags at home, their beards and their parkas identified them as law students. They would be gone after commencement, Peter predicted; they would decamp for Charlestown or the South End. The hopeful young couple, discovering themselves pregnant, would sell their folly and flee to a western suburb. The students' places, the couple's house, would be taken by other people. Homes allowed themselves to be commandeered by whoever came along. Not like cats; cats remain aloof. Not like dogs; dogs remain loyal. Like women, he made himself think, willing misogyny to invade him, to settle in, so that in another few years everybody would assume he had been in its possession forever.

The Noncombatant

"IF THEY FINISH UP THE WAR I'll never be a nurse," complained his oldest daughter.

"Why not?" Richard asked.

"There won't be any more battles," she said, and frowned at him from the foot of his bed. He remembered that she was reading a child's biography of Florence Nightingale: she must see herself gliding from tent to tent in the dusty Crimea, bringing comfort to brave British Tommies.

"You could be a peacetime nurse," he said. "Like the ones who helped me when I was operated on." In fact he had not found them helpful, those pitying, red-armed women. He had metastatic cancer. He was forty-nine.

"Nurses in the hospital, Uglies," this uncompromising eight-year-old was saying. "Will the war get over?"

"Yes." The war in Europe was already over. Now, in the beginning of July 1945, the war in Asia was winding down. Richard heard exultation in radio commentators' voices. He saw relief on servicemen's faces. His family had arrived in this little Cape Cod town three days ago, and when, that afternoon, Catherine had run from the parked car into the grocery store for some milk and bread, two young soldiers, safe now from battle, had felt as free as schoolboys to whistle, while Richard watched from behind the windshield.

Though he no longer shared their hunger, he understood it. In her little cotton dresses Catherine was indeed very pretty. The two lines of worry that stood guard between her brows enhanced the softness of her large brown eyes. She had been raised a Quaker, and she retained the stillness she had learned as a child. She was fifteen years younger than he.

Their two younger daughters were Catherine's replicas. The oldest, this fierce girl who wanted the war to continue, resembled him. She had his narrow pewter eyes and fair skin. "If I can't be an army nurse, I'm going to be a doctor, like you," she said.

"A good second choice," he commended. He saw that her face had already been made rosy by summer, whereas his, he knew, was still pale as sand.

But by the second week of July he was beginning to look better. Within his body there seemed to be a temporary lull in combat. Since coming here he had been able to reduce his painkillers. That made him more alert. Waking up was no fun, but by ten in the morning he could sit more or less comfortably on the screened porch of their rented house. He watched his children playing under a low, gnarled tree. He answered mail he'd received during the recent hospitalization. He listened to Catherine's fluting commentary as, near him on the porch, she sorted laundry, or peeled potatoes, or bent over the jigsaw puzzle.

Every afternoon Catherine walked with the girls to the beach. He watched them until they were out of sight, then picked his way back to the dining room turned sickroom. His bed was here because the bathroom was on this floor—near, though not always near enough. By the time the family returned he'd be waiting for them on the porch. Catherine sometimes carried the three-year-old. She'd remind the older girls to run around to the back of the house and wash their feet under the tap. "And don't make too much noise. Think of Mrs. Hazelton!"

Most days Mrs. Hazelton wasn't there to be thought of. The girls knew she was absent when her bicycle wasn't leaning against the shed, which doubled as her home when she was renting out the house. Whenever the bike was gone (they told their parents) they felt free to peer into Mrs. Hazelton's window and announce to each other—and later to anyone who'd listen—the marvels inside. Richard remembered the first day of this inventory: how eagerly they had interrupted each other, the eight-year-old and the six-year-old.

"A teeny, tiny sink, and—"

"One bed. A puffy blanket?"

"Comforter," said the attentive Catherine.

"A kettle. Gold?"

"Copper, I'm afraid," Catherine said, smiling.

"A rocking chair. A bureau. A rug like a snake?"

". . . Ah. Braided."

"A black stove-thing, fat."

"That's for cooking children," Richard teased.

"Oh, Daddy," said the oldest, and "She's not a witch," said the middle. But the youngest cried. She had been ready to cry anyway, regarding some other matter. "Mrs. Hazelton is a good witch," Richard explained.

But she might have been the wickedest witch, for all Richard and Catherine knew. They knew only that their landlady was a recent widow and that she worked at the library. They knew that she was tall and spindly; they guessed she was about Richard's age. Her hair was striped with gray and somewhat wild, as if she were perpetually standing on a bridge in a windstorm. She wore government issue pants and men's shirts open at the throat.

"There are pictures on her bureau," the girls told him.

"Pictures of what?" he idly inquired.

"You know, Daddy. People's faces."

"Photographs?"

"Yup," said the middle daughter. "Men. They all wear caps with sivors."

A few minutes later: "Sivors?" he asked.

"Visors," explained the oldest.

The one-room, one-windowed shed that Mrs. Hazelton retired to while renting her house stood in the northeast corner of the backyard, separated from the family by the victory garden of tomatoes, beans, and lettuce. "There'll be squash after we go home, and pumpkins last of all," Catherine said, grinning at this future abundance. Mrs. Hazelton left vegetables for them in a basket on the back steps. Once in a while they saw her on hands and knees, yanking weeds out of the soil. She wore an overlarge officer's cap. Occasionally they caught sight of her leaving in the morning or returning in the early evening. But often the bike was still gone at nine o'clock, when the littlest girl was fast asleep and the older ones were in bed with their books. And sometimes it wasn't until midnight that Richard, reading in his downstairs bed until the hour of the final medication, heard wheels crunch on unyielding soil. He'd look up from the page and wait for the second sound. There: the slam of the little house's door.

By THE THIRD WEEK in July he felt well enough to walk to Main Street and back every evening before dinner. In the beginning he walked between his two older children. Then one day he took the youngest along, too, in the old-fashioned stroller that allowed child to face parent, that allowed this parent to gaze at the sweetness of dark brown eyes and the arabesque of lips. He never again left the little look-alike behind.

By the end of July he was taking two walks a day—the one before dinner with all his daughters, and a later one alone, under a sky still patrolled by searchlights. On the first of these nights on the town he had stopped at a pink ice-cream parlor. Working girls sat at tiny round tables. Groups of women and children ate enormous sundaes. The pain within him, never altogether absent, flared. He blamed the harem atmosphere of the place.

The next night he went to a bar. Though he was not much of a drinker, he felt immediately comfortable. Here the walls were of no particular shade, and the dark booths sheltered both military and civilian customers. The radio gave them news from the Pacific. He sat at the counter, making one beer last a long time, testing his pain. The pain did not worsen, as if demonstrating that it could be merciful. Main Street was still busy when he emerged, but his own street was dark. Halfway home he urinated in the shelter of some stunted pines.

Catherine laughed when she smelled beer on his breath. "You old lush."

"I'm celebrating."

"Are you!" she said in her sweet melodious way, while a different tune twanged between them: What on earth have we got to celebrate?

THERE WERE VISITS. Banice Bass came, recently discharged from the navy. (Richard had preferred the army. He might have been a major by now. But the military hadn't wanted a sick, overage doctor, even one in remission, and certainly not one with a pregnant wife.)

The MacKechnies and their four children recklessly used up gas coupons to drive from Providence. Rationing would end soon, they all agreed. Catherine was saving drippings in a can on the back of the range, but that too would no longer be necessary. "The war will stop, and my battle will begin," he said to Mac on the porch.

"Cobalt," Mac said right away.

"Yes, we'll try cobalt," Richard said, sighing. And he would volunteer for an experimental protocol and hope he wasn't put in the placebo group.

It was raining. The wives had taken all the girls to a Betty Hutton movie. The MacKechnie boys grumbled quietly over the jigsaw puzzle. Boughs shifted and leaves rustled under the onslaught of rain. There was thunder in the distance and the hoot of ships. Without making a sound a figure pedaled down the strip of earth that was her own path, and onto the street. She wore no rain jacket, no hat. She lifted her wet head; she biked urgently toward the storm, as if it, at least, loved her.

THE BARTENDER WAS A FRIENDLY CHAP. The three or four regulars were also decent fellows. Their talk was always of the end of the war—how long do we have to wait, for Christ's sake? How many more of us need to be lost? A faded, stringy couple usually occupied one of the middle booths. A group of high-spirited middle-aged women often commandeered a table in the back of the room. One had artificially black curls. Another wore a lot of red. A third had a swishy sort of glamour; she could have played Rita Hayworth's aunt in the movies. One night they brought along a new woman. She had untidy hair and a mannish way of dressing . . . He nodded down the length of the bar. Mrs. Hazelton nodded back.

The nods were exchanged on subsequent but not consecutive nights. Sometimes she was there, sometimes she wasn't.

RICHARD'S BROTHER CAME to visit. Their families were close. His brother's children were old enough to appreciate the gravity of their uncle's situation. A mishap occurred: after lunch his middle daughter fell out of the tree. She blacked out for a moment. Richard's brother, also a doctor, examined her thoroughly—Richard and

Catherine anxiously held hands—and pronounced her unhurt. But everybody was shaken. And then, just before dinner, they discovered a puddle under the refrigerator. The food was still edible, but the interior was warming. Catherine knocked on Mrs. Hazelton's door. No answer. So the sisters-in-law prepared the meal, and the nine of them were already on the porch, eating their salad and hot dogs and corn ("The butter is *supposed* to be melted," the middle girl pointed out), when Mrs. Hazelton cycled past. "We'll get her," said his children, scrambling from the porch.

She was indeed a witch, if cleverness with stubborn household servants was any test. He watched from the kitchen doorway. Catherine sat at the table. Mrs. Hazelton opened a low door that revealed the refrigerator's innards. Then she squatted before it, reaching in to twist something and pull something else. Presently a buzzing indicated that the machinery was working again. She beckoned to Catherine. Squatting, they examined the refrigerator together. Why had she chosen Catherine to instruct? he wondered. Wasn't he the officer here? Both women rose—the graceful younger one in a dotted dress and the angular older one in her dead husband's garments—and they turned toward each other, then toward him. For a moment they loomed larger than life: Grave Acceptance and her grim sister Defiance. Then they became two people again: sweet Cathy and the backyard widow, whose eyes, blue as a gas flame, flickered at him.

August began. His pain decreased. He wasn't deceived, but he took advantage of the situation. One night they hired a babysitter and saw a movie. Another night they went out to dinner. Catherine's charm almost distracted him. How lucky he had been in her, and in their children, and in his work—and yet how willingly he would trade the pleasures of this particular life for life itself. He would hide in a cave, he would skulk in an alley, he would harness himself to a plow—anything to remain alive.

On August 6 the bar radio shouted out the news of Hiroshima. Many of the patrons applauded. People stood rounds of drinks for one another. Mrs. Hazelton turned from her companions and stared at Richard. Her palms lay flat against her thighs, as if they were lashed there.

On August 9 the destruction of Nagasaki was announced. Mrs. Hazelton was not present. Richard left early. At home he found Catherine knitting by the radio. She turned her large eyes toward him. "This is terrible," she said.

"All wars are terrible." He lowered himself to the floor near her feet. "The bombs may end the war and save lives. Killing to cure, darling." They listened together to the radio's ceaseless gloat.

In the coming days the town began to swell with civilians and servicemen asking one another for news from Japan. The day after the bombing of Nagasaki, Richard and the girls could hardly make their way through the sidewalk crowds on Main Street. A woman they didn't know, wearing a ruffled turquoise sundress, bent over the stroller and emotionally kissed his youngest daughter, all so fast that the child merely stared instead of crying.

Catherine reported that the beach was packed. A noisy blimp hovered over the water on August 11, enchanting some children and terrifying others. Eventually it moved slowly westward and out of sight. Meanwhile a new concessionaire had appeared, a vendor of cotton candy, which he swirled out of a vat. The girls had never seen such stuff before. When they came home their cheeks were laced with fine pink lines, like the faces of alcoholics.

On August 13 the bar was so full that Richard could find no stool. It was better anyway to drink standing. His pain had sharpened again. The underweight elderly couple shared their booth with strangers. The bartender was very busy. His son was working, too . . . a wiry young teenager whose presence behind the counter was buoyantly illegal.

ON THE AFTERNOON OF AUGUST 14 Richard felt restless. After his family left for the beach he walked to Main Street. The bar was open, and all the regulars were there. The bartender and his son had attached tan and peach crepe paper streamers to the center of the ceiling. Then they had twisted the streamers and tacked their ends high on the walls. The carnival effect was spoiled by the lingerie hues. "All the red, white, and blue ones were sold," the bartender explained. Some of the streamers had become dislodged and hung down like flypaper. The place grew more and more packed. Seven or eight people crowded into each booth. The lively women had already installed themselves in the back of the room. They had acquired some men—a couple of officers and a fellow with a dog collar. Mrs. Hazelton was not among the party.

The air was stifling. Richard took his glass to the doorway, but the frequent comings and goings jostled him, so he went onto the street with his drink—another illegality. A sailor was openly fondling a woman's breasts. Three of his companions were sharing a bottle on a bench. They were committing this breach right in front of the public library, diagonally across the street from Richard. On the third floor of the Woolworth building—the only building in town even to have a third floor—figures bobbed about at the windows, throwing confetti. The card shop was full of boisterous customers. The tobacco shop, the drugstore . . .

Someone, somewhere, set off a firecracker, then a string of them. Meanwhile the noise in the bar behind him had become a steady roar. "Victory!" he heard. "Defeat!" he heard. "Surrender!" Laughter thickened. Church bells began to ring—from the Episcopalians at one end of town and from the Congregationalists at the other. Automobiles blared their horns, though there were no automobiles moving on the street, since the street was filling with people—all sizes and ages of people, all shades of clothing and hair; people singing, shouting, hugging, crying, dancing alone and in pairs and in threes and in groups. Someone was playing an accordion. Someone was blowing a trumpet. An army truck poked its nose into the street from a side road, backed up, disappeared. Then a squad of soldiers arrived, not to contain the revelry but to join it, for this was the end of the war, and everyone was part of the glory. A small boy all by himself wandered crying into Richard's view and then was snatched up by someone, presumably his mother. Were the police opening the jails? Was that the meaning of the latest siren? He leaned against the window of the bar and noticed that he still held his half-full glass. He undid one of the lower buttons of his shirt and poured the beer into his garments. It spread onto his stomach. Some of it dripped below his loose waistband and cooled his abdomen, failing to quench the fire within, but diminishing it a little bit, for a little while. He threw the glass into a trash barrel.

From the grocery on the other side of the street came shouts and cheers. From the barbershop, from the dentist's office. Someone was running along the library path, past the three sailors on the bench—but there were twenty people on the bench by now, there were thirty! She raced slantwise toward him, crossing the street without seeing its inebriates. Her hair streamed backward like a figurehead's.

He saw that she was not laughing, not crying, not shouting, not delirious with delight. She was raging. Her fury was finally unleashed. He caught her as she tried to run past. She gasped, tensed, raised her fists. Then she recognized him, and threw herself moaning into his embrace. They stood like tens of thousands of celebrants across their mad nation, locked in victory. He felt his dying staunched by her wrath, her passionate unsubmissiveness. It was as if she were a savage new drug, untried, unproven: a last desperate chance. She arched her back and gazed at him for a moment, the blue flames of her eyes seeming to lick his forehead, his nose, his chin, his forehead again—though perhaps she was merely avoiding looking anywhere else, down at his soggy trousers, for instance, whose wetness she could surely feel through her own. Then she turned her head rapidly from side to side, making her hair shake with the force of the refusal. He released her. She flew into their bar. He slogged toward home, drenched but not defeated, not yet defeated, not yet.

Vaquita

"Someday," said the minister of health to her deputy assistant, "you must fly me to one of those resort towns on the edge of the lake. Set me up in a striped tent. Send in kids who need booster shots. The mayor and I will split a bottle of cold Spanish wine; then we will blow up the last storehouse of canned milk . . ."

The minister paused. Caroline, the deputy, was looking tired. "Lina, what godforsaken place am I visiting tomorrow?" the minister asked.

"Campo del Norte," came the answer. "Water adequate, sewage okay, no cholera, frequent dysentery . . ."

Señora Marta Perera de Lefkowitz, minister of health, listened and memorized. Her chin was slightly raised, her eyelids half lowered over pale eyes. This was the pose that the newspapers caricatured most often. Pro-government papers did it more or less lovingly—in their cartoons the minister resembled an inquisitive cow. Opposition newspapers accentuated the lines under Señora Perera's eyes and adorned her mouth with a cigarette, and never omitted the famous spray of diamonds on her lapel.

"There has been some unrest," Caroline went on.

Señora Perera dragged on a cigarette—the fourth of her daily five. She usually smoked it at this late-afternoon hour, in Caroline's soothing presence. The ministerial office was large and white, with beautifully carved walls. Gray oblongs indicated the recent presence of paintings. The draperies looked like a collection of ribbons.

"What kind of unrest?" the señora asked.

"A family was exiled."

"For which foolishness?"

The deputy consulted her notes. "They gave information to an Australian writing an exposé of smuggling in Latin America."

"Horrifying. Soon someone will suggest that New York launders our money. Please continue."

"Otherwise, the usual. Undernourishment. Malnourishment. Crop failures. Over-fecundity."

Señora Perera let her eyelids drop all the way. Lactation had controlled fertility for centuries, had kept population numbers steady. In a single generation the formula industry had changed everything; now there was a new baby in every wretched family every year. She opened her eyes. "Television?"

"No. A few radios. Seventy kilometers away there's a town with a movie house."

Golden dreams. "The infirmary—what does it need?"

Again a shuffling of papers. "Needles, gloves, dehydration kits, tetanus vaccines, cigarettes—"

A trumpet of gunfire interrupted the list.

The minister and her deputy exchanged a glance and stopped talking for a minute. The gunshots were not repeated.

"They will deport me soon," Señora Perera remarked.

"You could leave of your own accord," Caroline said softly.

"That idea stinks of cow shit," Señora Perera said, but she said it in Polish. Caroline waited. "I'm not finished meddling," the señora added, in an inaudible conflation of the languages. "They'll boot me to Miami," she continued in an ordinary tone, now using only Spanish. "The rest of the government is already there, except for Perez, who I think is dead. They'll want my flat, too. Will you rescue Gidalya?" Gidalya was the minister's parrot. "And while you're at it, Lina, rescue this department. They'll ask you to run the health services, whichever putz they call minister. They'll appreciate that only you can do it—you with principles, but no politics. So do it."

"Take my bird, take my desk, take my job . . ." Caroline sighed.

"Then that's settled."

They went on to talk of departmental matters—the medical students' rebellion in the western city; the girl born with no hands who had been found in a squatters' camp, worshipped as a saint. Then they rose.

Caroline said, "Tomorrow morning Luis will call for you at five."

"Luis? Where is Diego?"

"Diego has defected."

"The scamp. But Luis, that garlic breath—spare me."

"An escort is customary," Caroline reminded her.

"This escort may bring handcuffs."

The two women kissed formally; all at once they embraced. Then they left the cool, almost-empty ministry by different exits. Caroline ran down to the rear door; her little car was parked in back. Señora Perera took the grand staircase that curved into the tiled reception hall. Her footsteps echoed. The guard tugged at the massive oak door until it opened. He pushed back the iron gate. He bowed. "Good evening, Señora Ministra."

She waited at the bus stop—a small, elderly woman with dyed red hair. She wore one of the dark, straight-skirted suits that, whatever the year, passed for last season's fashion. The diamonds glinted on its lapel.

Her bus riding was considered an affectation. In fact it was an indulgence. In the back of an official limousine she felt like a corpse. But on the bus she became again a young medical student in Prague, her hair in a single red braid. Sixty years ago she had taken trams everywhere—to cafés; to the apartment of her lover; to her Czech tutor, who became a second lover. In her own room she kept a sweet songbird. At the opera she wept at Smetana. She wrote to her parents in Kraków whenever she needed money. All that was before the Nazis, before the war, before the partisans; before the year hiding out in a peasant's barn, her only company a cow; before liberation, DP camp, and the ship that had sailed west to the New World.

Anyone who cared could learn her history. At least once a year somebody interviewed her on radio or television. But the citizens were interested mainly in her life with the cow. "Those months in the barn—what did you think about?" She was always asked that question. "Everything," she sometimes said. "Nothing," she said, sometimes. "Breast-feeding," she barked, unsmiling, during the failed campaign against the formula companies. They called her *La Vaca*—The Cow.

The bus today was late but not yet very late, considering that a revolution was again in progress. So many revolutions had erupted since she arrived in this plateau of a capital, her mother gasping at her side. The Coffee War first, then the Colonels' Revolt, then the . . . Here was the bus, half full. She grasped its doorpost and, grunting, hauled herself aboard. The driver, his eyes on the diamonds, waved her on; no need to show her pass.

The air swam with heat. All the windows were closed against stray bullets. Señora Perera pushed her own window open. The other passengers made no protest. And so, on the ride home, the minister, leaning on her hand, was free to smell the diesel odor of the center of the city, the eucalyptus of the park, the fetidness of the river, the thick citrus stink of the remains of that day's open market, and finally the hibiscus scent of the low hills. No gunshots disturbed the journey. She closed the window before getting off the bus and nodded at the five people who were left.

In the apartment, Gidalya was sulking. New visitors always wondered at a pet so uncolorful—Gidalya was mostly brown. "I was attracted by his clever rabbinic stare," she'd explain. Gidalya had not mastered even the usual dirty words; he merely squawked, expressing a feeble rage. "Hola," Señora Perera said to him now. He gave her a resentful look. She opened his cage, but he remained on his perch, picking at his breast feathers.

She toasted two pieces of bread and sliced some papaya and poured a glass of wine and put everything on a tray. She took the tray out onto the patio and, eating and smoking, watched the curfewed city below. She could see a bit of the river, with its Second Empire bridge and ornamental stanchions. Half a mile north was the plaza, where the cathedral of white volcanic stone was whitened further by flood lamps; this pale light fizzed through the leafy surround. Bells rang faintly. Ten o'clock.

Señora Perera carried her empty tray back into the kitchen. She turned out the lights in the living room and flung a scarf over Gidalya's cage. "Good night, possibly for the last time," she said, first in Spanish and then in Polish. In her bedroom, she removed the diamonds from her lapel and fastened them onto the jacket she would wear in the morning. She got ready for bed, got into bed, and fell instantly asleep.

SOME BITS of this notable widow's biography were not granted to interviewers. She might reminisce about her early days here— the resumption of medical studies and the work for the new small party on the left—but she never mentioned the expensive abortion paid for by her rich, married lover. She spoke of the young Federico Perera, of their courtship, of his growing prominence in the legal profession, of her party's increasing strength and its association with various coalitions. She did not refer to Federico's infidelities, though she knew their enemies made coarse jokes about the jewelry he gave her whenever he took a new mistress. Except for the diamonds, all the stuff was fake.

In her fifties she had served as minister of culture; under her warm attention both the national orchestra and the national theater thrived. She was proud of that, she told interviewers. She was proud, too, of her friendship with the soprano Olivia Valdez, star of light opera, now retired and living in Jerusalem; but she never spoke of Olivia. She spoke instead of her husband's merry North American nieces, who had often flown down from Texas. She did not divulge that the young Jewish hidalgos she presented to these girls found them uncultivated. She did not mention her own childlessness. She made few pronouncements about her adopted country; the famous quip that revolution was its national pastime continued to embarrass her. The year with the cow? I thought about everything. I thought about nothing.

What kind of cow was it?

Dark brown, infested with ticks, which I got, too.

Your name for her?

My Little Cow, in two or three tongues.

The family who protected you?

Righteous gentiles.

Your parents?

In the camps. My father died. My mother survived. I brought her to this country.

. . . whose air she could never breathe. Whose slippery words she refused to learn. I myself did not need to study the language; I remembered it from a few centuries earlier, before the expulsion from Spain. Nothing lightened Mama's mood; she wept every night until she died.

Señora Perera kept these last gloomy facts from interviewers. "The people here—they are like family," she occasionally said. "Stubborn as pigs," she once added, in a cracked mutter that no one should have heard, but the woman with the microphone had swooped on the phrase as if it were an escaping kitten.

"You love this sewer," Olivia had shouted during her raging departure. "You have no children to love, and you have a husband not worth loving, and you don't love me anymore because my voice is cracking and my belly sags. So you love my land, which I at least have the sense to hate. You love the oily generals. The aristocrats scratching themselves. The intellectuals snoring through concerts. The revolutionaries in undershirts. The parrots, even! You are besotted!"

It was a farewell worthy of Olivia's talents. Their subsequent correspondence had been affectionate. Olivia's apartment in Israel would become Señora Perera's final home; she'd fly straight to Jerusalem from Miami. The diamonds would support a few years of simple living. But for a little while longer she wanted to remain amid the odors, the rap blaring from pickup trucks, the dance halls, the pink evangelical churches, the blue school uniforms, the highway's dust, the river's tarnish. To remain in this wayward place that was everything a barn was not.

LUIS WAS WAITING for her at dawn, standing beside the limousine. He wore a mottled jumpsuit.

"Much trouble last night?" she asked, peering in vain into his sunglasses while trying to avoid his corrupt breath.

"No," he belched, omitting her title, omitting even the honorific. This disrespect allowed her to get into the front of the car like a pal.

At the airport they climbed the steps of a tipsy little plane. Luis stashed his Uzi in the rear next to the medical supplies. He took the copilot's seat. Señora Perera and the nurse—a Dutch volunteer with passable Spanish—settled themselves on the other two buckets. Señora Perera hoped to watch the land fall away, but from behind the pilot's shoulder she could see only sky, clouds, one reeling glimpse of highway, and then the mountainside. She reconstructed the city from memory: its mosaic of dwellings enclosed in a ring of hills, its few tall structures rising in the center like an abscess. The river, the silly Parisian bridge. The plaza. People were gathering there now, she guessed, to hear today's orations.

The Dutch nurse was huge, a goddess. She had to hunch her

shoulders and let her big hands dangle between her thighs. Some downy thatch sprouted on her jaw; what a person to spend eternity with if this light craft should go down, though there was no reason you should be stuck forever with the dullard you happened to die with. Señora Perera planned to loll on celestial pillows next to Olivia. Federico might join them every millennium or so, good old beast, and Gidalya, too, prince of rabbis released from his avian corpus, his squawks finally making sense . . . She offered her traveling flask to the nurse. "Dutch courage?" she said in English. The girl smiled without comprehension, but she did take a swig.

In less than an hour they had flown around the mountain and were landing on a cracked tar field. A helicopter stood waiting. Señora Perera and the nurse used the latrine. A roll of toilet paper hung on a nail, for their sakes.

And now they were rising in the chopper. They swung across the hide of the jungle. She looked down on trees flaming with orange flowers and trees foaming with white ones. A sudden clearing was immediately swallowed up again by squat, broad-leaved trees. Lime green parrots rose up together—Gidalya's rich cousins.

They landed in the middle of the town square, beside a chewed bandstand. A muscular functionary shook their hands. This was Señor Rey, she recalled from Lina's instructions. Memory remained her friend; she could still recite the names of the cranial nerves. Decades ago, night after night, she had whispered them to the cow. She had explained the structures of various molecules. *Ma Petite Vache* . . . She had taught the cow the Four Questions.

Señor Rey led them toward a barracks mounted on a slab of cement: the infirmary she had come to inspect. The staff—a nurse-director and two assistants—stood stiffly outside as if awaiting arrest. It was probable that no member of any government had ever before visited—always excepting smugglers.

The director, rouged like a temptress, took them around the scrubbed infirmary, talking nonstop. She knew every detail of every case history; she could relate every failure from under-medication, from wrong medication, from absence of medication. The Dutch girl seemed to understand the rapid-fire Spanish.

Surgical gloves, recently washed, were drying on a line. The storeroom shelves held bottles of injectable ampicillin and jars of Valium—folk remedies now. A few people lay in the rehydration room. In a corner of the dispensary a dying old man curled upon himself. Behind a screen Señora Perera found a listless child with swollen glands and pale nail beds. She examined him. A year ago she would have asked the parents' permission to send him to a hospital in the city for tests and treatment if necessary. Now the hospital in the city was dealing with wounds and emergencies, not diseases. The parents would have refused anyway. What was a cancer unit for but to disappear people? She stood for a moment with her head bowed, her thumb on the child's groin. Then she told him to dress himself.

As she came out from behind the screen she could see the two nurses through a window. They were walking toward the community kitchen to inspect the miracle of soya cakes. Luis lounged just outside the window.

She leaned over the sill and addressed his waxy ear. "Escort those two, why don't you? I want to see Señor Rey's house alone."

Luis moved sullenly off. Señor Rey led her toward his dwelling in resentful silence. Did he think she really cared whether his cache was guns or cocaine? All she wanted was to ditch Luis for a while. But she would have to subject this village thug to a mild interrogation just to get an hour's freedom.

And then she saw a better ruse. She saw a motorbike, half concealed in Señor Rey's shed.

She had flown behind Federico on just such a bike, one summer by the sea. She remembered his thick torso within the circle of her arms. The next summer she had driven the thing herself, Olivia clasping her waist.

"May I try that?"

Señor Rey helplessly nodded. She handed him her kit bag. She hiked up her skirt and straddled the bike. The low heels of her shoes hooked over the foot pieces.

But this was not flying. The machine strained uphill, held by one of the two ruts they called a road. On the hump between the ruts grass grew and even flowers—little red ones. She picked up speed slightly and left the village behind. She passed poor farms and thick growths of vegetation. The road rose and fell. From a rise she got a glimpse of a brown lake. Her buttocks smarted.

When she stopped at last and got off the bike, her skirt ripped with a snort. She leaned the disappointing machine against a scrub pine and walked into the woods, headed toward the lake. Mist encircled some trees. Thick roots snagged her shoes. But ahead was a clearing, just past tendrils hanging from branches. A good place for a smoke. She parted the vines and entered, and saw a woman.

A girl, really. She was eighteen at most. She was sitting on a carpet of needles and leaning against a harsh tree. But her lowered face was as untroubled as if she had been resting on a silken pouf. The nursing infant was wrapped in coarse striped cloth. Its little hand rested against her brown breast. Mother and child were outwardly motionless, yet Señora Perera felt a steady pulsing beneath her soles, as if the earth itself were a giant teat.

She did not make much of a sound, only her old woman's wheeze. But the girl looked up as if in answer, presenting a bony, pockmarked face. If the blood of the conquistadors had run in her ancestors' veins, it had by now been conquered; she was utterly Indian. Her flat brown eyes were fearless.

"Don't get up, don't trouble yourself . . ." But the girl bent her right leg and raised herself to a standing position without disturbing the child.

She walked forward. When she was a few feet away from Señora Perera, her glance caught the diamonds. She looked at them with mild interest and returned her gaze to the stranger.

They faced each other across a low dry bush. With a clinician's calm Señora Perera saw herself through the Indian girl's eyes. Not a grandmother, for grandmothers did not have red hair. Not a soldier, for soldiers did not wear skirts. Not a smuggler, for smugglers had ingratiating manners. Not a priest, for priests wore combat fatigues and gave out cigarettes; and not a journalist, for journalists piously nodded. She could not be a deity; deities radiated light. She must, then, be a witch.

Witches have authority. "Good that you nurse the child," Señora Perera said.

"Yes. Until his teeth come."

"After his teeth come, chica. He can learn not to bite." She opened her mouth and stuck out her tongue and placed her forefinger on its tip. "See? Teach him to cover his teeth with his tongue."

The girl slowly nodded. Señora Perera mirrored her nod. Jew and Indian: Queen Isabella's favorite victims. Five centuries later, Jews were a great nation, getting richer. Indians were multiplying, getting poorer. It would be a moment's work to unfasten the pin and pass it across the bush. But how would the girl fence the diamonds? Señor Rey would insist on the lion's share; and what would a peasant do with money, anyway—move to the raddled capital? Señora Perera extended an empty hand toward the infant and caressed its oblivious head. The mother revealed a white smile.

"He will be a great man," the señora promised.

The girl's sparse lashes lifted. Witch had become prophetess. The incident needed only a bit of holy nonsense for prophetess to become lady. "He will be a great man," Señora Perera repeated, in Polish, stalling for time. And then, in Spanish again, with the hoarseness that inevitably accompanied her quotable pronouncements, "Suckle!" she commanded. She unhooked the pin. With a flourishing gesture right out of one of Olivia's operettas, conveying tenderness and impetuousness and authority too, she pressed the diamonds into the girl's free hand. "Keep them until he's grown," she hissed, and she turned on her heel and strode along the path, hoping to disappear abruptly into the floating mist as if she had been assumed. *Penniless exile crawls into Jerusalem*, she thought, furious with herself.

When she reached the motorbike, she lit the postponed cigarette and grew calm again. After all, she could always give Spanish lessons.

SEÑOR REY WAS WAITING in front of his shed. He clucked at her ripped skirt. And Luis was waiting near the helicopter, talking to the pilot. He gave the unadorned lapel a hard stare. The Dutch nurse would stay until next Saturday, when the mail Jeep would arrive. So it was just the three of them, Luis said. She wondered if he would arrest her in the chopper, or upon their arrival at the airstrip, or in the little plane, or when they landed at the capitol, or not until they got to her apartment. It didn't matter; her busybody's career had been honorably completed with the imperative uttered in the clearing. Suckle. Let that word get around—it would sour all the milk in the country, every damned little jar of it.

And now—deportation? Call it retirement. She wondered if the goons had in mind some nastier punishment. That didn't matter, either; she'd been living on God's time since the cow.

ALLOG

THERE WERE FIVE APARTMENTS in the house on Deronda Street. There were five mailboxes in the vestibule: little wooden doors in embarrassing proximity, like privies.

Nobody liked to be seen there—not the middle-aged widower, not the Moroccan family, not the three old ladies.

The widower got too few letters.

The Moroccans got too many, all bills.

The soprano got some, enough, too much, too little; what did quantity matter. Every concert series in Jerusalem had her name on its list. Do-good societies would not leave her in peace. But the one letter she craved rarely appeared, and when it did come it was only a thin blue square, as if it had been first ironed and then frozen. She extended her palm, the missive floating on it. Decades ago she had indicated with the same gracious gesture, after sufficient applause, that her accompanist might now take a bow. The letter weighed less than a peseta; inside would be perhaps four uninformative sentences in a jumble of Polish and Spanish. She might as well burn it unopened. Chin high, eyes dry, she climbed the stairs.

Tamar, who lived with her grandmother across the hall from the soprano, picked up their mail on her way home from school. Unlike the others, she didn't care who saw her correspondence. She was seventeen. Her parents, in the United States on an extended sabbatical, wrote once a week. A great number of elderly Viennese who had fetched up on other shores wrote to her grandmother. But her grandmother didn't like to go to the mailboxes, or anywhere else for that matter. When Tamar's grandmother did go out—to exhibits, to lectures, to the market—she did so because as a woman of cultivation she was obliged to transcend her dislike of society, though not to conceal it.

Mrs. Goldfanger, on the ground floor, loved society. But she crept from her apartment to the mailboxes like a thief. She wanted to be alone when puzzling out the Hebrew on the envelopes, making sure that everything in her box was truly addressed to Mr. Goldfanger or Mrs. Goldfanger or Mr. and Mrs. Goldfanger or the Goldfanger family; and not to the Gilboas, who ten years ago had sold their apartment to the Goldfangers, newly arrived from Cape Town. The Gilboas still received advertisements from tanning salons, which Mrs. Goldfanger felt justified in throwing away. But some morning a legacy might await them in the Goldfanger box. Such things had been known to happen. And then what? She would have to run after the mailman, hoping that he was still crisscrossing Deronda Street like the laces on a corset. If he had completed his route she would have to go to the post office with the misdirected letter, and join the line that backed all the way to the delicatessen; and she would have to explain in her untrustworthy Hebrew that Gilboa, who had just received this letter from a bank in Paris, was away, gone, exiled, and had left no forwarding address.

So Mrs. Goldfanger's relationship with her mailbox, as with many things, was an anxious one. How strange it was, then, that one August morning, having deciphered the first envelope and also its return address, she gathered up all the others without looking at them—let the Gilboas wait another day for their emeralds. She flew up the stairs, a smile on her pretty face.

Mrs. Goldfanger was eighty-five. Her doctor said she had the heart of a woman of thirty, and though she did not believe this outrageous compliment, it strengthened her physical courage, already considerable. She was not afraid of the labor of tending her husband—she could lift him from bed to wheelchair, from wheelchair to bed; she could help him walk when he wanted to. But her sadness was deepening. To diaper him seemed the height of impropriety, and listening to his unintelligible gabble was someday going to break her thirty-year-old heart. The assistants she hired were often indifferent; if they were kindly they soon got better jobs.

But now . . . she knocked at the door above her own. Tamar's grandmother opened it, dressed as usual in slacks and a blouse. No one had ever seen her in a bathrobe.

Mrs. Goldfanger leaped into the apartment like an antelope. "It's come!"

Tamar's grandmother examined the official envelope and then handed it to Tamar, who had wandered in from the balcony, where she was breakfasting in her skimpy nightgown.

Tamar, too, examined the envelope. "The hepatoscopist has landed," she said.

A YEAR EARLIER the state of Israel had entered into a treaty with an impoverished Southeast Asian nation. Under the treaty Israeli citizens could purchase the assistance of Southeast Asians for the at-home management of the elderly. The foreigners were not to be hired as nannies, house cleaners, or day care workers—able-bodied Israeli citizens were available for that work, not that they relished it. The Asians' task was to care for sages who had outlived their sagacity.

The employers undertook the expense of airfare—round-trip airfare: workers were not supposed to hang about when their charges died. Citizenship was no part of the deal. Weren't these people already citizens someplace else? The Law of Return did not apply to Catholics, which most of them nominally were, nor to hepatoscopists, which some of them were said to be.

As soon as a bureau had been established, Mrs. Goldfanger had applied for an Asian.

"What's a hepatoscopist?" she asked Tamar's grandmother now.

Tamar's grandmother said: "Hepatoscopy is the prediction of the future by an examination of the entrails, specifically the liver, of a mammal. Properly a sheep, more practically a rodent."

"Oh."

"All those stray cats," Tamar murmured. "Useful at last."

In the weeks following Mrs. Goldfanger's application, Tamar's grandmother had accompanied Mrs. Goldfanger to a series of office visits. The younger old woman had helped the older old woman fill out the required forms. Every time a packet of papers arrived in the mail, Mrs. Goldfanger brought them up to Tamar's grandmother. She settled herself at the table in the dining room. Sunlight slanting through the blind made her rusty hair rustier—more unnatural,

Tamar mentioned later. "Henna is a natural substance," her grandmother reminded her.

And now the Asian was here. Or would be here in three weeks' time. Mrs. Goldfanger was to go to the bureau at ten o'clock on a morning in September to be introduced to the newcomer and to sign the necessary final papers.

"Shall I come with you?" Tamar's grandmother said, sighing.

"Oh, not this time." Mrs. Goldfanger paused. "That there should be no confusion," she confusedly explained. "But thank you very much, for everything. I just wanted you to know."

So it was alone, three weeks later, that Mrs. Goldfanger journeyed to the dingy office that she now knew so well. Her hand alone shook the hand of the serious man. Her voice alone welcomed him, in English. His English had a lilt, like the waves that lapped his island country. Mrs. Goldfanger, unassisted, told the bureau official that she understood the necessity for employer and employee to visit the office once every four months (later she wondered briefly whether the visits were to occur four times every one month). Her smile beckoned the man to follow.

His satchel was so small. He wore tan pants and a woven shirt and another shirt, plaid, as a jacket. She hoped that cabs would be numerous at the nearby taxi stand; she wanted him to see immediately that the country was bountiful. Providence smiled on the wish: three cabbies were waiting, and the first promptly started his engine. But before the pair could get into the vehicle a schnorrer approached. Mrs. Goldfanger gave him a coin. Joe felt in his own pocket. Oh dear. "I've paid for us both," she explained.

DURING JOE'S FIRST AFTERNOON at the Goldfangers', he spent several hours on the balcony fixing the wheelchair. Because he was on hands and knees he could not be seen above the iron railing, wound about with ivy; but on the glass table, in plain view, lay an open toolbox and an amputated wheel. Coming home from school, Tamar paused under the eucalyptus, squinted through the ivy with a practiced eye, and saw the wheelchair lying on its side, the kneeling figure operating on it. Whatever he was doing was precise, or at least small; it required no noticeable movement on his part. He maintained his respectful position for many minutes. Tamar, under the tree, maintained her erect one. Finally his bare arm reached upward—blindly it seemed, but in fact purposefully—and the hand, without wandering, grasped a screwdriver. The girl went into the building.

In the succeeding days there were signs of further industry at the Goldfangers' apartment. The rap of hammering mixed with the mortar fire of drilling. The soprano noticed the new servant standing in front of the Goldfangers' fuse box in the shared hall, his fingers curling around his chin. Soon the stereo equipment rose from its grave; remastered swing orchestras that Mrs. Goldfanger had not been able to listen to for months issued from the open doors of the balcony into the autumn warmth.

"Joe is a wonder," Mrs. Goldfanger said to Tamar and her grandmother. "He's descended from the angels."

Tamar's grandmother narrowed her eyes. The indentured were often industrious. A good disposition was natural to people born in the temperate zone. Sympathy flourished in mild climates; it withered in torrid ones; and in *this* country, amid five million wound-up souls, it was as rare as a lotus. People here had mislaid civility a century ago.

Mrs. Goldfanger gushed on about Joe; Tamar's grandmother kept her knowledge of human nature to herself. "My husband is lucky," Mrs. Goldfanger said.

Mr. Goldfanger's decline had been gradual, though Tamar and her grandmother remembered that he had moved in already trembling. The children in the ground-floor apartment opposite the Goldfangers' had never known him as other than a speechless gremlin. Those funny pointed ears, hair sprouted right out of them, and he always looked as if he were going to speak, but he never did, not one word. They had been warned not to mock him.

This family, referred to as Moroccan by everybody in the building, had all been born in Israel—father, mother, three children. The epithet derived from the previous generation and would no doubt abide for several hundred years. The Moroccan mother got vigorously tarted up for the holidays and for nights out, but at other times she hung around in an unclean satin robe. She had apricot hair and freckles and a mischievous smile. Her children were always underfoot—under her feet, under everybody else's. Her husband ran a successful tile business; some of the most praised kitchens in Rehavia owed their gloss to him.

He was artistic—or at least he had an artistic eye—but he was not handy. The entire family, in fact, was all thumbs. All ears and all eyes, too; they couldn't help but be aware of the cleverness of the Goldfangers' new aide. Such fingers! And so, every ten days or so, when one of their appliances would break down: "Joe! Joe!" they'd call. "That damned toaster!" And Joe, leaving the Goldfangers' door open in case his patient needed him, would walk across the hall and diagnose and maybe repair the thing, and softly return.

"We must be careful not to take advantage of Joe," the mother said one morning. The father eyed her with pleasure. Her comments tickled him, as did her languid behavior, so different from the energy of the women who bought his tiles. She was indolent and forgetful, but she didn't crave much; she'd been wearing that red schmatte since their honeymoon. She loved the children in an offhand way—sometimes she called the older boy by the name of the younger, sometimes the daughter by the name of her own sister. "Take advantage of Joe?" he said. "What do you mean?"

But as usual she couldn't or wouldn't say what she meant, just sat smiling at him across the disarray of their dining table. So he got up, kissed her good-bye, and left the apartment. Across the hall he could hear Joe's calm voice. What do we need with these people? he wondered in a brief spasm of irritation. Didn't the country have enough trouble? Next time he'd take the toaster to the Bulgarian fixer. Then the mood passed, and he thought maybe Joe could use that flecked jacket he hadn't worn for years—a bit too vivid for his own complexion; perfect for a yellow man.

The soprano had friends and acquaintances in the Spanish-speaking community and in the musical one, and she went to a lot of recitals. However, she spent most of her time writing and revising letters to the home she'd left.

> *Besides you, Cara, I miss most the peasants. Do you remember how they used to welcome me whenever I went on tour?—crowding around the train, strewing my path with flowers? I miss their flat brown eyes.*

In fact her tours had been flops. In Latin America, trains to the provinces were just strings of dusty cars. Their windows were either stuck open or stuck closed. The soprano traveled with her accompanist—a plain young woman glowering behind spectacles—and the pair were untroubled by admiration or even recognition. But the singer had imagined throngs of fans so often that the vision in her mind's eye had the clarity of remembrance. She saw a donkey draped with garlands. Her hand was kissed by the oily mayor of a town whose cinema doubled as a concert hall. The mayor's wife was home preparing a banquet. Many people came to the concert and still more to the banquet, and the floor of the mayor's rickety mansion rocked with stomping and the room rocked with cheers.

In this ambitious country there is no peasant, no one to love the earth. The collectives pay mercenaries to farm; the countryside is a fiefdom now. The giants of the desert are gone. I am quoting my neighbor across the hall, a woman of strong opinions.

The soprano scratched her letters by hand, sitting on her balcony. She spent a week composing each one. For whose sake were those literary efforts? Tamar's grandmother inquired. Ah, to entertain her best friend back home, the soprano said, adjusting a soft shawl. She owned its replica in several shades—the gray of dawn, the violet of dusk, the lavender of a bruise.

Nobody cares for singing. We have become a country of string players, all Russian, all geniuses. Then there's the fellow with a fiddle and a cup who stands outside a big department store. He makes a living, too.

"Of course I no longer perform," she'd told Joe.
"Your speaking voice is music," he'd said, or something like that.

Joe grew up in a village by a river. The houses were on stilts. He trained as a pharmacist.

She imagined him mixing powders crushed from roots. He told her that in some of the villages of his country the pharmacist had to behave as a doctor. "Aided by American Police Corps," he said.
"Peace Corps, surely."
On the afternoons that she dropped in at the Goldfangers', she and Joe exchanged tales about high-minded Americans. Then,

when she indicated by a tiny droop that the visit was over, he escorted her upstairs to her door.

Come to me, Carissima. Bring your damned parrot. Come.

THE WIDOWER OCCUPIED the whole of the top floor. He was sad but alert. Not for him to be left out when other people were getting favors.

"There isn't a cab driver in the whole damned city I can trust," he confided to Joe as they climbed the stairs with the widower's groceries. "The Arabs? Don't make me laugh. The Russians are all crooks. That stuff's not too heavy for you, is it? Some muscles! Still, you could leave one bag on the landing and then go back for it. And I'll take the cabbage." He grabbed a pale head from the top of one bag, as well as the brochure that had constituted his mail of the day.

The widower was currently a vegetarian. Vegetables are lighter than chickens. Joe usually carried the weekly purchases in one trip, a sack in each arm, like twins. He managed the new television, too.

"I don't suppose you play chess," the widower said one day.

"I play chess."

Soon they were playing two or three evenings a week. If Mrs. Goldfanger was staying home they played after Joe had put Mr. Goldfanger to bed. The widower's apartment was a hodgepodge of office furniture and supplies for his stationery store, which was also a mess. The two men settled themselves on straight-backed chairs at one corner of a metal table stacked with cartons.

If Mrs. Goldfanger was going to a concert or a bridge game they played at the Goldfangers'. The widower brought down his board and his chessmen and a bottle of wine and a vegetable pie. Joe provided oranges and tea. The widower set up the game on the living room coffee table. After pie and wine, the widower dragged a hassock to the table. He spent the evening on the hassock, hunched over the set. Joe sat on the flowered couch. Mr. Goldfanger, sitting wordlessly beside Joe, often fell asleep with his head on his caretaker's shoulder. At those times, Joe, reluctant to shift his body, asked the widower to move the chessmen for him.

ON SATURDAY MORNINGS, while Mrs. Goldfanger was attending services and Tamar's grandmother was reading German philosophy and the soprano was swimming in the Dead Sea with other émigrés and the widower was playing with his grandchildren at his daughter's house and the Moroccan family, in its best clothes, had pranced off to some celebration, the youngest on Rollerblades—on Saturday mornings, Tamar knocked on Joe's door.

"Shall we take a walk?"

In response Joe posed the question to Mr. Goldfanger.

Mr. Goldfanger looked warmly at Joe.

"Tov," Joe said. His Hebrew was already better than Mrs. Goldfanger's, but he was too shy to use it with anyone in the building except the Moroccan children. He spoke English with the adults.

Joe pushed the empty wheelchair out of the apartment and out of the building. He parked it under the eucalyptus. He locked its wheel. Then he went back inside. Then he reemerged, walking backward, his hands extended with their palms up. Little Mr. Goldfanger tottered forward, his palms resting on Joe's. Mr. Goldfanger's gaze at first did not stray from his own sneakers, but he gradually lifted his eyes until they met Joe's. The two proceeded to the waiting chair. They executed a quarter turn, and Joe nodded and Mr. Goldfanger sat down and Joe settled him and then resettled him and took his own position behind the chair and unlocked the wheel.

"Here I come," Tamar called from her balcony. She had run upstairs to get a sweater, she said; to grab a book, she said; really to watch the pas de deux from above, like a princess in her box.

Sometimes they walked to the botanical gardens, sometimes to Liberty Bell Park, and most often to the Goldman Promenade, where they gazed across the forested valley at the walls of the Old City.

In English laced with Hebrew they talked about Tamar's future in television newscasting or video production.

"Of course I will live in Tel Aviv."

"I have heard of Tel Aviv. The action is there."

They talked about Joe's past—his island country.

"Little bits of islands, really. In the shape of the new moon."

"Connected?" she wondered.

"There are bridges. Sometimes you need a boat."

"So much water. You must find us dry."

"Well . . . I have heard of the Galilee," he said, respectfully.

"Do you have reptiles?"

"Oh, many lizards."

"And jungles?"

"And jungles."

"I've never seen a jungle."

"Before coming here I'd never seen a desert."

If Mr. Goldfanger were asleep in his chair, they might talk about him. In Joe's opinion, Mr. Goldfanger, despite or because of his inarticulateness, knew more than most people. "The secrets of plants. The location of water underground."

"Some ministry would pay for that information."

"He is like one of our allogs, grown too old for council duty, but still to be revered."

"Allog?"

Joe thought for a while. "It means a kind of chieftain."

"Allog, all'gim," Tamar said, Hebraizing it. Then she turned it into verbs, passive and active and reflexive. Joe listened patiently.

"The elderly allog, the wise one," he said, "is consulted on great questions."

"Allog emeritus," Tamar said.

Joe was silent again. Then: "I think perhaps you are very clever."

Tamar gave an ashamed whinny. "And the young allog—the one who is still in charge?"

"He makes decisions for the group. Also he acts as troubleshooter. And a sort of confessor, since the churches are not very helpful anymore."

"Is it true that you examine entrails?" she asked quickly.

"That practice died out when the missionaries came."

"When was that?"

"In the sixteenth century."

"JOE WAS EDUCATED BY THE JESUITS," the soprano said to Tamar's grandmother. "Another glass of wine?"

Tamar's grandmother nodded. "Then he was trained as a paramedic," she said.

"Pharmacist," the soprano corrected.

A barbed silence followed, gradually softening into a companionable one. There were few jobs for either paramedics or pharmacists on Joe's little island, the two women agreed when dialogue resumed. Joe's wife, a teacher, also could not find employment at home. She worked as a housekeeper in Toronto. Each hoped to be able to send for the other, and for the eight-year-old daughter who had been left in the care of her grandparents and was so unhappy with the arrangement that she refused to go to school. "She is on strike," Joe had said.

"The classroom," Tamar's grandmother observed, "is the crucible of reactionaries."

If Tamar ever went on strike her grandmother would enthusiastically undertake to educate her at home, emphasizing eighteenth-century German philosophy. This prospect kept Tamar in school, most of the time.

BUT SOME OF THE TIME she was repelled by even the thought of her classmates, greedy and self-absorbed . . . One such day she knocked at the Goldfangers' door.

"Surprise!"

"No school today?" Joe said calmly.

"No school," she lied. "Shall we take a walk?"

Mr. Goldfanger was agreeable. They set out. Tamar suggested that, since it was a weekday and everything was open, they visit one of the downtown cafés where you could browse the Net. Joe said that Mr. Goldfanger would not enjoy that activity. Tamar wondered if he had ever been exposed to it. They were walking while they argued. In the end they just pushed the chair along the busy streets.

They stopped in a dry courtyard to eat the lunch Joe had prepared. A fix-it shop and a dusty grocery opened onto the yard, and a place that sold ironware.

"Delicious orange," Tamar said. "When they did practice hepatoscopy, what did they discover about the future?"

Joe unwrapped a sandwich and handed her half of it. "The discoveries were about the past—about transformations that had occurred. Just one bite, dear man."

"Transformations? What kind?"

"People into fish. Trees into warriors."

Men into nursemaids? She waited, but he didn't say that. Caretakers into guardians, then.

"Girls into scholars," Joe said with a smile. "What a fat book."

The fat book was *The Ambassadors*. She was trying to improve her English reading skills. The first paragraph was as long as the entire Tanach.

Mr. Goldfanger was beginning to smell. Tamar picked up the debris from lunch and walked with it to a Dumpster in one corner of the courtyard. Her approach flushed a few scrawny cats.

She turned from the Dumpster and saw, across the yard, that the two men had been joined by a third. The third was a beggar, the kind with a story. She didn't need to be within range to hear the familiar patter. Wife recently dead. Children motherless and shoeless and without textbooks; was the foreign gentleman aware that children who couldn't afford textbooks had been known to commit suicide? She drew nearer until she could hear the spiel directly. How impossible it is to find work in this country which gives all its resources to Ethiopians who are no more Jews than you are, sir. Sir!

Joe was standing now, one hand resting on Mr. Goldfanger's head. With his own head slightly inclined he listened to the beggar. The fellow wore a junk-pile fedora over his skullcap. He held out his hand in the classic gesture.

Joe dug into his own pocket for shekels. The beggar put them deep into his long coat. Then he extended his palm toward Mr. Goldfanger. Mr. Goldfanger laid his fingers trustingly on the hand of his new partner.

"That will be that," Joe said to the beggar, his Hebrew not at all shy.

"Sir," the beggar said, bowing and stepping lightly away.

They walked home in sweet silence. On the corner of Deronda Street they ran into the Moroccan woman, and a few buildings later the widower caught up with them. In the vestibule they collected the mail. Joe got a letter from his daughter.

WINTER CAME, and with it the rains. Joe fitted an umbrella to Mr. Goldfanger's wheelchair. That served for misty or even drizzly days, but when it poured they had to stay inside. They listened to music while Joe cleaned and darned. The soprano loaned them her own two recordings of arias—LPs, not remastered.

Joe patched a leak for the widower. He fixed a newel. He accepted a spare key to the apartment across the hall and put it into his sewing box. One or another Moroccan child, forgetting his own key, knocked on the door at least once a week. Joe baked cookies while Mr. Goldfanger napped. The kids forgot their keys more often.

One afternoon the soprano stopped in at the Goldfangers' after attending a string-trio recital. Mrs. Goldfanger was playing solitaire and Mr. Goldfanger was watching her. The soprano sipped a brandy and talked for a while with Mrs. Goldfanger, their voices tinkling like glass droplets. Joe, coming in with a plate of cookies, remarked that the visitor looked pale. The summer will correct that, she told him. She refused his customary offer to escort her upstairs.

At her own door, about to insert the key, the soprano was seized. She slumped forward; then, with an effortful spasm, she pushed her hands against the door so that she fell sideways and lay aslant, her bent knees touching each other. Her upper body rested on the stairs leading to the top floor. Her head was in majestic profile.

Tamar saw the legs when she herself drifted upward on her way home from play rehearsal. She didn't scream. She turned and ran down to Joe's and beat on the door. Joe opened it. After a glance at her open mouth and pointing finger, he bounded up the stairs, removing his jacket as he ran. Mrs. Goldfanger, needlessly telling Mr. Goldfanger not to move, followed Joe. Tamar followed Mrs. Goldfanger. The Moroccan woman heard the footfalls of this small army and opened her door and started up the stairs, her children surrounding her. Tamar's grandmother, whose head cold had kept her in bed all day, opened her door. She was wearing an ancient bathrobe with a belt. The widower descended from his flat.

The Moroccan husband, coming home from work, pushed through the vestibule. He saw at first two open apartment doors, his own and the Goldfangers'. Mr. Goldfanger sat on the flowered couch, finishing off a snifter of brandy, though spilling most of it. The Moroccan husband saw his wife, halfway up the stairs, rising from a nest of their children. He then saw Tamar with her arm around Mrs. Goldfanger. He brushed past them all. Tamar's grandmother stood in her doorway, costumed as a Chasid. Now he saw his old flecked jacket in a heap on the floor; now he saw the soprano, flat on the landing where Joe had hauled her. The soprano's skirt was hiked up and one shoe had come off. A siren wailed.

They were none of them unused to death. The children had lost a beloved older cousin in a recent skirmish. Television kept them familiar with highway carnage. The Moroccan father had fought in one war, and the widower in several, and Tamar's parents had also served. During her stint in the army the Moroccan mother had been elevated to assistant intelligence officer, a job she executed skillfully while seeming to laze about. Tamar would be inducted after high school, unless she joined her parents in the States as they urged her to do. Three years earlier her most envied friend had been blown up in a coffee shop. The two old ladies had sat at many deathbeds.

Joe knelt over the corpse, attempting mouth-to-mouth resuscitation. Then he said she was gone, and cried.

JOE AND HIS FAMILY changed nothing in the soprano's apartment. They even kept the shawls. The little girl used them to cover her dolls. She went to the local school. She looked like a daughter of privilege in the plaid skirts of the nuns' academy she had refused to attend. She played with the Moroccan daughter. She was picking up Hebrew quickly.

The widower continued his chess matches with Joe. When Joe was working—he continued his attentive care of Mr. Goldfanger—they played as before in the Goldfangers' apartment. When Joe was at home they played there. Mrs. Joe cooked a spicy stew. After a while the widower inquired as to the ingredients—meat, it turned out, and sweet potatoes, and nuts. After a further while the widower asked for the recipes. His own cuisine took a promising turn.

They played at a low teak table, elaborately carved. Like the rest of the furniture, it had originated in Latin America and had accompanied the soprano into exile. The walls were still decorated with photographs of the deceased at various stages in her career. The child sat on the floor next to the table like a third player, following the moves.

Mrs. Goldfanger worried that the change in Joe's fortune would alter their relationship. Of course she was happy for him, though she did think . . . she did think . . . well, couldn't the apartment have been left to a family member?

"There was no family," Tamar's grandmother said.

"And she was of sound mind, I suppose," Mrs. Goldfanger said, sighing.

"Thoroughly."

In fact very little in the building changed. Though Joe lived in the apartment that had been bequeathed to his wife, he was always available for night duty. Sometimes he made dinner on those evenings, though more often his wife cooked; and the Moroccan children dropped in, and the widower, and sometimes Tamar, and sometimes even Tamar's grandmother; and when Mrs. Goldfanger came home it was as if a little party were being conducted on her premises. Mr. Goldfanger had always liked a crowd. He became restless only on the brief occasions when Joe left the room; as soon as Joe returned, and their eyes met, he settled into his usual calm vacancy.

As the treaty was renewed and expanded and a citizenship clause inserted, more of Joe's countrymen arrived, to take a wider variety of jobs. One, it is said, became a skilled schnorrer. The noun *allog* entered the accommodating vocabulary. The word became disconnected from the idea of chieftain; but it gained the connotation, at least in Jerusalem, of Resident Indispensable. In heedless Tel Aviv it sometimes refers to the janitor.

CHANCE

WHEN OUR SYNAGOGUE was at last selected to become the new home of a Torah from Czechoslovakia—a Torah whose old village had been obliterated—the Committee of the Scroll issued an announcement, green letters on ivory, very dignified. Our presence was requested, the card said, at a Ceremony of Acceptance at two in the afternoon on Sunday the sixteenth of November, nineteen hundred and seventy-five.

Nothing in the invitation suggested that the Committee of the Scroll had chafed under the dictatorship of its chairwoman, the cantor's wife. But my parents and I heard all about it from our neighbor Sam, a committee member. Sam said that the cantor's wife wanted the Ceremony of Acceptance to take place on a Friday night or a Saturday morning—not on the pale Sabbath of the gentiles. The group united against her. Here in America's heartland Sunday was the proper day for special ceremonies, they said. Also we'd get better attendance—faculty from the university, interested non-Jews, maybe even the mayor. Then the sexton expressed dismay that the Torah would enter the premises three weeks before the date of the ceremony.

It would lie in the basement—a corpse! he cried—because the Leibovich-Sutton nuptials were scheduled for the first Sunday after its arrival and the Lehrman-Grossman ones for the second.

But what could anyone do?—weddings must never be postponed. Sam and the sexton cleared out a little room off the social hall directly under the sanctuary, and the rabbi blessed the room;

and they fitted its door with a lock. The congregation continued its busy life.

Lots of activities went on weekly in our synagogue. The Talmud class met on Monday nights. Hebrew for Adults was taught on Tuesdays. Wednesdays belonged to committees. On Thursdays from six to eight a university professor conducted a seminar on Chasidic thought. Friday nights and Saturday mornings were devoted to worship, and on Sundays children straggled into the hateful old school building next to the new sanctuary. Parents had to pay for Sunday school (some also paid their kids); the other courses were free and open to anyone.

On a Monday morning the Czech Torah arrived by plane. The cantor, the rabbi, the sexton, and Sam laid it reverently in the little cleared-out room. They locked the room, and there it remained, its presence unsuspected by the Talmud class, the Hebrew students, the scholars of Chasidism, and the committees. Perhaps the sexton visited it sometimes. The Torah study group left it entirely alone.

THE TORAH STUDY GROUP was *not* open to anyone. It met on Sunday nights, in private homes, usually at our house but sometimes at the cantor's apartment. His flat had a formal dining room, my father told me: panels and dark wallpaper and a weak chandelier. When the Torah study group assembled at the cantor's long mahogany table, no one sat at the head or the foot. The men huddled near the center, three to a side. The cantor's wife insisted on protecting the table with a lace cloth. The complicated geometry of the cloth was distracting, even more distracting than my mother's habit of dealing in a singsong voice when the Torah study group met at our house.

"Why is the cantor's wife so stern?" I asked my parents.

"She's from Brussels," was my father's reply.

"They have no children," my mother explained.

"Or maybe Antwerp," said my father, sighing. "The chips snag on that goddamn lace."

The round Formica table in the breakfast area of our kitchen didn't require a cloth. It seated eight easily. At my fourteenth birthday party, in September, some dozen girls had squeezed around it to eat pizza and make voodoo gourds under the supervision of Azinta, a sophomore at the university, our then live-in.

For the Torah study group, our table was usually adorned with a single bowl of pretzels. But on the Sunday evening after the Lehrman-Grossman wedding it wore a centerpiece of Persian lilies and freesia. My parents had attended the wedding and its luncheon, where my mother found a paper daisy under her plate, signifying that she had won the flowers.

I was fiddling with the blossoms. "Dede o savalou!" I sang. I was still partial to voodoo despite Azinta's having left us.

"Oh, shut up," my mother said, though agreeably. "Help me with this food."

I joined her at the counter that separated the kitchen from the breakfast area. Halloween had passed. Outside the window our backyard was covered with leaves. A pumpkin was softly decaying on the windowsill.

My mother sliced the beef to be served later to the group. She sliced the cheese and the tomatoes and the rye. I arranged the food in horizontal rows on a long platter. I laid pickles here and there, vertically, like notes. She slid the platter into the refrigerator.

I turned on the hanging lamp over the table. Its brilliant cone would soon illuminate not only the Lehrman-Grossman flowers but seven glasses of beer or cider. (The cantor's wife provided only ginger ale.) Later in the evening the light would fall upon the sandwich materials. (The cantor's wife left a plate of hard pastries on the sideboard.) In the hours of play the lamp would light up the faces of the six learned men and the one woman.

It was seven thirty. My father emerged from his study, and stretched. The doorbell rang.

The cantor and the rabbi came in, one immediately after the other. These two spent a lot of time as a pair. They got together not only to conduct services and prepare bat mitzvahs and report to the officers; they also went skating in winter and took bicycle rides out to the farm area in spring. I had seen them on their bikes. The cantor's buttocks lapped over his seat like mail pouches. The rabbi's curls stuck up on either side of his cap like the horns of a ram. Sometimes the cantor's wife went biking, too. She maintained her strict posture even on a ten-speed.

"Hello, hello," the cantor said to us all, remembering not to pinch my cheek.

"Hi," the rabbi said to my father and me.

My friend Margie's father arrived next, along with her grand-father. Margie's father was treasurer of the synagogue. Also he ran a successful finance business. Margie referred to him as "the usu-rer." After his wife's death he had invited his own father to live with him and Margie. Margie called him "the patriarch." The patriarch's moist mouth protruded from a ruche of a beard. His son kept him supplied with white silk shirts embossed with further white, and shawl-collared sweaters.

The usurer's walk had a dancer's grace. He greeted my mother with a friendly hug and me with an imperfect kiss, lips not quite touching my skin. The patriarch raised his hand in a general blessing.

Sam, who had to trot over only from next door, came last. I let him in. The others were already seated at the round table in the kitchen. My mother had transferred the Lehrman-Grossman flow-ers to the counter.

Sam barely reached my shoulder. He was in his fifties, and worn out. "Hello, darling," he said glumly.

I followed him into the kitchen and he took the empty seat next to my mother. I placed my own chair at a little remove, behind my mother's right shoulder. But I didn't plan to remain seated. I would soon stand and begin to move around the group, pausing above one person and then another, looking at the fan of cards each held. I was allowed this freedom on the promise of silence and impass-sivity. The tiniest flare of a nostril, my father warned, might reveal to some other player the nature of the hand I was peeking at. So I kept my face wooden. Eventually I'd settle on a high stool next to the counter, and hook my heels on the stool's upper rungs, and let my clasped hands slide between my denimed thighs. Hunched like that, I'd watch the rest of the game.

Now, though, I sat behind my mother's silk shoulder. She was wearing the same ruby-colored dress she'd worn to the wedding. I could see just the tip of her impudent nose. My mother was a de-voted convert, but she could not convert her transcendental profile. Even in the harsh glow of the lamp, she was, in the words of my nasty great-aunt Hannah, a thing of beauty and a goy forever.

Two of the men—the slate-haired cantor and the young rabbi— were also handsome enough to withstand the spotlight. The patri-arch was elderly enough to be ennobled by it.

The usurer had a reputation for handsomeness. Margie told me he was pursued by women, not all of them single. At the table he warmly accepted the cards dealt him as if his love for each was infinite. When he folded—turned cards down, withdrawing from a game—he did it with an air of fatherly regret. The overhead lamp greased his hair and darkened his lips.

Our neighbor Sam was less than handsome. His small curved nose was embellished with a few hideous hairs. His upper lip often rose above his yellow teeth, and sometimes stayed there, on the ledge of his gum, twitching. His upper body twitched a lot, too. "Maybe he a duppy," Azinta had suggested one September day, looking through our broad kitchen window at Sam raking leaves in the next backyard. "Cannot lie properly in he grave. Tormented by need to venge self."

Azinta—christened Ann—was the daughter of two Detroit dentists who were extremely irritated by her adoption of island speech. They became even more irritated when she left us in October to share quarters with Ives Nielson, the owner of a natural food shop called, more or less eponymously, the Red Beard. My mother spent a long evening on the telephone with Azinta's mother, trying to reassure her. I eavesdropped on the extension in my bedroom.

"A phase, I'm certain," my mother said. "Azinta—Ann, I mean—wasn't happy with the philosophy department."

"She could have switched to premed instead of to that Swede."

"A short-lived rebellion," my mother predicted.

"Like yours?" the dentist said.

Duppy or not, Sam was suffering from all his tics tonight. His shoulders moved up and down in defeated shrugs.

My father was not handsome, either. I had recently and suddenly become aware of his lack of looks, as if a snake had hissed the secret in my ear. I was ashamed of my awareness. His bald head shone grossly back at the lamp. His big pocky nose gleamed, too. His cigar glowed. Only his voice revealed his soul—the velvet voice of a scholar. He was a professor of political theory. His smile was broad, and there was a space between his two front teeth. He used that space to good effect at the lake in the summer. Lying on his back in the water, he could spout like a whale.

∾

WHATEVER I KNOW ABOUT POKER I learned from watching the Torah study group. I learned that a royal straight flush was the best possible hand. This made sense—what could be grander than king, queen, and offspring, with a ten as steward, all under the tepee of an ace? Four cards of the same denomination were next best, and extremely likely to win the pot; then three of one value and two of another—that was called a full house; then five of the same suit, a flush; and so on down to a pair. Sometimes nobody had a pair, and the highest card won all the money.

I learned that whoever was dealing chose the form of the game. The deal passed from player to player in a clockwise direction. Betting within each round followed the same clockwise rule. Some games were called Draw; in those each player held his cards in his hand, not revealing them to anyone. He had to guess other players' holdings from their behavior and their betting and how many cards they drew. Other games were Stud; each player's cards lay overlapping on the table, forming a wiggly spoke toward the center, some cards faceup and some facedown. The down cards were called "the hole." A player could look in his own hole but not in anybody else's.

During my twenties I kept brief company with a fellow who played in a big-money weekly, and I discovered from him that my parents' pastime had been poker in name only. "Two winners?" he said, laughing. (In my parents' Stud games the best hand usually divided the money with the worst.) "What's Chicago?" he wondered. The lowest spade in the hole split the pot with the high hand, I diffidently told him. "Racist nomenclature, wouldn't you say?" he remarked.

"Oh dear."

"I'm sure the gatherings were pleasant," he quickly added.

White chips stood for nickels, red for dimes, blue for quarters. My mother was forbidden to deal her frivolous inventions like Mittelschmerz, where the most middling hand won, and Servitude, where you had to match the pot if you wanted to fold. The ante was a dime in Draw and a nickel in Stud. You couldn't bet a dime in Stud until a pair was showing, and the amount of the raise could be no greater than the initial bet, and there were only three raises each round. In short: very small sums were redistributed among these friends. Even between them my parents rarely recovered the price of the sandwiches.

And yet everybody—or at least every man—played with ardor, as if something of great value were at stake: a fortune, a reputation, a king's daughter.

THE PATRIARCH DEALT FIRST that evening. "Five-card Draw," he announced. "Ante a dime."

He dealt five cards to everybody. From my chair I could see only Sam's cards and my mother's. Sam had a jack/ten and I knew he'd draw to it. My mother had a low pair and I knew she, too, would draw.

The patriarch turned to his left. "If you please."

"Ten cents," the cantor responded, and tossed in a red chip.

"Raise," the rabbi said. Two red chips. He was sitting to the left of the cantor and to the right of Sam. I couldn't see Sam's face, only his crummy cards. Of the rabbi I could see only a portion of his curls.

"Call," Sam said, matching the rabbi's bet. He put in two red chips.

"Raise," my mother said, on her silly pair of fives.

The usurer smiled and called. Dad passed a hand over his brow and called. The patriarch folded. Everybody else called.

The draw began. The cantor drew one card, the rabbi two, Sam three. My mother drew two. She picked up the five of clubs and a queen. The usurer drew one, and seemed to welcome the newcomer. My father drew one, and frowned, but that message, too, could have been false.

The next round of betting began with my mother. She bet ten cents. The usurer folded. Dad folded. The cantor folded. The rabbi tossed in a red chip. Sam folded, his shoulder shuddering.

The rabbi and my mother laid their cards on the table. He had three nines to her three fives.

Did it happen exactly that way? A deck of cards has fifty-two factorial permutations—fifty-three factorial times two if you use jokers. (The Torah study group didn't play with jokers, though my mother had made a plea for their inclusion.) Fifty-two factorial is an enormous number. Roughly that many angels dance on any pin. Furthermore, two decades have passed since the night the rabbi's three nines (missing the spade) beat my mother's three fives (missing the diamond) in the first game of the weekly group. I would be wise to distrust my memory.

Yet I can see the moment as if it were happening now. The two of them inspect each other's cards. My mother then smiles at the rabbi, looking up at his eyes. The rabbi smiles at my mother, looking down at the pile of chips.

"I was dealt two pairs," says my father's thrilling voice. "But I didn't improve.

"I was dealt one pair," my mother says.

"You raised on a pair?" my father says. "God help me."

"I improved!"

"Insufficiently," the usurer says, and smiles.

The rabbi leans forward and sweeps the pile of chips toward him. A white one rolls onto the floor. I pick it up, and idly stow it in the front pocket of my jeans.

At the Torah study group I learned the politesse of dealing, at least as it was practiced there. In Stud games, though everyone could see all the up cards, it was the custom for the dealer to name them as they appeared. Also he commented on the developing hands. "Another heart, flushing," the cantor might have said in the second game, dealing to the rabbi. "Possible straight," he said, as a nine followed an eight in front of Sam. "Good low," as a four followed a six in my mother's display. "No visible help," he sympathized when the usurer's jack of diamonds took on an eight of spades like a bad debt. "Who knows?" he would shrug sooner or later; and then, reverting to the Yiddish of his ancestors, "Vehr vaist?" *Vehr vaist?* was the standard interpretation of some unpaired, unstraightening, unflushing medium-value hodgepodge. If the player behind this mess didn't fold when he received yet another unworthy card, the dealer's "Vehr vaist?" became ominous, reminding us that there were cards we couldn't see, things we couldn't know.

On Sunday nights it was my job to refill the drinks, and to tell people on the telephone that my parents were out. This work kept me pretty busy. One of the calls was always from Margie.

"What's he wearing?" she inquired by way of hello.

"A cassock."

"Stop that! Torturer . . ."

"Gray pants, gray striped shirt, tan sweater."

"Thanks. I'm absolutely devouring Rebecca at the Well, next week's portion. Are you going to the ceremony for the Czech scroll?" And without waiting for an answer, "What are you wearing?" And without waiting for that answer, either, "I'm wearing an exceedingly biblical outfit. How old do you guess Rebecca was when she watered the stranger's camel?"

"Thirty."

"Thirteen!"

I went back to the game. The deal had gone around to the cantor again, or so I think I remember. Seven-card Stud. Now I stood behind the patriarch. My mother was wiping her glasses with a handkerchief. She wore glasses over her Wedgwood eyes to deflect admiration, my father had told me. His great-grandmother had achieved the same thing with a matron's wig.

"The pair of queens bets," the cantor said, nodding to the patriarch.

"Ten cents," the patriarch said.

"I call," the cantor said, making the cadence sound like the beginning of a declaration of love. Some thirty years earlier, just out of high school, he had fought on the beaches of Anzio. I figured he had picked up his rich tenor on the march north. He had met his wife in Paris, after the liberation.

Sam did not conceal his disappointment in the cards he was being dealt. But disappointment was different from misery. He became noticeably miserable when the game ended and he had to go home. Sam had two sons, but both had escaped from his gloomy house. One was a physiotherapist in New York and the other was something unspeakable on the West Coast—at any rate, Sam wouldn't speak of him.

As far as I was concerned, Sam's wife was as dead as Margie's poor mother. She was just a pale face seen briefly at the kitchen window or an arm pulling down a second-floor shade. One rainy morning, when I was home from school with a cold, she ran down her front path after the mailman in order to give him a letter— perhaps one she'd forgotten to post, perhaps one that had been wrongly delivered. The mailman took the letter. Mrs. Sam turned and walked slowly back up the path. The wind further unsettled her scant red hair and her pink wrapper was coming undone and the rain lashed her squirrel face.

"Why is Mrs. Sam so strange?" I'd asked my mother.

"She drinks." My mother knew about drinking. She worked in a family-service agency.

At ten thirty, right after the patriarch had taken an entire pot by winning both high and low, Mother pushed back her chair. "Count me out."

"Already?" Sam moaned.

The men continued to play. My mother took the platter from the refrigerator and plugged in the coffee while I removed the empty beer glasses from the table and cut a defrosted carrot cake into eight slices. My mother loaded the glasses into the dishwasher, and I resumed my perch on the high stool and at last allowed myself to observe the rabbi. I did this at Margie's behest. I myself was in love with our chemistry teacher.

The rabbi was about thirty. He had a doctorate in sociology as well as a certificate of ordination, and he knew how to play the guitar. He was haltingly eloquent. Since his arrival two years earlier, attendance at Saturday-morning services had swollen. Every Friday night, Margie washed her hair with shampoo and then with flea soap, which added body. On Saturday mornings she put on a velvet skirt and a blouse with romantic sleeves. She walked to the synagogue. After services she descended to the social hall and drank the sweet wine and the seed cookies the Sisterhood provided. Sooner or later she edged toward the rabbi. The women behind the refreshments stiffened. Poor motherless vamp! Margie said something about the Torah portion. The interpretation was always borrowed from the Hertz commentaries but the vivacity was all her own. The rabbi gave her a kindly reply. She moved away.

The game now being dealt was seven-card Stud. The rabbi unabashedly peeked twice at his hole cards. His eyes were as black as calligrapher's ink. There were faint smudges under them. His hair made my fingers tingle. All at once I became unable to reconstruct the chemistry teacher's face in my mind. The white chip I had picked up earlier scorched my groin. I was no longer peeking at the rabbi for Margie's sake; now I was feasting my eyes on him for myself. I noticed that he had stopped checking on his pair. Through the medium of the darkened kitchen window, he was feasting his eyes on my mother.

That chilly replica of our kitchen in the window was like a

photograph that a son of mine might one day look at; he'd cautiously name me and my parents and wonder about the identity of the other five figures—the theatrical man with the gray hair, the bearded old fellow, the Latin lover, the shrimp, the young man burning up inside. I thought of my inquisitive descendant, not yet born, and then I thought of the Czech Torah, alone in its locked room, waiting to be born again. I shivered and shook myself—not like a dog, I hoped, again eyeing the rabbi. Maybe like a water nymph?

The rabbi lost to the patriarch, as I recall. It was now the last game. Dad announced pot limit, an unbuckled end to the evening. Pot limit was five-card Draw: any number of raises allowed, and you could bet the amount that was already on the table.

My father dealt. Chips hit the table immediately. Dad's was the only hand I could see. He wisely folded a jack/ten when it was his turn, but everybody else stayed in for three raises. At the draw everybody took two cards except for the rabbi, who took none.

There was a hoarse murmuring at this display of strength or nerve.

"Check," the patriarch said.

"Check," the cantor echoed.

The rabbi bet the pot. It amounted by then to five dollars or so.

"Too rich for me," Sam said, and folded.

But the usurer, smiling his tolerant smile, raised back. The patriarch and the cantor folded.

And then the rabbi raised again. I stepped down from my stool and slid behind the patriarch. I heard a squish: the pumpkin on the windowsill had imploded. I passed the cantor and stopped behind the rabbi. He held four spades to the king, and the nine of clubs.

Shocked by this four-flush that our man of God was so recklessly promoting, I nonetheless managed to obey my father's directions. I did not snicker, did not gasp, did not smile, did not frown, did not incline my head farther or change the angle of my shoulders or grip the back of the rabbi's chair any tighter than I was already gripping it. But my forehead felt as if a flame had been brought very near, and I wouldn't have been surprised to learn that my hair was on fire.

The usurer glanced up in order to evaluate the rabbi's face. He could not have avoided seeing mine, too. Who could fault him for misinterpreting my close-wrapped excitement?—I must be looking down on a royal straight flush, he'd have thought; or at least four of a kind.

"The pot's yours," the usurer said graciously to the rabbi. He showed his straight, which he was not obliged to do. The rabbi collapsed his own fan of cards with one hand and collected the discards with the other and merged his nothing with the other nothings. He was under no obligation to show what he'd held. I knew that good poker strategy recommended allowing yourself sometimes to be caught in a failed bluff. But a successful bluff is best not proclaimed, particularly one that you guess has been aided by the kibitzer behind your back. My father told me later that my face resembled a tomato.

Though the ceremony to receive the Czech Torah was scheduled to begin at two o'clock, the entire congregation and a host of other people had assembled by a quarter before the hour.

We crowded into the pews of the sanctuary—an octagonal room paneled in light oak, its broad windows unmediated by stained glass. The room glowed in the radiant afternoon.

My parents and I had arrived at half past one. I entered between them as if they were marrying me, but they let me take the seat on the aisle. I watched people come in. Mrs. Sam leaned noticeably against her husband. His body adopted a matching slant, and he seemed to be doing the walking for them both. Margie swished down the aisle on her grandfather's arm. She was wearing an outfit that Azinta must have helped her assemble—an orange caftan, an orange turban, and silver earrings the size of kiddush cups. The mayor nodded to several acquaintances. The university provost nodded to no one. Other Christians looked stiffly appreciative, as if they were at a concert. Azinta held hands with her Viking lover. She wore a pioneer's high-necked dress in a brown shade that just matched her skin. I wondered if she was now speaking with a Scandinavian accent.

At exactly two o'clock Mrs. Cantor marched across the bimah to the lectern. In a manly voice she welcomed us. "This is a momentous occasion," she boomed. "It is the culmination of the efforts of many people." Her speech was brief. Perhaps it was not meant to be brief, but by the time she had reached the fifth or sixth sentence, our attention was diverted to the rear of the sanctuary.

The cantor stood in the open double portal. He was wearing the white robe of the Days of Awe. His arms were wrapped around the Czech Torah, not confidently, as when he carried our Law on Shabbat, but awkwardly, as if he held something fragile. The scroll, swaddled in yellowing silk, might have been an ailing child.

The cantor moved forward. His footfalls were silent on the thick carpet of the aisle. There was no organ, no choir. There was no sound at all. Behind the cantor walked the rabbi, also enrobed. His eyes were fixed on the spindles of the Torah that poked above the cantor's white shoulder. Behind the rabbi marched the officers of the temple, talliths over their business suits. The usurer's tango glide was restrained.

The little crowd of talliths followed the two white robes down the middle aisle and across the front aisle and up the three stairs to the bimah and across the bimah toward the lectern. The cantor stopped short of the lectern, though, and turned to face the members of the congregation. The rabbi turned, too. The elders, unrehearsed, bumped into their priests, and there was some shuffling on the platform, and one old man almost fell. Soon everyone was still. The cantor's wife had disappeared. But I saw her green shoulder bulking in the front row. Then I lost sight of it as the congregation, without any signal, rose.

"Oh God of our fathers," the cantor began. His plummy voice broke. "God," he began again, and this time he kept talking, though his face glistened like glass. "We of Congregation Beth Shalom accept this sacred scroll, the only remnant of Your worshippers of the village of Slavkov, whose every inhabitant perished in Majdanek. Whenever we read from this Torah we will think of our vanished brothers and sisters and their dear children. God, may we be worthy of this inheritance."

He began a Hebrew prayer, which I might have followed, but I was thinking of what I'd learned in confirmation class about the village of Slavkov. Its Jews were artisans and peddlers and money lenders. Some of them read the Holy Books all day long in the House of Study. Then I thought about things I only guessed: some of them drank too much and others coveted their neighbor's silver and one or two of them lay with peasant women. A few little boys plotted to set their cheder on fire. On Sunday nights a group of men gathered in a storefront, putting troubles aside for a few hours, consulting the wise numeracy of a pack of cards.

The cantor ended his prayer. He handed the scroll to the rabbi. The rabbi held it vertically in his arms. He turned toward the ark. The president of the congregation opened the ark. The rabbi placed the Czech Torah beside our everyday one.

The congregation sobbed. I sobbed, too, weeping over a confusion of disconnected things, *vehr vaist*: Margie who missed her mother and the rabbi who lived alone; childless Mrs. Cantor and forsaken Mrs. Sam; the sons and daughters of the Jews of Slavkov, who had dreamed of love and were ashes now. My cheeks flamed. I gripped the pew in front of me, looked at my knuckles, looked up, and met the usurer's rueful gaze.

TOYFOLK

IN THE TOWN SQUARE Fergus was trying out his rudimentary Czech. "Stores are on the ground floors," he remarked. "People
above."

"I speak only English," snapped the news vendor, in German. His
left hand rested on the awning of his wheelbarrow. Index and middle fingers were missing—their ghosts pointed at Fergus's throat.

"The cobblestones were light gray once. Dark gray now," Fergus
persisted.

"I have other magazines in the bottom of the barrow," the news
vendor said, in French.

Fergus shook his head, though without censure. An old church
stood aslant in the middle of the square. The minute hand of its
clock twitched every sixty seconds. Would you go mad, hearing
that forever? Would you come to need it, like kisses? A line of
customers stuttered into the bakery, and the greengrocer moved
sideways and sideways, sprinkling water on his cabbages. Under
the October sun the whole little enterprise—church, stores, peaked
facades—glistened as if shellacked.

"Good-bye," Fergus said to the news vendor.

"Au revoir, Toyman."

Fergus walked away, smiling.

He was a division head of ToyFolk. He came to a new place
after a site had been selected, and he supervised the building of the

factory and the hiring of the workers, and managed the facility for a while—ten years, usually; well, it never seemed that long.

The knitting shop—what a careful pyramid of yarns. A cat with a passion for some middle ball could set the whole thing tumbling. The druggist's window displayed old-fashioned brass scales. Then came the premises of an estate agent. A middle-aged woman sat composedly at a typewriter; a young woman peered into a computer screen with an expression of dismay.

And this next place? Perhaps the window meant to be revealing, but it had too many small panes. There was merchandise inside— women's accessories? He thought of Barbara, and of his daughters and daughter-in-law; and he went in.

Bells fixed to the door announced his presence. Something flipped onto his head and then bounced onto his shoes. A knitted clown.

"Oh!" said a woman's voice.

"Ah," said a man's.

Fergus picked up the clown and remained squatting, examining the miniature buttons of wood that ran down the torso. Each button had been carved by hand. He cradled the toy in his own hand, two fingers supporting the head. Finally he stood up, creaking just a little, and looked around.

Dolls. Dolls crowding each other on shelves like slaves on shipboard. Dolls democratically sharing a pram. Dolls of all sizes sitting one atop the other, the largest on a rocker, exhaustedly supporting the rest.

Noah's ark, the animals assembled on deck to wait for the dove.

Jack-in-the-boxes. Punch and Judy, on their sides, locked in each other's arms. A pint-size printing press.

Teddies . . . His eyes didn't sting, really; they remembered stinging. They remembered his children asleep, favorites crooked in their elbows. They remembered the plush of his own bear.

The man who had said "Ah" and the woman who had said "Oh" stood in front of a case of toys. They were in their middle forties. Barbara had been at her lanky best then—the rigors of child rearing past, the predations of age still ahead. For this woman, now staring at him with such assurance, beauty must be an old habit. Her pale face was surrounded by hair once blond and now transparent. Her chin was delicately cleft as if by a master chiseler. The irises of her gunmetal eyes were rimmed with a darker shade. She wore a flowered skirt, a blouse of a different flowered pattern, a shawl embroidered with yet another species.

The man's eyes were a gentle blue. He had a courtier's small beard, but he was dressed in black garments that suggested the peasant—baggy trousers, a loose vest over a T-shirt.

Fergus walked toward a shelf of windup toys. He stepped sideways. In a case, tiny ballerinas posed before a mirror, and through the mirror he saw that a curtained archway led to a stockroom.

He glided again, and now the mirror gave him the handsome man and woman in their awful clothes.

"Is this a store?" he asked, turning toward them. "A museum?"

"We are a secondhand toy shop," the man answered. His accent was French. "That makes us a kind of museum. Most travelers come in only to look. But we get the occasional collector."

"We started out as a collection ourselves," the woman said. Her accent was Gallic, too. "We are also a workshop."

The man shrugged. "I turn out some wooden things."

"Bernard repairs appliances for the entire population."

"Anna exaggerates."

"My name is Fergus."

Bernard nodded. "The American. The president of ToyFolk."

"This town has no secrets," Anna explained.

Fergus laughed. "Not president. A division head."

"ToyFolk will bring prosperity," Anna said. "Everybody says so. Will you have some tea?"

Each new posting had brought its special friends. In Burgundy he and Barbara had hit it off with a cartoonist who raised sheep. In Lancashire they spent every Sunday with the dentist and his wife, disorganized, comical, their three children just the ages of Fergus and Barbara's own. In the Canaries the mayor, a bachelor, cleaved to them with nervous ardor. And now came this pair, served up like a final course. Toy people. What a blast.

"We always *have* brought prosperity," Fergus said, smiling at his hosts from the chair they had unfolded. Anna sat on a footstool; Bernard said he preferred to stand. "When we move on things are better than they were—they seem so, anyway. Delicious tea—blackberry?"

And your family?" Anna asked.

all married, living in different states. Barbara joins me
k; she's in Minneapolis visiting our grandchild."

"I like your action figures," Bernard said abruptly. "They remind
me of my lead soldiers. Only instead of pouring lead your factory
molds plastic—yes?"

"Yes. Limbs and torsos and heads." Fergus cleared his throat.
"Research indicates that as the market for action figures grows,
the market for old-fashioned playthings grows also. So you and I
are . . . collaborators."

"To be sure! But toys are not our living. We support ourselves
with repairs."

"You support me," Anna murmured. Then she raised her chin as
if staring down an enemy. She picked up a music box and put it on
her knees and wound it up. Two figures in formal clothing twirled
to "Cheek to Cheek," off tune here and there.

"I've tried to fix that cylinder," Bernard said, shrugging again. "It
resists me. Will you come back for dinner?"

"I have appointments this evening," Fergus said. "And the innkeeper has invited me for a schnapps."

"Tomorrow, then," Anna said, as the song wound sourly down.

HE CAME, FLOWERS IN ONE HAND, wine in the other. In the rooms
above the shop the couple lived snugly, kept company by overflow
toys. Dolls fitted their rumps into the corners of chairs, peered over
the top of a highboy. Cherry-colored rattles flourished in a pewter
mug.

"They were dangerous, those rattles," Bernard said gravely.
"Imagine putting paint on a plaything for a mouthing child. Some
toys were foolish then."

"Some are foolish now," Fergus said. "There's a list, every Christmas, you hear it on the radio in France, in England . . ."

"Here, too," Bernard said. "And was anything ever deadlier than
a slingshot?"

"Sanctioned by the Bible," Anna said. "Marbles, though . . . down
the throat . . ." She shuddered, then produced that soldierly smile,
and busied herself ladling the stew.

Photographs lined the passageway from kitchen to bathroom.
Snapshots, really, but blown up and matted in ivory and framed in

silver as if they were meant to hang in a gallery. All were of the same child—blond, light-eyed. At two she was solemn, in a draperied room, sharing a chair with a rag doll. At four she was solemn against the sea; this time the doll was a naked rubber baby. At six she smiled, clutching Raggedy Ann. At eight the girl with her Barbie stood straight as a stick in front of a constructed pond—could it have been the one at the Luxembourg Garden? Slatted chairs, smoking pensioners, and a toy boat sailing off to the right.

No further pictures.

He found himself unable to swallow.

After coffee he walked back to the inn across the floodlit square—the mayor had recently planted a light next to the church. At tables outside the café a few tourists bent toward each other in puppet conversations. In doorways pairs of men stood motionless. Smoke floated from their pipes. The news vendor stood beside his barrow. The church clock ticked.

Fergus looked up at tiled roofs, then at the mountains beyond. Visiting grandchildren would recognize this scene as the source of tales, he thought with a brief joy. The clock ticked. That girl.

IT WAS STILL AFTERNOON for Barbara. She was babysitting while their daughter did errands. "Hello!" she heard Fergus say, fizzing with anxious love. "How are you?"

She was fine, and the kids were, too. She had made telephone rounds yesterday. As usual he refused to take the whole for the parts, and asked after each in turn, and the spouses, too. "And the little fellow?"

"A genius, I do believe," she said. Their grandchild was six months old.

"Of course. And the rash?"

"Prickly heat, entirely gone." She would not fret him about the little patch of eczema. Then they talked about friends in France and England and the Canaries—Barbara kept up with everyone—and then Fergus asked whether she thought their son was really enjoying law school, and Barbara, who knew he hated it, said law school wasn't supposed to be enjoyable, was it? Perhaps he'd like practice. "Not everyone can be as fortunate in work as you've been." Immediately she regretted the remark; he did not want to be luckier than his children.

"The kids were my work," he said.

"Well, don't tell that to ToyFolk; they might renege on that nice retirement package." She thought of all those years on all those living room floors, the five of them, and wooden blocks and doll houses and action toys. The school conferences. The older daughter's flirtation with anorexia and the younger's brief attachment to a thug on a motorcycle. The army-brat hardness of all three of them . . . "Darling. They're on their own at last."

She heard two sounds, the first a resigned sigh, the second a catch of breath, as if he were constructing one of his catastrophes.

"I can't wait to see you," she said.

"Oh, and there's this couple . . ."

A cry upstairs. "The baby's awake."

"Till soon," said his soft voice.

Two nights later Fergus visited Anna and Bernard after dinner. In the living room Anna was repairing the headdress of a Japanese doll in a kimono. The kimono had an elaborate design of reeds and a river. The doll's face was dead white: faithful to life, the color of a powdered geisha. "Is that hair real?" Fergus asked.

"Some of it," Anna said.

"A museum would give—"

"She is not for sale."

At the dining table Bernard was playing chess with one of the druggist's sons. Bernard introduced Fergus to the boy, and motioned him to a chair; but he did not interrupt the play or his affectionate commentary. He revealed his plans to the child, offered suggestions for an opposing strategy, tolerated the distortion of his advice, allowed young Mirik to progress toward gentle defeat. The boy, cheeks aflame, said: "Tomorrow?"

"Tomorrow." Bernard's hand rested briefly on the plaid shoulder. Then Mirik ran through the living room, pausing to bow toward Anna.

"No knack for the game," Bernard summed up. "Such a sweet youngster."

On the night before Barbara's arrival Fergus came for another of Anna's stews. He brought brandy along with flowers and wine. After the meal Anna said her palate was as discriminating as flannel and she would excuse herself from wasting fine cognac.

Fergus said to Bernard, "I'd like to see your workshop."

"Let's take the bottle there."

From the stockroom downstairs they descended farther, spinning around a staircase to a stone basement. "This was once the wine cellar," Bernard said. An overbright fluorescent bar in the ceiling made Fergus's eyes water. Bernard pulled a string, and now the only light came from the church's flood lamp spilling weakly through a small high window. The two men sat at the worktable, surrounded by shelves of toasters and vacuum cleaners and radios, or their shadowy ghosts; by dolls without heads and marionettes without strings.

"Where did you learn toy making?" Fergus asked.

"Ah, I taught myself. I like to carve, and I am mechanical by nature, and I trained as an engineer. I was employed by a company in Paris."

"I studied engineering, too, at Georgia Tech. But it wasn't my bent. Management was more to my liking."

"A talent for organization, affability, languages. You could have been a diplomat . . ."

"I'm not canny. And I worry too much."

Bernard lit a pipe. "That must make you valuable to ToyFolk."

"Well, it does. I've never seen you smoke," Fergus said.

"Anna coughs."

What had felled the child in the photographs? A missile to the eye, a marble in the esophagus? A train wreck, the middle cars humping upward, the engine falling onto its side? Drowning? There were microorganisms resistant to medicine that could lodge in the chest and emit poisons; sooner or later the patient lay dead. He had spent his children's childhoods making mental lists of dire events, to forestall them.

He looked across the worktable at the smoking man, then looked away. His eye fell on a rectangular wooden box at the end of the table. One of its faces was glass. He reached for the thing. A crank protruded from the side. "Is this an old automaton?"

"A new one."

Fergus turned the crank. A bulb went on inside the box. A

castle had been painted on the back wall. Three carved soldiers in breeches and jackets with epaulets pointed their rifles at a blind-folded figure in a peasant's smock. One soldier had a blond beard, another a jutting brow, the third a frivolous nose. Fergus continued to turn the crank. The soldiers lurched in unison. There was a tiny blasting sound. The blindfolded figure fell forward. The light went out. Fergus kept at the crank. The light went on: the scene as before—executioners poised, villain erect and waiting.

Fergus worked the toy for a while. Then he said: "What will you do with this?"

"Oh . . . we're fond of the estate agent's children, and at Christmas . . ."

"You have a rare talent."

"Oh, rare, no . . . It passes the time."

Fergus turned the crank again. "Yes," he said. "What doesn't pass the time? Managing factories, mastering languages, raising families . . ." He had said too much. "More brandy?" he asked, and poured without waiting for an answer, as if the bottle were still his.

Bernard drank. "Your action figures . . . they all have the same face, yes?"

"The same face," Fergus admitted. "Headgear distinguishes them, and costume . . . Children, young children, identify clothes, equipment, color."

"Features are too . . . subtle?"

"Well, research indicates . . ."

Bernard said: "After all, this is not for the estate agent's children." He paused. "I would like to give it to you."

"Oh, I—"

"Because you value it."

"—couldn't take such a gift." But he took it.

BARBARA RODE ON A LITTLE TRAIN that chugged through the mountains. From her window she looked up at pines, down at a miniature town. She recognized it as charming: the ideal final posting for her sentimental man.

When the train halted she stepped briskly off, carrying one small suitcase and a sack of paperback novels. She wore new harlequin glasses bought in the hope that they would soften her bony face.

She leaped toward Fergus and he leaped toward her.

Then Fergus shouldered Barbara's books and picked up her suitcase. "Only a few blocks to the inn," he said. "Wherever we live we'll be able to walk everywhere. In two months we'll know everybody here. Have you eaten?"

"There was a nice little buffet car. I'll bet you know half of the citizens already. Let me take the books."

"I've met the officials," he said, not relinquishing the sack. "The lawyer, the estate agent," he enumerated as they walked downhill past soft old buildings. "A doctor, too; I met him at a party the contractor gave. All rather wooden, except for a crazy news vendor who speaks in tongues, sort of."

At the inn she met the innkeeper. Then: "What a model room!" she said when Fergus brought her upstairs. "That fat quilt. Stencils on the highboy. And what's this?" she said, spotting the automaton.

She listened to a description of a husband and wife who were devoted to toys. Then she picked up the box and turned the crank and watched an execution several times. "The chin below the blindfold," she said at last. "Such defiance. I'd like to meet the man who made this."

"You will. Are you tired, darling?" her husband asked.

"Not too tired. Darling."

FIVE DAYS WENT BY before Fergus and Barbara could get together with Bernard and Anna—five days of meetings, of house hunting, of the hiring of a tutor. "Though I'm not sure I have the stomach for another language," Barbara said. "I'll mime my way around."

At last the four met on a Saturday night in the dining room of the inn. Under his vest Bernard wore a button-down instead of a T-shirt. He looked like a woodman. Anna wore a cocktail dress— Fergus remembered that his mother had once owned one like it: blue taffeta, with a wide skirt.

The innkeeper sent over a bottle of wine. They bought a second bottle. Guests of the inn and citizens of the town came into the big room in pairs and groups.

"Saturday night," Anna remarked. "It's always like this."

At ten o'clock the innkeeper brought out his collection of big band records, and there was dancing in a glassed-in terrace that overlooked the square. Fergus danced with Barbara, then with Anna.

"I like your wife," she said.

"I like your village. I think we'll be happy here."

"I suspect you're happy everywhere."

"Happy enough," he said, cautiously. "We have a taste for small things."

"Here you can make a lot out of a little. Old tragedies like the news vendor's. His father had a fit and chopped off his fingers when he was twelve . . ."

"Good Lord." The music stopped.

"He speaks half a dozen languages, more when he's sober. Life's a game to him."

Music again: the big band records repeated. Couples again took the floor. Fergus smiled at the people he'd already met and wondered which would become intimates, which only friends.

"What other scandals can you tell me?" he asked.

"Bernard and I are a bit of a scandal . . . not being married, you know."

"I didn't know. That's not much of a scandal these days," he said lightly.

She gave him an offended stare. Though the floor had become crowded, he maneuvered her sideways, backward, forward, without colliding with anyone. He had always been a skillful dancer.

"*I* am married," she said at last. "Bernard isn't. I've seen you watching the photographs. Isn't she pretty?"

"She is your image."

"We lived in Paris. My husband owned jewelry shops. I designed brooches, necklaces. Ten years ago Bernard persuaded me to move in with him. I thought to divorce."

Divorce was not on his list of unbearables; it was simply unthinkable. "Custody?" he asked.

"We'd divide her."

"She liked dolls."

"She was careless with the antiques."

"Yes, well . . ."

"The bastard sent the whole collection in a taxi across town," she said, heatedly now. "As if they were groceries. He sold his business, and decamped with our daughter. I traced them to New York but never any further."

"That's kidnapping," Fergus said. "It can't be done."

"No? It was done."

"She would be . . . eighteen?"

"She *is* eighteen," Anna chided softly.

The song had not ended but they had stopped dancing. He stood with his heels together, stiff as a palace guard. Her fingers caressed the silk of her skirt. He took her right hand in his left and placed his own right on the small of her back and moved forward lightly, mechanically. "You and Bernard were young enough to have children together."

"Oh, young enough," she said, and nodded; this time she was not offended. "But I would have no further children until my first child was returned. Loyalty. It's how I'm made."

She smiled that brave little smile. Her spite uncoiled like a paper snake; Fergus felt its twitch. He imagined Bernard beset by his own longings: raising a rifle to his shoulder and training its sight on the hollow of her neck . . . Because the music was ending at last, and because Anna's outdated dress demanded some appreciative flourish, Fergus whirled her once and then urged her backward over his left arm. He did not bend over her as custom demanded, but instead looked fiercely at Barbara and the toyman standing profile to profile against the floodlit square.

BARBARA FELT THE BEAM cast by his eyes, and turned to face it. He was holding Anna so oddly, like a garment. Anna, one hand clawing his upper arm, righted herself, looking aggrieved. Barbara tactfully shifted her own gaze to the square, where smoke rose from the pipes of standing men; and a café waiter stacked chairs, one on top of another on top of another; and the news vendor, the hour of repose come round, lifted the handles of the barrow and trundled it across the cobblestones, his footfalls managing to keep time with the church clock; ten unsteady steps . . . click; ten steps . . . click; ten steps . . .

"Tomorrow is Sunday," she heard Fergus loudly saying. His shoulder brushed hers. "We have to call the States early, because of the time difference," he said, somehow getting it wrong even after all these years, or pretending to; anyway, he rushed her away from their new friends with only the skimpiest of good-byes.

Fergus, in pajamas, sat on the billowing quilt, clipping his toe-nails into the wastebasket. Barbara, in her nightgown, brushed her short hair.

"I thought they'd lost her," he said.

"They lost sight of her."

"Bernard, a bereaved father, I thought. Well, bereaved in a way. His children were never allowed to be born." He got up and moved the wastebasket back to the corner of the room and put the clippers on the highboy.

"He's made other people's children his," Barbara said. Fergus, considering, put his elbow on the highboy. "A reasonable alternative to the terrors of parenthood, some would say," she added.

He gave her a look of distaste.

She countered with one of boldness. "Maybe even preferable."

"Some would say," he hurried to supply, sparing her the necessity of repeating the phrase, she who had experienced motherhood's joys in such reassuring milieus—just listen to that faithful clock. "Well, we know better," he said.

And waited for her assent.

And waited.

TESS

NO MATTER HOW EARLY the hospital counsel gets to work—and he is very early this Tuesday in May—the attending physicians are there already, each of their unremarkable cars in its assigned place in the garage. The nurses have also arrived, the counsel knows; but most of them travel by bus. The clowns' purple wagon is parked at an annoying diagonal, occupying two spaces. Maintenance should speak to those jokers. The bicycles of the residents are chained tightly to posts.

The counsel locks his car and moves swiftly through the garage. Within its gloom his fair hair looks like dust. His first task today is to draft a preliminary argument, and it will take several hours. The hospital is at last going to sue the state for reimbursement for Tess—poor Tess, the counsel thinks; pretty Tess.

TUESDAY WAS MY DAY OFF. That Tuesday I stopped at the diner on the way to the train.

I was always a good waitress. When I had to leave the Sea View a month before the baby because of some law about lifting and stuff, Billie said not to worry. I could come back whenever I was ready. She raised my pay, too, so I could afford the old lady I'd lined up to watch the kid. It turned out I didn't need the old lady, but Billie gave me the raise anyway when I came back.

Billie must have been surprised to see me but she only asked did I want a cup of coffee.

∽

TESS IS PRETTY. The feeding tube entering her body near the mid-line provides every nutrient a two-year-old has been discovered to require, even a two-year-old who cannot talk or walk or for that matter make any purposeful motion, though she does hold up her wobbly head, and she will more or less clasp an offered finger. Another tube burrows through her chest and into her superior vena cava; outside her body this line is connected, through a cheery plastic device, bright aqua, to four more tubes drawing essential minerals from translucent bags. Nourished abundantly, Tess has round limbs and plump cheeks. Pretty.

She is pretty also because of her hazel eyes and she is pretty especially because of her eyelashes: long, brown, and curly. These lashes could adorn royalty. She is sometimes called "Princess" by the staff. Tess is pretty because of her translucent pallor, alarming though it can be. After a transfusion she is pretty in a party girl's way, as if she has been lightly rouged.

I DIDN'T WANT COFFEE, just wanted to lay eyes on big old Billie. So I stood there. She said nobody would take me for thirty-six in those jeans and that leather jacket, why didn't I get me a student pass for the train, whack a student or something. Both of us laughed.

I never knew how long two years was until this two years.

TESS'S SPARSE SILKY HAIR, washed daily and kept trimmed by one nursing assistant or another, is the same brown as the lashes. The nose is merely a blunt little wedge. But the mouth is gorgeous, the upper lip with its two peaks resembling a miniature suspension bridge. A designer lip, thinks the nursing student who is select-ing Tess's wardrobe today (a light rose top and a deeper rose bot-tom and lime green socks; this nursing student has a flair for style). Tess's lower lip creases into two tiny pillows when she frowns, and stretches into a crescent when she smiles.

The smile . . . It is a curious thing, that smile. It seems responsive, seems to mimic a smile initiated by someone else, anyone else, any-one who accompanies the greeting with a hearty gesture, bending or even squatting beside Tess's wheeled padded chair. Strangers, un-aware that Tess is deaf, talk to her in standard baby. "Heartbreaker," they wheedle. "You adorable girl," they pronounce. (Tess's gender is unmistakable; all her garments have ruffles.) "You have exceeded the cuteness quotient," said a pharmaceuticals representative who met Tess in the lobby while she was on an excursion to its tropical fish tank. Tess smiled. Her friends—she has innumerable friends within this hospital, her home since she was medevaced from the seaside hospital she was born in—her friends know she cannot hear, but they talk to her anyway, for to see faces in action, lips moving, is instructive for Tess, according to the neuro-audiologist. Tess smiles at these efforts, too. She smiles also at toys placed on the tray of the special stroller—a yellow plush rabbit with black felt eyes; a plastic merry-go-round that revolves whenever somebody pushes a button. But she has been seen to smile at no one and at nothing: carelessly, even mindlessly it is feared, her head against its supports aslant like a chickadee, or like a robin, or—one much-traveled resident thinks to herself—like that flirt, the ostrich.

This resident possesses a dangerous combination of optimism and inexperience. She is one of the few people around Tess to imagine the child's future—or, more accurately, to redesign it, for each of the caretakers imagines it. But the resident—she has plans. Knowing that Tess's neurological deficits are multiple and tangled, the determined little doctor reads history after case history. She thinks about what she reads. She is thinking now while supposedly snatching a much-needed nap in the on-call room. Elbows on the desk, slender brown fingers probing her dense hair, she thinks about clever neurons taking over from failed ones.

> I LIKE THAT SLOW TRAIN. It goes from town to town, and at the first three stations you can still see the ocean. Then the train runs behind pines like the ones in Maine. I was born in Maine. It runs past factories. It stops in the city.
> I got off there, in the city.
> I was scared, but I didn't turn back.

THE RESIDENT THINKS about synapses creating themselves; and she remembers that there are areas of Tess's damaged brain that have not yet been fully scanned; and she says to herself that until Tess reaches some plateau—and she's not there yet, she's still climbing—why, no cap can be put on her progress.

The older doctors are less sanguine. Neurological deficiencies united with gut deficiencies make a grim prognosis. These physicians doggedly do their jobs. The neurology attending follows the case. He may write a paper; no name has yet been attached to Tess's particular agglomeration of troubles. The surgical attending replaces the feeding tube when necessary. She works with speed and grace. The tube is Tess's lifeline: she will never have use of her upper digestive tract, never be able to employ her mouth for eating or drinking, never bite or chew. Nonetheless—the dental attending reminds the nursing staff, his pale eyes intense—the twelve teeth Tess has already sprung must be brushed frequently with a little stick tipped with foam rubber, for despite the inutility of the tiny incisors they are subject to decay. (Also they enhance her smile.) The infectious-disease attending—who at this moment is scowling at another child's lab report floating from the printer—prescribes for Tess's frequent infections. He is a Bengali trained first at home and then here. Even as he battles the microbes that invade Tess, he wonders, as if from afar, which one will carry her off. Already there are antibiotics that, for her, might as well be barley water. "She is a fly in our web," he said once to a nurse, surprising her not only with the thought but with his clipped voicing of it. He is usually so silent.

The case of Tess is discussed periodically by the staff, with at least one of the weary attendings present. When immediate concerns about Tess's condition have been voiced—"Her cranial circumference is not enlarging," the resident reported yesterday; "Hmmm," said the neurology attending—the talk turns to her near future, to her disposition, to her removal from the unit, from the single-crib room containing Tess-specific toys, mobiles, and that padded stroller; containing, also, amenities common to all patients' rooms: giraffes prancing on a frieze; a window looking out on other hospitals; television, sink, wastebasket; hamper for dirty linen; bin for dangerous waste; and, attached to the wall above the crib, a box of rubber gloves. There's a bathroom for the use of parents and guests. Tess's bathroom is entered by the cleaning person every morning, and by her mother, who visits once or twice a month these days, though in the beginning she came more often.

IN THE CITY I waited for the subway. I lit up, and a black girl in a uniform told me I couldn't, but she was nice, she let me finish the butt. The subway came. It was after rush hour but still crowded, so I hung on a strap in front of a woman and her two children. They were cute, Mexican maybe, such big eyes, and I made funny faces at them so they'd laugh. But the mother went stiff, so I stopped. I looked at myself in the black window. Round head, round glasses, buzz cut. Maybe Billie thinks I look like a girl that's still in school but I think I look like a boy that's turned eighty without ever growing up. There's a disease like that. I read about it once.

I always liked to make funny faces at kids.

EXCEPT FOR THE CLEANING PERSON and Tess's mother, no one uses the gleaming bathroom. Tess's father, who had no fixed address at the time of Tess's conception, had left the state altogether by the time of her birth. The cost of the child's residence here, the cost of her care, the cost of Tess—this is presently borne by the hospital. The cost is one of those enormous figures flung by newspapers at a horrified public. To the accounting department Tess is an impressive statistic. To the hospital counsel she is always a worry. And today she is a task.

What else can I do? the counsel asks aloud, partway through his draft. Alone in his office, he directs his question to Tess, seven floors above. *The Utilization Committee is breathing down my neck. Two years. Those pricks can count.*

There have been efforts to move Tess into a facility. A facility is certainly her destination if she continues to live. The Sisters of Evangelista would take her, would love to take her, would love to love her; but they are not a hospital, and their medical services are unequal to the demanding body of this tyke. The bags hanging from Tess's pole must be continually replaced; the cylinder of nutrients attached to the feeding tube likewise. And the places where she's pierced must be kept uncontaminated; and physical therapy must be performed; and visual stimulation . . . Tess needs expert servitors. Loved by the Sisters, she'd be dead in a week.

So how lucky Tess is, thinks one of the nurses, who is Tess's primary today, and is gently swabbing the area around her feeding tube . . . how lucky Tess is to make her home in the unit, with its trained staff. Here she sees dozens of smiling faces. (Tess now smiles at the primary.) Here the practiced hands who tend her do so unresentfully, for they tend not only Tess but also patients who howl, who hurl little fists, who fiercely suck bottles and pacifiers; who vomit and hiss and grow quite red in the face; whose harelips get fixed and whose stomata get repaired and whose bacterial infections succumb to medications and whose viruses succumb to the passage of time; who often get better; who at last leave, though they may be back. (Tess scowls.)

I TOOK THE ESCALATOR up from the subway. The wall there got decorated by kids from some art school. They used bottle caps and other junk they found. I always touch it. My friend the wall.

When I got off the escalator the bus to the hospital was just rolling up.

I didn't turn back then, either.

Billie says you can always count on me.

CLOWNS SASHAY INTO THE UNIT on Tuesdays and Fridays, and every day there are volunteers to wheel the child into the activity room so she can look at other children. Other children look at her. They find comfort in her placid refusal to make noise, in her willingness to share toys—that is, to have a toy snatched from her tray and replaced by a different toy. One thing is as good as the next to this little girl who has never grabbed; who has never sucked; who will never—thinks the fashion-minded nursing student with sudden envy—feel envy; who will never—the exhausted resident may be forced to conclude—discriminate between Tess and non-Tess.

Today's volunteer, understanding Tess's limitations, is nonetheless hopeful that the soft fingers curling around her own extended forefinger, with the chipped peach polish on its nail, can be induced to grasp a plaything, a hollow plastic chicken drumstick from the Let's Make Dinner set. It lies now on the tray of the special stroller. Tess, seated in the stroller under the scepter hung with bags, has accepted the substitution of drumstick for forefinger. She is slumping. The volunteer wonders if the supports are properly placed, but her heart sinks at the thought of lifting and readjusting child and tubing. Instead she edges the drumstick along the tray, Tess's four fingers still surrounding it (her thumb does not oppose, or at least not yet). The drumstick, a ghastly yellow, at last reaches the charming mouth with a little assist upward from the volunteer's chipped nails. Tess's lips part at the drumstick's kiss.

Want, the volunteer silently begs. *Want.*

Along comes a nursing assistant who bends down and blows at Tess's hair as if it were a candle, and Tess smiles in the warm breeze ... Next week, the volunteer promises herself; next week we'll work on the thumb.

In fact, even without the aid of her thumb, Tess's limp fingers, encountering her feeding tube, sometimes weakly tug on it. The primary nurse and the fashion-minded nursing student comment on this later, when they are readying Tess for a nap. They confer bleakly about the possibility, in a month or two, that Tess's aimless pull will be just strong enough to cause discomfort and even to do damage. For now, though, clothing snapped around the tube deflects the incompetent hand.

Sometimes she has trouble going to sleep. She whimpers, cries a little: a soft wail that she herself cannot hear. The nursing student would like to stay with Tess—would like to pick her up and cuddle her, an intervention that is performed many times during the day, not just for Tess but for all the little patients, the fussy and the bored and the hot and the insomniac, by volunteers and nursing students and nursing assistants and nurses and once in a while by residents when they are too tired to do anything else, and even by attendings. The infectious-disease attending, his glasses two gold circles and his mustache one black rectangle, has sometimes been found in a chair rocking a feverish baby, as if this effort and not the IV febrifuge would bring the temperature down.

The nursing student, raising her eyebrows at the primary, reaches toward Tess. The primary shakes her head, and covers Tess with a light blanket. "Princess will comfort herself." The two women leave the room.

When the cleaning person enters, pushing his mop and bucket and trundling his supply cart, he finds Tess still awake, though no longer whimpering.

≈

I WENT INTO THE HOSPITAL. Those crazy fish, flipping around in the tank all day. I took the elevator upstairs. Then I sat down. When she was born I couldn't tell there was anything wrong with her, though the doctor knew, right away. "I have some concerns, Loretta," was what he said. They rushed her down the hall. They were going to operate then and there but they decided to send her here in the chopper.

TESS IS LYING partly on her side (a rolled baby blanket props her back). From this position she can see a mirror hung on the slats of her crib, a mirror which reflects her visage. It is claimed that babies as young as three days recognize the presence of eyes. Tess's mentation is far above that of a three-day-old infant—the staff would rear like warriors were anyone to suggest otherwise. And indeed an expression of soulfulness passes over her face whenever she sees it mirrored—an expression of further soulfulness, that is, for her eyes and mouth always suggest soul, to the staff's relief. The lashes, however, sometimes make her caretakers uneasy. There is not a woman connected with the unit, from the surgeon to the volunteer, who has failed to wonder at the assignment of these eyelashes to this young lady: an example of the profligacy or carelessness of Whoever's In Charge. And yet every woman, and every man too, has also at some time privately praised the assignment, for although the staff would be attentive to an ugly child—they are already attentive to ugly children, to children whose features have been flung any which way onto their faces, as if by a raging Hand—still, comeliness inspires a tender leap of the heart, a frisson of identification, softening the shackles of Tess's imprisonment, easing her warders' vigil.

I SAW THE CHOPPER FROM MY BED. I had signed the permissions. By the time I got to the city, two days later, in Billie's car, with Billie in her baseball cap driving, my child was hooked up to about a hundred machines. "Is it a baby?" Billie asked. "Or is it a sprouting onion?" You'd think that would have made me mad, but it didn't, it made me feel better. Billie always has a handle on things.

After a few months there were only two tubes, the feeding one down below and the one that stuck right into her heart.

The medicines from all the bags went through an aqua thing that looked like a clothespin and then into the heart tube.

So I could sit and hold her. One day I held her too tight and something tugged and I found out ten minutes later that the tube into her heart had gotten loose from the clothespin and instead of liquids going in, blood was coming out, slowly though, there were just a few splotches on my skirt, but the nurses said they had to flush the line. One did it and the other watched.

THE CLEANING PERSON dutifully scrubs the rarely used bathroom. He mops the floor of the room. He empties the wastebasket into his rolling cart. And then, just before leaving, he pauses.

Tess is still gazing into her own eyes.

The cleaning person, like the infectious-disease attending, is Asian; but whereas the doctor was born in the Subcontinent, the cleaner hails from the Pacific Rim. He has five children. They are all healthy, and they go to school every day—except perhaps for the oldest, who leaves the house at the proper time but with a secretive look in his eyes. Nonetheless, no bad reports have reached the father's ears. The cleaning person is grateful for his children's health, for his job, for the United States of America, a country which rescues its ill babies and repairs its malformed ones, sometimes (he has heard) before they come out of the womb—such meddling, he doesn't understand it.

He has known Tess for the two years of her life, and he considers her beauty angelic. Angelic beings, he knows, need no justification for existence. (Unlike the infectious-disease attending, whose belief system does not include the heavenly Hierarchy, the cleaning person is a devout Christian.) But Tess is not an angel, despite her looks; she is a human, despite her flaws; and he has overheard (his English comprehension is good) that these flaws will be the death of her. In his country, if Tess had been born at home she would have been allowed to die. If she had been born in a hospital, she would have been helped to die. *Why you here?* he wonders. Pain and death and sorrow he understands as part of the design that God has created—but life like this?

The eyelashes lower. The cleaning person pulls off his thick yellow gloves and puts on a pair of thin rubber ones from the box on the wall and runs his protected finger down her plump cheek, once, twice, three times, recklessly, for such a gesture is against the rules and he would be reprimanded for making it. It is hard to know, though, who among Tess's overworked court of doctors, nurses, nursing assistants, and volunteers; not to mention directors, Utilization Committee members, accountants, and the fellow who removes dangerous waste—who would bother to chastise him. Anyway, the cleaning person caresses her cheek unreproved, and tosses the rubber gloves into the wastebasket, and shuffles into the corridor.

I STAYED IN THE CHAIR near the elevator even after the Chinese man left my daughter.

I wasn't afraid anymore. I was glad I hadn't said anything to Billie, though. You can't let the baseball cap she wears fool you. She takes everything hard.

TESS'S NEXT-TO-LAST VISITOR is the counsel, so much taller than the cleaning person that his pale hair grazes a mobile. He has drafted the preliminary statement to the court, he silently informs the now sleeping child. He doesn't touch her, and his stance is not reverential like the cleaning person's, but reflective. His thoughts are not in the interrogative mood, but the mildly threatening conditional: *If we are to continue to save you, why, someone must be made responsible.* Responsible in a financial sense is of course what he means.

THE TALL GUY pushed the elevator button over and over and it finally came.

I went into the room.

She looked okay, sleeping on her side, though when I lifted the blanket and undid a couple of snaps I saw that she still had the diaper rash. Her skin just burned itself off sometimes because she didn't crawl or even roll, just lay there in her stuff. She might turn over someday, one of them said. She'd never eat and drink and she was deaf and she was impaired but really she knew me always.

I put the blanket back on. I watched her ear for a while. All those windings and curves. My little girl's little ear.

I got the toy she liked best from the windowsill. The red floppy dog. They always forgot it. I put it in a corner of the crib. Then I unscrewed the end of the heart tube from the aqua clothespin and I slipped it under the blanket so the blood would pool quiet and invisible like a monthly until there would be no more left.

Fidelity

When old Victor Cullen, housebound, his sight dimming fast, filed a report from his bed with the invented dateline of Ataraku, Japan, his editor at *World Enough*, elderly himself but with mental and physical gears fully engaged, didn't know what to do. So he did what he'd always done: edited the piece (never much work except for those damned ellipses), corrected the galleys, checked the blues. With the help of the art director—also Victor Cullen's friend and colleague—he fooled around with photographs of Matsushima and Tsuwano and Aomori and came up with convincing composites. An impoverished young artist who happened to be Japanese was let in on the mischief. She did a fine wash drawing of an imaginary Shinto temple. The editor sent the proofs up to Godolphin, the town Victor and Nora Cullen had moved to twenty years ago, no, twenty-one; leaving New York, no, forsaking New York. Godolphin was just outside of Boston. Their daughter practiced medicine there.

Nora telephoned right away.

"Greg," she said softly. "This Ataraku . . . it doesn't—"

"I know," he said, cutting her short; her voice still had the power to liquefy him. "It's okay. Victor's fans adore whatever he writes."

That much was true—the magazine's readers never tired of praising the keen eye and ear, the turns of phrase, the research. Every Victor Cullen contribution to *World Enough* inspired enthusiastic letters to the editor—letters in longhand, letters pecked on derelict typewriters, letters composed on word processors, and nowadays e-mail. "Ataraku: An Edgy Serenity" reaped the usual harvest.

It had been a prank, Greg figured: the prank of a furious old monarch, assisted by loyal retainers. King Victor. Maybe he'll rest now.

Almost immediately came Stwyth, Wales, whose entire population was named Pugh.

After Stwyth came Mossfontein, South Africa: such extravagant gardens.

Greg, in his third-floor office, edited Stwyth and Mossfontein and gave them pride of place in consecutive issues. The publishers on the twentieth floor published them. Did anyone in that suite even read the rag? *World Enough* made money; that was all the conglomerate wanted to know. *World Enough* had always made money despite its refusal to take ads from hotels, airlines, cruise ships, and package tours. Instead, whisky distillers, cigar makers, purveyors of tweeds and cashmeres willingly bought space; also antique booksellers and rug dealers and, increasingly, retirement communities and facilities for assisted living.

Victor next filed a story from Akmed, a Nile village, though the envelope bore the familiar Godolphin postmark. Young Katsuko, the artist, drew the ruins outside Akmed with the precision of Piranesi. The art director, back in the office after hip surgery, spread out on Greg's desk photographs of Egyptians from bygone issues. "They're not all Egyptians," he admitted. "Some are Jordanians. This one's an Afghan." Such wisdom in those seamed faces, Greg thought—they'd glow on the page. The art director cleared his throat. "Are we paying Victor the usual?"

"No. More."

"Good. I don't like to think of Nora scrimping," he said, not meeting Greg's eyes. "The daughter's divorced now, can't help much."

"THE EXUBERANT CASTLE OF LUBASZ," Victor's latest smoothly began, "is our temporary abode; it lies twenty kilometers from Budapest. In our bedroom an extraordinary armoire . . ."

Greg and the art director studied the new piece. They arranged and shot interiors to fit Victor's prose. Greg's own armoire carved with bearded cherubim was pressed into service. Victor had reported that the genitalia of the cherubim were as long as their beards. One would think he'd actually seen this unrestrained bit of furniture. But Victor had never laid eyes on the thing, had he; Greg found it on Third Avenue after the Cullens left town.

Nora must have described the armoire. Greg squinted at the galleys and then through them; he saw Victor propped in a bed trying to imagine the work of a Hungarian craftsman. "Well, Greg has this sort of closet under the skylight," Nora might have indiscreetly remarked. She was eighty now; slippage was to be expected.

"Does he really," Victor would have drawled. Then, snapping, "And how do you happen to know that?"

Two decades ago, on a September morning—Greg still recalled the stinging clarity of that fall day—she had trundled by early-morning train from Boston to Manhattan. Her handbag was stuffed with designs for fabric. The appointment with the vice president of the fabric company lasted an hour; then, flushed with success, she hurried down Madison and arrived at the restaurant further flushed, eyes shining. "They bought three, Greg. And they want some more silly beasts for children's curtains—kangaroos, wombats. This commission comes in so handy. How are you?"

They were both nearing sixty then. For so long he had played the role of neighbor and friend, guest at the feasts, editor of the articles. And on the rare occasions that Victor traveled alone on assignment, Greg escorted Nora to this concert and that party, expecting nothing more than to kiss the silken cheekbone and then return to his cramped apartment and its priceless view of the sky. But now they lived in different cities: a different convention obtained.

"How am I, Nora? I am dying for love of you."

"A knightly compliment," she said, and picked up the menu. "What on earth is Arctic char?"

"Not a compliment. I mean it."

Her startled gaze rose from the menu but paused before meeting his. She stared at his necktie, or at the tip of his goatee, maybe he should shave it off . . .

"Look at me, Nora."

She still didn't meet his eyes. But alarm was slowly fading from her face, and a soft acceptance replaced it. And his heart leaped like one of her kangaroos.

"Look at me," he pleaded.

"I don't dare."

Those three words were the closest to an admission of love he would ever hear. They were enough. During the next five years, until the onset of Victor's illness, she arrived once a season, like a quarterly dividend. They spent the afternoon in his not-quite-wide-enough bed. The sky told them when it was time to leave for her train—a merciless five o'clock sky, royal in December, slate in March, turquoise in June, cornflower in September.

THE ARMOIRE WITH THE BEARDED CHERUBIM that had kept them company in Greg's skylighted room was not in fact Hungarian. It was Albanian. As he edited "The Castle of Lubasz" Greg worried about this discrepancy, as if someone might peek through the small lie and discern the larger one. But suppose some indulgent readers did spot the falsehood? They'd only smile, and continue to buy enough whisky, cashmere throws, first editions, signed etchings, and retirement condominiums to keep advertisers happy; they'd continue to write appreciative letters to the editor. They weren't going anywhere, were they?—for if they did shiver with wander-lust, any other travel magazine, full of Galápagos tips and Parisian hideaways and Middle East excavations, would serve them better. The *World Enough* demographic ideal was content to sit in a leather chair islanded on a Persian rug, and smoke a cigar and read.

Greg stopped worrying.

The final envelope, rather flat, was on his desk the day the Cullens' daughter called from Godolphin. "They're gone," she said, and halted. "Both," she said.

Icy tongs gripped his vocal cords. After a while, "*Both?*" he managed.

"They died twelve hours apart. She probably swallowed something, Uncle Greg." There was a prolonged sniff. "Even though I was here, and my kids . . ."

They talked some more and then hung up. Greg opened the envelope.

Azula

The kingdom of Azula is shaped like a circle, not a perfect one, for its volcano juts westward as well as upward, but, rather, a circle with a bulge. Azula is completely surrounded by a river. The river was thought to be a lake until a current was discovered, flowing counterclockwise. The water reflects the sky—our sky, a faithful and steady blue.

Azula was established in 1678 by a land grant from Rudolfo the Fifth to a rogue musician. The country flourished under the musician's rule. Now it is nearly deserted. But the mosaics on the floor of the royal mansion have hardly faded since the days of glory. Beetles in constant motion add to the complicated mystery of the tiles . . . In our cobwebbed suite, ecru draperies droop, like flesh from an old elbow . . . There is no roof. The nearby hospital for incurables is considerably decayed—the veranda on its second story should not be stepped on, as Nora discovered almost to her destruction. Two cured lepers inhabit the place.

In fact, Azula is a haven for couples: crows, who mate for life, dwell in noisy twosomes in our ruined rafters; and we are served by a man and woman lawfully married; and a pair of cassowaries occupy the courtyard. Their flightless majesties resemble huge pillows whose feathers have burst through their casings. Necks curve seductively; faces ardently woo.

Amenities? A plank for a toilet, a bucket for a shower, an unvarying diet of fish and root vegetables, ragged shrimp nets for sheets. And the blessed absence of needles, conversation, trays, periodicals, grandchildren, and enemas.

Here we wait, beetles below and crows above and cassowaries without. The lepers tend the garden. The female servant cooks and the male servant fishes. And Nora and I swim and dine and embrace, ah, my lovely; my lined darling . . . Get that clever artist to draw the author's beauteous spouse; forget my battered mug.

Soon the volcano will erupt or the earth crack open; or perhaps one hot afternoon we will simply fail to emerge from the river, will sink into that blue that never changes, unlike the fitful New York sky you and she watched those afternoons Greg you bastard.

No, no, Greg silently screamed. I was a paladin. I kept her happy for you, Victor you fool.

His pencil was twirling between his fingers as if it had a will of its own.

Victor you fool, his mind kept repeating as if it, too, acted without his control. *Nora my dearest.* He moaned helplessly.

His fingers tightened; the pencil stopped twirling. "Rudolfo" would not do: a name out of operettas and Christmas ditties. Call the king "Godolpho." And the river—can its end really be its beginning, or . . . He felt rather than saw the art director shamble in.

For the contributors' page, Greg gave Katsuko a studio photograph of Nora to work from. The art director added a snapshot from his own wallet. When Katsuko submitted the finished drawing, she remarked in that uninflected way of hers that she wished she had known the subject. Greg looked at the picture, and there in brown ink on cream paper was Nora: the playful mouth, the luminous irises, even the slight pleating of the lids. One eyebrow lifted, the lips parted, *Oh, Greg, sometimes I have to escape from his intensity, I get scorched, you are so cool, darling, like a winding-sheet.*

To illustrate "Azula" the collaborators ignored *World Enough*'s extensive files. Instead they performed a rare misdemeanor: they rifled the expense account. They flew to Cairns to photograph cassowaries. They went to Istanbul to hunt down mosaics. They found a leper hospital in Jerusalem.

Then the two exhausted old men took the jumbo back to New York. They arrived early in the morning. At Greg's apartment they dropped their satchels in the living room and hung their neckties on the cherubim and, in suits and shoes, lay down side by side on the skimpy bed. Steadily they watched a sky streaked with gray and puckered with small clouds. Shortly after noon the streaks and puckers disappeared. A quantity of satin stretched before their eyes like a chivalric banner. "True blue," Greg said. The art director stood up on the bed and pointed his lens and clicked and clicked.

IF LOVE WERE ALL

I.

"BEFORE YOU CAME HERE—what did you do?" Mrs. Levinger asked during Sonya's first month in London.

"Books."

"Wrote?"

"Kept."

"Well then. Think of this enterprise as a balance sheet. On balance the children are better off. Don't you have a handkerchief, Sonya? Take mine."

The sort of incident that triggered this exchange—the removal of a child from his cohort by medical personnel—would occur frequently, but Sonya had just witnessed it for the first time: the kindly faces of doctor and nurse; the impassivity of the other children, imperfectly concealing their panic. Many wore cardboard placards, like Broadway sandwich men. LONDON, LONDRES, LOND, ENGLAND, the boards variously said.

"There is something a little wrong with your chest," the doctor had told the child, in German.

"We will make it well," the nurse said, in French.

The little boy spoke only Polish and Yiddish. He spoke them one after the other as he was led away. Then he screamed them, one after the other, stiffening his legs so as not to walk. "Mama!" he called as he was lifted up, though his mother was no doubt dead. "Big sister!" he cried as he was carried off, though his big sister, a girl of eight, had fallen to the floor.

"You will get used to it," Mrs. Levinger said to Sonya. "Oh dear."

Sonya was an American in town for the war. For several summers in the recent past she had led a gypsy life on the Rhode Island coast—danced on the beach, shared a one-room house with an aging tenor who loved her to distraction. These facts were a matter of indifference to Mrs. Levinger and the rest of beseiged London . . . or would have been a matter of indifference if Sonya had broadcast her history. But she said little about herself. When, during the previous year, friends in Providence (her home during the three seasons that weren't summer) begged to know why she was going abroad, throwing up her jobs (she taught Hebrew at Sunday school and she kept accounts for various small enterprises) . . . when people posed these questions, Sonya answered, "Because of the hurricane."

Her beach house had four slanted walls and an uncertain roof. No electricity, no running water. The hurricane of 1938 had lifted the place from its cement foundation and spun off with it. Not a stick of Sonya's belongings had ever been recovered—not the wood-burning stove, the chemical toilet, the teapot, the garments hanging on hooks. In the weeks that followed the storm she sat in her hillside Providence apartment and stared at the center of town, also ravaged but gradually repairing itself. But her own life would not be repaired; she was already sliding into unrelieved respectability. Somebody would sooner or later ask her to marry him—despite middle age, despite lack of beauty, somebody sometimes did. The tenor had already proposed. She feared that, no longer buoyed by her annual summer of freedom, she would weakly say yes.

She had offered herself instead to the American Joint Distribution Committee, affectionately called the Joint. She went to New York for an interview. The interviewer, an overweight man in shirtsleeves and a rumpled vest, said, "Good that you speak Hebrew."

"I don't, you know," Sonya told him. "I have enough biblical Hebrew to teach classes Aleph and Beth."

"If you are sent to Palestine your Hebrew will improve," he said. And, glancing down at her dossier: "You speak French."

"I studied French in high school, that's what it says. Once, in Quebec, I ordered a glass of wine. And Yiddish—I haven't used it in decades."

Their eyes met. "The situation in Europe is desperate," he said. "Thousands of Polish-German Jews have been expelled by Germany and refused by Poland and are starving and freezing and dying of dysentery in a no-man's-land between the two countries. Many are children. Several organizations are working together to help—and working together is not, I see you studied Latin as well, our normal modus operandi. Two Jews, three opinions, I'm sure you understand." He checked his verbal flow with a visible effort. His mouth opened and closed several times but he managed not to speak.

"I'll do any job," she said in this interval. "I just don't want you to count on languages."

"Do you sing? We find people who sing are comfortable in our work."

"I am moderately musical." Very moderately. She thought of the tenor. She could still say yes. But she did not want to become a caretaker.

The fat man's gaze loosened at last. He looked out the window. "All agencies are working together to get these people from Zbąszyń into England. For this, for all our efforts, we need staff members who are efficient and unsentimental. Languages are of secondary importance. The Joint trusts my judgment."

She signed a sort of contract. Then she said, "You should know, I am occasionally sentimental."

A smile, or something like it, landed on his large face and immediately scurried off. She suspected that, like many fat men, he danced well.

Sonya took the train back to Providence. After several months she learned that she would be sent to London and there loaned to another organization, one helping refugee children. She put the books of her clients into order. After several more months, there came a steamer ticket. She stored her furniture, and gave herself a farewell party in the emptied apartment. She took the train again and in New York boarded a ship bound for Southampton. The fat man—his name was Roland, she remembered—showed up to say good-bye, carrying a spray of carnations.

"How kind," she said.

"It is not the usual procedure," he admitted.

By the time she arrived in England the displaced Polish-Germans were already rescued or lost. War had been declared. She was sent to Hull for a year, to help settle as domestics German-Jewish women who had already arrived. Then she was reassigned to London.

There the Joint found her a bed-sitter in Camden Town. The landlady and her family lived on the ground floor; otherwise the place was home to unattached people. Each room had a gas fire and a stove. It took Sonya a while to get used to the smells. She had to get used to footsteps, too—there was no carpet, and everyone on the upper floors traveled past Sonya's room. There was an old lady with twittering feet. "My dear," she said whenever she saw Sonya. A large man looked at her with yellow-eyed interest. His slow footsteps sounded like pancakes dropped from a height. An elderly man lightly marched. With his impressive bearing and his white mustache he resembled an ambassador, but he was the proprietor of the neighborhood newsstand. Two secretaries tripped out together every morning after curling their hair with tongs. (The first time Sonya smelled singed hair she thought the house was on fire.)

And there was a lame man of about forty, their only foreigner. Sonya didn't count herself as foreign; she was an American cousin. But the lame man—he had a German accent. He had dark skin and bad teeth. Eyebrows sheltered glowing brown eyes—eyes that seemed to be reflecting a fire even when they were merely glancing at envelopes on the hall table. His legs were of differing lengths—that accounted for the limp. Sonya recognized his limping progress whenever he came up or down the staircase: ONE pause Two, ONE pause Two; and whenever he passed her door: ONE Two, ONE Two, ONE Two.

THE CHILDREN CAME, wave after wave of them. Polish children, Austrian children, Hungarian children, German children. Some came like parcels bought from the governments that withheld passports from their parents. These children wore coats, and each carried a satchel. Some came in unruly bands, having lived like squirrels in the mountains or like rats by the rivers. Some came escorted by social workers who couldn't wait to get rid of them. Few understood English. Some knew only Yiddish. Some had infectious diseases. Some seemed feebleminded, but it turned out that they had been only temporarily enfeebled by hardship.

They slept for a night or two in a seedy hotel near Waterloo station. Sonya and Mrs. Levinger, who directed the agency, stayed in the hotel, too, intending to sleep—they were always tired, for the bombing had begun. But the women failed to sleep, for the children—not crying; they rarely cried—wandered through the halls, or hid in closets, smoking cigarettes, or went up and down the lift. The next day, or the next day but one, Sonya and Mrs. Levinger escorted them to their quarters in the countryside, and deposited them with stout farm families, these Viennese who had never seen a cow; or left them in hastily assembled orphanages staffed with elderly schoolteachers, these Berliners who had known only the tender hands of nursemaids; or stashed them in a bishop's palace, these Polish children for whom Christians were the devil. The Viennese kids might have found the palace suitable; the Hungarians would have formed a vigorous troupe within the orphanage; the little Poles, familiar with chickens, might have become comfortable on the farms. But the billets rarely matched the children. The organization took what it could get. After the children were settled, however uneasily, Sonya and Mrs. Levinger rode the train back to London, Mrs. Levinger returning to her husband and Sonya to solitude.

For months she nodded at the dark man and he at her.

They said "Good evening."

One day they left the house at the same time, and walked together to the underground.

He lived two floors above her, he said. She already knew that from her attention to footsteps.

His room contained an upright piano left behind by a previous tenant. He managed to keep it in tune. "A piano is so rare in furnished . . . digs," he said, seeming to relish the British word.

He was on his way to give piano lessons. His pupils were London children whose parents thus far refused to have them evacuated. She was on her way to her office. He left the Tube first. "I hope we meet again, Miss . . ."

"Sofrankovitch," she said. She didn't tell him that the honorific was properly "Mrs." Her childless marriage had ended long ago.

After that, as if the clock previously governing their lives had been exchanged for a different timepiece, they ran into each other often. They met on the narrow winding High Street. They bought newspapers at the kiosk manned by their distinguished-looking housemate. They queued at the greengrocer's, each leaving with a few damaged apples. They found themselves together at the fishmonger's. Both were partial to smoked fish, willing to exchange extra ration coupons for the luxury.

Often, at night, after he came home from work, after she came home, they sat by her gas fire.

"Providence," he mused. "And the place of the hurricane?"

"Narragansett."

"Naghaghansett," he rolled out, his vowels aristocratically long, his consonants irreparably guttural.

"Something like that," she said, and smiled into the shadows.

Eugene had never visited the United States, though as a young man he had studied piano in Paris. "Yes, I heard Boulanger." Except for that heady time he had not left Germany until three years earlier, when one of the other refugee agencies helped him emigrate to London. Still short of forty then, his parents dead, his sister safely married in Shanghai, his ability to make a living secure—he was one of the easy repatriation cases, she supposed.

His father, he told her, had fought for the kaiser.

She had been a young woman during that war. Yes, she knew that Germany had once been good to its Jews, its Jews faithful to their rulers.

He stretched his long, unmatched legs toward the meager blue flames. "I'm glad we met."

One noontime—mirabile dictu, the New York fat man might have said—they ran into each other far from home, in Kensington Gardens.

"I am attending a concert," Eugene said. "Come with me."

"My lunch break . . . not much time."

"The performers also are on lunch break," he said. "You won't be late. You won't be very late," he corrected, with his usual slight pedantry.

They hurried along the streets leading toward the river, passing bomb craters and shelters of brick, of cement, of corrugated iron. Their own shelter, back in Camden Town, was an underground bunker, a crypt, safer than these. But it trembled sometimes, and then little children cried and women paled, and men too. Sonya soothed whichever toddler crawled into her lap, and smiled encouragement at the child's mother. It was hard to breathe. Suppose the thing should cave in—they would all suffocate. Being struck above ground, being blasted, being shattered into a thousand pieces like her beach house, that would be better than not breathing . . . There were times she did not go into the shelter at all, but stayed sitting on the floor in her blacked-out room, arms around shins. Behind her on the windowsill bloomed a sturdy geranium, red in the daytime, purple in this almost blindness. And if the house should be hit, and if she should be found amid its shattered moldings and heaps of glass and smoking bricks, her head at an odd angle, her burnt hair as black as it had been in her youth . . . if she should be found in the rubble, people would think, if they thought anything at all, that she had slept through the siren. She might have taken a bit too much, the wineshop keeper would say to his wife—he no doubt guessed that his customer sometimes sacrificed food for whisky. She was working so very hard, Mrs. Levinger would remark.

Eugene led her to a church. Sonya looked up at the organ loft. A few parishioners on their own lunch breaks settled into the empty pews. One slowly lowered his forehead onto the back of the pew in front of him, then lifted it, then lowered it again.

Downstairs, in a small chapel, a dozen people waited on chairs and two performers waited on a platform. The standing young man held a viola by its neck. The young woman sat at a piano, head bowed as if awaiting execution. A note on the mimeographed program mentioned that these twenty-year-old twins had recently arrived from Czechoslovakia. The performance began. The sister played with precision. Eugene's fingers played along, on his thighs. The brother made love to his instrument. In the intervals between selections the attentive audience was entertained by faint sounds of organ practice from above. The concert lasted less than an hour. When the twins and their guests filed upstairs, Sonya looked for the parishioner who had banged his forehead against the pew back, but he was gone.

As Eugene had promised, Sonya was not very late getting back to work. Still, Mrs. Levinger had already returned from lunch. She was on the telephone. She gave Sonya a distracted nod and hung up.

"The next batch is here," she said. "The French ones."

THE USUAL SETUP: at one end of a large room, volunteers stood at bridge tables; at the other end, a trestle table holding loaves of bread, and biscuits, and plates of sausages, and jugs of milk.

Forty children who had been fending for themselves for six

months now huddled in the middle of the room as if, were they to approach the food, they would be shot.

One girl's hair was the color of lamplight.

Mrs. Levinger hoisted herself onto a folding chair and grasped its back for a moment while her rump threatened to topple her. Then she stood up. Once standing she did not falter or shake.

Sonya made note of various details—it was part of her job. There was a small pale fellow who looked sick, but the doctors hadn't detained him. Hunger and fatigue, probably. Two little girls gripped each other's hands. Many children carried smaller children.

The fair-haired girl carried an instrument case.

Mrs. Levinger welcomed them in French. They were being sent to villages in the Cotswolds, she said. Hills, she elaborated. They could keep their belongings. Siblings would not be separated. The host families would not be Jewish. But they would be sympathetic.

"I am not Jewish, either," said a dark boy.

"Ah, Pierre," reproved a bigger boy. "It's all right, in this place."

The children made their slow silent way to the trestle table.

Soon all were eating—all except the tall blond girl with the instrument. She seemed about to approach Mrs. Levinger. But it was a feint. She swerved toward Sonya. "Madame . . ."

"Oui," Sonya said. "Voulez vous—"

"I speak English." Her eyes were gray. She had a straight nose, a curly mouth, a small chin. "I do not wish to go into the countryside."

"What is your name?"

"Lotte," she said with a shrug, as if any name would do. "I am from Paris. I wish to stay in London."

"Your instrument . . ."

"A violin," Lotte said. "I tried to sell it when we ran out of food in Marseilles, but no one wanted to buy it. I am skilled, madame. I can play in an orchestra. Or in a café—gypsy music."

"I wish," Sonya began. "I cannot," she tried again. "There is no arrangement in London for refugee children," she finally said. "Only in the villages."

"I am no child. I am seventeen."

Sonya shook her head.

The lids dropped. "Sixteen. Truly, madame."

"Call me Sonya."

"Merci. Madame Sonya, I am sixteen next month, if I had my papers I could prove it, but my papers were lost, everything was lost, even the photographs of my father, only the violin . . ." Lotte swallowed. "I will be sixteen in three weeks. Please believe me."

"I do." Mrs. Levinger was glancing at them; other children needed attention. "You must go to the Cotswolds now," Sonya said. "I'll try to make some better arrangement."

Lotte said, "Empty words," and turned away.

"No!" Was she always to be denied sentiment, must she be only efficient forever?—she who was moderately musical. "I love gypsy tunes. Look, this is my address," she said, scribbling on some brown paper. "I will try to find you a café, or maybe a . . ."

Lotte took the paper. Sonya's last sight of her was on the train, a different train from the one Sonya herself was taking. Lotte stood in the aisle, clasping the violin to her thin chest.

"I WOULD LIKE TO GIVE YOU A RING," Eugene said.

"Oh!"

"I may be interned."

"It won't happen," she said, fervently. But it was happening every day. Aliens suspected of being spies—Jews among them—were shut up in yellow prisons.

Eugene said, "My other suit, my piano scores—they can fend for themselves. But my mother's ring—I owe it respect. It eluded German customs, it eluded also my own conscience."

She glanced at him. In the light of the gas fire his skin looked as dark as the geranium.

"I should have sold it to repay my rescuers," he explained. "But it is only a little diamond. And it meant much to my mother."

"Ah . . . your father gave it to her."

"Her lover gave it to her. My mother was born in Lyon; in Berlin she retained her French attitude toward marriage. And then, of course, my father was so much older."

"Older?" A dozen years separated Sonya and Eugene—she had recently turned fifty-two without mentioning it.

"Twenty years older." Eugene fished in his pocket. Something twinkled. He put it into her palm.

Two weeks afterward he was taken away.

II.

By the beginning of Sonya's second year in London she had acquired women friends and men friends and a favorite tearoom and two favorite pubs and several favorite walks. She had adopted the style of the women around her—cotton dresses, low-heeled shoes—but she spurned the brave little hats. She swept her gray hair back from her brow and pinned barrettes behind her ears. Her hair curved like annoyed feathers below the barrettes.

She knew where to get necessaries on the black market. Occasionally, for her small clients, she used that knowledge. Sometimes she used it for herself—a bottle of contraband cognac was stashed at the bottom of her armoire waiting for Eugene's return.

She went to lectures in drafty halls. She went to briefings with people who had recently returned from Vichy and Salonika and Haifa. She went to patched-together concert operas and to stunning theatricals—once, in a theater, she heard Laurence Olivier's voice rise above the sound of bombs.

She attended exhibitions of new watercolors. A few times, during the summer, she bathed at Brighton. "You must play!" Mrs. Levinger ordered. She received letters from friends in Rhode Island and her aunt in Chicago and the fat man in New York and the tenor and Eugene. She kept track of that first tubercular boy, visited him in his seaside sanatorium. The Yiddish of her childhood stirred, necessarily, during the early visits, but after a few months she discovered that the new words he was learning stuck to him like burrs. Soon they spoke only English. Together they watched the slate-colored sea. Sitting next to his little chaise, his translucent hand in hers, she told him about the hurricane that had sliced her own life in two. "A tall wave smashed onto our cove."

"A hill of water," he experimented. "Yes, yes! A mountain."

She kept in touch with the sister, too, in her berth in a cottage. A year after the boy was taken away, Sonya and Mrs. Levinger presided over the reunion of the children, the girl rosy, the boy pale but free of disease. The foster mother agreed to take him, too. "For she pines, she does," said that kindly soul.

～

"OF COURSE YOU REMEMBER Roland Rosenberg," Mrs. Levinger said.

"Of course." They shook hands. He was a little less fat, but it would be tactless to say so. They spoke of work in an unnecessary way—it was as if she knew by heart the papers in his shapeless briefcase, as if he could trace each line on her face back to the situation that had drawn it there. But they did talk, some, in a gloomy restaurant. His table manners were terrible. His handkerchief was a disgrace. That peculiar smile recurred now and again—upturned lips, a look of wonder. Mark Twain, he told her, was a passion with him. Someday he wanted to follow Twain's journey around the world.

"And the composers you like?" she idly asked.

"Franz Lehár is my favorite."

Lehár: beloved by Hitler. "Oh dear," Sonya said.

"Shameful, isn't it. The Joint should fire me."

There was no cab. When was there ever a cab? He walked her home. "I will be back someday," he said.

"Good." Good? What were they doing to Eugene?

"THE NEW YORK TIMES, PLEASE," she said one evening, and took the paper from the distinguished gentleman. Standing at the kiosk, she looked at the front page. The war occupied most of it, though there were city scandals, too. The Dakotas were suffering a drought. She folded the paper under her arm—she would read it by lamplight, at home; there were no air raids nowadays.

From his recess he rumbled: "How are you, Miss Sofrankovitch?"

She turned back. ". . . Okay, thanks."

"I have newspapers from Belgrade today, a rare event."

"Ah, I don't read Yugoslavian."

"No? You read French, perhaps. I have—"

"Not really. And not German, either," she anticipated. "I can read elementary Hebrew, Mr. . . ."

"Smith."

"Smith." She peered at him, and at the darkness behind him. "My own parents sold newspapers," she confided.

"Indeed."

"Yes, in a store. They sold cigarettes also. Candies, notions. Notions—an Americanism—perhaps you are not familiar with it."

"Haven't a notion!" He turned his attention to the next customer. Business first, of course; but how urgently Sonya now wanted to describe to him that small round couple, her parents, that pair of innocents to whom she had been born long after they had given up the idea of family. By then the store itself was their issue—a close, warm cave. In it she grew into a tall girl; graduated from high school, from normal school; from it she married a handsome and untrustworthy boy. She kept the marriage going, and the store too, until both parents were safely dead.

Mr. Smith disposed of his customer. Sonya leaned across the shelf of newspapers. The interior, big enough for two if the two were disposed to be friendly, was adorned with magazines clipped to bare boards, and advertisements for beer. The place was redolent of tobacco, the fragrance of her childhood. She remembered Eugene's bad teeth, made browner still by his cigarette habit. She inhaled. "I sold the place during the Depression," she told Mr. Smith. He leaned against a poster: LOOSE LIPS LOSE LIVES. She withdrew her upper body from the booth and again stood erect, continuing her history. "I sold the living quarters, too. I rented an apartment and also bought a . . . house, a house on the shore. It was destroyed by the hurricane, but perhaps here you didn't know of the hurricane."

"Oh, we knew of it. We saw photographs. *Comment donc!*" he said, turning to another patron who must have been familiar, a little Frenchman in a floorwalker's frock coat and polished shoes.

Sonya turned away and walked up the High Street toward home.

Home? A wallpapered room with a gas fire. A round table and turnup bed and desk and armchair and radio and lamp and battered armoire. A little locked jewel box in which reposed her mother's wedding ring; the silk handkerchief from the tenor which he himself had received from a famous mezzo; Eugene's diamond. Yes, home. Her home was wherever she was. "You have no nesting instinct," her husband had accused when he was leaving. "Lucky for us we never had a child. You would have kept it in a bureau drawer."

No mail for her. Up the stairs, then. She boiled two eggs on the stove and put a slice of bread on the toasting fork. She had no butter and no jam but she did have a glass and a half of wine in yesterday's bottle, and she uncorked it gratefully. She read the paper during this repast, saving the obituaries for last, nice little novelettes, it was unlikely that she'd ever recognize anybody on that page until Roly-poly Rosenberg burst a blood vessel; no, really, he wasn't the apoplectic type, and he was losing weight, anyway . . . she read of the tenor's death.

He had collapsed while singing to a large audience of soldiers at Fort Devens. He was seventy-three. His career had spanned six decades. He had sung all the great roles, though never at the Met. His radio program was popular during the thirties. Its signature song was "The Story of a Starry Night." He left three daughters and eight grandchildren.

There had been only seven grandchildren when she left; otherwise she could have written the obituary herself.

That night she wept for him. Of course she had been wise not to join her destiny to his. She was not meant for the settled life—not she, not Sonya, not this human leaf that had appeared unexpectedly in an overheated notions store and gotten popped, as it were, into a jelly glass by the proud but bewildered storekeepers. Oh, they had loved her, Mama and Papa; and she had loved them; and she had loved her husband for a while, and some others after him; and she had loved the tenor, too. But her love was airy, not earthbound, and so she could be scooped up like a handful of chickweed by Roland Rosenberg and flung onto the stones of London, there to send out shallow creepers into this borough, that block of flats, the derelict basement over by the river. The children. Sleeplessly she counted them. Some were in the city now. There were two small boys living with a mother who had become deranged when the oldest son was shot dead at the border; those tykes took care of her. There was a family with a dim-witted daughter who herself had borne a dim-witted daughter. "That shouldn't happen; offspring regress toward the average!" Sonya objected, as if laws of heredity would acknowledge the error and revise the little girl's intelligence. Mrs. Levinger ignored her outburst. There were teenage girls from Munich working as waitresses who refused to confide in Sonya, though they allowed her to buy them dinner. And . . .

The scratching at the door could have been a small animal. Had it been preceded by footsteps? Sonya was out of bed immediately, her left hand on the bolt, her right on the knob. Was that the smell of cigarettes? She opened the door.

Lotte stepped across the threshold. Her eyes swiveled from corner to corner. She saw the round table and laid her violin carefully under it. Then she turned and fell into Sonya's arms.

THEY FEASTED ON BACON in the morning. Lotte had carried it from the farm. Sonya fried it along with a hoarded tomato, and toasted her last two pieces of bread. They dipped the toast into the grease.

"Now we have to talk," Sonya said, when they had wiped their fingers on her only napkin. Lotte's fingers were more deliberate than delicate—rather like Eugene's at the piano.

"The family," Lotte began. "They were kind. The church organist befriended me. There was a boy at school, too: an English boy, I mean," and Sonya knew what she meant—the local boy's attention supplemented but didn't supplant the calf love of the immigrant boys already attached to her. Such an enchanting sweep of lash.

"The family," Sonya prompted.

"I left a letter. Don't send me back. Let me stay here with you."

It was against the organization's rules. But the organization's rules often got ignored. South of the river five teenage boys from Bucharest lived in one room, supporting themselves who knew how, though pickpocketing was suspected. Sometimes Mrs. Levinger hauled them in. "It's not good for the Jews, what you're doing." The boys looked at their feet.

"They endanger our enterprise," Mrs. Levinger said later to Sonya.

"A couple of them actually work as plasterers."

"Well, we do need plasterers," said Mrs. Levinger, deflected. "Rumor has it that they steal only from rich drunks."

"Rumor! Rumor has it that Winston is planning an invasion. I'll believe that when it happens. We're probably going to be invaded." Sonya imagined Mrs. Levinger picking up the fireplace shovel and banging the heads of Germans foolish enough to enter her office.

Meanwhile the young Romanians lifted wallets in Mayfair. And an unlicensed pair of Polish doctors kept an unlicensed clinic in Clapham Common. Belgians who had arrived with diamonds in their hems sold those diamonds on the black market and decamped for South America, bestowing not one shilling on the agency that had brought them to London, a different agency, but still. "Not against the rules," Mrs. Levinger mentioned. "Not *comme il faut*, however." Sonya thought of Eugene's mother's little stone.

"I'll sleep on the floor," Lotte was saying now. "I'll get a job. I'll pay my share. You'll see."

"WHAT'S THIS ABOUT A FRENCH GIRL?" Mrs. Levinger said a few days later. "I had a letter from a family . . ."

"She's with me."

They exchanged a steady look. "We can manage a small allowance," said Mrs. Levinger.

"If that becomes necessary," Sonya said—in a rather cold voice, since she was almost in tears—"I will let you know."

It did not become necessary. On Saturday Lotte asked Sonya for a few shillings; also, could Sonya borrow a screwdriver from someone in the building? Well, she'd try. Mr. Smith was at his kiosk. The twittering old lady had gone to live with her daughter. The yellow-eyed man was out. Eugene was of course not in, either. Sonya finally knocked on the secretaries' door, expecting no luck. But the secretaries owned an entire tool chest; they'd built a hutch for their window. They were raising generations of rabbits. "How . . . sweet," said Sonya.

"Cash," explained one of the young women. "The nobs still love their lapin."

Sonya came downstairs with the screwdriver to find Lotte returning from the High Street with a brass lock and two keys. Within an hour she had affixed it to the door of the armoire. Then she stowed her violin next to the cognac. She locked the closet. For a moment she sank into the chair. "Safe," she said, and sighed. Sonya forbore to mention the bombings; perhaps they wouldn't start again.

Returning the screwdriver, Sonya ran into the landlady. "I have a . . . guest."

"I noticed, dearie. I'll have to charge a bit more."

Every day Lotte went out looking for work. She came back disappointed. At night they went to concerts. It was like having Eugene back. "At St. Aidan's—there's a choir singing tonight," Lotte would say; or "A basso over at Marylebone—just got here from there." Scattered musicians formed makeshift ensembles.

"How did you hear about this?" Sonya asked as they drifted home from a trio.

"I went to a music store looking for a job . . . met some other string players . . ."

Lotte began to play on street corners. Sonya warned her to watch for policemen. At first she played in outer London. But though small bands of admirers collected (she reported matter-of-factly to Sonya), too few coins fell into the open case at her feet. She moved toward the center of town. She played in Picadilly; in the Strand; near Whitehall. "I saw Churchill," she exclaimed. Everyone knew that Churchill was directing the war from underground offices, but there were rumors of look-alike doubles, hundreds of them, deployed to fool the enemy and maybe the populace.

In Lotte's new sites she collected enough money to meet the landlady's rise in rent, to buy cheese and smoked fish and peaches, to insist that Sonya always take the greater share. "You are my patron, my benefactor, my angel."

"I repudiate those roles. This peach is heavenly."

"My mother, then . . . no, no, you are too young."

"Hardly too young."

"Big sister!"

Sonya was still on loan to Mrs. Levinger from the Joint, but Mrs. Levinger's mandate had altered. Few refugees managed to get in now, but there was plenty to do for the ones already here. Families were starving. Sonya made rounds with ration books, with money, sometimes with piecework from factories—she might have been a foreman sweating workers. Lotte fiddled for coins.

One spring evening Sonya decided to cross the river before going home. No raids for a long time now, just a few planes every so often, scared off by the ack-ack guns. On the embankment she saw a clown . . . no, it wasn't a clown, it was a girl. Yes, it was a clown: Lotte.

She was near a bombed-out site beginning to be rebuilt. Those plasterers—were the Romanian boys among them? Lotte wore wide plaid trousers underneath her usual skimpy jacket. She had found a diplomat's homburg—snatched it, maybe—and she had blacked the space between her upper teeth and darkened some of her freckles. Her pale hair foamed beneath the hat. She played the street repertoire that she practiced at home—Kreisler, Smetana, Dvořák—with exaggerated melancholy and exaggerated vivacity. "To make their eyes water," she'd explained. "To give them a swooping finale."

After the swooping finale she walked among the loiterers, her hat upside down in her hand. When she came to Sonya she bowed. Teasingly she shook the hat. Sonya reached into the pocket of her raincoat but Lotte moved on.

The listeners drifted away. A smiling Lotte returned to Sonya. "Let's feast!"

"Those clothes!" Sonya smiled back.

The homburg turned out to be a trick hat, collapsible. Lotte shed the wide trousers with one twist of her nimble hips, revealing a pleated skirt, one of the two she owned. With trousers and hat in one hand and the violin in the other she led the way to a pub.

They sat in a corner booth, the two of them—three, counting the instrument. Lamplight streamed through stained-glass windows into the noisy place.

"I did well today," Lotte said, handing the money to Sonya, who knew better than to refuse. "But I would prefer a steadier income."

"You should be at school," Sonya moaned.

"Soon I will find a place in an orchestra. Or a nightclub."

Sonya ordered a second whisky.

Roland Rosenberg appeared the next week and stayed for forty-eight hours. Though still fat he was thinner and worn. But: "You are losing weight, Sonya Sofrankovitch," he had the nerve to say. "Take care of yourself."

And then—Lotte's mad dreams came true. A restaurateur heard her, hired her, provided crepe trousers and a sequined jacket. Café Bohemia was a hodgepodge of banquettes, murals, gilt, and salvage. Sonya dropped in one or two nights a week.

There were no more eye-watering swoops, no more glittering glissandi. She played Brahms, Liszt, Mendelssohn. She looked twice her age, Sonya thought. But then Sonya herself probably looked twice hers.

Lotte found a trio—two old men and one old woman—who wanted a second violinist. "They play very well," Lotte commended, "though none of them is Jewish." The recitals were free, but the performers were paid, sometimes, by a foundation in Canada. Lotte had to rifle the account she shared with Sonya to buy a blue dress with a collar—the sequined outfit was not considered appropriate.

She had every right to rifle the account. She was contributing more than Sonya. She bought a fold-up cot and no longer had to sleep on the floor. She bought a second geranium, and whisky, though she herself drank only an occasional glass of wine. And when Sonya turned fifty-three, Lotte bought a pair of train tickets. They journeyed to Penzance for a weekend and stayed in a hotel and walked on the beach, holding hands like sisters.

ONE pause Two. ONE pause Two.

A Sunday afternoon. Lotte was out playing with the quartet.

ONE Two, ONE Two.

Sonya opened her door. This time it was he.

THE WAR HAS GONE ON so long it seems like peace, Sonya wrote to her aunt. *One day is like another. No new horrors, just old ones.* She wondered if the letter would get by the censors.

Eugene was busy. Perhaps, to compensate for his unfair internment, someone was pulling strings. So many people were making so many unseen efforts. Sonya and Mrs. Levinger continued the quiet tasks of their agency, more and more of them against the rules. The yellow-eyed man upstairs spent weeks at Bletchley Park, the center of code-breaking efforts. Lotte fiddled on corners when she had a free afternoon. Mr. Smith, so adept at inviting confidential disclosures, was discovered to be a spy and was arrested.

Eugene wrote reviews for newspapers. Sonya helped occasionally with sentence structure. New families wanted him to teach their children, who were practicing Czerny in formerly grand neighborhoods now sparkling with shards. He gave performances, too. He joined Lotte's quartet from time to time and played trios with Lotte and the cellist and duets with Lotte. When the two could, they practiced in the church where Eugene and Sonya had listened to the Czech brother and sister. "Such a good piano," Eugene said.

Sonya brought her families to the concerts—the couple and their retarded daughter, once; the half-crazy mother and her little boys, several times; the young waitresses; the pickpocket plasterers.

Of course—she told herself—all couples who played together developed affinities. Some had affinities from birth—consider those Czech twins, consider the Menuhins. Eugene and Lotte were not brother and sister, though they could be father and daughter. Twenty years lay between them. She calculated again. Twenty-four! She thought of the tenor . . . Eugene's brown profile bent over the keys. His mouth grimaced, sucked. Lotte nestled her chin onto her handkerchief. The fingers of her left hand danced. There were dark patches under the arms of the blue dress. At night, on her cot, she sometimes cried out, in French.

One evening Sonya came home to an empty room smelling of cigarettes. She put the milk she was carrying on the sill next to the geraniums. There was a chapel a block away—an ugly little dissenters' place. She went there and sat in a back pew and rested her brow on the back of the pew in front of her, and lifted her head, and brought it down again on the wood, and lifted it, and brought it down.

III.

THE FIRST OF THE DOODLEBUGS struck a week after the D-day landings. They struck again and again. They were not like the bombs of the earlier Blitz. There was no time to get to a safe place; there was no safe place. People simply flattened themselves, waiting to be hurled, impaled, shattered, blown to bits, buried alive. If they were far enough away from the site they might be spared.

"The end is near, the end is near," the landlady told Sonya. "The end is near," sighed the parents of the damaged daughter. "Hitler's last gasp," Mrs. Levinger declared. Sonya thought that the Führer seemed to have a lot of wind left in his lungs, but all she said was that the demented mother and her boys must be gotten out of London. "Maybe that house in Hull." For half an hour they discussed the pros and cons of the children being incarcerated in a virtual bedlam, each woman supplying the other's arguments like the friends they had become. They resolved on a more farm-like retreat, and Sonya made the arrangements.

Work continued, rebuilding continued; even concerts.

One day at half past noon Sonya was eating an apple on a bench in Hyde Park when she heard the familiar hum. She continued to chew. She saw the flying bomb, there was just one, it was only a bomb, they were all only bombs. Some, she'd been told, failed to explode. This one exploded, south of the park. She was still chewing.

Smoke rose, dark gray and thick, and the sounds she heard now were sirens and further explosions and buildings crashing and shrieks, and footsteps, her own among them, for she was running across the park, her apple still in her hand, toward the bomb, because the place of the bomb was the place of that church, wasn't it? And they were rehearsing this noontime, weren't they? She ran across the King's Road; and now she was part of a mob, some rushing along with her, some against her. Sides of houses had vanished. Faces were black. She stumbled over a woman, stopped; but the woman was dead. She ran on. An arm poked out of a heap of stones. She stopped again and this time helped a fireman dig at the stones and extricate a woman, still alive thank God, and a baby protected by the woman's other arm, the baby too was alive thank God thank God. The smoke made it hard to breathe. Buildings kept falling. There was the smell of scorched flesh. Sonya reached the street of the church. The church was blasted. There was already a cordon; how fast the municipality had worked; no more than ten minutes had passed; these brave people; but she would simply have to get under the rope. Her apple was gone. She stooped. "Miss!" Somebody strong yanked her by her hips. She whirled into the arms of a red-faced man in a helmet and saw, over his shoulder, Eugene, his brow dark, bruised in fact, and Lotte, filthy. They were holding hands. In her free hand Lotte held the instrument case. They had not been in the church, they explained when she reached them. They had lingered at home.

The barrage continued for months. Only storms kept the planes away. Sonya prayed for a hurricane. Churchill conceded that London was under attack. The flying bombs did not cease until three weeks before victory.

But earlier still—five weeks before victory—Lotte and Eugene left for Manchester. The director of the new civic orchestra there had heard Lotte playing with the quartet, had offered her a job. There would be pupils for Eugene.

Lotte had been sharing Eugene's bed since the day the doodlebug struck the church. But the night before leaving, she scratched on Sonya's door. She put on the old clothes—the hat, the plaid trousers. She played "Someday I'll Find You" and "I'll See You Again."

In the morning all three walked to the Tube and rode to the

station. Even next to Eugene and Lotte, Sonya saw them as if from a distance—two gifted émigrés, ragged, paired. Father and daughter? Step-siblings? Nobody's business. As soon as they boarded the train they found a window and stared through it, their loved faces stony with love of her. She wondered how long Lotte would flourish under Eugene's brooding protection, how soon she would turn elsewhere. She was French, wasn't she, and Frenchwomen were faithless . . . His mother's diamond! She lifted her left hand in its disreputable glove and pointed toward the place of a ring with her right index finger.

On the other side of the window Eugene shook his head. *Yours,* he mouthed.

So Sonya sold the ring. It fetched less than she'd hoped—the stone was flawed. She bought a voluminous raincoat made out of parachute material. She bought new gloves and some dramatic trousers. She stashed the rest of the money.

IV.

"It's been a long time," Sonya said, once Mrs. Levinger had left them alone.

"Oh, I wanted to visit," Roland said. "When I was in Lisbon, in Amsterdam . . . But each time, something sent me elsewhere." He shifted in his ill-fitting jacket. He had lost more weight. Mrs. Levinger had hinted that he was some kind of hero.

They left the office and walked into wind and rain. Sonya's new coat swirled this way and that; it got drenched though it was supposed to be water-repellent; it dragged her backward. Finally she lifted its skirts, so as to be more easily blown to wherever he was taking her.

A pub. They sat down. Sonya knew he would not mention the nature of the work he had done, and he didn't—not during the first beer, not during the second. So: "Where now?" she asked, resting her worn-out hands on the worn-out table.

He told her about the Displaced Persons camps. He was going to the one at Oberammergau. "I hope you will join us. Your persistence, your intelligence, your accommodating nature . . ." She waved away his words with her right hand and he caught it mid-air. "I will stop this talk, though it is not flattery. I invite you to Oberammergau."

"I speak no German."

"But you are musical," he reminded her. He caught her other hand, though it couldn't be said to be in flight, was just lying there on the table. "Sonya Sofrankovitch. Will you come?"

She was silent for several moments. His odd smile—would she ever get used to it, to him?—told her how much he wanted to hear *yes*.

"Yes," she said.

Purim Night

CAMP GRUENWASSER WAS PREPARING for Purim, that merry celebration when you must drink until you cannot distinguish the king from the villain, the queen from the village tart.

"Purim?" Ludwig inquired.

He was twelve—pale and thin like all the others. But Ludwig had been pale and thin Before, during his pampered early boyhood in Hamburg. While hiding out with his uncle he had failed to become ruddy and fat.

"Purim is a holiday," Sonya said. She was fifty-six, also pale and thin by nature. She had spent the war in London; now that it was over she was codirector of this camp for Displaced Persons. What a euphemism: fugitives from cruelty, they were; homeless, they were; despised. "Purim celebrates the release of the Jewish people. From a wicked man."

"Release. Released by the Allied forces?"

"No, no. This was in Shu, Shu, Shushan, long ago . . ." She said *long ago* in English. The rest of the conversation—all their conversations in the makeshift, crowded office where Ludwig often spent the afternoon—was conducted in German. Ludwig's was the pedantic German of a precocious child, Sonya's the execrable German of an American with no talent for languages. Her Yiddish was improving at Camp Gruenwasser, though. Yiddish was the camp's lingua franca, cigarettes its stable currency.

"Shu, Shu, Shushan," Ludwig repeated. "A place of four syllables?"

Sonya briefly closed her eyes. "I was repeating an old song, a line from an old song." She opened them again and met his reddish-brown gaze. "Haman was the name of the wicked man. The heroine was a queen, Esther. Speaking of queens . . ."

"We were not."

"We were not what?"

"We were not speaking of queens."

"Even so," Sonya said. "A set of chessmen came in with the allotments yesterday. It is lacking only a pawn. A stone—can you employ a stone?"

"Yes. Also my uncle keeps his corns in a box for just such purposes."

Sonya dragged a rickety chair to the wall underneath a shelf, and climbed up on it, and retrieved the box of chessmen. She gave it to Ludwig.

He was scurrying off when Ida said, "Wait." Ida was the secretary, a Person who had been a milliner Before. "I will tell about Purim, you should know, a Jewish boy like you."

He paused mid-flight, back against the wall, eyes wide as if under a searchlight. "In Shu, Shu, Shushan long ago," Ida said in English, with a nod to Sonya, then continued in German, "there was a king, Ahasuerus; and a general, Haman; and Mordecai, a wise Jew who spent his time by the gates of the palace. King Ahasuerus's queen offended him so he called for a new queen. Mordecai . . ." and she used an unfamiliar word.

Sonya ruffled through her German-English dictionary. *"Procured*? I'm not sure . . ."

". . . *procured* his niece, Esther," Ida said, her dark eyes insistent. "Mordecai refused to bow down to Haman. Haman arranged to murder the Jews. Esther, the new queen now, urged Ahasuerus to stop the murder. The Jews were saved."

"Procured . . ." Sonya still objected, and Ludwig, still pinned to the wall, said, "It was a miracle, then."

"A miracle," Ida said, and nodded.

"I do not believe in miracles, especially miracles accomplished by the *fuck*." The word wedged its Anglo-Saxon bluntness into the German polysyllables. The vocabulary of children had been augmented by American servicemen. But the GIs were not responsible for the hasty and brutal lovemaking Ludwig had witnessed in forest huts, in barns by the side of the road, in damp Marseille basements.

"A girl with good looks and a beautiful hat can work miracles," Ida said. "Withholding the fuck. And that word, Ludwig, it is improper." She returned to her typewriter. Ludwig ran away.

Sonya, who had more to do today than three people could accomplish in a week, strolled to the narrow window. It was February, mid-afternoon. Shadows were deepening in the courtyard formed by the long wooden barracks so hastily abandoned by the Wehrmacht that Persons continued to find gun parts, buttons, medals, and fragments of letters (*"Heinz, Leibling, Der Kinder . . ."*). There was still a triangle of sunlight in the courtyard, though, and ragged children were playing within it, and Ludwig should be among them, would have been among them if he weren't a peculiar child who preferred the company of adults.

The year was 5707 by biblical reckoning and 1947 by the Christian calendar. The Purim party would begin after dinner. There would be pastries—hamantaschen: Haman's hats. Without those pastries the holiday might as well be ignored; without those pastries the megillah—the tale, written on a scroll—might as well be stuffed into a cistern. Tonight's necessary hamantaschen—they would be a joke. Men who had been chefs Before knew how to bake Sacher tortes, linzer tortes, all kinds of sweets; but where was the sugar, where the nuts? Today, using coarse flour and butter substitute and thin smears of blackberry preserves, they would bake ersatz hamantaschen, one or two per individual. Sonya did not know whether the practical bakers considered babies individuals, though babies certainly counted to the Red Cross and the American command—each infant received its own vitamin-laced chocolate bars and its own Spam and its own cigarettes. Sonya could not procure sufficient tinned milk, however . . . As for the meal preceding the party, it would consist of the usual dreck: watery spinach soup, potatoes, and black bread. Eisenhower had decreed that the Displaced Persons camps be awarded two thousand calories per Person per day; decent of him, but the general couldn't keep count of newcomers, they came in so fast.

"In my atelier I served the most distinguished and cosmopolitan women," Ida mused, her hands at rest on the typewriter keyboard. "I fashioned turbans and cloches and toques."

"Cartwheels and mantillas," encouraged Sonya, who had heard this reminiscence before.

"I spoke five languages. I made—"

"Sonya!" came the voice of Roland, Roland Rosenberg, Sonya's codirector. "Sonya?" and he followed his voice into the office, his eyes flickering over the beauteous Ida and coming to rest on Sonya's narrow visage. He still had a fat man's grace, even a fat man's circumference, though he was losing weight like all the staff. "Sonya, the Chasids in the north building refused to share their megillah. They boycotted the general service."

"The Enlightenment Society also boycotted," Ida remarked. "They held a seminar on Spinoza."

"The blackberry jam—there's so little of it. Goddamn!" Sonya said. She was subject to sudden ferocity these days. It was the Change, Ida told her knowingly, though Ida herself was only thirty-five.

"Poppy seeds—why couldn't they send poppy seeds," said Roland. "I requested poppy seeds." Consulting a list, he left as unceremoniously as he had entered.

"Roland, it's all right," Sonya called after him. "The kindly German farmers—they will certainly butcher some calves for our party." She was in the doorway now, but he had rounded the corner. "Whipped cream will roll in like surf." She raised her voice, though he was surely out of earshot. "General Eisenhower—he will personally attend."

"Sonya," Ida said in a severe tone. "It is time for your walk."

ABOUT PURIM LUDWIG HAD DISSEMBLED. Feigning ignorance was always a good idea; know-it-alls, he'd observed, tended to get beaten up or otherwise punished. In fact, he'd already heard the story of Esther, several times. First from the young man in the room next door, the one with the radiant face. Ludwig, recognizing the radiance, predicted that the young man would get caught in the next X-ray roundup. Meanwhile the feverish fellow did a lot of impromptu lecturing, even haranguing. Did he think he was the Messiah? grumbled Uncle Claud. One day last week he'd gathered a bunch of children around him and recited the Purim tale. He made a good thing of it, Ludwig thought from the periphery of the circle; he almost foamed at the mouth when reciting the finale, the hanging of Haman and his ten sons, the slaughter of the three hundred conspirators. Then the story had been taken up in the schoolroom on the second floor of the north building, where grimy windows overlooked in succession the one-storied kitchen and the grubby garden, all root vegetables—well, this was a stony patch, said Uncle Claud, his voice rumbling like a baron's; we cannot expect the chanterelles we scraped from the rich soil in the south of France. Past the garden a road led between farms to the village of tiled roofs. Beyond the village green hills gently folded. The Judaica teacher, not looking through the window at this familiar view, had begun the Purim story by reading it in Hebrew, which maybe half a dozen kids could understand. He translated into Yiddish and also Russian. His version, a droning bore in all three languages, insisted that the Lord, not Esther, had intervened to save the Jews. The history teacher said that night that there was no justification for this interpretation in Scripture. A day later the philosophy professor referred to the story as a metaphor.

"Metaphor?" Ludwig inquired, and presently learned the meaning of the term. He loved learning. He liked to hang around the office because Roland, without making a big thing of it, let fall so many bits of knowledge, farted them out like a horse. Sonya, too, was interesting to observe, hating to argue but having to argue, hating to persuade but having to persuade. She'd rather be by herself, reading or dreaming, Ludwig could tell; she reminded him of his mother . . . And Ida with her deep beautiful eyes and her passionate determination to go to Palestine; if only Uncle Claud would fuck her, maybe all three would end up in the Holy Land, well, not so holy, but not a barracks, either. He'd heard that people there lived in tents with camels dozing outside. But Uncle Claud preferred men.

Even without the story, Ludwig would have noticed Purim. The Persons in the camp—those who were not disabled, paralyzed with despair, stuck in the TB hospital, too old, too young, or (by some mistake in assignment) Christian—the Persons were loudly occupied with the holiday. In the barrack rooms, behind the tarps and curtain strips that separated cubicle from cubicle, costumers rustled salvaged fabrics; in stairwells, humorists practiced skits; in the west building, raisins fermented and a still bubbled. In the village, Persons were exchanging cigarettes and candy bars for the local wine. "Sour and thin," sneered Uncle Claud, who hid among his belongings a bottle of cognac procured God knew how. Uncle Claud smoked most of his cigarette allotment and also Ludwig's, and so he rarely had anything to barter. The cognac—Ludwig thought of it as a foretaste of the waters of Zion. "Zion has no waters," Uncle Claud insisted. Every night he gave Ludwig a fiery thimbleful, after their last game.

They owned a board. Sometimes they were able to borrow chessmen, but usually they rented those of a Lithuanian in the next room, the fervent Messiah's room. The Lithuanian didn't care for chess but happened to own the set of his brother, now ashes. He wouldn't lend, wouldn't sell, would only lease. Claud had to relinquish a cigarette for the nightly pleasure.

But now . . . Ludwig parted the shredded canvas that was their door, sat down on the lower bunk beside his uncle. "Look!" he said, and shook the box Sonya had given him like a noisemaker.

Claud smiled and coughed. "The Litvak—he can kiss my backside."

When Sonya left the office, Ida resumed typing. She was doing requisitions: for sulfa drugs; for books; for thread; for food, food, food.

Dear Colonel Spaulding,

You are correct that the 2000 calories Per Person Per Day are Supplemented by Red Cross packages and purchases from the village. But the Red Cross packages come unpredictably. Some of our Persons will not eat Spam. And though we must turn a blind eye to the Black Market, it seems unwise to encourage its use. Our severest need now is dried fruit—our store of raisins is completely wiped out—and sanitary napkins.

Yours Very Truly,
Sonya Sofrankovich

Ida ran a hand through her hair. It was as dense and dark as it had been ten years earlier, when she was captured, separated from the husband now known to be dead, oh Shmuel, and forced to work in a munitions factory. Not labor camp, not escape from labor camp, not the death in her arms of her best friend, oh Luba, not recapture, not liberation; not going unwashed for weeks, not living on berries in the woods, not the disappearance of her menses for almost a year and their violent return; not influenza lice odors suppurations; not the discovery in the forest of an infant's remains, a baby buried shallowly, dug up by animals; not the one rape and the many beatings—nothing had conquered the springiness of her hair. Her hair betrayed her expectance of happiness. And where would she find this happiness? Ah, b'eretz, in the Land. Milliners, she had been informed by the emissary from the Underground, barely concealing his disgust . . . Milliners were not precisely what the Land required. Do you think we wear chapeaux while feeding our chickens, Giverit? Perhaps you intend to drape our cows with silken garlands. Sitting on a wooden chair, hands folded in her lap, she told him that she would change careers with readiness, transform herself into a milkmaid, till the fields, draw water, shoot Arabs, blow up Englishmen. Then she leaned toward this lout of a pioneer. "But if cities arise b'eretz, and commerce, and romance— I'll make hats again." He looked at her for a long time. Then he wrote her name on his list. Now she was waiting for the summons.

Meanwhile she typed applications for other Persons. Belgium had recently announced that it would take some. Australia also. Canada too. America was still dithering about its immigration laws, although the Lutheran Council of the American Midwest had volunteered to relocate fifty Persons, not specifying agricultural workers, not even specifying Lutherans. But how many tailors could this place Minnesota absorb?

She typed an application, translating from the Yiddish handwriting. *Name: Morris Losowitz*; yes, she knew him as Mendel but Morris was the proper Anglicization. *Age: 35*; yes that was true. *Dependents: Wife and three Children*; yes that was true, too, though it ignored the infant on the way. *Occupation: Electrical Engineer*. In Poland he had taught in a cheder. Perhaps he knew how to change a lightbulb. *Languages Spoken in Order of Fluency: Yiddish, Polish, Hebrew, English*. Strictly true. He could say "I want to go to America," and maybe a dozen other words. His wife spoke better English, was more intelligent; but the application wasn't curious about her.

Ida typed on and on. The afternoon darkened further. Her own overhead lightbulb shook on its noose. In the big hall above her ceiling raged a joyous battle: walls were being decorated, the camp's orchestra was practicing, the Purim spielers were perfecting their skits.

She stopped, and covered her typewriter with the remnants of a tallith. She locked the office and went into the courtyard. Two members of the DP police stood there, self-important noodles. They grinned at her. She passed children still playing in the chill dark. She entered the east building. What a din: groups of men, endlessly arguing. And those two Hungarian sisters, always together, their hands clasped or at least their knuckles touching. She'd heard that they accompanied each other into the toilet. In the first room there was a vent to the outdoors and somebody had installed a stove, and always a cabbage stew boiled, or a pot of onions, and always washed diapers hung near the steam, never getting entirely dry. Hers was the next room, hers the first cubicle, where a nice old lady slept in the bed above, preferring elevation to the rats she believed infested the place, though there had been no rats since the visit of a sanitary squad from the British occupation zone. But the lady expected their return, and never left her straw mattress until mid-afternoon.

She was up and about now, gossiping somewhere. From beneath the bed Ida dragged a sack and dumped its contents onto her own mattress—a silk blouse, silk underwear, sewing utensils, glue, and a Wehrmacht helmet, battered and cracked. And cellophane; cellophane wrappers; dozens of cellophane wrappers, hundreds; some crushed, some merely torn, some intact, slipped whole from the Lucky Strikes and Camels that they had once protected . . . She began to work.

SONYA, EJECTED FROM HER OFFICE by the solicitous Ida, had only pretended to be taking a walk. When out of range of the office window she doubled back to the south building. Two women there were near their time, though neither was ready to be transported to the lying-in bungalow. In their room they were being entertained by three men rehearsing a Purim spiel: a Mordecai with a fat book, an Ahasuerus in a cloak, and a fool in a cap with a single bell. A fool? The Purim spiel had a long connection to the commedia dell'arte, Roland had mentioned. This fool played a harmonica, the king sang *Yedeh hartz hot soides*—Every heart has secrets—and

Mordecai, his book open, rocked from side to side and uttered wise sayings.

Sonya next went to the storehouse. Someone had stolen a carton of leftover Chanukah supplies donated by a congregation in New Jersey. Not a useful donation—the camp would be disbanded by next December, every resident knew that for a fact, all of them would be housed comfortably in Sydney, Toronto, New York, Tel Aviv . . . Still, shouted the Person in charge, this is a crazy insult, stealing from ourselves; why don't we rob the swine in the village?

The TB hospital next, formerly the Wehrmacht's stable. The military nurse who ran the place snapped that all was as usual, two admissions yesterday, no discharges, X-ray machine on its last legs, what else was new. Her assistants, female Persons who had been doctors Before, were more informative. "Ach, the people here now will sooner or later get better probably," one said. "They'll recover, *nu*, if God is willing, maybe if he isn't, if he just looks the other way. Choose life. Isn't it written?"

Sonya went to her own bedroom. As camp directors she and Roland occupied private quarters—a single narrow room with a triple-decker bed. Roland slept on the bottom, Sonya in the middle, once in a while an inspector from headquarters occupied the top, where else to put him? There was a sink and a two-drawer dresser. Sonya opened the lower drawer and reached into the back. Why should she too not dress up for the Purim party? Choose life, choose beauty, choose what all American women long for, a little black dress. She grabbed the rolled-up garment she had stashed there two years ago and brought it into the weak light and raised it and shook it. It unfurled reluctantly. She took off her shirt, slipped the dress over her head, stepped out of her ski pants. The dress felt too large. There was a piece of mirror resting slantwise on the sink—Roland used it for shaving. She straightened it. Then she backed away.

A witch peered at her from the jagged looking glass. A skinny powerless witch with untamed gray hair wearing the costume of a bigger witch.

She had been a free spirit once, she thought she recalled. At the young age of fifty she had dwelled on a Rhode Island beach; she had danced under the moon. She had known the Hurricane. She had lived in a bed-sitter in London and had worked for the Joint

Distribution Committee. She had saved some children. She had known the doodlebugs. In a damp pub in 1945 she had accepted Roland Rosenberg's invitation to run Camp Gruenwasser with him. She had allowed his fat, freckled hand to rest on hers.

She peered closer at the tiny witch in the glass. And then some disturbance in the currents of the air caused the mirror to hurl itself onto the wooden floor. There it splintered.

Roland would have to shave without a mirror. Maybe he'd grow a beard. She was attempting to pick up the shards when he came in.

"Sonya, stop." He walked down the hall and fetched the communal broom and dustpan—a large thistle on a stick, a piece of tin. She was sucking her finger when he returned. He looked at the cut. "Run it under water for a long time." She ran it under water for a long time. When she turned around the damage was swept up, the implements had been returned, and he was lying on the lowest bed, eyes closed, as if it was this recent effort that had exhausted him, not two years of constant toil.

She closed their door. She unbuckled his worn belt. She unbuttoned his flannel shirt. What color had it been originally? It had long ago faded to the yellowish green of his eyes. She unbuttoned the cuffs, too, but did not attempt to remove the shirt—it was up to him whether or not to take it off; he was a sentient being, wasn't he? Was he? He had all the vitality of a corpse. But when she roughly rolled down his trousers and pulled them off and rolled down his undershorts and pulled them off, she saw that he was ready for her. When had they done this last—three months ago? Six? For them, as for the Persons, one gray day got sucked into the next. Yet there were joys: letters from relatives thought dead, meat sometimes in the soup, and tonight a party . . . She stood and lifted her little black dress over her witch's body. It ruffled her witch's coiffure. She left the dress lying on the floor. She straddled Roland's erection, brushing him back and forth, side to side, until she felt a spurt of her own moisture, and he must have felt it, too, for, alert, he gripped her upper arms and turned them both over at once as if they were a single animal, a whale in green flannel maybe. She looked up at him. "Roland, I love you," she said, for the first time ever. And she did, she loved the whole silly mess of him: the effeminate softness of his shoulders, the loose flesh under his chin, the little eyes, the breath redolent of processed meats, the sparse eyebrows, the pudgy hands, the fondness for facts. Were these not things to love? Oh, and the kindness. He thrust, thrust . . . "Ah," she said. And even in her pleasure, her witch's pleasure, she heard the stealthy opening of the door. She turned her head and met Ludwig's rodent gaze.

BY THE TIME ROLAND AND SONYA ARRIVED at the great hall—a big room with a little stage—the thrown-together orchestra was playing: strings, one trumpet, woodwinds, an accordion, a balalaika, three guitars, one drum. Candles in tin cans were burning side by side on the rim of the stage and on a ledge around the room and at the windows. Each thick candle, Sonya noticed, was made up of a clutch of little, twisted candles, the Chanukah kind. There were also several chanukkiyahs. A broad table held a mountain of hamantaschen. Another table sagged under bowls of liquid. "Let's hope no one got hold of the methanol," Roland said. At another camp, mostly Polish Persons, two men had gone blind from drinking the stuff.

Roland was dressed, he claimed, as Dionysius—that is, two sprigs of juniper were pinned to his scant hair, one falling onto his forehead, the other nestling within his humble nape.

Most costumes were equally rudimentary. Where could Persons get fabric, jewels, gauzy shawls? Yet some had indeed procured such items. A wife had made a royal garment for her husband. It was a short black silk cape, formerly the lining of their only coat. They wouldn't need a lined coat in Palestine, this loving spouse explained to Sonya. She had adorned the cape with little white fur tails which on close inspection turned out to be the inner stuff of sanitary napkins. Several young Mordecais wore, in front of their ears, scholarly coils: the strapping tape from Red Cross packages. One Esther had saved a beaded dress from her dead mother's wardrobe. Another wore a dirndl skirt and a jersey shirt that said ENGLEWOOD HIGH SCHOOL. A Catholic family slipped in shyly wearing Easter finery; after years in a cardboard valise the clothing too seemed to be cardboard. Ludwig and his uncle Claud had encased their upper bodies in splintery barrels that had held potatoes. Their heads were crowned by circlets of dry leaves. SCHWARZ KÖNIG was painted on Ludwig's barrel. Uncle Claud was the white queen.

King, queen, wise man, and the occasional hero: cigar stubs identified Churchill, a cigarette holder Roosevelt. No one came dressed as Haman. Haman adorned the yellow walls, though. He was painted in green, painted in black tar, drawn in pencil, cut from brown paper. There were several Hamans in relief, made from a sturdy papier-mâché. "What is this stuff?" Sonya asked the history teacher. "The *Stars and Stripes,* pulped," he told her. Many Hamans were rendered feet up, head down. Each wore a little black mustache.

The orchestra fluted, blared, strummed. Persons danced, changed partners, danced again. The pile of hamantaschen diminished, was replenished. The two Hungarian sisters entered, hand in hand. A skit was performed in one corner. Ida entered, wearing a hat. A skit was performed on the stage. Someone sang, dreadfully. Three men dragged in the upright piano from the corridor, although the orchestra had specified that it did not require a piano, did not want a piano, certainly could not employ that piano, which was missing seventeen keys. The orchestra leader swiped at one of the three moving men with his baton, an umbrella spoke. Roland intervened. The piano, with bench but without pianist, remained, near the string section. The radiant young man from the south building entered, wrapped in a blue and white tablecloth with permanent stains; Sonya guessed that it, too, came from Englewood, New Jersey. The philosophy teacher . . .

Was that woman Ida? Sonya had never before seen her in lipstick. She must have been hoarding it forever; lucky it hadn't pulverized. And that brilliant red silk blouse, how come *it* wasn't dust . . . Ida blew a kiss to Sonya and asked Mendel to dance. Mendel's wife, vastly pregnant, smiled acquiescence. Mendel was dressed in a long black jacket whose wide belt bore a buckle covered in silver foil. Sonya guessed his puritan garb was intended as Lutheran. Ida danced with others. Her hat glistened in one part of the room, glowed in another. It was a heavy cloche with a narrow brim, and it was covered with hundreds of shining bows, or perhaps butterflies, or perhaps ecstatic transparent birds. They caught the light of the candles, transforming that light into ruby twinkles, turquoise wings, flashes of green. Were they silk, those bows butterflies birds? Were they diamonds? Were they real winged creatures? Ida whirled by. Below the iridescent helmet her hair thickly curled; some curls, damp and enticing, clung to her neck. "We have guests," Roland said in Sonya's ear.

She had been ignoring the three American officers, though she had identified their rank, she had noticed their medals, she had recognized the famous grin. "Roland, I am exhausted, my charm whatever there was of it is used up, would you take care of them for a while, Roland? And tell them that your wife will be with them shortly."

"Wife?"

"Everybody thinks we're married, why upset that cart . . ."

"I wish you were my wife. I would like you to be my wife."

"Yes," she said, acknowledging his wish, maybe even acceding to it; and then she backed up, backed up, until she collided with the accordionist moving forward. The Persons' orchestra was taking a break. Sonya sat down at the ruined piano.

She played "You and the Night and the Music." The missing keys were mostly at either end; the absence of middle A and the B-flat below middle C was a nuisance, but she fudged. She played a Strauss waltz and the waltz from *Faust*. The smoke thickened like roux. The air in the room was clouded and warm and vital; life itself might have originated in these emanations from burning tobacco. She played "Smoke Gets in Your Eyes." She played "The Merry Widow."

The noise increased. There was some yelling: another skit. She saw Ida waltzing with the general. Ida looked up at him from under her hat. As they turned, Sonya saw an inquiring look on her lovely face. As they turned again she saw the look change into one of admiration. As they turned again she saw the look become one of pleasure.

"She's fucking him," Ludwig said, in English. He had taken off his black king's barrel. He was seated on the bench beside her. He smelled of brandy. "I am employing a metaphor," he explained.

The general danced a two-step with Ida's cubicle mate, the little old lady who came alive at dusk. He danced the Kozachok with a group of Ukrainians. He danced another waltz with Ida. And then, twenty minutes later, Sonya and Roland and Ludwig and Ida and a dozen others stood at the gates to wave good-bye to the jeep carrying the three officers. The general touched his cap—handsome headgear, really, with all that gold insignia, but no match for Ida's.

Sonya predicted that the camp's rations would soon increase, but they did not. She hoped that Ida might get a private gift—silk stockings, maybe—but nothing appeared. She even thought that the new immigration act would be rushed through the United States Congress.

"It was only a dance," Ida said.

"Two dances. And you were ravishing."

"He's a soldier," Ida said, sighing. "Not a king."

But then something did happen. The allotment of cigarettes per Person was officially increased. The augmented allotment, however, was not to be distributed (a formal letter ordered) but to remain in the disposition of the directors. And that, Sonya and the newly bearded Roland discovered, was enough to change things significantly—to get butter, milk, greens, sanitary napkins; to buy a sow, which enraged some but fed others; to pay a glazier from the village to fix broken windows; to procure gas for mendicant trips to Frankfurt, which resulted in more butter, milk, greens, and sanitary napkins; and finally, with the aid of a bundle of additional dollars contributed by Americans, to enable a sizable group of Displaced Persons, including Ida, to bribe its way overland to Brindisi, where waited a boat bound for Haifa.

One day Mendel's wife, who had replaced Ida as the directors' secretary, handed Sonya a letter.

We have reached Palestine, wrote Ludwig, in Hebrew. *We have been saved, again.*

THE COAT

"OTHER CAPITALS," BEGAN ROLAND, and paused for breath as he sometimes did. Sonya waited with apparent serenity. ". . . are in worse shape," he concluded.

They were standing on the Pont Neuf, holding hands. All at once they embraced, as if ravaged Paris demanded it.

Roland Rosenberg was sixty and Sonya Rosenberg was fifty-eight. They had directed Camp Gruenwasser since 1945, but finally the place had been able to close, its last Displaced Persons repatriated to Romania. So the Rosenbergs, too, had left, traveling westward on first one train and then another. Each was dressed in prewar clothing, each lugged a single misshapen suitcase. They looked like Displaced Persons themselves; but their American passports gave them freedom, and their employment by the Joint Distribution Committee gave them cash.

Paris was giving them dusty cafés, a few concerts with second-rate performers, black bread, and this old bridge called New. Recovering from their embrace, they turned again toward the river. "The Old World," Roland said, "is a corpse."

Sonya—who had spent the war years in blistered London and the five decades previous in Rhode Island—knew the Old World only by reputation. Cafés, galleries, libraries, chamber recitals; *salons de thé*; polyglots in elegant clothing conducting afternoon dalliances before returning to one of the great banking houses . . . A derelict barge sailed toward them, sailed under them; thin children without shoes played on its deck.

ON THEIR THIRD DAY, coming out of a brasserie near the Bastille, Roland suffered a heart attack. He spent a week in the hospital. Sonya sat by his side in a long room with metal cots and wooden floors that, like Camp Gruenwasser's infirmary, stank of carbolic acid. She displayed an outward calm, she even felt calm—he would survive this attack, the French doctors told her, with emphasis on the *this*—but she could not prevent her long fingers from raking her long hair, hair that had turned from gray to white during the war and its aftermath.

When Roland was released they traveled by train to Le Havre and by ship to New York. The Joint got them a place on lower Fifth.

It was a meandering apartment with mahogany furniture and gilded mirrors and draperies in a deep red. Circus wagon, Sonya might have called that shade, but she knew that colors had acquired new names since her departure in 1939, a decade ago—names borrowed from wines and liqueurs: cassis, port, champagne, chartreuse. The apartment was rent-free—that is, the Joint paid its rent to the regular tenant, who was away in California for a year. At the end of the year Roland and Sonya would find something more to their mutual taste, whatever that turned out to be. At Camp Gruenwasser they had shared an office and then a bedroom; they had married six months ago, but they had not yet together made a home.

Right away Sonya got her hair cut. The actress Mary Martin was playing a navy nurse in a Broadway show. Mary Martin's hair was clipped close to the scalp, like a boy's. All over Manhattan women were trying that coiffure, most of them just once—even the prettiest face looked plain without surrounding fluff. But the cropped style suited Sonya's long head and steady eyes. "You're always beautiful to me," Roland said when she came nervously home from the beauty shop. The effect of his declaration was stronger because of the flatness of its tone. "I'll love you until the day I die," he added, again without emotion; and she knew that to be true, too. Let the day be slow in coming, she thought, again smelling the carbolic of the hospital.

Roland's skin was still pasty but he was less often short of breath—a new medicine was helping. The Joint kept asking him to make speeches; well, of course, who knew more about the plight of European Jews during the previous two decades; who could judge better the situation of those who were left on the continent; who could better suppose the future? He came home from speech giving with his shirt moist. Thank God the apartment building had an elevator.

The apartment's permanent tenant was a woman, they thought—they judged partly from the four-poster's silk spread, creamy yellow. Eggnog? There was a crumpled, lace-trimmed handkerchief in the back of one of the dresser drawers; it smelled of perfume. The tenant read German; German books were everywhere. "She is German," concluded Sonya.

"Or Austrian or Swiss," Roland said. "Or Lithuanian."

"She's no Litvak," Sonya insisted, helplessly remembering Baltic Persons shivering in Gruenwasser's under-heated barracks. "She's an aristocrat."

"There are Lithuanian aristocrats," began the reasonable man, but Sonya was already enumerating the signs of *hoch* culture: mille-fleur paperweights, framed eighteenth-century drawings, volumes of Rilke and Novalis, a shelf of novels in French. And the family photographs on the desk: a bespectacled father, a fine-featured mother—how would *she* fare with a Mary Martin chop?—five blond daughters in the loose children's dresses of the twenties. The photographs seemed unposed—perhaps a favorite uncle had taken them, Roland suggested. The girls, very young, played in a garden; mountains rose in the distance. Slightly older, they occupied a living room—three lolled on a couch, another sat at a piano, the littlest looked out the window. At the foot of a gangplank the entire family stood close together, as if bundled. They were all in coats except for the father, who carried his over his arm. Mama wore an asymmetrical hat. The girls—teenagers now—wore cloches.

"They got out in time," Roland said.

"They're not Jewish. Intellectuals, though, liberals . . ."

"National Socialism had no use for them. Which one is our landlady, do you think?"

Sonya peered at the faces, alike but different—one wore glasses, one had very full lips . . . Roland coughed, touched his chest. "The curly one," Sonya decided.

And so, the identity of their more-or-less landlady more-or-less established, they turned to other things. Roland's job at the Joint kept him busy, and Sonya was playing hausfrau and taking long walks. She got to know the butcher, the grocer, the fishmonger. She was a steady customer at the hardware shop and the lending library and the dry cleaning establishment. She patronized a coffee shop on Fourth Avenue, and established an ersatz friendship with its proprietress. Through the Joint she and Roland met apprehensive immigrants and were kind to them. And Sonya made two real friends: women who'd known one of her cousins—a jewelry designer on the East Side, a social worker on the West. Sometimes, on weekends, Sonya and Roland went to the movies with these women and their husbands, or out to a restaurant. "Normal life," she exulted. She thought of Ida, the camp secretary, maybe safe in Israel née Palestine, maybe killed by mortar fire.

There was an armoire in the room they called the study. Sonya had stored her few summer dresses in the right side of it, and Roland's one summer suit. He had a winter suit, too. Insufficient; the Joint asked him to provide himself with a tuxedo at its expense. He was more and more in demand as a speaker, requested now by organizations of wealthy philanthropists, not just Zionists and socialists. Roland reluctantly bought a tuxedo at Macy's, and Macy's altered it to fit. It was delivered on a Saturday.

"I'll hide it in that armoire," he said. "And I'll hope that I don't ever have to pull it out, that those fellows find somebody else to harangue them. Just thinking of their dinners I get heartburn," and he groaned in his easy chair.

"Don't get up, I'll put it away," Sonya said quickly.

She opened the left door of the armoire; and held the tuxedo high, like a lamp. It was shrouded in the new element plastic. She attempted to hang it and encountered resistance. Something was already hanging there. She opened the right door and thrust the tuxedo among the summer clothes. Then she took down the something.

It was a long black narrow coat of soft wool. It was doublebreasted: buttons on its right side, buttonholes on its left, and so—she had to look down at her own striped cotton blouse to be sure—it was a coat designed for a man. It had a shawl collar of fur—brown fur, mink probably. Her friend the jewelry designer had a mink jacket, its glossy hairs similar to this. There was a producer who lived on West End Avenue; Sonya had seen him in his famous mink greatcoat.

She peeked into the living room. Roland was dozing now, the newspaper in disarray across his lap. She took the coat from the wooden hanger and, carrying it across her two extended arms, brought it into the bedroom.

There she put it on. The stripes of her blouse peeped between the crescents of fur like some other species. This coat needed a brandy-colored silk scarf costing perhaps one month of Roland's salary, perhaps two. A bit of black would suffice. She reached into her middle drawer, pulled out a black slip, draped it within the collar. There.

Women's slacks were just catching on. They were not generally for street wear, unless the streets were in the Village. Sonya had adopted them enthusiastically. They suited her long stride. She could buy men's pants off the rack. She was wearing black trousers today, and oxfords.

A pier glass stood between the two bedroom windows. She walked slowly toward it.

What a distinguished gentleman. How well the white-haired head sat above the fur collar. The owner of this coat must be a slender fellow—the garment barely skimmed Sonya's thin frame. A man like this had had the cash to get out of Vienna, then get out of Paris, then get to New York—not like the little shoemaker Yenkel and his numerous children, not like chess-playing Claud, smoking and coughing on his lower bunk . . .

She took off the coat and brought it into the living room. Roland was awake. She showed him the garment like a saleslady, displaying the fine workmanship of the buttoned right cuff. The other cuff, she discovered, had lost its button.

"Very nice, but no use in California," Roland said. "So she left it in New York."

"He."

"He, I suppose. We might have figured. A woman irons." There'd been no ironing board when they arrived; they'd had to buy one. "A woman would have chosen different draperies—a softer color. Yes: this is a man's apartment."

"There's no spice rack above the stove," Sonya said. Roland gave her a thoughtful look. She turned from him and laid the coat at an angle on the Biedermeier sofa, its shoulders against the strict back, its skirts spread on the seat.

"But the photographs," Roland said suddenly.

"Oh, your first guess must have been right." She turned from the coat and walked back to Roland. "The pictures of that pretty family were taken by the coat's owner, our landlord, the beloved young uncle."

"No longer young," he said, sighing.

"Still beloved," and she touched his arm.

SHE TOOK THE COAT to the neighborhood yarn shop—its missing button preyed on her conscience like a hungry pet. "Can you match this?" Sonya handed the buttoned right sleeve to the woman on the other side of the counter. The rest of the coat remained in her protective embrace.

"Ach, you don't meet such buttons anymore. May I see the others?" Without waiting for permission, the woman leaned forward and grasped the coat under the arms and took it from Sonya and laid it on the counter. She examined the carved leather hemispheres on the breast. She raised little green eyes to Sonya's. "We have nothing like this here. I would not know where to look, though in Budapest . . ." and she trailed off sentimentally. "But maybe!" She thrust her ringed hand into the coat's pocket, a pocket that Sonya had not guessed was there, so flat it was, so cleverly disguised by the seam. "Ach," she said again. "He knew it was loose, ripped it off, kept it safe."

"Who?"

"Your employer." Sonya had pulled on an old cardigan sweater against the October chill. She supposed she did look like a housekeeper. "A tailor should sew this on; don't try it yourself."

The tailor on University Place did the job while she waited. A sudden wind swept newspapers against the shop's grimy window. Once outside, Sonya noticed that the temperature had dropped. So she put on the coat.

Only three blocks to home—one westward, two north. She was moving like a chess knight. No, a king. No, no, how self-important—minor nobility.

Roland wasn't yet home. So she let the coat sit in his chair until, after five, the elevator began swishing up and down. Then she stowed it.

The next afternoon it kept her company in the kitchen while she cooked. Another afternoon, while she lay on the bed reading, the coat slumped on a rosé chaise.

She did not wear it again until after the Christmas holidays. Then there was a cold snap. Her own coat was warm, yes; but would not the old gentleman's be warmer still?—its lining, unseen between silk and wool, was light yet effective. When she held the fabric between thumb and fingers, something slid within, as if alive.

She bought it a scarf—not real silk, something synthetic, oh, these new fabrics. The color was perfect—cognac. She bought cashmere-lined leather gloves on sale. In a thrift shop she found a hat in the shape of a squat cylinder, mink-dyed squirrel.

Her daily walks became longer. She began on Fifth, turned onto Broadway at Union Square, stayed on its sunny side. In half an hour she was among the émigrés. She would not enter the cafeterias, where forgotten journalists argued all afternoon. But there was a café run by a sly man with a twirled mustache, and that place she did patronize. He was Bulgarian, she thought—her work at Camp Gruenwasser had made her adept at guessing nationalities. At the Bulgarian's were newspapers, chess games, waiters in discolored white jackets. Soon Sonya had her own table by the window, and she could order her omelet by raising an index finger. The coat lay on its side across the other chair. Hat and gloves and scarf nestled under the sleeping arm. Keys and wallet reposed in her trousers.

She went to art-gallery openings, which were free, as were the canapés and champagne. She went to noontime concerts in churches, also free, though lacking refreshments. Warmly she stood in the unimproved area behind the library and fed pigeons. She went to a Saturday-morning service at a Reform temple—Roland always slept late on weekends. She went to a big Conservative synagogue. She went to an old shul, and sat downstairs.

She did not think of the coat as lawfully hers, oh no. But in its illicit protection she became a personage. Immigrant men hoping to adapt to the New World were buying fedoras and secondhand broad-shouldered suits. Unwittingly they looked like gangsters. In print dresses their wives resembled charladies. Sonya, American by birth, graduate of a teacher's college and an accounting course, never out of the country until she was past fifty . . . Sonya was preserving the Old World of *Ringstraßen*, universities, coffeehouses, salons, museums, bunds and diets and parliaments and banks. She walked and walked. Truck drivers shouted coarse phrases to one another. Shopgirls out for lunch wore glistening lipstick. Sometimes she paused at a department store window and bowed at her reflection.

ONE MARCH WEDNESDAY she went to a student recital at a private school. It was an Episcopalian establishment, but some German-Jewish families had been sending children there for a few generations. The school occupied a block of brownstones whose shared walls had been removed, so that behind the burghers' facade was a surprising interior: hallways hung with kindergarten art, an aquarium, the buzz of hopeful activity. A little auditorium was embedded within the whole. Sonya found a seat in the middle of a middle row. She saw from the program that she was to be treated to recitations, musical performances, a ballet . . .

"Your grandchild is performing?" said the person next to her: a hammered pageboy under a beret, a badly reconstructed nose.

"Yes . . . she will dance."

"Ah," the woman said, slightly friendly. "What is her name?"

"She is my daughter's child," said the barren Sonya. "*My* name is . . ."

The headmaster mounted the stairs to the stage, and Sonya's neighbor turned her worshipful gaze toward him, so Sonya had to be content with the botched rhinoplasty of the profile.

". . . Gruenwasser," she finished.

But the woman was no longer listening. Who wanted to listen to a refugee from God knows where? Delicate voices on the stage were singing Stephen Foster. The children's chorus at the camp had managed Berlioz; well, they'd been directed by a once-notable baritone from Dresden. He was in Argentina now. She wondered how he was faring among the gauchos.

The recital ended. Half an hour later, stepping out of the elevator, Sonya heard the telephone ringing in the apartment.

"Mrs. Rosenberg? This is Dr. Katz at the Montefiore hospital . . ." She threw keys and wallet onto the telephone table. ". . . has sustained a heart attack, he's very much alive . . ." She unbuttoned the coat and allowed it to drop to the floor. ". . . and conscious. His condition is stable . . ." She stepped away from the fallen coat, kicked it, got the room number, hung up, grabbed her raincoat from the closet—really, spring had come at last—and retrieved wallet and keys from the table. She snatched up a square of challis, and ran down the five flights of stairs and hailed a taxi. In the cab she slid the challis over her head and tied it under her chin. Roland had given it to her for her birthday, to wear as a scarf around her neck— paisley, it was all the rage. Oh, let her have another birthday gift from him next year; let him buy her another babushka. Let him live.

"Thank you for coming."

"Thank you for inviting us." Where should they sit? Sonya wondered. She watched Roland settle himself in his customary chair, and so she took her own. Their hostess sat at ease on the sofa.

She was not the curly daughter, she was the one with full lips. The lips were still full—she could not be more than thirty-five, after all—and the long hair was still blond. "I want to meet you," she'd said on the telephone, in a husky voice that she must have been told many times was irresistible. Well, maybe it was irresistible; *they* hadn't resisted. "You left me a nicer apartment than the one I left you," she'd gone on. "Nothing out of place; and those improvements!" The spice rack, Sonya supposed; the ironing board, a chair leg that no longer wobbled, added plants . . . the button? "Besides," she'd chuckled. "You forgot your tuxedo."

Now Madame Schumacher—"Can't I be Erika?" she'd requested—poured generous tots of sherry. "You're living on the West Side?" she asked.

In their new building the elevator always clanged. They had no second bedroom. On Roland's bad nights he sat up reading and Sonya slept on the living room couch. There she dreamed of London and the bombs. But the place caught afternoon sun. They had purchased cotton rugs and secondhand furniture. Then they had splurged on a Finnish chest painted with stylized flowers. They used it as a coffee table.

"The West Side, yes," Sonya said.

"An easy bus ride to Carnegie Hall," Roland said. They talked of music, and of the mayor, and of films.

"Were you in Hollywood?" Sonya asked. Direct questions were not her habit; but she was a quarter century older than this beautiful woman, and her navy shirtwaist gave her the modest authority of a nanny. She had abandoned the Mary Martin hairstyle. Her straight white hair just grazed the shirtwaist's collar.

"The whole family is in the movie business, none of us in front of the camera. I did some translations, this and that . . . I was divorcing when I left New York and I am thoroughly divorced now." She gave a graceful shudder. Her accent was light, not at all guttural, just a sometime transposition of Ws and Vs, as in "diworced." The sisters had all learned English from their tutor, she said; and she, Erika, had worked on French during a summer spent with an aunt, such a beautiful apartment, you could see the Seine. Sonya thought of ailing Paris, the oily river, the bridge.

More conversation, then silence. They would not see each other again: the woman of the world, the pair of pensioners. When Sonya and Roland got up to say good-bye, Erika stood also and left the room and came back with the tuxedo over her arm. "I didn't notice it when I first came home. It was hiding behind Franz's old coat."

"Oh Yes The Coat," Sonya said.

"My ex-husband's. I kept it out of malice, he loved it so. I think I'll give it to the Writers and Artists Thrift Shop."

"Our organization distributes clothing to the needy."

"I'll remember that," Erika said. She'd forget it before the elevator reached the lobby.

On the sidewalk, Roland pointed to the tuxedo, which Sonya carried over her arm. "I'll never wear that thing again."

"Who knows? 'With proper care you can live another twenty years,'" she said, quoting his doctor.

"Proper care does not include after-dinner speeches in a monkey suit."

"Yes, well." And the coat, the coat . . .

"The tuxedo . . . will do for a shroud."

. . . the coat: she would haunt the Writers and Artists Thrift Shop until the thing appeared. She'd buy it and stash it in the Finnish chest; maybe in that relic the Old World would find repose. And if not, let it writhe. Love, love . . . "A shroud? Up yours," snorted Sonya, startling him, making him smile. "I intend to keep you around. Darling, let's have dinner out."

She took his arm and led him to a new Italian place on East Twelfth, one which the courtly old gentleman in the fur-collared coat had never had a chance to patronize.

MATES

KEITH AND MITSUKO MAGUIRE drifted into town like hoboes, though the rails they rode were only the trolley tracks from Boston, and they paid their fares like everyone else. But they seemed as easy as vagabonds, without even a suitcase between them, and only one hat, a canvas cap. They took turns putting it on. Each wore a hiker's back frame fitted with a sleeping bag and a knapsack. Two lime green sneakers hung from Mitsuko's pack.

That afternoon they were seen sharing a loaf and a couple of beers on a bench in Logowitz Park. Afterward they relaxed under a beech tree with their paperbacks. They looked as if they meant to camp there. But sleeping outside was as illegal twenty-five years ago as it is today; and these newcomers, it turned out, honored the law. In fact they spent their first night in the Godolphin Inn, like ordinary travelers. They spent their second night in the apartment they had just rented at the top of a three-decker on Lewis Street, around the corner from the house I have lived in since I was a girl.

And there they stayed for a quarter of a century, maintaining cordial relations with the downstairs landlord and with the succession of families who occupied the middle flat.

Every fall they planted tulips in front. In the spring, Keith mowed the side lawn. Summers they raised vegetables in the back; all three apartments shared the bounty.

Anyone else in their position would have bought a single-family house or a condo, maybe after the first child, certainly after the second. Keith, a welder, made good money; and Mitsuko, working part-time as a computer programmer, supplemented their income. But the Maguires kept on paying rent as if there were no such thing as equity. They owned no television, and their blender had only three speeds. But although the net curtains at their windows seemed a thing of the moment, like a bridal veil, their plain oak furniture had a responsible thickness. On hooks in the back hall hung the kids' rain gear and Keith's hard hat and Mitsuko's sneakers. The sneakers' green color darkened with wear; eventually she bought a pair of pink ones.

I taught all three of the boys. By the time the oldest entered sixth grade he was a passionate soccer player. The second, the bookish one, wore glasses. The third, a cutup, was undersized. In each son the mother's Eastern eyes looked out of the father's Celtic face; a simple, comely, repeated visage; a glyph meaning "child."

Mitsuko herself was not much bigger than a child. By the time the youngest began high school even he had outstripped his mother. Her little face contained a soft beige mouth, a nose of no consequence, and those mild eyes. Her short hair was clipped every month by Keith. (In return Mitsuko trimmed Keith's receding curls and rusty beard.) She wore T-shirts and jeans and sneakers except for public occasions; then she wore a plum-colored skirt and a white silk blouse. I think it was always the same skirt and blouse. The school doctor once referred to her as generic, but when I asked him to identify the genus he sighed his fat sigh. "Female parent? All I mean is that she's stripped down." I agreed. It was as if nature had given her only the essentials: flat little ears; binocular vision; teeth strong enough for buffalo steak, though they were required to deal with nothing more fibrous than apples and raw celery (Mitsuko's cuisine was vegetarian). Her breasts swelled to the size of teacups when she was nursing, then receded. The school doctor's breasts, sometimes visible under his summer shirt, were slightly bigger than Mitsuko's.

The Maguires attended no church. They registered Independent. They belonged to no club. But every year they helped organize the spring block party and the fall park cleanup. Mitsuko made filligreed cookies for school bake sales and Keith served on the search committee when the principal retired. When their eldest was in my class, each gave a What I Do talk to the sixth grade. At my request they repeated it annually. Wearing a belt stuffed with tools, his mask in his hands, Keith spoke of welding's origins in the forge. He mentioned weapons, tools, automobiles. He told us of the smartness of the wind, the sway of the scaffolding, the friendly heft of the torch. "An arc flames and then burns blue," he said. "Steel bar fuses to steel bar." Mitsuko in her appearances before the class also began with history. She described Babbage's first calculating machine, whose innards nervously clacked. She recapitulated the invention of the Hollerith code (the punched card she showed the kids seemed as venerable as papyrus), the cathode tube, the microchip. Then she, too, turned personal. "My task is to achieve intimacy with the computer," she said. "To follow the twists of its thought, to help it become all it can." When leaving, she turned at the doorway and gave us the hint of a bow.

Many townspeople knew the Maguires. How could they not, with the boys going to school and making friends and playing sports? Their household had the usual needs—shots and checkups, medications, vegetables, hardware. The kids bought magazines and notebooks at Dunton's Tobacco. Every November Keith and his sons walked smiling into Roberta's Linens and bought a new Belgian handkerchief for Mitsuko's birthday. During the following year's special occasions, its lace would foam from the pocket of the white silk blouse.

But none of us knew them well. They didn't become intimates of anyone. And when they vanished, they vanished in a wink. One day we heard that the youngest was leaving to become a doctor; the next day, or so it seemed, the parents had decamped.

I had seen Mitsuko the previous week. She was buying avocados at the greengrocer. She told me that she mixed them with cold milk and chocolate in the blender. "The drink is pale green, like a dragonfly," she said. "Very refreshing."

Yes, the youngest was off to medical school. The middle son was teaching carpentry in Oregon. The oldest, a journalist in Minnesota, was married and the father of twin girls.

So she had granddaughters. She was close to fifty, but she still could have passed for a teenager. You had to peer closely, under the pretext of examining pineapples together, to see a faint crosshatching under the eyes. But there was no gray in the cropped hair, and the body in jeans and T-shirt was that of a stripling.

She chose a final avocado. "I am glad to have run into you," she said with her usual courtesy. Even later I could not call this remark valedictory. The Maguires were always glad to run into any of us. They were probably glad to see our backs, too.

"You are a maiden lady," the school doctor reminded me some months later. We have grown old together; he says what he pleases. "Marriage is a private mystery. I'm told that parents feel vacant when their children have flown."

"Most couples just stay here and crumble together."

"Who knows?" he said, and shrugged. "I'm a maiden lady myself."

The few people who saw Keith and Mitsuko waiting for the trolley that September morning assumed they were going off on a camping trip. Certainly they were properly outfitted, each wearing a hiker's back frame fitted with a sleeping bag and a knapsack.

The most popular theory is that they have settled in some other part of the country. There they work—Keith with steel and flame, Mitsuko with the electronic will-o'-the-wisp; there they drink avocado shakes and read paperbacks.

Some fanciful townspeople whisper a different opinion: that when the Maguires shook our dust from their hiking boots they shed their years, too. They have indeed started again elsewhere, but rejuvenated, restored. Mitsuko's little breasts are already swelling in preparation for the expected baby.

I reject both theories. Maiden lady that I am, I believe solitude to be not only the unavoidable human condition but also the sensible human preference. Keith and Mitsuko took the trolley together, yes. But I think that downtown they enacted an affectionate though rather formal parting in some public place—the bus depot, probably. Keith then strode off.

Mitsuko waited for her bus. When it came she boarded it deftly despite the aluminum and canvas equipment on her back. The sneakers—bright red, this time, as if they had ripened—swung like cherries from the frame.

How to Fall

"FAN MAIL!" brayed Paolo. "Come and get it."

Every Monday and Tuesday Paolo lugged a canvas sack from the studio to the rehearsal room at the Hotel Pamona. Until recently Paolo had been Paul. The change in name was going to get Paul/Paolo strictly nowhere, in Joss's opinion; but teenagers had to transform themselves every month or so—he had read that somewhere. Before dropping off the mail, Paolo picked up lunch for the television brass and brought it back to the studio. He told Joss that he hoped to become a comedian. The letters that came out of the sack smelled of deli. Some envelopes had greasy stains.

"Missives!" He swung the sack onto the round table in the corner, loosened its neck, and allowed some of the letters to spill out—fussy business, too many little motions; but Joss kept his mouth shut. He wasn't in the coaching game. Besides, silence was what he got paid for.

Happy Bloom had been rehearsing his opening monologue—the one he delivered in a tuxedo, the one with the snappiest jokes—in front of the wide mirror between the windows. But when he saw Paolo he whirled, stamped, and called a recess. He loved his fans. He got quantities of letters, all favorable. He was "the New Medium's New Luminary"—*Time* magazine itself had said so when it ran his picture on the cover the previous December. Churchill had been on the cover the week before, Stalin the week afterward, you'd think Happy had conferred with those guys at Yalta. But Happy was bigger than a statesman; he was an honorary member of every American family. On Thursday nights at five minutes to eight the entire nation sat down to watch *The Happy Bloom Hour* . . . And on Friday nights, as maybe only Joss knew, Heschel Bloomberg, wearing a gray suit and horn-rims—without greasepaint, without toupee, unrecognized—welcomed the Sabbath with the other congregants in a Brooklyn synagogue.

Joss admired the funnyman's faith. Himself, he hadn't been inside a church in eighteen years, not since the morning his daughter was baptized. But he had graduated from a Jesuit high school; he had believed in things then . . . "I like the routine in the shul, no improvising," Happy told him. "The cantor's a baritone, not bad if you like phlegm."

The Heschel Bloomberg placidly worshipping on Friday night reverted to Happy Bloom on Saturday morning. Writing and rehearsals started at nine; he usually threw his first tantrum by ten. But today was Tuesday—the show already shapely, the skits established. There'd be only a couple of outbursts.

Now Happy settled himself at the table to devour his mail. Joss strolled over to one of the windows and breathed New York's October air. Happy might snuggle with the country; he, Joss, belonged to this stony metropolis which kept forgetting his name—oh well.

"There's a fan letter for *you*, Mr. Hoyle," Paolo said, and did a Groucho with his eyebrows. He extracted a pale green square from the heap and walked it over to Joss, heel-toe, heel-toe, poor sap.

No return address on the envelope. Joss opened it. Slanted words lay on a page the color of mist. He brought the letter up to his nose. No scent.

Dear Mr. Jocelyn Hoyle,

I'm a big reader (though small in physique). Television leaves me absolutely frigid. I don't ever watch hardly. Those wrestlers—shouldn't they sign up at a fat farm? Happy Bloom smiles too much. Much too much too much.

But I admire your face. Your long mouth makes thrilling twitches. Your dark eyes shift, millimeterarily. Those eyes know hope. Those eyes know hope deferred. Those eyes know hope denied. Oh!

The Lady in Green

Joss looked up. "This is a fan?" he inquired of the city. He sniffed the paper again.

～

THE SECOND LETTER ARRIVED the next week, on show day, at the studio—they rehearsed there Wednesdays and Thursdays. Happy was screaming at the orchestra; at the properties-and-scripts woman, who held the whole enterprise together (she had a name but he called her "the Brigadier"); at the writers; at the cameramen; at Joss. Paolo came around, the sack of mail on his shoulder. Joss took the letter from Paolo and put it into his pocket, unopened.

The show went all right. They had a fading tenor for the next-to-last number leading into Happy's windup monologue, the sentimental one. Joss stood listening to the tenor in what passed for the wings. The studio had some nerve calling this a stage, wires and cables all over the joint. He'd worked Broadway, rep, vaudeville; the worst house he'd ever played in had kept itself in better shape than the New Medium. The two circuses he'd traveled with were tight as battleships; well, circuses couldn't afford bad habits . . . *Nessun dorma*, sang the has-been. He was at the point in his decline that Joss liked best: ambition flown; to hell with the high notes; emotion at last replacing resonance. He wore a tux and makeup but he might as well have been naked. Joss could sense the paunch under the corset, could imagine the truss, too—oh, the eternal sadness of fat men.

They all had a quick one afterward—Joss and the producer and the Brigadier drinking whisky, the tenor brandy, Happy his usual ginger ale. Then Joss ran down into the subway. Searching his pocket for a token, he found the letter.

> *Dear Mr. Hoyle,*
>
> *Ho! I've found you! Id est, I looked you up in Who's Who in American Entertainment. Also in newspapers in the New York Public Library.*
>
> *You were born in 1903, in Buffalo. You've been an acrobat. So have I—in my dreams. You served in the armed forces during the War. You have a wife and a daughter.*
>
> *Such calm lids, such haunted eyes. Your expression is holy.*
>
> *I wonder where you went to college after that Jesuit high school. Who's Who doesn't say.*
>
> *The Lady in Green*

He'd been a poor boy, but they were all poor boys at the school.

He liked every subject, history best. Father Tom's breathless ora-tory made history alive. Father Tom's eyes were green and moist, like blotting paper. The way the fathers lived, there behind the school . . . a quiet, chuckling sort of house, with Brother Jim their beloved fool. Joss, too, would teach someday, he thought then—history maybe. The fathers mentioned a scholarship to the state university. But he came to see that it was not Father Tom's subject he loved, not even the teaching of it—it was the delivery. He loved jesting, too: not jokes like Brother Jim's, not words at all, but glanc-ing and byplay and pratfalls. He had joined a troupe right after graduation, disappointing his mentors and breaking his mother's heart. Now this letter-writing individual wanted him to relive those times . . . In the late-night uncrowded subway car he stood up, briefly enraged, and shook himself, twitching in the black glass of the window like a marionette. The window threw back his face: the same face the lady had called holy. A man slid uneasily along the bench away from him.

When Joss got home he put the second letter on top of the first, in the bottom drawer of the dresser, underneath his sweaters. He could have stuck it between the salt and pepper cellars on the kitchen table for all his wife cared.

Mary was asleep, lying on her back, her thin hands side by side on the coverlet. She would have watched the program in the dark-ened living room, bourbon at her elbow, already wearing night-gown and wrapper. Already? There were days she never got dressed at all. Tomorrow, on their walk to the train, she would tell him about his performance in a flat voice. How the camera had cut him in half not once but several times. How it had dropped him entirely during the production number. How Happy held the audience in the palm of his hand. How Joss had outlived his usefulness . . . but she wouldn't say that.

The specialists he'd brought Mary to always first acknowledged the tragedy of their daughter's condition, then suggested that Mary's attachment and grief were excessive. You *could* have a second child, these specialists said . . . You *should* have a second child. You are only in your twenties, Mrs. Hoyle . . . Later: You are in your thirties . . . You are not yet forty.

Hospitals had been tried; baths; insulin. Nothing made a differ-ence. She had been a darling little thing with soft lashes when they met, but the small down-turned smile on her pointed face might have warned him of her fragility . . . A second child? He had too many children as it was. He had his sad-sack kid brothers, he had his damaged wife, he had Happy. And he had Theodora, Teddie, his one issue. Every Friday they went to visit her. It was Friday now, wasn't it—he glanced at the clock as he wearily undressed: 1:00 a.m. In a few hours he and Mary would walk to Grand Central and take the train and get off the train and take a bus and get off the bus and walk two blocks. They'd come to the iron gate. The guard would nod: he knew them.

Teddie knew them. She made that hideous moan, or she covered her eyes with huge hands. Sometimes obesity seemed the worst thing about her. She wore cotton dresses made by Mary, all from the same childish pattern—short-sleeved, smocked, white collared. The fabrics were printed with chickens or flowers or Bambis. Sometimes Joss felt shamed by Happy Bloom's drag—lipsticked face and fright wigs and bare masculine shoulders emerging from an oversize tutu, or yellow braids flopping onto a pinafore—but why should Joss feel shamed? Happy was the one who should feel shamed, big famous comedian aping big retarded girl. Aping? Happy had never seen Teddie. "How's your daughter?" Happy would ask maybe once a year, his gaze elsewhere. "The same," Joss always said.

Though she was not always the same. He sometimes sensed a change. The exhausted staff shrugged. "Not growth," one of the doctors warned, his English infirm. "Not expect growth, no." Okay, but once in a while her unforgiving expression softened a little, or her vague look of recognition slid into an equally vague one of welcome. If she could only talk. Perhaps she understood, a little. When they were alone—when Mary had left for one of her desperate walks around the fenced-in pond—he told Teddie that he loved her. He held her fat fingers. He kissed her fat cheek.

"HOYLE!"

Joss took his place at the table with Happy and the Brigadier and the writers. They revised, argued, laughed. Every so often Joss dropped his hand into his pocket and fingered this week's letter from the Lady in Green. He knew it by heart—he memorized each one now, like a script, easy as breathing.

Happy Bloom's loud good humor—I guess the public wants it.

Happy and the writers avoided the raw subject of the recent war. But the Europe exposed by the war had inspired many of Happy's inventions—the British dowager, for instance; the French floor-walker; even the milkmaid who yodeled first and then warbled in Yiddish.

But you—the silent consort—are what the public needs.

The public needed the dowager's meek husband? The floor-walker's intimidated customer? The milkmaid's goat—a horned, garlanded, Joss-faced goat who raised itself on two hooves and executed a double flap and a shuffle?

I absolutely adore the dancing goat.

Happy and Joss would be wallpaper hangers this Thursday. Costumed in overalls, they would lift a protesting clerk, chair and all, out of an office. They would heedlessly paper over bookcases, radiators, paintings. The rolls of wallpaper wouldn't match. Happy would disappear into a doorless closet to decorate its inner walls. Joss would paper over the recess. There'd be shouts from the imprisoned Happy, in a variety of accents. He'd sing a few bars of "Alone"; he'd sing "Someday I'll Find Me." At last his head would burst through the paper, that round lovable head: the teeth, slightly buck anyway, goofily enlarged; a multitude of curls spilling over the brow; the eyebrows darkened and the eyes kohled. While Happy mugged to applause, Joss's back would be turned to the audience—the silent consort, papering a window.

"THE SHOW WAS FUNNY," Mary acknowledged on the train that Friday. "You were funny." Her smile turned downward as it had in her young womanhood—but it was a smile; it was.

Teddie, sitting, looked away when they came, and banged her forehead against the hip of an attendant. After a while she stopped banging. The weather was mild for January; they sat on metal chairs in the brown garden. The paint on his chair was chipping. At these prices, you'd think . . . It was better not to think.

You know something? He depends on you! Maybe you depend on each other.

And maybe she too endured a mutual dependence, a marriage of convenience, a spousal alliance like his with Happy. Poor Happy—overbearing mother, two greedy ex-wives, years on the circuit, years in radio, and then, at last, seized by the new men of the New Medium.

Joss was doing third lead in a musical at that time, playing a father-in-law. The thing was holding on. Demobilized servicemen liked it. People were traveling again: out-of-towners liked it. It gave him a chance to hoof a little.

Happy called him. "*The Happy Bloom Hour* needs you!"

"My face on a screen?" Joss said. "I can't see that. I was a flop in Movieland . . ."

"It's not the same, kid. This screen is just a postcard. People aren't looking for handsome on it. They're looking for uncular."

"What?"

"Like an uncle," screamed Happy.

"Avuncular."

"Sure, what you say. That turkey you're in, Joss . . . how long can it last? Television: it'll be forever. Us together." Joss said he'd think about it. "Yeah, think. I've got your shtick worked out already. You'll be mute, won't even have to smile."

Once, early days, they had a near disaster on camera. A guest came on drunk; he flubbed, froze, fell over the cables, passed out. And one of the girls had a hemorrhage backstage and was rushed to the hospital. The props were in the wrong places because they had not yet found the Brigadier. They had to improvise an entire number. Happy wriggled into his tuxedo and pulled on a pageboy wig, blond. Joss grabbed a tweed jacket from the assistant producer. He came on slowly, the love-struck, ruined professor. He sat down heavily at the stage upright piano and played "Falling in Love Again." The orchestra kept still. Happy leaned against the piano and sang the song with a Marlene Dietrich accent, nice, *W*s and *R*s pursed just as Joss would have done them, corners of the mouth compressed. The wheeled camera came close and Joss saw that it was focusing on his own face and he squeezed out some water. The papers made a lot of them that week, Mr. Bloom and Mr. Hoyle, bringing sensitivity to burlesque, melding tragedy with comedy, mixing tears and laughter, all that stuff.

Dear Mr. Hoyle,

What an article, that one in the <u>Post</u>, telling secrets, all about

Happy Bloom's writers, and the people who have quit, and the ones who have stayed. And the rehearsals in the Hotel Pamona. Fans will be hanging around the Pamona all day now, won't they?

The rehearsal site had been known for months. Fans already hung around. But unwigged and un-made-up and bespectacled, Happy Bloom was as anonymous in a New York hotel as he was in his Brooklyn house of worship. At five o'clock he whisked unnoticed through the side door, a revolving one.

I myself will be in the lobby of the Pamona next Monday, April 13th, at noon.

The Lady in Green

ON SATURDAY:

"Lunch? Monday? Out?" screamed Happy.

"Can't be helped," Joss said. "You fellows work on the patter number—I'm not in it."

And then Happy, in one of his turnarounds, said, "My dentist is threatening me like the gestapo, all my gums are falling out. Okay, *everybody* goes out to lunch on Monday. Paolo will kill himself when he doesn't find us. Don't bother to come back until Tuesday morning. My dentist will bless you, Hoyle . . . But we start at *eight* on Monday, not nine," he yelled.

Monday they did start at eight, and at quarter of twelve the gang skedaddled, kids on holiday. Only Joss was left.

He straightened his tie and adjusted his blazer in front of the big mirror. First position, second, third . . . He grasped the barre and raised his right leg, high. It might be a good bit: mournful male balletomane. Would it be funnier in whiteface? Suppose he played a bum trying to play Ghiselle? A church bell rang. He was so sallow. Still on one foot, he let go of the barre and pinched his cheeks; he had seen Mary do that twenty years ago. He resumed his normal stance, left the room, shut the door and locked it.

He rode the elevator to the lobby.

The elevator doors parted. He stepped out.

On a chair beside a palm, facing not the elevators but the registration desk, sat a female in glasses. The forest green of her jacket and pleated skirt hinted more at uniform than suit. Her legs were bare. Her ankles were warmed by bobby socks. She looked about fourteen years old.

Joss walked slowly forward. She had a bony nose with a little bump. Her dark hair was curly and thin. She was probably Jewish or one of those hybrids. He looked at the feet again. One laced shoe had a thickened sole and heel.

Her age had angered him, and now her defect turned anger into fury. It was a familiar tumble. Whenever one of his brothers showed up at the door—just a loan, Joss, something to tide me over—he was only vexed. But: I have *kids*, Joss—when he heard that he wanted to kill the jerk, and then he wanted the jerk to kill him.

He paused, waiting for his rage to peak and subside. Meanwhile the girl took off her glasses. He walked forward again. He slipped behind her chair and placed his hands over her eyes. Unstartled— she had perhaps sensed his approach—she placed her hands over his. For a few moments they maintained this playful pose. Then he slid his avuncular hands from beneath hers. He glided around to the front of the chair and stood looking down at his correspondent.

"I am Jocelyn Hoyle," he said.

"I am Mamie Winn." Her gaze didn't falter. Her small round eyes were a flat brown. She put on her glasses again.

"You haven't had lunch, I hope," he said. "Tell me you haven't had lunch."

"Otto believes that young people should be introduced to alcohol early," Mamie said to Joss across the booth, and then she said to the waiter who was inquiring about drinks, "Kir, please."

"What?"

"White wine with a splash of cassis."

"Forget the cassis, Mamie," Joss said. "Draft for me," he said to the waiter. Perhaps Cassidy's had been a mistake. He wondered if he could be arrested for plying a minor. He didn't know her age exactly; that would be his defense. He did know she was in tenth grade, the prosecution would point out. The waiter served the drinks.

"Otto?" Joss inquired.

"He lives in the next apartment. From Vienna. The University of Chicago is the only true American university, Otto says. All the others imitate European ones. So I want to go to Chicago." She sipped her wine, leaving lipstick on the glass. She had much to learn about cosmetics. "Is your daughter in college?" she asked.

"Thanks," Joss said to the waiter, who had brought their specials, both plates on one forearm. "She's in boarding school," he said to Mamie: the practiced lie. "Your penmanship is excellent."

"Oh, cursive. I practiced a lot when I was young."

"And your writing, too."

"I go to a private day school"—and she named it. "On scholarship. We are required to wear a uniform." She fingered her pleated skirt.

"Ladies in green."

"Rich bitches." A bold smile. "So ignorant! *National Velvet* is their idea of a masterpiece."

Mamie came from a large, loose, wisecracking family. "Happy Bloom could be one of my uncles," she said. The men were sales representatives, the women salesladies, an optimistic crowd tolerating in its midst members who were chess players and members who were racetrack habitués and members who were fat and thin and good-natured and morose and peculiar—"My great-aunt walks the length of Manhattan every day"—and even Republican. She loved movies and gin rummy and novels. She had a very high IQ—"That just means I'm good at IQ tests," she said with offhand sincerity—and because of her intelligence she'd been sent to the green school. "The uniform—it's equalizing, that's good; it's a costume, that's good too . . ."

"Mamie," he said. *Enough babble*, he meant. He leaned across his corned beef. "Why these letters. Why to me."

She reddened. It was not beautifying.

"A bit of fun?" he asked, helpfully.

"At first. I thought, hey, he'll answer . . ."

"There was no return address."

"Answer another way, get Happy Bloom to mention ladies, or green. Some trick. But then, I don't know, I didn't need an answer anymore. I just wanted you to read the words, to wonder. When you look out of the screen with that face, it's like a carving, you're looking for me, you're looking at me . . ."

"Yes," he soothed, thinking of the camera's red bulb, the thing they had to look at.

"At school, they all have boyfriends." She was all at once lonely and forty, and nothing had ever happened to her and nothing would. "I love your silence," she said after a while.

"My silence—it's imposed."

"Everybody at home talks all the time. I love the way you dance."

"The silent character—Bloom made it for me."

"I love the way you fall down."

He had mastered the technique young, while still at the Jesuits'. He had gone to every circus, every vaudeville show. He studied clowns and acrobats. And in the first troupe and then the second he spent seasons watching, imitating, getting it right. He practiced on the wire, he practiced with the tumblers. Never broke a bone. Learned how not to take the impact on the back of the head or the base of the spine or the elbows or the knees. Knew which muscles to tighten, which to relax . . .

She said: "You make me want to fall, but with my, you know, I can't." She paused. "I *have* fallen," she confessed. She took off her glasses. Her little eyes softened. Would she ever be pretty? "Actually, I have fallen in love," she said. "With you," she added, in case he'd missed her drift.

There were several things he could do at this juncture, and he considered each one of them. He could award her an intent, sorrowful look, he knew which one to use; and from this and her flustered response there would develop, during future meetings, a kind of affection. Stranger romances had flourished. When she turned twenty he would be . . . Or he could talk smart: prattle tediously about the Irish in America, his hard boyhood, the Jesuit fathers, the early jobs, the indifference of the public, the disappointing trajectory of his life. Bore her to fidgets, push her calf love out the swinging doors . . . Or he could offer to introduce her to Paolo, what a pair . . . Or he could pretend to get drunk and stumble out of Cassidy's leaving her to pay their bill. She probably had a couple of fives tucked into that orthopedic shoe.

He did none of those things. Instead he reached his hand across the table and gently pulled the nose, the nose with the little bump.

They lingered over their lunch and then walked the length of Fifth Avenue. Walking, she hardly limped at all.

"I don't do sports," she told him. "Steps are sometimes difficult," she added mildly.

They discussed, oh, the Empire State Building and the dock strike and hizzoner: the idle conversation of two friends who have met after a long silence, and who may or may not meet again. At the subway entrance on Eighth Street they paused. He took both her hands and swung them, first side to side, then overhead. London Bridge is falling down. Then he let them go.

"This afternoon has been . . .," she began.

"Yes," he said.

She clumped down the stairs. He stood at the top, watching her grow smaller. Soon she would turn. He'd watch until then . . . "Pardon," said a woman in a hat, edging past him, rushing downward, blocking his last view of the girl.

THAT THURSDAY THEY did a takeoff of *On the Town*—they couldn't make fun of the war, but dancing sailors were fair game. A movie tapster danced with them, another guy on his way down. But the spoof was too short. Three minutes to go before the good-night monologue, signaled the Brigadier. So Happy said "Sweet Georgia," under his breath—they'd done that number together on the circuit a dozen years earlier, feet don't forget. It was a Nicholas Brothers routine. So what?—they'd never claimed originality, Happy stole most of his jokes. The Brigadier said "Georgia" to the orchestra, and then she hooked the Hollywood fellow off the stage, and there they were, Joss and Happy, dancing, just dancing. Happy flapped into the wings thirty seconds before the finish, to get out of the sailor suit and into the tux. Joss kept cramp-rolling. He felt Mamie's eyes on him and his on hers. He double-timed into a leap, why not, and he kicked midair, heels meeting, and dropped onto his feet and then slid down slantwise, perfect, thigh taking the weight, and now he was horizontal. The camera's lens lowered, smoothly following him; those guys were getting better. Elbow on floor and chin on palm and body stretched out and one leg raised, foot amiably twitching, Joss grinned. Yes: grinned.

"What made you smile? They'll get rid of you," Mary griped an hour later.

He touched her hair. So dry, you'd think one of her cigarettes would set it on fire. "I was smiling at you," he said.

THE STORY

"PREDICTABLE," said Judith da Costa.

"Oh . . . hopeful," said her husband, Justin, in his determinedly tolerant way.

"Neither," said Harry Savitsky, not looking for trouble exactly; looking for engagement perhaps; really looking for the door, but the evening had just begun.

Harry's wife, Lucienne, uncharacteristically said nothing. She was listening to the tune: a mournful bit from Liszt.

What these four diners were evaluating was a violinist, partly his performance, partly his presence. The new restaurant—Harry and Lucienne had suggested it—called itself the Hussar, and presented piroshki and goulash in a Gypsy atmosphere. The chef was rumored to be twenty-six years old. The Hussar was taking a big chance on the chef, on the fiddler, on the location, and apparently on the help; one busboy had already dropped a pitcher of water.

"It's tense here, in the dining room," Judith remarked.

"In the kitchen—don't ask," Harry said.

In some accommodating neighborhood in Paris, a restaurant like the Hussar might catch on. In Paris . . . but this was not Paris. It was Godolphin, a town that was really a western wedge of Boston; Godolphin, home to Harry and Lucienne Savitsky, retired high school teachers; Godolphin, not so much out of fashion as beyond its reach.

One might say the same of Harry. His preferred haberdashery was the army/navy surplus store downtown. Lucienne, however, was genuinely Parisian (she had spent the first four years of her life there, never mind that the city was occupied, never mind that she was hardly ever taken out of the apartment) and she had a French-woman's flair for color and line. As a schoolgirl in Buenos Aires, as a young working woman in 1950s Boston, she had been known for dressing well on very little money, and she and her brother had managed to support their widowed mother, too. But Lucienne was well over sixty now, and perhaps this turquoise dress she'd bought for a friend's grandson's bar mitzvah was too bright for the present company. Perhaps it was also too tight for what Lucienne called her few extra pounds and what Harry called her blessed corpulence. He was a fatty himself.

In the da Costas' disciplined presence Harry was always a little embarrassed about their appetites, his and Lucienne's. Certainly they had nothing else to be ashamed of: not a thing! They were well educated, as high school teachers had had to be in their day (she'd taught French, he chemistry). Lucienne spoke three languages, four if you counted Yiddish. Harry conversed only in Brooklyn English, but he understood Lucienne in all of her tongues. They subscribed to the *New Yorker* and *Science* and *American Heritage*.

These da Costas, though—they were *very* tall, they were *very* thin. Judith, with her pewter hair and dark clothing, could have passed for a British governess. Justin was equally daunting: a high brow and a lean nose and thin lips always forming meaningful ex-pressions. But there were moments when Justin glanced at Judith while speaking, and a spasm of anxiety crossed his face, entangling itself with the meaningful expressions. Then Justin and Harry briefly became allies: two younger brothers who'd been caught smoking. One morning at breakfast Harry had described this oc-casional feeling of kinship to his wife. Lucienne looked at him for a while, then got up and went around the table and kissed him.

PAPRIKA BREADSTICKS! The waiter's young hand shook as he low-ered the basket. Judith took none; Justin took one but didn't bite; Lucienne took one and began to munch; Harry took one and then parked another behind his ear.

"Ha," Judith said, mirthlessly.

"Ha-ha," Justin said.

Lucienne looked at Harry, and sighed, and smiled—her wide

motherly smile, reminding him of the purpose of this annual evening out. He removed the breadstick, brushing possible crumbs from his shoulder. "What do you hear from our kids?" he said to Justin.

"Our kids love it out there in Santa Fe. I don't share their taste for the high and dry," Justin said with an elegant shrug.

"You're a Yankee from way back," Harry said.

The da Costas, as Harry well knew, were an old Portuguese-Dutch family who had begun assimilating the minute they arrived in the New World—in 1800, something like that—and had intermarried whenever an Episcopalian would have them. Fifty years ago Justin had studied medicine for the purpose of learning psychiatry. His practice still flourished. He saw patients in a free-standing office, previously a stable, behind their home, previously a farmhouse, the whole compound fifteen miles north of Boston. Judith had designed all the conversions. The windows of Justin's consulting room faced a soothing stand of birches.

The Savitskys had visited the da Costas once, three years ago, the night before Miriam Savitsky's wedding to Jotham da Costa. At that party they discovered that there were backyards in Greater Boston through which rabbits ran, into which deer tripped; that people in the mental-health professions did not drink hard liquor (Justin managed to unearth a bottle of Scotch from a recess under the sink); and that the severe Judith was the daughter of a New Jersey pharmacist. The pharmacist was there on the lawn, in a deck chair: aged and garrulous. Harry and his new son-in-law's grandfather talked for a while about synthetic serotonin. The old man had died three months ago, in January.

Cocktails! The Hussar did provide Scotch, perhaps knowing no better. The fiddler's repertoire descended into folk—some Russian melodies. Harry guessed that Lucienne knew their Yiddish lyrics. The da Costas ignored the tunes. They were devotees of early music. To give them their due—and Harry always tried to give them their due—they perhaps did not intend to convey the impression that dining out once a year with the Savitskys was bearable, but only marginally. Have pity, he told himself. Their cosseted coexistence with gentle wildlife must make them uncomfortable with extremes of color, noise, and opinions. And for their underweight Jotham,

who still suffered from acne at the age of thirty-seven, they'd probably wanted somebody other than a wide-hipped, dense-haired
lawyer with a loud laugh.

"The kids' apartment out there . . . it's adorable," Lucienne said.

"With all that clutter, how can anybody tell?" Harry said.

"Mostly Jotham's paints and canvases, that clutter," Justin bravely
admitted.

"Miriam drops her briefcase in one room, her pocketbook in
another, throws her keys on the toilet tank," Lucienne said. "I raised
her wrong," she continued, in mock repentance.

"They like their jobs. They both seem happy," Judith said, turning
her large khaki eyes to Harry—a softened gaze. Justin said, "They
do," and Lucienne said, "Do," and for a moment, the maître d' if he
was looking, the fiddler if he was looking, anybody idly looking,
might have taken them for two couples happy with their connection by marriage. Sometimes what looked so became so. If Jotham
was a bit high-strung for the Savitskys, if Miriam was too argumen-
tative for the da Costas, well, you couldn't have everything. Could
you?

"Many people have nothing," Harry said aloud, startling Judith, alerting Justin's practiced empathy—"Yes?" the doctor encouraged—and not at all troubling Lucienne, who was on her fifth
breadstick.

THE APPETIZERS CAME—four different dishes full of things that
could kill you. Each person tasted everything, the Savitskys eager,
the da Costas restrained. They talked about the Red Sox, at least
the Savitskys did. The team had begun the season well, and would
break their hearts as always, wait and see. The da Costas murmured
something.

The main course arrived, and a bottle of wine. Judith poured:
everyone got half a glass. They talked about the gubernatorial
race. The da Costas were staunch Democrats, though it sometimes
pained them. "No one cares enough about the environment," Judith
said. Harry nodded—he didn't care about the environment at all.

The fiddler fiddled. They talked about Stalin—there was a new
biography. None of them had read it, and so conversation rested
easily on the villainy they already knew.

Harry finished the rest of the wine.

They talked about movies that both couples had seen, though of course not together.

There were some silences.

Lucienne would tell the story tonight, Harry thought.

She would tell the story soon. The da Costas had never heard it. She had been waiting, as she always did, for the quiet moment, the calm place, the inviting question, and the turning point in a growing intimacy.

Harry had heard the story scores of times. He had heard it in Yiddish and in French and occasionally in Spanish. Mostly, though, she told it in her lightly accented English.

He had heard the story in many places. In the sanctuary of the synagogue her voice fluted from the bimah. She was sitting on a Survivor Panel that time. She wasn't technically a survivor, had never set foot in a camp, but still. He'd heard it in living rooms, on narrow backyard decks, in porches attached to beachfront bungalows, in restaurants like the Hussar. Once—the only instance, to his knowledge, she'd awarded the story to a stranger—he'd heard it in the compartment of an Irish train; their companion was a priest, who listened with deep attention. Once she'd told it at the movies. They and another couple had arrived early by mistake and had to occupy half an hour while trivia questions lingered on the screen. That night she had narrated from his left, leaning toward their friends—a pair of lesbian teachers—on his right. While she spoke she stared at them with the usual intensity. Harry, kept in place by his wife aslant his lap, stared at her: her pretty profile, her apricot hair, the flesh lapping from her chin.

Whatever language she employed, the nouns were unadorned, the syntax plain, the vocabulary undemanding: not a word that couldn't be understood by children, though she never told the story to children, unless you counted Miriam.

He could tell the thing himself, in any of her tongues. This was how it went:

I was four. The Nazis had taken over. We were desperate to escape. My father went out every morning—to stand in line at one place or another, to try to pay the right person.

That morning—he took my brother with him. My brother was twelve. They went to one office and were on their way to a second. Soldiers in helmets grabbed my father. My brother saw the truck then, and the people on it, crying. The soldiers pushed my father toward the truck. "And your son, too." One of them took my brother by the sleeve of his coat.

My father stopped then. The soldier kept yanking him. "Son?" my father said. "That kid isn't my son. I don't even know him." The German still held on to my brother. My father turned away from them both and started walking again toward the truck. My brother saw one shoulder lift in a shrug. He heard his voice. "Some goy," my father said.

So they let my brother go. He came running home, and he showed us the ripped place on his sleeve where they had held him. We managed to get out that night. We went to Holland and got on a boat for Argentina.

THE DESSERT CAME. Four different sweets: again they shared.

Lucienne said, "We will go to Santa Fe in September, for the holidays."

Judith said, "We will go for Thanksgiving."

"And the kids will come east for . . . in December," Justin said.

The young couple spent half their vacation with one set of parents, half with the other. "More room in their place," Miriam told Harry and Lucienne. "More food here."

The bill came. They paid with credit cards. The nervous waiter hurried to bring their outerwear—two overcoats, and Judith's down jacket, and Lucienne's fur stole inherited from her mother.

"Judith," said Lucienne. "I forgot to mention your father's death."

"You sent a kind note," Judith said, in a final manner.

"My own father died when I was a little girl," Lucienne said. "But when my mother died—I was fifty already—then I felt truly forlorn, an orphan."

"Dad's life satisfied him," Judith said.

The fiddler had paused. A quiet moment. Justin leaned toward Lucienne.

"You were a little girl?" he said softly. "What did your father die of?"

The patrons were devotedly eating. A calm place. A growing intimacy.

"Where?" he asked.

She lifted one shoulder, and lifted her lip, too. "Overseas," she said. She stood up and wrapped herself in her ratty stole; and Harry had to run a little, she was so fast getting to the door.

Rules

One autumn Donna's Ladle—a soup kitchen for women, operating out of the basement of the Godolphin Unitarian Church—became all at once everybody's favorite cause. "There are fashions in charity just as in bed slippers," sniffed Josie, who had been working as a part-time volunteer since the Ladle's beginning, six years earlier. "Don't count on this popularity to last, Donna."

Donna never counted on anything to last. But she was grateful for the new help regardless. A group from a local synagogue undertook to deliver cooked delicacies. The members of Godolphin Helping Hands raked each other's closets for clothing contributions. Maeve, a nearby Catholic women's college, posted the Ladle's flyer on its bulletin board. As a result, a few eager students appeared almost every day in the lower depths (Josie's phrase)—the big basement dining room with its scabby walls, the ancient kitchen presided over by a black oven, a couple of side rooms whose high windows let in little light. Some students needed firsthand material for term papers on poverty. The others showed up out of simple good-heartedness. "Mother Theresas in designer jeans," Josie said privately to Donna. But to the Maeve students, Josie was a model of patience, repairing the Cuisinart whenever they broke it, and demonstrating a restrained kindness toward the guests that the girls meant to emulate, really they did. They just couldn't help overreacting to the tragic tales they heard. They were frequently in tears. Their eyes, even when red with weeping, were large and lovely.

"Those kids are prettier at that age than I ever thought of being," Donna remarked at a staff meeting. "Is it their faith?"

Beth said, "It's their smiles. All those buckteeth bursting out at you." And she smiled her own small sweet crescent. "Orthodontia can be a cruel mistake."

Pam went further. "Orthodontia is child abuse."

Her colleagues laughed with her at this distortion. Boyish Pam, round Beth, and lanky Donna were not caseworkers, not sociologists, not child advocates—they were just the full-time staff of the Ladle and its director, three overworked young women—but they had seen children who had been abused. They had broken bread with the abusers. They had witnessed—and put a stop to—beatings by enraged mothers. "You can't hit anybody here," they each knew how to say in a voice both authoritative and uncensuring. A few weeks ago, Pam, turning white with fury hours after the event, reported to the others that she had interrupted Concepta peppering her grandson, a *niño* of eighteen months.

"Peppering him?" Donna asked. "Peppering him with what?"

"Peppering him with pepper. She had him on her lap and she was shaking the pepper jar over him as if he were a pizza. I don't think any got into his eyes. But I wanted to strangle the bitch." Pam bit her lip and bent her curly head.

"What happened next?" Donna mildly inquired.

"I said, 'Please stop that, Concepta. You can't hurt people here.' And I sat down beside her and she handed the kid over with a giggle. 'We were only having fun,' she told me. I bounced him on my lap and he stopped crying and after a while I handed him back. What else could I do?"

"Not a thing," Beth said softly, her plump little hands stirring in her lap.

"Not a damned thing," Donna said.

Reporting incidents to the authorities was out of the question. Donna's Ladle rarely knew the last names of its guests, or even their real first names if they chose to glide in under a nom de guerre. Their addresses, if they had any, were their own business. This peppering was thus far an isolated event. Concepta usually came in alone, drunk but not drinking. ("You can't drink here" was another rule. Shouting and doping were also forbidden. All four rules were frequently broken.)

"Did you suggest the children's room?" Donna asked Pam. The children's room, opening off the dining room, contained donated toys, most broken, and puzzles and games, most missing at least one piece.

Pam lifted her narrow shoulders. "I'd suggested that earlier, before she decided to season him. But Concepta didn't want her *niño* anywhere near Ricky Mendozo, and Ricky was in the children's room that morning. 'Might catch it,' Concepta said."

Ricky Mendozo's mother had AIDS. Ricky himself was a sickly child, often hospitalized. Donna and Pam and Beth understood Concepta's reluctance to let her grandchild play with the runny-nosed, frequently soiled Ricky. As far as the staff knew, Ricky did not have AIDS. But the staff didn't know very much.

Some things they did know. They knew that the little kids who came in liked stuffed animals and trucks and toys you could ride and toys you could climb into. They liked crayons and paint. They didn't like to put things away. They liked to hurl things around, and to hurl themselves around, and to sit on laps. They enjoyed ice cream, though they were fearful of getting themselves dirty. They were loud and possessive and self-centered, but they had learned somewhere that when you grabbed a toy from another child you had to shout "Share!"

But when their mothers or aunts or grandmothers or father's girlfriends retrieved them after lunch, something frightened uncoiled within certain of these stained, smelly little persons. The children did their part in the rough ceremony of reunion—"Where the fuck's your cap?" "Did you make a mess like always?"—by producing an article of clothing or feinting at mopping some milk. But the staff felt their hearts sink, and the Maeves claimed that theirs broke in two, at the premonition of outrage that might follow, back in the welfare motel, or the dirty apartment, or the room grudgingly loaned by a sister-in-law, places where even the bare-bones rules of Donna's Ladle did not prevail. "He had such a nice morning," a Maeve moaned to Josie one mild November afternoon, as the voice of Nathaniel's mother shot through an open basement window from the sidewalk: "You do what I say, hear? Or else!"

" 'Or else' may mean no more than a slap," Josie said to the worried girl. "And he did have a nice morning. That's important."

It was important to keep the children's room open, even though maintaining the play area meant that there were fewer hands making lunch in the kitchen. Some children had become regulars—Nathaniel, Cassandra, Africa, Elijah. Others visited from time to time. These days—because of the Helping Hands clothing drive—the Ladle's youngest guests wore outfits that had originated in Neiman Marcus and Bloomingdale's.

But the erect and solemn girl of about seven who appeared one December morning was not wearing the castoffs of a Godolphin child—not of a twentieth-century child, anyway. Her long dress of gray flannel might have belonged to an early citizen of Massachusetts Bay, if it had not had a back zipper. The woman who accompanied the child was garbed also in a long plain home-sewn dress. They wore identical brown capes. Each had a single braid, thick and fair. The child's straight-browed smoky eyes resembled her mother's. But the girl lacked the scar that ran down the left side of the woman's face, from the lower lid to the middle of the cheek.

When they arrived, Beth was circulating through the large basement dining room with a tray of knishes. "Hello," she said. "I'm Beth."

A silence followed. "Yes," the woman said at last.

At Donna's Ladle the staff restricted its questions to matters of food and comfort. And so: "Would you like a meat pastry?" Beth said, bending down to the child. "Take two." But the child, with murmured thanks, took only one. Beth straightened up. "We're glad to have you with us," she said. "Please feel at home. We serve lunch at noon. Sit at any table. Breakfast fixings are on the buffet against the wall. The quiet room is behind you," she said, pointing with her free hand to a narrow room with three cots. "The children's room is next to it." She backed away. "Feel at home," she repeated weakly, realizing that this couple would not feel at home anywhere.

Beth reported her encounter to Donna, who was concocting a sweet-and-sour sauce in the kitchen. Donna handed the wooden spoon to a volunteer and moved to the pass-through, from which vantage she could see the entire dining room.

"On the right," Beth said.

Donna was distracted by the sight of twenty-year-old Bitsy crooning to a stuffed animal. "Off her meds?"

"Yes. Says they addle her."

Donna shifted her gaze to the next table and saw the new guests. They were seated side by side. The child's hands, clasped, rested on the table. The mother's hands lay in her lap. Each was attentive to the space in front of her eyes . . . to the vision of some New Jerusalem, Donna suspected.

"Adventuresses, do you think?" Beth said. "I'll go have a chat with poor Bitsy."

"Actresses on their lunch break," suggested Pam, at Donna's other shoulder. "What's that Arthur Miller play?"

"*The Crucible*," Donna said. Pam moved off.

"They're like from another world," said a Maeve who had replaced Beth.

And Josie had replaced Pam. "Weirdos."

Donna didn't reply. These newcomers were not the poor she had always with her. She was used to cheats and crazies, drunks and dealers. She was fond of little retired chambermaids whose voices still shivered with brogues; they relied on the Ladle to augment their pitiful pensions. She liked hot-tempered sisters from the South and the South Bronx; she viewed with puzzled respect magicmongers from the islands; and she was even accustomed to certain outspoken religious zealots—shrews of Christ, Josie called them. But plain-living puritans—what were they doing in her facility?

The pair didn't look needy. But the Ladle's policy must hold: no prying. Among the guests were a few batty gentlewomen who might well possess million-dollar trust funds, who probably lunched at the Ritz on the days that the Ladle was closed. They were served without question. So, too, would this mother and daughter be served. It was the rule.

In the months that followed, Donna and Beth and Pam learned a few facts about the mother and daughter, facts which they shared at the weekly staff meetings. The woman's name was Signe. The child's was Rhea. Signe was separated from Rhea's father, a clergyman. Mother and daughter lived in two basement rooms just over the line in Boston. They received a monthly check from the clergyman. It met their wants. "But only barely," Signe said to Donna. It was after lunch. The dining room was emptying out; the three were alone at a table. "We are grateful to the Ladle for our breakfasts and lunches."

"I'm so glad. But there are other sources you could tap, too," Donna responded. "The state government supplements inadequate incomes, and the city itself—"

"No."

After a few minutes Donna said idly, "We sometimes hear of jobs. Tailoring work."

"Rhea is my work."

Donna looked at the severe little girl, who was reading a thick book. The Bible? Donna wondered. She squinted at the title.

"It was Grimm's," she reported later that week. "In the Modern Library edition. No pictures. Impressive."

"Signe teaches her at home," Beth said.

"Isn't that against the law?"

"No," Pam said, and then looked down at her hiking boots. She was terrified of seeming to show off.

"Tell us," Donna said, and laughed.

Pam ran both hands through her curls. "There's a law that even provides for home schooling, sets down regulations. But the person who teaches has to take a test, and a curriculum has to be followed, and materials . . . Signe would probably meet the requirements, but I doubt she's deigned to apply."

Signe and Rhea spent most mornings in the children's room. Shortly before lunch they selected places at a table in the dining room. Before they ate they bowed their heads in silent prayer, and then quietly and with perfect manners dispatched whatever was set before them; then they returned to the room. There Rhea sat on a low chair beside her mother with her book, turning pages, rarely looking up.

A Maeve named Michelle—the fifth of seven children—took a sisterly interest in Rhea. She offered to play with the girl. She offered to walk with her to the park. On one occasion she offered to tell Rhea some Navajo fables. "I'm minoring in folklore," she confided to the children's room at large. "I'm majoring in American women. I'm writing my senior paper on Donna."

Donna was scraping dried oatmeal from the easel. She raised her eyes. "Don't you dare."

"Oh, it's almost finished," Michelle said.

Michelle's invitations to Rhea were always met with a polite refusal—from the child; the mother listened without comment.

"There's a lovely pulpit upstairs," Michelle said one morning. "Should we have a look at it together?"

"No, thank you."

"Wouldn't you like to see my dormitory? It's just a few blocks away."

"No, thank you."

Donna had to take Michelle aside. "I think perhaps—if you're just nearby, like an old tree, she'll eventually come to you."

"She's so lonely," Michelle wailed.

"Little Cassandra would love to build a block tower."

"Cassandra's no challenge."

"Yes, well, but," murmured Donna. "Okay?"

When Rhea did play she played by herself: arranged the dollhouse or drew elaborate diagrams that looked like plans for lace tablecloths. Meanwhile Signe actually did crochet, her hands and hook converting a ball of wheat-colored thread into a long, loose fabric. The ball of thread lay in a canvas sack, and since the fabric she made dropped slowly into the sack, too, none of the staff knew whether Signe was making afghan strips or dresser scarves or just yards of trimmings. The woman was as silent and as absorbed as her daughter. Once in a while, though, when one of the toddlers became difficult, she would put down her crocheting, rise from the chair, and pick up the whining or bawling or flailing child. The child grew instantly quiet, either borrowing Signe's composure or becoming paralyzed with terror. After a few minutes Signe set the youngster down and returned to her work, her scar glistening like the trail of a tear.

The winter wore on. There were two fistfights. There was a fight with knives; the police had to be called. Concepta was caught drinking in the bathroom and was barred for a week. An elderly guest was found dead in her rented room. Another was found almost dead in an alley. Pam began to lead after-lunch discussions on subjects like self-esteem and expectations. Cassandra and her mother stopped coming to the Ladle. Over dessert one afternoon Donna wondered aloud what had become of them. Her table erupted with answers.

"They went south."

"They went to New York."

"The gran took them back."

"She married that son of a bitch."

Donna was impressed by this group confabulation. She lit a rare cigarette. Cassandra and her mother would return. Or else they would not.

"But all those explanations can't be true," Michelle said to Donna as she took away the dishes.

"Sure they can. Seriatim. Anyway, it's not our business, toots."

"Whose business is it?"

"The parole officer's. You've got to take some things as you find them, Michelle."

Michelle wheeled furiously away. She deposited her stack of dishes in the pass-through. Noisily scraping a chair, she sat down beside a guest who had once practiced law. Donna heard the girl enthusiastically propose that the former lawyer write down some of her experiences. The delighted guest understood this as an invitation to dictate her autobiography. "I am born," she began.

Donna considered rescuing her acolyte, thought better of it, took refuge in the children's room. Within a few minutes she was sitting cross-legged on the floor. Ricky Mendozo was sniffling in her lap. Nathaniel and Elijah were lining up trucks, squabbling lightly. Bitsy lounged in the doorway, a teddy bear under her arm.

"The sauce on the fish was funny today," Bitsy said. "Did you make it, Donna?"

"Josie made it."

"The volunteer that looks like a parrot?"

"She has red hair and dresses colorfully," Donna sidestepped.

"What's in that sauce, huh?"

"Yogurt and mayonnaise."

"Where's my Nathaniel!" said Nathaniel's mother, bursting past Bitsy.

"I prefer lemon butter," said Bitsy.

"You, Nathaniel. Ain't you ready?"

Nathaniel ran toward Donna. Ricky, still in Donna's lap, gave him a feeble kick. Nathaniel yelled and punched Ricky. Nathaniel's mother slapped Nathaniel. Elijah threw a truck at Bitsy.

The trouble swirled and then settled. Donna got help from Michelle, who thereby escaped from the lawyer's reminiscences. By three o'clock most of the children and their mothers had been bundled out. Beth and some volunteers were putting the kitchen to rights. Michelle was singing to Africa. Pam was managing to calm Elijah's gorgeous turquoise-eyed mother, who claimed that her social worker had recommended prostitution as a career. Donna was mopping the dining room.

"Good-bye," said a low voice: Signe's. She was carrying her sack and several books. Rhea too had books within each elbow. Their capes, widened by their burdens, looked like bat wings.

Many guests made use of the public library. Free toilets, a choice of periodicals, chairs to snooze in. But Signe and Rhea actually borrowed and returned books. They patronized the museum, too; a volunteer had spotted them at a lecture on Dutch Interiors. And Pam had once seen them at the statehouse, listening to a debate on the budget. Those events were probably part of Rhea's schooling. They were fine arts and social studies field trips, just like the ones taken by schoolchildren, but uncomplicated by questions of who would sit next to whom on the bus. Rhea would end up better educated than her cohorts. "She'll get into Harvard," Pam had predicted. "That's more than I did." But Donna thought that the girl would be better off in a classroom, learning to tolerate and interact and share. Schools weren't meant only for the likable. There must be a place for this scarily self-possessed miniature of her mother. Let Signe crochet in the corridor if the two couldn't bear separation. Let them practice their queer habits somewhere else.

"Good-bye," Donna said.

She watched them go. She leaned on her mop, letting her distaste for the pair flood her cheeks. The motherly slaps and threats and insults she countenanced every day at the Ladle didn't bother her as much as Signe's austere silence. She wondered if Signe controlled her girl by means of some drug undreamed of by the street-smart clientele of the Ladle—brimstone, maybe, bubbling on the stove in their basement apartment.

"Am I glad them two is gone," Africa's aunt said, finally coming out of the john. She tied Africa's knitted hat so tightly that the child's face bulged beneath it.

"Which two?"

"Which two? The devil and her child. They give me the creeps. And is you the cutest cookie God ever made?" she inquired of Africa, who burbled something in return.

"Isn't the devil a man, Ollie?"

"He can put on a dress, honey. Do you happen to have an extra buck or two? Pampers is so expensive."

Pampers were indeed expensive. They were regularly stolen from stores and resold on the street; the entrepreneurs involved made a tidy supplemental income. Donna gave Ollie both money and Pampers, and was rewarded by a mammoth embrace that made her grin—it was so easy, so emphatic, so momentarily sincere, so ultimately meaningless.

"Hug me again," Donna demanded.

Ollie complied. Then: "How about another Pamper?"

Donna gave her the rest of the box. Ollie and Africa jounced away. "You're the devil," Donna called after them, laughing. As for Signe—she was merely a visitor from a strict, drear world.

Donna turned her thoughts to current problems. The Helping Hands had dropped the Ladle in favor of animal rights. The Maeves' attendance had slackened, though Michelle remained faithful. The price of vegetables was going up; even broccoli was almost out of sight. Mice were running free in the pantry. Tomorrow, Thursday, might be a nightmare. Pam was to lead an after-lunch discussion of empowerment, and who knew what would ensue? Last month the empowerment session had ended in disarray: the former lawyer had lengthily cited cases; Bitsy, in disgust, had poured iced tea down a new guest's back. Perhaps tomorrow's meeting would be more orderly. A representative from the governor's office had promised to drop in. Donna hoped he wouldn't get the iced tea.

IN FACT, THE EMPOWERMENT discussion went well. The guests who attended drafted a petition protesting budget cuts. Bitsy caused no trouble: she stayed in the children's room with Michelle and Elijah. In the dining room Elijah's mother sat next to the governor's representative and with judicious obscenity explained exactly how this state had failed her. A knapsack containing all her belongings lay on the table in front of her; she punched it for emphasis. The governor's representative jotted down some notes, but mostly he stared hungrily at Elijah's beautiful mother—at her glossy hair, braided like an Indian bride's; at her ivory skin; at her long blue-green eyes.

Toward the end of the discussion Donna saw the supermarket's boy trundle in a case of young asparagus, as mauve as a rabbit's nose. "Donation!" he yelled. The pantry mice, she'd noticed, had swallowed all their poison. They must be back behind the walls, dying.

AND NOW IT WAS Friday afternoon. Free Food had just delivered several baskets of very soft tomatoes. The staff would stew them as soon as possible. Pam and Donna were separating the merely over-ripe from the absolutely rotten.

"I got a glimpse of Signe's handiwork the other day," Pam said.

"What's it like?"

"Like nothing I've ever seen. It's a hollow coil that seems to turn inside out every so often. I can't imagine its purpose."

"A noose, maybe?"

Pam shuddered. "She probably rips it out every night, like what's her name."

"Penelope. But Signe does make their clothing. She can do use-ful needlework."

"Maybe the coil is her hobby," Pam said. "Ugh," she added, as a tomato imploded on her palm.

Most of the guests had left. The staff and the volunteers mopped the floors and cleaned the kitchen and stacked chairs and tables. Michelle, on her way to a weekend with her boyfriend, ran by—a toothy smile, a pair of fast denimed legs. "Oh, Donna, I forgot to put away the cleaning bucket in the children's room. Have to catch the bus. Sorree!"

Donna waved her on and went into the empty children's room to fetch the bucket.

But the children's room wasn't empty. Signe and Rhea sat on their low chairs, facing each other. They were reciting something in words Donna couldn't catch—a tuneless but emotional song consisting of questions and responses. Signe intoned the questions. Rhea declared the responses. The child's eyes were closed, her sparse lashes long on her unmarked cheeks. Signe's eyes were open, watching the girl with consuming interest. "You can't—," Donna began, lurching forward, banging her shin on Michelle's pail.

Rhea opened her eyes. Both Signe and Rhea turned to look at Donna, who was standing on one leg now, rubbing the other. We can't what? they seemed to be inquiring. What rule were they breaking? They were not drinking. They were not doping. They were not yelling. They were not striking each other. The tone of their liturgy was charged but it wasn't abusive. How was Donna to finish her admonition—you can't look peculiar? You can't try to save your child from corruption? You can't pray?

"Sorry," she muttered. Limping, she pushed the wheeled pail out of the room. The harsh duet resumed. Rhea's words sounded like numbers. Perhaps she was reciting the populations of the world's capitals. Perhaps she was calculating square roots.

Whatever her catechism, it was soon over. Mother and daughter emerged, now in their capes, while Donna was putting away a stack of newly washed tablecloths. At the same moment a small figure with half a dozen arms and legs whirled into the dining room from the area of the bathroom, capturing the attention of all three. It was Elijah, in flight. He scooted diagonally across the empty dining room, a pinwheel shooting sparks. Then his mother ran in, too, her now unbraided satin hair streaming over her knapsack, a hunchbacked bird. "I'm going to get you!"

There was a swoop. The pinwheel was caught. His captor, however, was not the raven but the bat: Signe. She held him high, above her upturned face. He grinned down at her. Her cape hung in a column behind her. Elijah's mother skidded to a stop.

"My baby!" she demanded.

Rhea joined them.

"I a plane!" Elijah shouted, flapping his elbows. "Donna, I a plane!"

Rhea lifted her arms in imitation of her mother. Elijah's mother lifted her arms, too. "My baby," she said, in a softer voice. Signe placed Elijah in the girdle formed by Rhea's hands. Rhea held the child aloft for a moment, then passed him to his mother. She, too, held him for a moment, like a chalice, before settling him onto her shoulder and marching out.

Signe adjusted her cape. Then she turned to her daughter. They exchanged a long, silent stare—a gaze of peace and intimacy and intricately tangled pleasure. The space between them became briefly radiant. Donna, though blistered, watched. She wondered whether she would ever again pay honor to that meager virtue getting-along-with-people. She knew that she would never again claim to understand anything about mothers and children.

They left. Donna walked into the kitchen. It would be a pleasure to stew tomatoes until they burst through their skins.

Home Schooling

Nauseated, dizzy, I lay on the backseat of our dusty car, my head resting against the garment bag that held my father's two tuxedos. Beyond my raised knees I saw a mortar sky. Above the front seat rose my Aunt Kate's ponytailed head and shoulders, and my twin sister Willy's head, or at least the top of her baseball cap. Willy kept fiddling with the radio and singing French songs we'd learned from our parents. "Yaagh," I said every so often.

"Feeling better, hon?" Aunt Kate asked, not taking her eyes off the road. Just two days earlier she'd quit her graduate program in classics, chucked those Romans as if they were all losers, chucked her boyfriends, too. "They can cool their heels," she'd told us. "Your dad is my current boyfriend." We'd left Cincinnati the day before. "Feeling the same?" she asked me.

"Feeling worse."

"Let us know if you have to stop."

"I have to stop."

At the next opportunity Aunt Kate pulled over. I sat on a hump of grass and thrust my head between my thighs. New England dandelions, I noticed, were different from Ohio ones, though the grass seemed browner in late August than Ohio's. I could smell hamburgers from a highway McDonald's. If I hadn't been nauseated before, I would have been nauseated now. Aunt Kate stood nearby. Willy gazed at us from the car.

"It might be better if you did throw up," Aunt Kate said, not unkindly. "Car sickness is your specialty."

"Vomiting is *not* my specialty," I reminded her, though I spoke into my skirt and probably couldn't be heard. I can still remember that ugly plaid—turquoise and peach. At the time—we were ten—I thought it gorgeous. My nausea at last subsided. I thought of the delicacies that awaited us: clams and lobster. The streets of Boston were paved with them, my father had said.

My car sickness had something to do with my inner ear, our pediatrician had told us: I had an atypical vestibular canal. Willy's vestibular canal was less atypical, the doctor had tactfully said, when pressed. More normal, better—but he didn't say those things. Who cared? I had a more atypical memory than Willy. That is, she remembered a lot and I remembered almost everything.

Otherwise we were pretty similar in aptitudes and tastes, though we don't look alike—I am dark and she is fair, I have a blunt short nose and she has a long thin one. In those days we both wore braids.

I didn't throw up, not once on the two-day journey to Boston. My father had thrown up at the beginning of his illness, when the headaches began. He and my mother were already in our new home while we were driving and I was not throwing up. Our new home was a rented flat in a three-decker section of the city. My parents had flown ahead with two suitcases and my father's violin. "The doctors in Boston are better than the ones at home," my mother had explained. "No, not better—more experienced in Dad's disease."

"It's all that shellfish they eat," my father had playfully added.

When not in the hospital for treatments given by those fishy doctors, my father slept in the front bedroom with my mother. A congregation of mahogany furniture kept them company. On the highboy stood a stag line of Dad's medications. Mom's perfume bottles flared their hips at the pills. The violin in its case lay flat on top of a lower dresser. We didn't ask who was substituting for Dad in the quartet—maybe old man Premak. He, too, played in the symphony.

Aunt Kate had the middle bedroom. Willy and I shared the back room. Our window looked down on an oblong of brown earth rimmed with pink geraniums, an abscess of a yard. The view horizontally at our third-floor level was more encouraging—clapboard three-deckers like ours, their back bedrooms close enough to see into at night. These were children's rooms. We gave the children epithets: Nose Picker, Curls, Four-Eyes, Amaryllis. Amaryllis was a stalk of a girl with a beautiful drooping head. She was about thirteen. Beyond and between these nearer houses we could see bits of the other side of their street—more houses with front porches—and beyond that row still another set of back windows. "Like scenery," Willy said. I knew what she meant: the flat, overlapping facades destroyed perspective, turned the daytime view into backdrop. At night, though, when the near windows were lit, the rooms behind them acquired depth, even intensity. Nose Picker practiced his perversion. Curls read magazines on her bed. Amaryllis smiled into the telephone.

There were black-bellied hibachis on some of the porches. It was the era of hibachis. It was the era of consciousness-raising. The previous year our third grade had been told that women could be anything they wanted to be. We were puzzled by this triumphant disclosure; nobody at home had hinted otherwise. It was the year of war protests and assassinations. Hubert Humphrey kissed his own face on a hotel TV screen. There were breakthroughs in cancer therapy.

Whenever my father went into the hospital for his treatments he had to share a room with some other patient—sometimes an old man, sometimes a young one. They, too, were recovering from surgery and receiving therapy. My father wore a turban, entirely white, though with no central jewel. He and Aunt Kate, siblings but not twins, resembled each other more than Willy and I did—the same silky red hair, the same soft brown eyes. His eyes were dull now, and his hair had vanished into his sultan's headgear.

Most mornings Willy and I would find Kate and my mother at the kitchen table, silently drinking coffee. During the fall some brown light often made its way through the one spotted window, but by winter the only light came from a table lamp: a dark little pot whose paper shade was veined like an old face. We owned no appliances—a fortunate deprivation, for the kitchen had no counters. We kept crockery and utensils in a freestanding cupboard, drawers below, shelves above. Our canned goods marshaled themselves on a ledge above an ecru enameled stove. The enamel had worn off the stove in some places; it looked like the hide of a sick beast. Kate and Mom said that the atypically patterned stove was a period piece, a survivor; they seemed to feel a pet owner's affection for it.

A brand new refrigerator occupied most of the back hall. It was too big for the blackened space in our gypsy kitchen where a smaller refrigerator had once stood. In place of the vanished fridge my mother installed her Teletype. She nailed corkboard onto the wall above the instrument. From the corkboard fluttered pages of computer code. The Teletype was usually turned off in the morning, but when she was expecting a printout she turned it on, and when we came into the kitchen we could hear its hum. During breakfast the thing would seem to square its shoulders against an onslaught. Then the message would begin to type out. Paper rose jerkily from the platen. Sometimes what scrolled into our kitchen was a copy of the program my mother was working on, with its three-letter instructions and fanciful addresses:

TAK FEEBLE
PUT FOIBLE
TRN ELSEWHERE

We knew that such a series represented the transfer first of information and then of control. We understood the octal number system and the binary number system and their eternal correspondence. Fractions and decimals, however, were still terra incognita to us, and Willy, invoking her not atypical memory, hadn't yet bothered to learn any method of long division.

At breakfast Mom and Kate wore flowered wrappers trimmed with lace. They lingered over their coffee as if they had all the daylight hours to kill. Early in the fall, when Dad was home more often than he was in the hospital, when he was still getting up for breakfast, he told them that they looked like demimondaines and that Willy and I looked like semi-demimondaines and that we were his harem and the Teletype his eunuch.

When the New England winter settled in, my mother bought oatmeal, and on those dark mornings it bubbled on the stove. We hated oatmeal. But it was the glue of normality, the stuff that was supposed to stick to kids' ribs through a morning of math and grammar. So we spooned some into bowls and joined our mother and our aunt at the round table. They had already divided the newspaper between them; now each divided her section with one of us. The Teletype throbbed. Kate got up to pour more coffee. Her hips were as slim as a boy's. She sat down. The Teletype spat. After a while Mom got up. She bent over the machine, hair falling forward, hand splayed on lace-covered bosom.

It was not usual in those days for a programmer to have a Teletype installed in her home. But my mother was not a usual programmer. Her mind could sinuate into the circuitry of a machine. She understood its syntax and could make use of its simple doggy logic. "I have a modest gift," she earnestly told us. "I was just born with it, like freckles." Fifty years earlier—ten years earlier, even—a person with such a faculty would have had to divert it to accounting, or weaving, or puzzles. My mother had been born into the right generation for her talent. In that regard she was lucky.

She had landed a part-time job the week after our arrival. A month later she was offered the home Teletype and told that she could work as many hours as she pleased, at twice the original rate of pay. She had to attend the weekly staff conference; that was the only requirement made of her. But she considered contact with her fellow workers important, and anyway she always did more than people asked. So she and we went into the office two days a week, often staying until midnight. On those days she'd visit my father in the morning and then drive home to pick us up. I sat stiffly in the front seat and willed myself not to get carsick.

Computers were hulking giants then, with lights and switches and whirring magnetic tapes. Mom's machine growled in an air-conditioned warehouse, surrounded by a warren of offices with fiberboard walls and desks that were just planks on iron legs. Programmers hung snapshots and party invitations and straw hats above their desks. My mother's walls were bare; but in one corner of her office a pair of old school chairs with armrests sat at a 30-degree angle to each other. She had picked them up in a second-hand shop near the hospital. Between the chairs stood an oversize tin bucket filled with books and games. Under it all was a small fake Oriental rug.

Whenever I see the word *happiness* I think of that corner.

Few of Mom's coworkers were married, and none were parents. Some brought their dogs to work. One evening one of her fellow programmers took us to a wrestling match. We held our breath each time a fighter was pinned, sighed when he was resurrected. Later in the year a young woman took us to the flower show. Clubs from the suburban towns had created real gardens in real earth in front of painted houses. We brought home a pot of daffodils and a paper poppy. "I will extract some paper opium from this," our father said in his weakened voice. "We will have such dreams . . . Dreams!" he suddenly shouted.

But field trips were rare. Mostly we spent Mom's workdays in our corner.

An elderly secretary labored for my mother's group. She kept conventional hours, and it was a while before we had any commerce with her. But one December afternoon at about five she stopped us on our way back from the sandwich machine. She was seated at her typewriter, and she didn't lift her fingertips from the keys when she spoke to us, though the tapping ceased. "Harriet and Wilma," she said by way of greeting.

All we had to do was say "Hello, Miss Masters" and smile and skedaddle. But: "Harry and Willy," Willy corrected.

Miss Masters slid her hands onto her lap with an awful gravity. "Twins but not identical."

"Fraternal sisters," Willy said.

"What grade are you in?"

"Fourth," I said at the same time that Willy said "Fifth."

"My oh my," was the extent of Miss Masters's reply, but her tone was inquisitorial.

"She's advanced," I said, my explanation ruinously coinciding with Willy's "She's retarded." Then we did skedaddle. When we'd turned a corner I grabbed Willy by her bony shoulder.

"Do you *want* to go to school?" I demanded.

"Jeez. No."

"Well then."

My mother was sitting at her slab of a desk, writing code. Whenever she was bent over her work, her shoulder-length hair, abundant but limp, separated of its own accord and fell on either side of her neck. We settled down on our chairs with sandwiches and books, our presence unacknowledged. We understood that absorption, not indifference, made her ignore us, just as we understood that our father's sudden explosions were disease, not rage.

My mother's pencil scratched. We read and chewed. She began to hum—a sign that she had solved a problem. She straightened and moved her chair outward, and it protested faintly, *aagh*. I looked up and began to sing the words to the tune my mother was humming. The song was "Good Morning," from the movie *Singin' in the Rain*—we'd seen it twice in the revival house back home and once on somebody's television. Willy joined in, a third higher. We sang the words and Mom abandoned the melody and hummed continuo. The wrestling programmer, walking in with a flow diagram, stopped to listen to this makeshift serenade.

WHEN WE DIDN'T GO TO WORK with Mom we went to work with Kate. After my mother left for the hospital, after we had finished the housecleaning (Kate wore a blue bandanna over her hair) and had made a trip to the library and the Civil War monument and had perhaps listened to the organist practice in the little brick church or visited chilly Walden Pond, traveling by bus, or inspected the daily catch up in Gloucester, traveling by train, or curled up at home, listening to our aunt read her own translation of Ovid . . . after that, we set off for the Busy Bee Diner. Aunt Kate did a half shift at the Busy Bee, from four until eight.

On our walk to the diner we saw the children of the neighborhood engaged in their various childish activities: practicing hoop shots, or minding toddlers, or, at the variety store, fastening powerful gazes onto the candy counter so that Baby Ruths would leap into their pockets. Often we recognized the young people we'd spied on from our window—Nose Picker, his hands safe in his pockets; Curls, pretty; Amaryllis, gorgeous. Other kids, too. They wore hand-me-down clothes and they looked strictly brought up. They were all white, and most were fair. Not Amaryllis, though. Dark brows shaded dark eyes: a Mediterranean siren in this Hibernian tract.

We looked at the familiar strangers, and they looked back at us. Did they wonder about us? Parochial school students probably thought we went to public school. The public-schoolers knew we had never been seen in their cinder block building; did they notice that we didn't wear the pleated skirts and white blouses of Catholic scholars? How did they explain us to each other? We speculated about their speculations.

"Because of our delicate health we are tutored at home," Willy suggested.

"By our aged relative," I added.

Aunt Kate grinned.

The Busy Bee was owned and manned by the Halasz family. The Halasz rice pudding was made with ricotta; the Halasz chocolate pie contained nuggets of chocolate cake. When my father was out of stir, as Kate called it, we would bring home one of these desserts, and also a carton of barley beef stew. Though the food was very good, he didn't finish it.

We longed to practice short-order cooking behind the counter with Anton Halasz, and to try waitressing with Kate. But laws against child labor were more severe than laws against truancy. Mr. Franz Halasz, Anton's father, allowed us to work only in the kitchen, a high square room that the public couldn't see. Mr. Halasz, who wore a beret as a chef's hat, taught us to scrub up like surgeons. He taught us to pound herbs and then powder them between our palms, and to roll leaves of cabbage around chopped meat sweetened with rosemary, and to beat egg whites until they were as stiff as bandage gauze.

Some mornings Kate visited my father while my mother stayed home with us and the eunuch. We didn't resent not being left on our own. We knew that our competence was not in question, just as we knew that it was not hatred of men that caused Aunt Kate to snub the blameless advances made by some of the Busy Bee's patrons, and to keep Anton at arm's length, too. We knew it was not Willy's skinniness that prompted Mom to lay her cheek against my sister's some wintry mornings in the living room, and that it was not my tendency to vertigo that made her embrace me suddenly in the kitchen. And although Willy and I liked to check on what the neighbors were up to, it was not to watch Amaryllis brushing her hair that we perfected our spying techniques. It was to watch our two demimondaines. We saw the glances they exchanged in the beginning of that year; and then we sensed glances without seeing them; and eventually we sensed glances they didn't even need to exchange.

Often I got up at night—to use the bathroom, if anybody asked—but really to draw closer to the dark heat in the living room.

Sometimes Aunt Kate played Chopin or Schubert on the upright. Usually she lay on the couch, her knees bent, reading. Mom sat at the desk, coding. Music came from the hi-fi: *Rosamunde, Egmont, Siegfried*. The two women talked a little. One time, without pre-amble, my mother got up from the desk and crossed the room and dropped to the floor and laid her head on Aunt Kate's stomach. She began soundlessly to cry. Aunt Kate placed the book she'd been reading, still open, across her own forehead, like a sombrero. She held it there with her left hand as if against a gale. With her right hand she fondled my mother's foolish hair.

IN MARCH MY FATHER was transferred to a rehabilitation center. One Saturday afternoon my mother took us to see him there. We drove across the city. The place was near grim buildings of mostly undefinable uses, though one of them, we knew, was a popular roller-skating rink.

Dad was not connected to an IV. "A free pigeon," he said, flap-ping his elbows. His gait was unsteady but he could walk without a cane and without leaning too much on my mother—his arm around her shoulders was mostly an embrace. The four of us tramped up and down the corridors, as if not daring to stop. I think he guessed what was coming—the tumor's steady growth, the blindness in the right eye, the new operation, the new operation's failure . . . Along the polished linoleum the sick man marched, whispering into his wife's ear. Her hair separated, revealing her meek nape. We trailed behind.

At four thirty my parents finally sat down on my father's bed. They were going to share supper in the cafeteria, they said. It was always nutritionally appropriate. "Bilious," Dad confided. "Maybe you two would like to go out for pizza."

If we stayed we could watch her eat, watch him pretend to eat, eat ourselves—see! good children—swallowing the clam cakes, the stewed fruit. "But—," Willy began.

"Have fun," my mother said.

We trudged down the corridor. In each room lay two sad patients.

The pizza parlor, two blocks away from the hospital, had tiled walls and a feral odor. There were no booths, only tables. It was too early for the supper crowd. Except for a few solitaries in Wind-breakers we were the only customers. We ordered our pizza and sat down to wait for it.

Four girls burst in. We recognized them from the neighborhood. They must have traveled here by trolley and underground—from our spying we knew they didn't get driven anywhere. Roller skates hung from their shoulders. Amaryllis's were in a denim case.

"Hello," they said.

"Hello," we said.

They swept to the counter to order their pizzas. We studied their various backs (erect, round-shouldered, slim, bisected by a braid) and their various stances (jumpy, slouching, queenly, hands in back pockets) and their noses as they turned their profiles this way and that, and their languor or purpose as they visited the jukebox or the ladies' room, and their ease as they more or less assembled at their table, one always getting up for something, where are the napkins anyway, talking, laughing, heads together, heads apart, elbows glid-ing on the table. The girl with glasses—I was pretty sure her name was Jennifer, so many girls were Jennifers—sat in a way that was familiar to me, her right knee bent outward so that her right foot could rest on the chair, her left thigh keeping the foot in place like a brick weighing down a Christmas pudding. This position caused a deep, satisfying cramp; I knew that pain.

"Wilma," called the pizza man. Willy got up to get our pizza. The girls didn't watch her. Willy brought the pizza to our table, and we divided it, along with our salad. "Nicole," the pizza man said. The girl I'd thought of as Jennifer uncoiled and went to fetch the pizzas with Amaryllis. Nicole and Amaryllis set the big round pies carefully on the table. Then came an unseemly scramble. They laughed and grabbed and accused each other of greed, and some-body spilled a Coke. "Pig!" they cried. "Look who's talking." "Jen, you thief," said the bespectacled Nicole, laughing as Amaryllis overturned one wedge of pizza onto another, making a sandwich of it, doubling her first portion. "Jen, you cow!"

So Amaryllis was just another Jennifer. She raised her face. She was wearing a tomato-sauce mustache, beautifying. She looked directly at me. Then she looked directly at Willy. Four-Eyes—Ni-cole—raised her head, too, and followed Amaryllis's gaze—Jen's gaze. Then the third girl. Then the fourth.

We were all over them in a minute. We swarmed, if two boy-ish eleven-year-olds can be said to swarm over a quartet of nubile adolescents. Eleven-year-olds? Yes, we had celebrated our birthday the month before. We were officially teenagers, my father had said from his bed in the front room (he was out of stir that weekend), handing us each a leather diary, one brown, one blue. Any number between eleven and nineteen, inclusive, belonged in the teens mathematically, my mother explained; we might call ourselves one-ten or one-teen if we liked. Many languages used that locution, Aunt Kate affirmed.

We were one-ten; this interesting fact we told our new friends. We talked about pizza toppings. We discussed television programs we'd never seen. Boys in the neighborhood, too.

"You know Kevin?" Nicole asked.

"I know who he is," I lied. "Wicked." We knew that *wicked* meant "splendid."

Did we like Robert Redford? the Stones? Had we ever seen the gas-meter man?

No one asked us what grade we were in.

Did we skate?

Skating was our passion, Willy said. We had practically been born on little steel wheels. Next to watching television and pluck-ing our eyebrows . . .

"We come to the rink on a lot of Saturdays," said Amaryllis, who would never be Jen to me. She stood up, and her associates stood with her. "Maybe we'll see you here sometime. Here."

Hear, hear: here. Any further commerce between us would be off-neighborhood. We got it: we were known in their homes, and not thought well of. Maybe their families had glimpsed the whorish dressing gowns of our mother and aunt. Perhaps they were preju-diced against men in turbans.

The schoolgirls whirled out. Willy and I shuffled back to the hospital. My mother was waiting for us in the dim lobby. We three walked wordlessly to the car.

IN THE LATE SPRING my father came home for the last time. He could no longer eat, unless you count tea. "I'd like to play a little," he said to Kate.

Whenever the quartet or the symphony performed he sat up on

the stage, remote, as if the music lifted him away from us, as if his bow gliding back and forth drew him to some place we couldn't reach. He was separated even from himself: the fingers on his left hand seemed to dance on their own. Once, though, he had fiddled almost in our midst, at the wedding of my mother's youngest brother; standing, he played "The Anniversary Waltz" by request, borrowing an instrument from the hired trio. He was wearing his tuxedo on that occasion, and his red hair above the black-and-white garment gave him a hectic gaiety. My mother told us that "The Anniversary Waltz" was an old Russian tune, stolen and given words in order to fill a need in a movie musical.

In our rented living room my father did not play "The Anniversary Waltz." He played a few sweet things—some Mendelssohn and some Gluck—and Aunt Kate did well with the accompaniment; very well, really, since she was quietly sobbing. Then he played "Isn't It Romantic?" and Kate recovered and pushed through with a nice solo bit, Oscar Peterson-ish. We knew the tune and the lyrics, and we could have hummed along or even sung along. But we sat mute on the sofa, flanking our mother. Outside, the streetlamps illuminated the cardboard facades of the other houses. The sky was purple. My father wore a striped hospital robe over custard pajamas. His eyes closed when he reached the final note. Silence. From the kitchen the Teletype began to clatter.

"NO DEPENDENT CLAUSES," said the principal back home, in August. "No Middle Ages." She was muttering, but in a kindly fashion. She was trying to decide whether to enroll us in the fifth grade or simply to declare it skipped. "Tell me what you did learn."

Willy sat looking out of the office window at the playground. I sat looking at Willy. "What did you learn?" the principal gently repeated.

We kept mum. So we had to repeat fifth grade, or endure it for the first time, who cared, same difference. Willy did master long division. I never figured out how to forget.

Hanging Fire

Nancy at Cynthia's wedding had made a kind of hit. That is, one of Cynthia's uncles had fallen in love with her.

"My dear Miss . . . Hanks?"

"Hasken."

"That's what I said. Sweet girl graduate. Lovely green stalk. How old are you, Hanks—twenty?"

"Twenty-one," Nancy admitted. A pair of dancers hung above their table. Nancy shook her beaded bag over her plate. As her eyeglasses landed she grabbed for them. The dancers, revealed as Cynthia and her new husband, floated away.

"Glasses, and that filmy green dress—you remind me of a studious naiad," the uncle said. When his hand crept between goblets toward the girl's elbow, his wife at last claimed him. "I am not an old fool," he protested as he was led away.

Thus the wedding. The next afternoon, Nancy, in dungarees and T-shirt, slumped against the window of a Greyhound. The bus was rumbling northward along a New Hampshire highway. Her duffel bag lay in the overhead rack. Nancy drew a compact from her back pocket and opened it. That uncle might be no fool, but he had a poor eye for similarities. She was not a nymph. What she did resemble, though, was a tutor—a tutor of German literature, say: the sort of fellow who used to hire out to young gentlemen hiking in the Dolomites. He'd quote Goethe while his charges frolicked with barmaids. Nancy had seen pictures of such scholars in biographies—limp hair just covering the ears, and long chins, and gold-rimmed glasses. The likeness was remarkable. She ran a comb through her bangs, and wondered where the Dolomites were.

The trees along the highway were taller now, and greener: Maine. Nancy shifted in her seat and took out her worry beads. When in doubt, tell your assets. A bachelor's degree, cum laude; a boyfriend, Carl; a skill at certain languages; a good forehand. Yes, and she was an expert skier. She was discreet, too; for more than a year she had borne a hopeless passion for an itinerant tennis coach, and not a soul suspected. She'd do. Ahead waited her family, such as it remained—three kinswomen, couchant. She'd be fine.

At six the bus pulled into the Jacobstown depot. Nancy debarked, compact, comb, and beads in the back pocket, duffel bag over the shoulder. She walked quickly away from town. Sidewalks narrowed, then withered altogether. The road climbed a hill. At the top, a board on a pole marked the entrance to the Jacobstown Country Club. The girl sat down beneath the sign.

A few days earlier at around this time her relatives, driving back from her commencement, would have reached this spot—weary ladies with champagne headaches. Nancy could imagine their approach. Aunt Laurette would have been at the wheel of the Jeep, her heavy lips folded like arms. Nancy's mother would have been beside her, as thin as asparagus. Old Cousin Phoebe nodded in back. They chugged uphill, raising dust, awakening a vagabond on the grass . . . and, sitting up, Nancy saw that what had stopped today was a Renault, not the family Jeep. Two golden eyes glowed at her. "Miss Hasken?"

". . . yes."

"It's Leopold Pappas," he said, telling her what she could herself see, presenting her with a situation which she had herself invented, and many times: that on this hill, at this hour, he would appear, sweaty from the game just won, and invite her to ride with him, to leap, to soar . . . "Hey. Can I give you a lift?"

"I'll level with you. I walk on purpose."

"Oh. Good for the digestion."

". . . I suppose."

"See you at the club this season?"

She nodded.

He rolled away.

Blank-mindedness, for five or ten minutes. Then Nancy lumbered to her feet, hoisted the duffel bag, and tramped on. Soon she had reached her mother's property. The pines and firs were dense. She left the road, walked along a path, and reached a clearing. Still under cover of trees, she gazed at her home.

It was a low white house, silvery now in the summer evening. An ample porch encircled the first floor. Upstairs, dormers and turrets. The house was comfortable. Plays could be written here, or revolutions planned. At present, on the porch, three St. Petersburg countesses were enjoying high tea. Their posture seemed a shade too arrogant—one had to squint to be certain—yes, arrogant. Nancy sighed. She drew something from her pocket, raised it, took aim . . .

"Is that you, Nancy?"

"Yes, Mom." She walked across the lawn and swung a leg over the porch rail. Cousin Phoebe leaned forward and tapped her knee.

"What were you doing out there? Something silver flashed."

"Steel," the girl corrected. "A steel comb."

"Oh. I imagined it a pistol."

Nancy handed her the comb and swung the other leg over.

"Welcome," said the nasal voice of Aunt Laurette.

"Welcome," Mrs. Hasken said, gently.

"Welcome," Phoebe said.

They were drinking gin out of teacups. Mrs. Hasken was placid. Aunt Laurette grinned under her globe of orange hair. Phoebe was currying her skirt with Nancy's comb. They were not aristocracy after all—only stand-ins.

"Tut," Phoebe said. "Tut, tut, tut, tut, tut, my girl; it's not so bad to have come home."

Nor was it. Often during the semester just past, Nancy had furiously contemplated her future, coming up always with a single agreeable vocation: governess. But these days, who required a governess? Genteel spinsters took up other trades now, Nancy figured. Veiled, they turned up in Washington as prostitutes or lobbyists. As for her friends, some were settling into New York apartments. Some were hitching west. One had gone to live on a houseboat. But such enterprises were out for Nan. She had her family to consider . . .

They were at this moment considering her, regarding her coolly over their gin like the aunts they all more or less were, for Phoebe seemed closer than a cousin, Mrs. Hasken more remote than a parent. But whether aunts or ancestors, lineal or collateral, these dotty ladies were Nan's by blood. In consanguinity lay their claim—consanguinity, and affection.

She slipped from the rail and settled on the glider. Phoebe handed her a gin and mint. Her mother smiled. Laurette began to whistle.

"Hello, Nancy," said a housemaid at the window.

"Hello, Inez." Inez vanished.

"Did you dance a lot at that wedding?" Mrs. Hasken asked.

"Some, with Cynthia's uncles."

"Men are creeperoos," Laurette said. Each winter she flew to the Caribbean for two disappointing weeks. "Do I really resemble Simone Signoret?"

"Like sisters," Cousin Phoebe said.

"How's Carl?" Mrs. Hasken inquired.

"Since yesterday," Phoebe added.

". . . fine."

"You don't love him." Mrs. Hasken's pale eyes were spoked and rimmed with black. She had been a widow for ten years.

"No, I don't," Nancy said.

"He loves you," Phoebe remarked.

"The way of the world," Laurette said briskly. "Usually the shoe's on the other foot. Anyway, what's love? Duping, derangement. I like Carl."

"I say, take him," said Phoebe. "Or else, don't."

"Maxima Gluck is dead," said Mrs. Hasken.

"The old schoolteacher? Too bad."

"Also Mr. Sargent." Mrs. Hasken fastened her gaze on an inch of wicker. Cousin Phoebe massaged a veiny calf. Aunt Laurette calculated the price of the scenery.

Phoebe said, "We are thinking of adopting a twelve-year-old boy."

"Any particular one?"

"No. We might settle for a second TV."

"Your mother has taken up weaving," Laurette said.

Mrs. Hasken said, "We are otherwise unchanged."

"Since yesterday," Laurette said.

The porch glider hadn't much in the way of springs, and her partner the duffel bag was dead to the world, but Nancy tried to pump anyway. Glider scraped floorboard, halted. "I'll unpack," Nancy murmured, and fled.

Upstairs in her room, clothes flew around; finally a framed Carl emerged from a sweater. His face was as thin as hers. He was bespectacled also, and they had the same julienne hair. At college other students had often mistaken them for relatives—brothers, Nancy supposed. She left him on the desk and walked out onto a small wooden balcony. There she adopted a rentier's stance—arms spread, hands on the rail. She would track down an interesting job, she vowed. She would study Hesse and Mann. She would refuse to make a nightly fourth at bridge, and to pay calls on local drips. This austerity would clear her decks for action. Still she wondered: did the present deliver up the future, or must you chase your destiny like a harpoonist? Presently she heard her mother calling her for dinner. She ran inside and pulled off her clothes and put on a long black skirt and a blouse with conical sleeves, wearing which she felt like a schoolmaster, in drag. Piously she ate her meal. The evening passed.

Thus Nancy's first day home. The next few were inconclusive, but by the end of the second week she had wedded herself to the porch glider. In its embrace she was studying Laurette's collection of detective novels. She slept late each morning, and whenever she awoke found breakfast waiting, prepared by a joyous Inez. Inez had a lover, Nancy's mother reported from the far side of the table. Nancy inspected the ads. In town, Laurette, who managed a dress shop, was pushing her summer merchandise. Cousin Phoebe, under a tree, worked on her memoirs.

Dinners began with cocktails on the porch, ended with beer in the living room.

"Are you planning to get a job?" Mrs. Hasken occasionally inquired.

"Yes."

"Of course she is," Phoebe said.

"Soon," Laurette promised. "Let's go to the movies."

Every third evening the Jeep bounced into town. Laurette at its wheel. On the way home it was Nancy who drove, slowly probing a leafy darkness. In the front seat she and Laurette were as silent as lovers. The other two drowsed in back.

She felt pampered: an adored young nephew. She observed no

routine except to turn up three afternoons a week for her tennis lesson. On the court she was all energy . . .

"No slashing!" Leo shouted. "The racket is not a saber."

A July Monday, a turquoise sky. Nancy, at net, frowned. Leo lobbed a high one. Nancy held her racket stiff above her head, like a protest sign. The ball struck its face and ran down its neck. Leo joined her at net. During the winter a mild paunch had developed above his belt. His right knee bore a familiar scar.

"Not bad. Work on the angle," he said.

"Okay," she said. "See you Wednesday."

That night at dinner, Phoebe said, "I hear he's loose."

"What do you mean, loose?" Laurette snapped. "*Débauché* or incontinent?"

"Unbuttoned," Phoebe answered. "Last year he kept to himself. This year he's been seen with every bit of fluff in town. Are you aware that he used to teach Art History? And then loafed in Europe for several years? And is at last attending medical school? He's thirty."

"Thirty-one," Nancy said. "He's relaxed, is all."

"His eyes are like lozenges," panted Laurette.

Nancy began to arrive early for her lessons. Her costume didn't change, though—baggy seersucker shorts and a T-shirt. Brown hook-on lenses covered her everyday specs. She carried the newspaper. It became their custom to take a break halfway through the session, sitting side by side on a whitened bench. Leo, who'd grown fond of certain localities during his six months abroad, talked about his favorites. At a certain London hotel, where the tapestries are faded and the linen a wreck, you can feel heir to all that is gentle. Courtyards in Delphi are chalk by day, flame and cinnamon in the twilight. One hesitates to visit the Palais-Royal, yet behind that cold colonnade can be found an ice-cream parlor and a Romanian upholsterer.

"You love to travel," Nancy accused.

"Sure."

"People should stay put."

"Should they? You, too, might like to explore new places."

"Maybe the Dolomites," she mumbled.

Leo wore a battered felt hat, the hat of a peddler's pony. His amber eye reminded her of decongestant. She yearned to paint his throat.

"Let's go to the movies!" Laurette kept suggesting.

"Let's!" Nancy swooned the moment she sat down, watched the flick laxly, was always convinced that from this syncope she would emerge altered. Next to movies she liked best to be reading on the porch. By August she had abandoned detective fiction in favor of the fat, lazy novel.

Sometimes she biked into town and moped at the library. Long windows opened onto sprinkled grass. One day at about five thirty she looked up from her book and saw Leo on the far side of the lawn. Beside him stood a young woman lavishly dressed. In the street was his Renault. Leo examined a parking meter, his thumb over the coin slot, his chin on his chest—the meter had contracted something serious. His companion sucked in her stomach. Presently they walked on. Nancy left the library and pedaled toward home. As usual, she paused at a large rock just off the road, near the country club. This boulder overlooked Leo's home for the season, a one-room cabin that Nancy had mentally furnished with cot, braided rug, and, on a hook, the nag's hat . . . She stood watch for a while, then mounted her bike and churned home.

I miss you, wrote Cynthia. *What are your plans now?*

Nancy lay on the glider like a corpse. A straw hat, a boater, rested on her brow. *Sir Charles Grandison* guarded her crotch. Flies buzzed on the ceiling. It was eleven o'clock on a Monday, the first morning of Laurette's vacation. Laurette stalked onto the porch, wearing a housecoat and a headdress of rollers.

"Nan, I'm going to New York in a couple of weeks. Come along. We'll stay in a nice hotel."

"Okay."

Laurette sat down near the rail and presented her face to the sun. "We'll have a ball," she declared. "We'll get you an autumn outfit—a velvet pantsuit, maybe. Wherever did you pick up that hat?"

"In a charity ward. Will you badger the salespeople?"

"Yep." Laurette closed her eyes. "Though comedy is my true thing. My ex-husband chose me because I was droll."

Nancy remembered him, a chemist with an off-center mouth. He had married again, fathered four sons. "Why did you give him the gate?" she asked.

"Thought I could do better." The woman raised her head and blinked. Sunlight illuminated her orange hair. "Do I really—"

"Like sisters," Nancy assured her.

When Laurette had gone, Nancy peeked again at her other letter. *I love you*, it still said. *I consider that it's time we . . .* She stared at the flies for some minutes, during which Mrs. Hasken drifted onto the porch and sat down.

"Would you like the glider, Mother?"

"I don't think so." Her face was beautiful despite its extreme thinness. At fifty she had not yet turned gray. She was a woman who had worn hats, hummed tunes, laughed at radio wags. She had endured the illness and decay of the man she loved, and his dying. Alone, she'd attended ballet recitals in drafty barns, clapped at graduations, and waited up for Nancy, lying sideways on a couch whose brocade carved a cruel pattern into her cheek.

"Remember 'Glow-Worm'?" Nancy asked.

"I don't think so. That pas de deux?"

"Irma Fellowes pushed me across the stage like a broom."

"Chubby Irma. She's married now."

"How are you feeling?"

"Fine!" Fingers flew to cheek. "Don't I look fine?"

No. But Nancy had already spoken with their physician, a belly with a beard.

"High blood pressure," he'd said. "Under control."

"Shouldn't she be on a special diet?" Nancy had asked.

"No. How's life treating you?" he said.

"So-so."

"Ha-ha. Lots of chaps blushing you up?"

"Too few."

"Tsk. Get married, girl," he advised.

The message was coming through. Marry, said Laurette's hot eyes—or prepare to wisecrack your way down the years. Marry, warned Phoebe. Or you, too, may play the fool at someone else's court. "Marry!" Cynthia had wailed, her train a bandage around her arm. "Hey, Nan, get married yourself. Everyone wants to dance with you!" Marry, sighed Mrs. Hasken. Before I withdraw. *Marriage*, said Carl's letter, *would benefit us both*.

Why not? She was not the sort to set men on fire. She was lanky and ungifted. She was lucky that Carl wanted her. She thought hard about that decent young man, so hard that he appeared before her, scholar, don. To a bunch of small rowdies he might someday be the head. He smiled, nearly destroying her—he had a darling smile. She set him on the rail. Next she conjured up the man she wanted, and after checking him for details—the scar on the knee, the paunch—placed him beside his rival.

Nancy was sure the three of them could find contentment. Wearing knickers and caps, they'd hide out in a cave. Late on a January night they'd spy wolves sliding across the ice. When spring came they'd drift downriver in a homemade raft . . . She twisted on the glider as if in pain. Young women of twenty-one did not play Huck Finn. They got married, sensibly, or made themselves otherwise useful.

What was up, anyway? Truths ducked their heads whenever she drew near. Also she had begun to suffer from sinusitis. The next morning she rose at five and took a walk in the woods, and the day afterward, also. By the third day of tramping out at dawn she was reliably clearheaded in the morning, enraged by afternoon. She abandoned the sport.

That evening, using some grimy yellow paper, Nancy wrote: *Dear Carl, I can't, I'm sorry.* Merciful, she stopped there. *Fondly, Nan,* and mailed the thing.

"You don't look pleased," Leo said, the next afternoon. No sun, but the fog was scorching. They sat on their bench, Leo wearing his pony's hat, Nancy her straw one.

"Dysphoria," mumbled the girl, uncomfortable under his medical gaze. Her chest was abnormally flat, he'd notice; her shoulders too high; the long chin had been designed as a bookmark . . .

"Hey!"

She roused herself. "Hot," she explained.

"Too hot for tennis."

"Much."

Leo said idly, "Come down to my cabin for a glass of beer." Whereupon Nancy, in a panic, stammered, "I'm expected at home."

"Oh."

". . . half a glass. Would be okay. Do you own a half glass?"

"I'll halve one," he promised.

A path dived between the trees. Leo led the way. Nancy studied his nape. Soon they were approaching the cabin. She took the last steep run like a novice, arms outstretched, palms prepared to meet a wall. Leo, still ahead of her, opened the door, and she flew past him into the room. She flopped onto the cot and threw her straw hat onto a table. Leo squatted before a refrigerator. Nancy unhooked her Polaroid cheaters. He handed her a mug. She removed her glasses altogether. A blur seated itself in a chair.

"My uncorrected eyesight is 20/400," Nan opened. "The army would never admit me, except as chaplain. The foreign legion requires reasonable vision, also."

"Oh."

"Many important people have been myopic. It correlates with inventiveness and anxiety." She plucked at the table, found her glasses. Sighted again, she smiled at Leo as if she had outwitted him. "Do you play squash in addition to tennis?" she inquired.

"No. Ping-Pong's my other sport."

"Bridge is mine."

"I prefer poker."

"Oh yes."

"Yes."

Outside, the fog abruptly lifted. Sunlight flashed into the cabin. A yellow diamond fell upon the central oval in the braided rug. Nancy examined the intersection of quadrilateral and ellipse, and reviewed the method for calculating its area. From this exercise she went on to consider certain authors. Oscar Wilde. Thomas Hardy. Shakespeare; *Much Ado*; Beatrice and Benedick and their raillery. Profitable to avoid such nonsense. "We're alone in your cabin," she told Leo's scar. "I'd like to take advantage of the opportunity."

"Oh?"

"I'm in love with you."

"Oh. Nancy, I'm old enough to be your—"

"Grandfather. I'll overlook it. Will you marry me?"

". . . no."

". . . I didn't catch that."

"No."

"Unacceptable," she croaked. "You're the one I want."

"Only at the moment," Leo said, soberly.

"I'm not at all impoverished," persisted Nan.

"Nancy. Do cut this out."

"All right," Nancy said, fast, "then let's just dwell together. I'll be your slavey sister. Mend, darn, dish up the stew, rinse out the undies of your paramours . . ."

"No."

"No?"

"No."

Nancy soared. She felt detached, exalted. To be defeated, she realized, is also to be disburdened. One travels the lighter. Nevertheless . . . Leo's cough drop eyes shone. His enormous sneakers were like ocean liners. She longed to embrace his midsection and plunge her nose into his belly. She recalled the arid nights on Carl's pallet. There might be commerce between men and women that she was as yet ineligible for.

She remained on the cot, in an aggrieved slouch. Stretching one arm she managed to pick up her hat and place it aslant on her head. Then she rammed her fists into the pockets of her shorts. "Care to reconsider?"

"No, puss."

The boulevardier shrugged. "Then that's that."

Leo leaned forward "Hey. Listen. Listening? Fortune favors the brave, Nan. Life won't find you here. Go somewhere else for a bit. Fifty million Frenchmen can't be wrong . . . Hey, sweetheart, don't cry."

". . . rarely cry. Not crying now."

He crouched before her, his hands soothing her shoulders. "See the world, girl."

"Can't. Have an obligation."

"Sure. To yourself. Femme up a little. Try Paris."

"Le haute couture?" she asked, curious.

"La vie. Look at the swans in Zurich. Study the healthy life in Amsterdam. Learn love from Italians, in Rome."

"I'd hoped to pick up some pointers from you. In Jacobstown," Nancy said, crustily. Leo, laughing, kissed her twice: hard, cousinly busses. Since a rejected suitor could expect no more, they had to suffice.

At five Nancy biked up to the porch. The women smiled as she swung one leg over the rail. Having decided against rooming with Carl, the girl thought, and having failed with Leo, content yourself with riotous reunions like this one. You may recollect that you have an obligation. Every so often you can chase crazily after the impossible. Diverting! Still astraddle, she endured a vision of herself in the seasons ahead—a dandy's jacket, a ruffled shirt; praised, indulged; androgynous beyond repair. She blinked the rascal away.

Early the next morning a spare person trousered in denim and stoled in duffel slid out of the Hasken house. On the porch stood three solemn but uncrushed figures. Eyeglasses glinting, Nancy walked steadily. At the bus depot she leaned against the storage boxes. Istanbul? Too thievish. And Zurich was too square. In Amsterdam one could be run down by a bike. She crossed to the counter, bought her ticket, and gazed for a while at the coffee machine. She would make up her mind at Cook's. Briefly Nan wished she'd enjoyed a more bracing adolescence, wished she'd put to sea before. Then, supporting her duffel bag, she climbed onto the southbound bus.

Unravished Bride

"TELL ME ABOUT YOURSELF," Marlene chattered to this Rafferty fellow. The wedding was going to her head, as all weddings did. There was nothing majestic about the suburban parish church, but the late September day was beautiful, and the bride, Marlene's cousin's daughter, was certainly pretty—she resembled Marlene's grandmother. The groom was a salesman for the Raffertys. He was handsome in an untrustworthy way: hair too abundant, eyes too calculating, smile erupting with teeth. He might have passed for a young Kennedy. His name, however, was O'Riordan.

Somehow during the reception Marlene had become separated from her husband and their children. At these family affairs Paul and the kids always looked so interesting, or just so Jewish, that they got snapped up like savories. So she had begun to move alone through the receiving line, like a widow—no: like a maiden. Then this Hugh Rafferty materialized at her side. Marlene kissed the bride, Peggy Ann, and told the groom she hoped he'd be very happy. Hugh did the same. They drifted together into the swirl, and Hugh grabbed two champagnes from a passing tray.

"Tell me about yourself." Not the most sophisticated of openings. But sophistication would leave this man cold—she knew that just by looking at him. She knew, too, that he had been gently bred and properly educated (Harvard, it turned out); he was respectful and observant; his wife was the sort who gets things done (she was director of publicity at a local college, he told Marlene with pride);

he loved his many kids. He sailed and skied and played tennis, but a paunch was rising anyway.

His eyes were bright blue and his smile was the turned-up kind that children put on cookies. She meant to slip away as she often did at parties, fearful that she was restraining people ambitious to be elsewhere. But Hugh pleasantly stood fast, telling Marlene about himself. He managed the family lumber business and lived on the South Shore. He was the third generation to do both; love of work and pleasure in home were strong in him. His smile must once have haunted the dreams of virgins . . .

"You were at Wellesley?" he said. "You'd think we'd have met."

"I was a fireman's daughter, on scholarship, from Detroit. It's my mother's relatives at this wedding, though she's gone, so's my father. My sisters are scattered," she babbled.

Paul came up. Marlene introduced the men, then said to her husband, "You've been a trooper with Aunt Tess. I was watching you. Is it her gout this time?"

"It's her gums."

"Are you a dentist?" Hugh asked.

"I'm a radiologist."

"It's all the same to Aunt Tess," Marlene said, and they laughed, and then Hugh excused himself, shaking hands first.

That should have been that. Meeting again seemed unlikely— Hugh halfway to the Cape, Marlene near to town; his crowd rich, hers high-minded. If O'Riordan were to take an ax to Peggy Ann, they might see each other at the funeral, or the trial. Otherwise, no.

They saw each other five days later. Marlene's avocation—she was an amateur biographer—sometimes took her to the Boston Public Library. Hugh's work demanded his presence at the company's Prudential Center office twice a week. He was headed there at quarter past twelve that Thursday; she was about to enter the library.

"Hello!" he called.

The usual flurries. And then—he so easily might not have said it—"Have you had lunch yet?"

"I . . . don't have lunch, usually."

"Then you can't have had it yet. Have it with me."

Once in a while at a college party some tall handsome boy, caught by her alert face, had danced with her . . . She walked next to Hugh, along Boylston Street, along Clarendon. She wished her friends could see her.

They talked easily. Neither liked to worry a subject to death. They passed up wine and shared a dessert. Afterward they retraced their steps. At the entrance to the library she turned and shook hands.

"Thank you very much," she said, looking up at him. "You've reminded me of the pleasures of having lunch."

"Let me do it again," he said relinquishing her hand and putting his own in his pocket. Don't make too much of this, his attitude said.

"I'm here every Thursday," she lied.

"Next Thursday, then? Tell me where you usually work."

"I drift from section to section," she said. "I could arrange to be in bound periodicals. Near *Fortune*, say."

"Fine. At about one?"

So it began—Thursday lunches. They feasted at taverns and went hungry at salad bars. They ate raw fish wrapped in seaweed. One Thursday when Hugh was in a hurry they sat at a doughnut counter. The next week he insisted on several courses at the Ritz.

At Christmastime they took an enforced break while Hugh and his family went south. In February, Marlene had a week-long flu; that Thursday morning, trembling, she called his office.

"Mr. Rafferty, please," she said to the secretary, who sounded gorgeous. "Ms. Winokaur calling."

"Marlene?" he said when he picked up. She had never before heard his voice on the telephone. Her bowels turned to water; but that was probably the flu. "Oh, I'm sorry," he said, when she told him she was too ill to come out. "Feel better." His voice was frank and unashamed. Anyone hearing the conversation would have assumed that they were merely two friends canceling a luncheon appointment.

And were they anything else? Their weekly meetings couldn't be more blameless if some Sister made them a threesome. They were as public as statues. They talked about politics, basketball, first communions they had lived through, the lives she investigated, the trees he loved. They talked about the few people they knew in common (the young O'Riordans were expecting a baby already). They were like college boy and college girl on that outmoded, rule-bound thing: a date. But dates were only the beginning, weren't they—the slow beginning of a series that became hurried, became precipitous, came to a head, and ended in either a broken heart or a ceremony in a stone church. "How did I get here?" more than one panicky bride had said to Marlene. How did *we* get here? Marlene wondered now. Where are we going?

On the first warm Thursday in May, they bought a bag of pretzels and ate them on the bank of the Charles. They sat on Hugh's raincoat. He loosened his tie. Hundreds of men all over the city were loosening their ties in the spring warmth. Yet she had to look away until she felt her flush recede.

They spent most summer Thursdays picnicking on the river or watching swan boats in the public garden. If it rained they sat at a sidewalk café under an umbrella. Their vacations happened to co-incide—temporally, not geographically; the Raffertys went camping in Wyoming, the Winokaurs exchanged houses with a family in Hampstead. September found them both back in town. It was almost a year since they'd first met.

The Thursday after vacation, they took a noontime cruise on the harbor. The boat was crowded and noisy. The ladies' room was out of order. Hugh spilled coffee on Marlene's skirt. He apologized, but his annoyance seemed directed at her.

"Sorry to be in your way," she said stiffly.

"Hey!"

And the boat returned so late that they had to take a cab across town. She huddled in the backseat corner and watched his profile. Many a college romance had not survived the summer vacation. As if you could call this romance! *How did we get here?* she echoed herself. *Where are we going? Suppose Paul found out?*

Suppose Paul found out what? She and Hugh had never kissed. They had never held hands. Once his knuckles had burned hers as he handed a menu across the table. Once, on the riverbank, he had flipped over onto his stomach beside her and she had placed her hand briefly on his blue-and-white striped back. He'd shuddered and turned his face away . . .

"Would you like to visit a hotel together?" he was saying now.

Her skirt was still soaked with coffee. "Are you inviting me or the cab driver?"

So he had to look at her. He was unsmiling, and his face flamed like a boy's.

"Yes," she said. "I would. I would."

They knew where to go. Twice they had lunched in the lobby café at the Orlando, a lively salesman's hotel, and they watched couples without luggage—handsome, well-dressed couples—checking in.

"Next Thursday, then," Hugh said.

"Next Thursday," Marlene agreed.

She had never stopped loving Paul. During the week that followed she loved him tenderly, gratefully—loved his short, muscular body, his preoccupied manner, his kindness to their children. One love had nothing to do with the other. Paul was the man she would contentedly grow old with. But though she and Hugh were both past forty, theirs was the brief happy fling of youth. Everything proved it: their indifference to the future, their bright, news-of-the-week conversation. He was her boyfriend. She was his girl.

She wore a new dress—silk, with a dropped waist. It was the color of Hugh's eyes. She looked beautiful, she hoped . . . even though her cheeks were a little too round and her slate-colored eyes disappeared when she laughed. Her headful of curls was in fashion. At a distance she could pass for a femme fatale.

And it was at a distance that they saw each other, that next Thursday. She was standing at the rear of the lobby when he came through the revolving door. The lobby café separated them. He made his way among the tables, lumbering a bit, bigger than most men, handsomer than all. The smile curved. It curved, it curved . . . but falsely; she could tell that at once. "You don't have to," she said, under her breath. Then his face was close to hers, so close that she could have kissed him, and who would have thought anything of that?—two old friends kissing, people did it all the time, Paul was always complaining that women he hardly knew embraced him at parties like tango dancers. She said it again. "You don't have to. Dear."

"I cannot," he told her.

She probably could have talked him into it. "I've put on my diaphragm," she could have said, and he would have understood that by that act she had already betrayed her marriage. Or she could have allowed her eyes to fill with chagrined tears. Or her enthusiasm, her delight, might have carried him along. But she didn't use those wiles.

"You don't have to," she said for the third time. "Although," she couldn't help adding, "everybody else does."

He took her arm and led her toward a table. "We're not everybody else," he said.

No, they were not everybody else, she thought while pretending to eat her salad. Everybody else—in Boston, in Paris, in Tel Aviv; Protestants, Catholics, Jews; black and white, young and old and rich and poor—everybody else played by today's rules. Young O'Riordan would turn up in this hotel within a decade. And Marlene's children, when the time came; and Hugh's children . . . Everybody else was up-to-date. But she and Hugh were throwbacks. They were bound to the code of their youth—self-denial and honor and fidelity—an inconvenient code that would keep them, she realized with a pang, forever chaste, and forever in love.

BINOCULAR VISION

FOR HIS FORTIETH BIRTHDAY my father was given a pair of binoculars. His medical colleagues teamed up on the present. He was neither a bird-watcher nor a sports fan, so the glasses just lay on his dresser like a trophy.

They didn't tempt me at first. I had already been disappointed by his ophthalmoscope, which didn't magnify a thing. (I also didn't like the coin-operated telescope on our Connecticut city's twenty-four-story building, the tallest in New England; as soon as I managed to focus on something through the telescope, my nickel ran out.) But one December afternoon, wandering in an aimless, childish way around my parents' bedroom, I picked up the binoculars, took them to a window that looked out on the street, and directed them toward a leafless tree. I saw a brown blur, so I fiddled with the wheels on the instrument. Now the tree was hyper-clear, making my eyes ache. Finally, after more fiddling, I saw the tree plain and even vaguely menacing, like my great-uncle at the last family party who had leaned so close to me that his tie swayed in front of my eyes. But when I thoughtlessly reached out to touch the tree's bark, I touched instead the windowpane.

The side window in my parents' room, like the windows of the other bedrooms in our end-of-the-row house, looked out at the second-floor apartment next door, also brick, where the Simons lived.

With the aid of the binoculars, I projected myself into the Simons' living room. Their fireplace was as dark as a cave. On the mantel crouched a humpbacked clock. In one of the two chairs flanking the hearth sat Mrs. Simon herself, her gray head bent. She was crocheting. I could not see the pattern of the work, nor the pattern on her dress, but I could see that her green chair wore a lace antimacassar and that a flared lamp on a table cast its glow on a pile of magazines. There was no television, of course—only rich show-offs had televisions then.

I went into my own bedroom. From there I inspected the Simons' dining room. An empty silver bowl occupied pride of place on the table. Perhaps Mr. Simon's colleagues had given it to him when *he* turned forty. I went into my sister's bedroom. From her window I peered at the Simons' little kitchen. Two cups and two saucers lay on the drainboard. A calendar hung on the wall, but no matter how much I fiddled with the wheels of the binoculars I could not make out the Simons' appointments.

From our last bedroom, reserved for guests, I got a dark glimpse of the Simons' big bedroom. I knew there was a small bedroom, too, for my friend Elaine lived in an identical apartment down the street. The small bedroom faced the backyard, a skimpy strip of grass and six little garages, one each for the six apartments. I would never get to see that bedroom. The room I did see had a double bed with an afghan at its foot, folded into a perfect right triangle. This application of geometry to daily life gratified my critical ten-year-old self.

DURING THAT MONTH, which included a school vacation, I discovered that Mrs. Simon was a great tidier. Often I would find her in the living room, readjusting an antimacassar or rearranging candy in a dish or polishing the glass door of the bookcase. Serious cleaning was done once a week by a regal mulatto woman, but sometimes Mrs. Simon would stand at the kitchen sink, her stubborn profile lowered, fiercely scrubbing something. Occasionally she lay down in the bedroom. And often she disappeared. Perhaps she was talking on the telephone in the hall, a windowless place my binoculars could not penetrate. Or perhaps she was walking a few blocks to Elm Street, as most of the women in our neighborhood did most days, in order to pick up some fish and vegetables, or a library book. Once in a while I ran into Mrs. Simon on just such an errand. We were the same height—I was a tall child and she a small and somewhat bent woman—and her expression was as steely as her curls. Our eyes met, with no mediating binoculars. "Hello," I'd whisper, suddenly shy. She never answered.

In the late afternoons, Mrs. Simon got busy. She stirred pots on the stove. She set the table in the dining room. She folded the evening paper several times, this way and that, and finally laid it on the arm of Mr. Simon's chair. Again she adjusted the antimacassars and arranged the candies.

Darkness came at 4:30. From the window of our spare bedroom, reading by flashlight, I kept track of the cars returning to the six garages. A floodlight illuminated the area. When Mr. Simon's car appeared, I would close my book, switch off my flashlight, and raise my binoculars.

Mr. Simon, a tall man, would unfold from his automobile. He'd pass a hand over his gray hair, raise the door of the garage, get back into the car, and drive it into the garage. He usually sat there for a while, giving me a chance to inspect his license plate, which had three numbers and two letters. I have forgotten them all. My eyes caressed the curve of his car trunk. I noticed the branch caught on the fender. Where had he been driving, to collect such a trophy? Was he a salesman? What did he do while Mrs. Simon and I were watching the clock for him?

In the midst of my musings, Mr. Simon would reappear, briefcase in hand, and roll down his garage door. That handkerchief, hanging from his overcoat pocket—might it slip out? Would the drop of the handkerchief be marked only by me, whose presence was as undetectable as God's? And if I alone saw cloth meet asphalt, could the handkerchief really be said to have fallen, or would it be like the tree I'd learned about in class, the tree that cracks unheard in the forest and thus provides a philosophical question for the ages? Surely Mrs. Simon, who sorted her laundry with as much finickiness as a forty-niner panning for gold, would notice a missing item. But the handkerchief clung to his pocket as Mr. Simon walked slowly across the backyard and toward the rear door of the apartment building.

I glided into my parents' dark bedroom. My mother was duplicating Mrs. Simon's activities in our kitchen downstairs, my father was saving people's vision in his office. I turned my magic glasses onto the Simons' bright living room, only a few yards away.

How I yearned to witness Mr. Simon's return. Alas, it always took place in that inner hall. It must be like my father's homecoming: the woman hurrying to the door; the man bringing in a gust of weather and excitement; the hug, affectionate and sometimes annoyingly long; and finally the separation, so that two little girls rushing downstairs could be caught in those overcoated arms. But at the Simons' there were no children. Perhaps the pair exchanged a dignified kiss.

Our dinner coincided with theirs. And then I had to help my mother with the dishes. It wasn't until evening that I saw the Simons again.

This was my favorite scene. The couple by the fireplace and the invisible guest. I could see how motionless Mr. Simon's long face was as he read the paper, page by slow page, and how stiffly he held his shoulders under the jacket he never took off. I could almost hear the tick of the mantelpiece clock.

I shifted my attention to Mrs. Simon. Cross and cross again went the needles. And up and down, up and down went the active lips, the unstoppable mouth, the mouth that never produced a word for me but spoke so easily and swiftly and continually when the beloved was home. Talking. Laughing. Talking again.

AFTER VACATION I visited the Simons less often. By the end of January I was dropping in only occasionally—for a moment at the end of an afternoon, say, to make sure that something was cooking on the stove.

Then, during breakfast one February morning, two policemen appeared at our back door. "Doctor, can you . . .?" My father did not pause even to put on his suit jacket; he just followed the sturdy officers into the yard, looking like their servant in his silk-backed waistcoat and his white shirtsleeves. They walked across the crusted snow and into the backyard of the apartment building next door. My mother stood at the kitchen window, her hand on her heart.

My father returned before we left for school. "It's Al Simon," he said to my mother. "He died during the night."

My sister continued to buckle her boots.

"Was he murdered?" I said.

"No," my father said. "What makes you ask?"

"The policemen."

My father sighed. Then, after a thoughtful pause, "Mr. Simon committed suicide," he told me. "In his car."

"Did he drive it off a cliff?"

My parents exchanged frowns and shrugs. Such a child, their looks said, all curiosity and no sympathy—and this the teachers call gifted? Then, still in a patient voice, my father explained that Mr. Simon had driven into his garage, closed the door from inside, stuffed the cracks with newspapers, reentered his car, and turned on the motor.

The next day in the obituary section I could find no hint of suicide, unless *suddenly* was the code word. But the final sentence was a shocker. "Mr. Simon, a bachelor, is survived by his mother."

I raced to my own mother. "I thought she was his wife!"

"So did she," my mother said, admitting me abruptly into the complicated world of adults, making me understand what I had until then only seen.

NEW STORIES

GRANSKI

"TWO FACES, ONE NOSE," Toby said. "A physiognomic curiosity. Which ancestor did we get it from?"

"Isaac Abravanel," Angelica replied, though the family's connection to that prominent Portuguese merchant had never been firmly
established.

The nose, whatever its origin, was a long thin wavy proboscis,
rather comely. Except for this similar feature, the cousins looked
nothing alike. Angelica had topaz eyes. Various dark colors shifted
in her hair. Toby's narrow eyes were gray, his hair a steady brown.

They were sixteen. During the school year, at home—she in Paris,
he in Connecticut—each kept au courant with songs, the proper
placement of studs, movies; of course they carried cell phones and
knew where to buy weed. But here in Maine they could be their
true selves. Their true selves were variously described by the family. Snooty agoutis, according to their younger siblings and cousins.
Good sports, according to Gramp, a good sport himself. Too damned
clever, said their mothers, who were sisters. The third sister, aunt to
Toby and Angelica, complained that they breathed air rarefied even
for this family, and we are already the most hyper-indulged characters on the face of the . . . Her statement dwindled as always. As for
Gran—tall, crop-haired, pale-eyed Gran—whatever she thought of
these particular grandchildren she didn't bother to say.

They were enjoying exceptional educations, Angelica in her
école, Toby in his boarding school. His French was almost as good
as her English. Here in Maine they played tennis, hiked, swam.

Gramp taught them to drive, then told them not to use the car. "Self-restraint is strength," he explained. "Also you can be arrested for driving without a license."

"Self-restraint is fear," Toby said one afternoon as they walked to the little boathouse. "We are a terrified clan. Since Antwerp."

Seventy years earlier the family had fled Antwerp for Haifa. The details of the disembarkation had been repeated again and again. Angelica could have drawn the scene. The youngest child, a little girl, ran down the gangplank, a fortune in diamonds sewn into her coat. Her two brothers followed—the older would become Gramp. Great-grandmother came next, face tragic above a fur-collared coat. She had left the graves of two other sons in the Shomre Hadas Cemetery. Great-grandfather brought up the rear. He had managed the departure from Belgium, he had swept his family to safety, his children now twice owed their lives to him. His portrait hung over Gramp's desk in the Manhattan brownstone.

"Great-grandfather was a *type*," Toby now remarked. "Cultivated European."

"Prescient," Angelica reminded him. "Without Great-grandfather you and I would never have been born."

"We were fated to be born."

"No, no, it was hap." Yesterday she had won bonus points for *hap* in bilingual Scrabble. "Hap and heroism."

Their heroic great-grandparents had settled in Jerusalem, thrived, worriedly saw the birth of Israel. Their grandfather, though, had remained only long enough to conceive a dislike for the coarse country. The end of the war found him on another ship, this one bound for Hoboken. (Two years later his younger brother emigrated to Cape Town.) The family had retained its banking connections: useful to both sons. In New York, Gramp made money from money. He was a dandy, he was musical, he married a renegade Yankee then working as a veterinarian's assistant. Grace Larcom— Gran, now—was an only child, born late in the life of her parents. She insisted on converting, or at least declaring herself converted, though Gramp said it was unnecessary. This big summerhouse in Maine was all Gran's straitened father and mother had to give her, and they gave it gladly. "They were relieved that I was chosen by a human being," she'd said to Angelica in her dry voice. "They were braced for an interspecies liaison." And decades afterward, summer after summer, Gramp and Gran's three far-flung daughters returned with their husbands and their growing families—Angelica's beautiful mother from Paris; Toby's artistic one from Washington; the third sister, the one who rarely finished a sentence, from Buenos Aires.

Angelica was a month older than Toby. That made her the oldest of the nine grandchildren. This accident of rank brought little privilege—everyone had chores to do—though she did get her own room on the third floor. The third floor was reached only by a set of shabby back stairs, but rising from the spacious front hall toward the balustraded second floor was a handsome central staircase. It separated into two staircases halfway up, an enormous Y. "Fit only for an opera house," Gran complained; still, she kept the carved posts in good repair. Except for this spectacular feature, the house was asymmetrical, and also disorderly. Parlor opened off parlor, and the pantry cupboards were decorated with stained glass stained more deeply by time, and a piano was covered with brocade edged in dusty fringe, and the whole place was strewn with heirlooms of little value if you didn't count the occasional signed piece of silver. "Impedimenta," Gran said. Dense pines protected the house from the prying sun. But here and there light unexpectedly winked—reflected from a copper shovel, from a chandelier long ago cut down from the ceiling and left unmourned on its side, from a decanter holding a cloudy amethyst liquid.

"That purple stuff has gone organic," Toby suggested. "One day a flatworm will crawl out of it and we'll have a new universe."

Through the cluttered house moved nine adults and two teenagers and seven children, seeking each other, avoiding each other, carrying books wine rackets flowers teddy bears. The smallest ones liked riding on the shoulders of their fathers and their uncles. Sometimes Gramp played pony to one or another of them. "You're killing me!" he complained, groaning with happiness.

Every summer the daughter who lived in Buenos Aires drew up a detailed schedule for ridding the house of unnecessary items; sooner or later she abandoned the project. Meanwhile the once-a-week cleaning was accomplished, more or less, by a mother and daughter from the nearby town. They had brown teeth. Meals were prepared by Myrrh, a large, hunch-shouldered, muttering woman who was Gran's second cousin with a few removes. Myrrh was paid for her work, and she dined with the family—it was her family, too. She endured without comment the nightly dinners, everybody talking at once; she endured the endless Sabbath-eve meal. Gramp had returned to religion in his later years, and he recited a long individualized blessing over the heads of each of his twelve offspring. The three daughters and the nine grandchildren took turns helping in the kitchen, obeying a complicated rotation devised by Gran. While cleaning up, Myrrh grunted an occasional brief command: "Here," or "Discard." Recently she had snapped "Cut that out" to Toby and Angelica, who were merely standing at the trash barrel hip to hip, scraping plates.

Myrrh slept in the room next to Angelica's. She spent most of the day in the house, though sometimes she took a walk with the youngest grandchild, who still spoke only her native Spanish. They came back looking peaceful, carrying pails of blueberries. They sat next to each other at the table. "Silent, depthful," Myrrh said one dinnertime: an actual remark, apparently addressed to Gran. "Reminiscent of Abigail the lumber woman, our progenitress." Gran nodded.

At night the kitchen became Gran's domain. Here she endured her famous insomnia. She read books about extinct mammals and examined her childhood collection of bird skeletons. "My cat brought me the corpses." She smoked. She worked chess problems and played an old flute. By day the flute rested on a table in the big useless front hall; the instrument, too, caught the light.

TOBY AND ANGELICA were drifting on the lake. He rowed from time to time. Her fingers trailed in the water. It was a cliché of a pose. Why strike a pose for this amusing relative, her favorite. He was like a brother, like a sister . . . "We are a terrified family?" she wondered aloud.

A different fellow might have forgotten he'd thrown out the phrase. Toby remembered. He remembered the dates of kings and presidents. He remembered all their Scrabble disputes. Could you really add *-tous* to *anathema*? You could; *anathematous* was right there in the *American Heritage*. He could recite entire paragraphs from the books they chose for the nine months each year they were apart. In Angelica's Paris house, in Toby's dormitory cell, the cousins read by arrangement Ransome, Colette, Naipaul . . . During the past year they'd read Russian novelists. They agreed to study Russian at university—no one in the family spoke it; it would be theirs alone. This summer Toby kept trying to Russify various words—Gothamgrad, the Volvoskaya, anathematouski.

His gray eyes searched her face. He was not smiling. "Terrified. Look at yourself, *moy* Angelica. You have every reason to be confident. Beauty—don't shake your head, *dushinka*. Those *ochi charnya*, your eyes are yellow, not dark, but I don't know the Russian for yellow"—as if he knew the Russian for everything else; the scamp had about five words. "You belong to a noble house . . ."

"Don't talk nonsense, Toby. Jews recognize only . . . nobility of purpose."

"Spiritual meritocraski, sure, but we're a first family all the same."

"—okay," she said, sighing.

"And yet . . . our importance rests on sand, and we all feel it. You feel it."

"The diamonds, you mean?"

"They're carbon. I mean a metaphysical sand . . . no, metaphorical," he corrected, suddenly sounding very young. "It shifts, the sand. It casts us out, or accepts us unwillingly. We don't belong anywhere, so each generation flees to some other place."

"Portugal," she said. There was a shameful legend: some ancestor had advised the Portuguese king against sponsoring Columbus's voyage. "We started in Portugal."

"We started in the desert, like everybody else."

They had reached a cove. "Literal sand," he said, hopping out, dragging the boat onto the tiny beach with Angelica still seated in its stern. He helped her get out; all the grandchildren had been taught good manners. They walked up a path, Toby leading the way. "*Terrified* was too strong," he said over his shoulder, giving her a glimpse of his rippling profile. "Uneasy . . . that's what we are."

But now she had indeed become terrified. His long straight hair, held back by a headband; his brown back; his buttocks taut within iridescent trunks. Like many Parisian teenagers, she found older men sexy. She planned to marry someone mature and experienced. She planned to teach in the Sorbonne like her father and his father.

She'd continue pencil sketching. Young men were a necessary feature of her life plan. She knew she would soon surrender to one, but this littermate? His shoulders, so bony . . .

They stopped in a clearing. An old stone fireplace, stumps, an abundance of pine needles. He turned to her.

"Will you, Angelica Laurentovna?" His voice was grave. Had he embraced her she would have spun away. But so respectful a request . . .

"Yes," she said, her terror melting.

She stepped out of her bathing suit. His eyes widened. He flipped his trunks off, flung them onto a branch. She lay down. Needles stabbed her back, her nape. He knelt, she spread, this was how, wasn't it; and he entered her like a . . . chemist, she thought, someone intent on transferring liquid from beaker to vessel without accident. He frowned. Helplessly she whimpered. He looked at her with hungry eyes, *merde*, his desire was more painful than the pain, at last thank God he closed those *ochi grayski*. He thrust once, twice, and all of a sudden it was over. His head slammed onto the pine needles. "God," he said. "Angelica, sorry, too soon," he said.

Poor boy, his first time, too. She turned wet eyes toward his burrowing head.

"Did it hurt a lot?" he mumbled.

"Yes."

"It won't next time, I promise."

It never hurt again. What a strange boiled stalk he had. It grew from fleshy mauve pads. Veins ran along it. It wore an opaque cloak during the few days each month they dubbed terafacient, though that their issue would be monstrous was not at all certain. "I think there has to be generations of inbreeding," Angelica said one night.

"We share approximately one-eighth of our genes," he said, spent, garrulous, his familiar nose pointing toward the bedroom ceiling. "But that's only statistical. We could share as many as half, our mothers could be as alike as twins, you never know, everything is chance."

"No, fate."

"And that hap of yours—whatever happened to hap?"

"Shh, not so loud. Our fate was decided long ago," she insisted. "Before dinosaurs, even before Jews."

They didn't return to the clearing in the pines. They met here instead, in Angelica's bedroom. Its furnishings had been flung upward by generations of Gran's forebears who never gave anything away, who never moved out of New England, who never had to flee to a new land with the family's assets distributed about the person of the youngest child. Beside the bed a copper pheasant stood in a brass bowl on top of a skeletal night table. The deep reds and greens of the darkening wallpaper had run into each other and become one rich color. A glass-fronted bookcase held medical textbooks. "They belonged to my great-uncle Jim," their grandmother had said. "Good old Jim. Never too drunk to make a house call."

The windows on the third floor were shaped like lozenges, with smaller lozenges their panes. These windows opened outward on a hinge. Their screens had been made to order a hundred years earlier, and were now full of holes. "Ridiculous diamond windows," Gran grumbled. "Maybe a century ago somebody anticipated my alliance with a great Antwerp house."

"I thought they thought you'd hook up with some inferior primate."

"My parents feared I might marry a monkey, yes. And maybe I did." Gramp had a monkey's long upper lip and wide nostrils. A tall, well-dressed monkey, an organ grinder's handsome pal. He and Gran were reputed to have had youthful arguments that involved broken crockery. But Gran's remark was said softly. This plain stick of a woman loved her playful husband. He loved her in return. Their love brought the three daughters back to the inconvenient summer house. "We are replicating an ancestral passion," Angelica told Toby.

"Any excuse will do," he said, and grinned.

In Angelica's nighttime room, she and Toby, black marble statues, rubbed each other into life. The medical books were obscured behind the discolored glass, but the young lovers knew the titles by heart, knew even their order on the shelves. *Principles of Otolaryngology, Textbook of Ophthalmology, Advances in Epidemiology . . .* "Which epidemics back then, do you think?" Angelica murmured into Toby's shoulder.

"Influenza, rheumatic fever, Jew hating."

Angelica looked past him at the copper pheasant in the brass bowl on her night table. "Rheumatic fever isn't communicable."

In one of the Antwerp graves lay a little boy who had died of rheumatic fever: Jacob, a year older than Gramp, his constant playmate. "So many decades ago . . . and I think of Jacob every day," Gramp had said in his monkey's grating voice. "Siblings can be closer than spouses."

Angelica wondered if the pheasant could ever be separated from the bowl. "Some people are struck down early," she said. The old truth seemed like new wisdom.

"Little Jacob? Yes. Not the Nazi boot: a bacterium. Hap, dear girl."

On the fourth Thursday in August the youngest grandchild at last deigned to speak the language she had long understood, and demanded, in grammatical English, to be taken with the other kids to a traveling carnival. She came back happy, with cotton candy in her hair and vomit on her clothing. "Loop the Loop, it was a mistake," her father confessed. She wisely refused dinner and allowed herself to be bathed by Angelica and put to bed by her mother. By chance one of Gramp's business pals turned up and took the child's place at the table. He was a Broadway angel; he saw the house as a stage set and the family as the cast of a three-act comedy and he said so at such annoying length that Gran put him on kitchen duty. Twice during the evening he draped his long arm around Angelica's shoulders.

"I'd like to give him a karate chopakoff," said Toby, much later, and he sliced the air with his flat, rigid hand and knocked the copper pheasant to the floor. The brass bowl shuddered for a while, as if thinking things over; then it fell, too. The rickety night table, deprived of purpose, collapsed. "Stop!" yelled Angelica's brother from the boys' room on the other side of Myrrh's. He was subject to nightmares, and the three crashes might have had nothing to do with his cry.

Shortly after midnight Angelica awoke to a different sound. Was it the wind in the pines, telling of autumn and separation? No: it was a large object being dragged along uncarpeted flooring. She heard grunts, also, and unpleasant words. Then she heard bumps.

It was a crate, wasn't it, perhaps with a frightened girl inside . . . It was a large wooden trough . . . After all, it was something ordinary, a suitcase, and it had reached the back stairs. It tumbled down.

Toby slept. Angelica pulled on shorts and a T-shirt and sped down the back stairs herself. She opened the door to the second floor's landing with its exquisitely carved railing. Myrrh was making her way down the rightmost branch of the grand staircase. She had her luggage in temporary control. What an old-fashioned valise it was, a hardened oblong with a chevron. It must have been elegant, once. Myrrh wore a yellow coat and a glazed brown hat, the outfit resembling a vile custard dessert she was in the habit of preparing. Her soliloquy had become louder. She reached the broad middle part of the staircase where the two large branches converged. She kicked her suitcase. It crashed into the front hall.

Gran came out of the kitchen. Smoking, still in her daytime costume of pants and sweater, she looked up at her relative. "Myrrh," she said. "What."

"Not another minute," Myrrh said, clumping down the final stairs. "Decadence. Hospitality betrayed. Are youth and beauty always to have their way?"

"The family is here for another two days, three at most."

"I am retiring to my brother's house tonight."

Gran puffed. "The arrangement is that you will stay here for the summer. As always."

"Funk the arrangement."

"Fuck. The first bus isn't until six o'clock."

"I am leaving this sinkhole now. I will walk if necessary."

Silence.

"Do you hear my words, Grace?"

Silence.

"I am capable of waking up the entire dissolute, spoiled-rotten household, aswim in its liquidity—"

Gran sighed. Her gaze rested on Myrrh, then traveled upward to Angelica, then traveled upward farther. "Girls! Get back to bed." Angelica looked over her shoulder in time to see three bedroom doors close, her own parents' last—she got a glimpse of Mama's interested dark eyes. Gran now glared at Angelica. "Shoes."

Angelica descended the stairs, edged around Myrrh, ran into the kitchen. Another cigarette smoldered there. She stubbed it out, found her deck shoes, returned to the hall. Gran tossed her something. She caught the something—the keys to the Volvo.

She had never driven at night, but it turned out to be easy to slip through the black-lacquer woods. There were some silver filaments—pine needles picked out by the moon. The long road ahead of them, their road, was soft and gray, like the dust in the fringe of the scarf on the piano. Would Russian prepositions be sensible? There were about a hundred tenses, she'd heard: the iterative, the durative, the . . . They reached the two-lane highway. In the back the elderly women were silent, the suitcase upended between them like a shared suitor. They reached the town.

"Où doit-on aller?" Angelica asked her grandmother.

"Après la gare, au droit."

"Cut the frog talk," Myrrh said, her voice piercing Angelica's nape. "Yid. Incesticator. Won't anyone outside do?"

"Myrrh," Angelica wailed.

"Exocrat!"

"Turn right here," Gran said. "Here!" and Angelica had to step on the brake, and reverse, and go backward. Finally she was able to turn. A few hundred yards along this road was a sign—BILL'S CABINS—and an office with a porch where a weak bulb burned. A narrow figure appeared under the bulb.

Gran opened her window. "Bill?"

"Miss Larcom?"

"Here's Myrrh, for a night. She'll take the 6:00 a.m." She thrust some bills at Myrrh. "For the cabin and the bus ticket." Myrrh dragged her suitcase out of the car and slammed the door and passed in front of the headlights—head bent under the hat, shoulders rounded within the coat: a figure she'd like to draw, Angelica thought, and she'd leave the drawing untitled and some shrewd gallery owner would call it *Exile*. Myrrh stopped at the porch.

"Cabin three," Bill said.

"Okay," Myrrh said.

"Drive," Gran said.

The ride home was shorter than the ride there—an eternal truth of the space-time continuum, Toby had once pointed out. Angelica and her grandmother went into the kitchen and sat down at the oak table. Gran turned off the lamp and lit a cigarette. Angelica handed Gran the keys, which caught the dull light from the window. The shadowy room slowly revealed its known treasures—pewter in a cupboard, the old stove with its cobalt pilot, some revolutionary's portrait, several upended brooms flaring from an umbrella holder.

"All in all," Gran said without preamble, "a continued liaison would be a great deal of trouble. For you, for him, for all of us. Your great-grandfather didn't rescue his line so it could get tangled up with itself like rotten old lace, like some altar cloth from Antwerp. I suppose I mean Bruges."

"Bruges, yes." Angelica swallowed. "You are part of the lace now."

"Not noticeably," Gran said. "The Larcom influence has not made itself felt."

Was that any wonder? The Larcoms had no golden-age ancestors, no diamonds hidden in coats, no displacements, no rebirths, no tragedies. No money.

Angelica said: "Consensual incest is not considered a crime."

"I believe you are quoting Toby. We're not talking about incest as criminal. Funk that. We're talking about incest as undutiful. Broadening the group to insure its survival—that is your responsibility, yours and your coevals." She lit a new cigarette, and in the flame of the match her eyes gleamed, the whites white, the irises almost white. "You will tire of this sooner or later," she said. "Tire of it now, beloved daughter of my daughter."

For sixteen years she had addressed Angelica by name only. The sudden endearment—a declaration, really—was worth ten of Gramp's long-winded blessings. What a rich phrase. You could live a life on the income it yielded.

Angelica gazed steadily at her grandmother. "I will do as you say." She offered her right hand to confirm the agreement. But Gran just continued to smoke.

THE NEXT SUMMER Gran lay ill in the Manhattan brownstone. Gramp crouched on a hassock in a corner of the bedroom. No one had the heart to open the house in Maine. The three daughters came, left, came again. Angelica's mother brought Angelica from Paris. During their sad week in New York—Gran had stopped talking—Toby's mother flew up from Washington with Toby. The two cousins were shooed out of the house. They sat in awkward silence at a delicatessen. They slouched through a museum.

"I have discovered astronomy," Toby said.

"Our stars are our destinies."

"That's astrology, as of course you know. What you and I need is a bed." What they needed was a bedroom full of cast-off furniture and a diamonded diamond window. But one more time, why not . . . She allowed herself to be led to a grimy hotel where, taking off only their lower garments, they each enjoyed a brief spasm of relief—first Toby, then Angelica, taking turns as if under a nurse-maid's eye.

"I will begin Russian next year," Angelica said, adjusting her sandal.

"Yes, well then, so will I," he said without conviction.

Gran died in August. An important rabbi conducted a dignified graveside ceremony. The Buenos Aires daughter began a eulogy of her own but broke down midway. Then prayers; then everybody wept: the three daughters, the three sons-in-law, the nine grand-children, the great-uncle from South Africa and his brood, the great-aunt from Jerusalem. One by one they threw clods of earth onto the pine coffin. And the Presbyterian relatives, Myrrh in-cluded, followed suit, and then offered condolences to speechless Gramp. They were odd, stubborn, unchosen: yet in Angelica's veins their Maine blood kept company with the overwrought Antwerp stuff; and maybe someday she would have a stark daughter who collected beetles and preferred Route 201 to the Boulevard Raspail and played a flute that caught the light . . . Cousin Myrrh was ex-tending her hand. Angelica took it.

All of Great-grandfather's descendants stayed the week, and then returned home, if that's what they called it. "Good-bye, be-loved mother of my mother," Angelica whispered to the thick indif-ference of the Air France window. "Good-bye, Tobski," she added, an afterthought.

THE LITTLE WIFE

THEY FLEW FROM BOSTON to Bangor on a mild February morning. Gail pretended to read a dumb novel selected by her group. Max brought some scientific tome. But he kept the volume closed on his knees, and on top of it he had opened the Beethoven score, opus 66, which he was practicing on his wide thighs. Gail playfully inserted a manicured nail between two of his busy fingers, and with uncharacteristic irritation he flicked her hand away.

They were in their late sixties, both retired. They were going to Maine to see their friend Fox, probably for the last time. Gail, fond of Fox, nevertheless looked forward to this finale with as much curiosity as dread. Every death foretold your own—there would be something to learn. She had been a schoolteacher; discovery was a lifetime habit.

I.

THERE IS AN ANECDOTE ATTRIBUTED, though not traceable, to Beethoven: In Vienna, seeing a passing woman, he remarked to his friend Janitschek, "What a magnificent behind, like the beloved pigs of my youth."

Long ago, when they were in college, Fox had instructed Max not to believe this tale. Fox had said that if anybody made the remark it wasn't Beethoven and not Janitschek, either, but Janácek, the Czech composer who lived almost a century later and who so loved the folk that he probably loved their livestock, too. Beethoven was a city boy, argued Fox; he knew pigs only as sausage. "But a

243

pig's behind is indeed a thing of beauty," Fox went on to say. Fox's uncle had been a gentleman farmer in Vermont, and during a few summers spent with him Fox had come to appreciate the plump joyousness of swine.

Max was acquainted with pigs mostly from the warnings in Leviticus. He did remember carcasses behind the window of the Italian butchery on Avenue J, which he had passed every day on his way to grade school. They hung there for all to see, upside down like Mussolini. "Dead and cured," Max told Fox.

"A pig deceased bears little resemblance to a pig alive," Fox informed him.

"How did you and your roommate find each other?" Gail asked Max a decade after college. They had just met. Seated next to each other at a bat mitzvah luncheon, they were asking each other question after question, rudely ignoring the other singles at their table.

"Fox and I? We were married by the university *shadchan*."

Gail understood; the housing office had placed them together as freshmen. "Not an obvious pairing," she ventured.

"We, too, wondered about it." In those days freshmen were assigned to room with fellows who resembled them in backgrounds, religious and athletic preferences, secondary educations. In none of those particulars—except, perhaps, that neither played a sport—did there seem to be a match between Foxcroft Whitelaw and Max Chernoff. One of Fox's grandfathers had been governor of Maine and the other a president of a small New England college; further in the past a Protestant divine had cast a wrathful glance over his own and succeeding generations. Max's ancestors, keepers of small unprofitable stores, receded namelessly into the shadowy *shtetlach* his grandfathers had abandoned. In their turn his Brooklyn parents abandoned most observances, though they did keep kosher to please the old folks. During the first years of their marriage, Max and Gail did the same in honor of those ancient grandparents, who sometimes took a meal with them. When the last grandparent died, the young Chernoffs gave up the practice, and soon they were boiling lobsters in their own kitchen.

Max hadn't always been Max. But entering college had given him the opportunity to discard the affected "Maurice" his parents had saddled him with. Later, though, when he'd become established as a historian of medicine, he was grateful for the dignity of "Maurice Leopold Chernoff" decorating both his books. Shortly after the publication of the first book a gift came in the mail: a recording of Maurice Abravanel conducting Maurice André and the Utah Symphony Orchestra in trumpet works by Ravel. *Foxcroft*, said the enclosed card. Max turned the record over and over in his hands. "Neither of us plays the trumpet, neither of us likes Ravel . . .," he wondered aloud.

Such a learned man; such a sometime dope. "He thought this had your name on it," Gail explained.

Music connected the roommates—perhaps the college housing office had been shrewder than it seemed. As a little boy, Max had been taught scales and finger exercises and "Für Elise" by a monstrously unmusical great-aunt. ("It's a wonder you can even hum," Gail remarked after meeting this redoubtable, still alive when they married.) Then he studied with a real teacher on Twenty-third Street. During the first semester of freshman year he sometimes played after dinner in the dormitory's common room—jazz, mostly, but also Bach and Chopin. He was an adept amateur. Fox, thoughtfully listening, mentioned that he himself had tried various members of the string family. Then, the day after Christmas vacation, while Max was memorizing formulas in their shared bedroom, he heard Fox returning to their shared living room, making more than the usual amount of noise. Small wonder: he was carrying a battered cello case and had to kick his second suitcase. From the cello case he withdrew a magnificent instrument. "I just thought," he said. Max hoped the thing was insured.

Fox turned out to be accomplished and dedicated. He was soon practicing an hour a day, and he joined a student quartet and played duets with Max in the common room on afternoons when neither had a lab and no one else was around. They both enjoyed these sessions, though the disparity between their instruments—Max's the dormitory's upright, Fox's the invaluable cello—and between their abilities reminded Max of the other disparities that sometimes grieved him. *Flatbush boys*, Gail thought when Max told her of this old distress; *is there any species so easily stung?*

Fox went to medical school in Chicago, Max in New York. Fox married before graduating. "A surprise to me, that early marriage," Max said to Gail at the fateful bat mitzvah. "He was wary of girls in college. Well, so was I . . ." Sophia Whitelaw was a bony, unadorned young woman who had flouted her aristocratic background, skipped college altogether, tramped around Europe like a hobo. At the wedding she danced with all the men and also with her sister, Hebe, an undersized ten-year-old in love with her horse.

"Foxcroft's sister-in-law is named—what?" Gail inquired. They were still only an hour into their lifetime companionship; each had just been issued half a chicken. "Hebe? As in heebie-jeebies?"

"As in the Greek goddess of youth."

Max was then working on his second graduate degree, in the history of medicine this time. "I find I prefer the library to the bedside," he told her. Gail was teaching fourth grade. (She would later take time off after the birth of their only child, a son, then return to the classroom for another thirty years.) Her hair was curly, her nose fixed. She read a lot and collected art deco jewelry. She had her choice of suitors, including a rich one who had loved her before the nose job, when she still wore an owl's profile, but she felt elevated by being chosen by a doctor, even if he was not planning to hang out a shingle. (For her part Sophia seemed to consider medical practice on a social level with window washing.)

Fox joined an endocrinology group in Maine. Max taught in Boston. The families sometimes spent weekends in each other's homes. The men listened to music and played duets; the children—the Whitelaws had a daughter, Thea—played checkers and, in later years, chess; the women went to the museum if they were in Boston and to crafts fairs if in Maine. Once Sophia drove Gail and Hebe (the Goddess of Youth visited her sister frequently) all the way to Lewiston to see some notable antique farming tools. The crone who collected and sold the stuff also dealt in jewelry, mostly worthless. But there, tossed onto a table, was a circle of diamonds banded in silver banded in black enamel. Gail put the bracelet on. What a transformation—she felt like a queen, or at least like a commoner with a royal wrist.

"I could bring the price down a little," said the witchy proprietress.

"Won't you have a birthday one of these years?" said Hebe, fondling Gail's upper arm.

"Filch the housekeeping money. Insist on a special gift," advised

Sophia. "Satisfy yourself," she urged, this Yankee who didn't wear even an engagement ring.

Gail slid the conspicuous shackle from her arm and shook her head: No. Some weeks later, Sophia, satisfying her own self, left husband and teenage daughter, Thea, and resumed her life of vagabondage—modified, this time; she was home as often as she was away. "No, I don't mind," Thea said, in her forthright way, when Gail asked. "It's fun when she's here, relaxing when she's gone."

II.

"SOMEONE IN YOUR LARGER COHORT has to die first," Max had mentioned early on. "To start the avalanche." In the first decades there were the accidents, the horrific early cancers, the suicides. And there were deaths of children, other people's children, thank God, but Gail was never without fear for her own boy. Luckily, the Whitelaw daughter and the Chernoff son turned into healthy adolescents and then healthy young adults—nobody nowadays considered male homosexuality an affliction, not out loud, anyway.

After a while came diseases predictable by any actuary. Somehow Fox and Sophia and Max and Gail avoided them. They couldn't avoid growing old, though. The men did it in differing ways. Neither stayed fit—neither had been fit to begin with—but Fox at least was naturally skinny. Max steadily gained weight—that was natural, too, or at least familial, or at least not pathological (he pointed out to Gail); extra flesh, his grandmother had assured him, is protection against various ills. A statistical analysis published in the *Journal of the American Geriatrics Society* supported this unlikely truth. Max's narrow shoulders contracted through the years and his broad hips broadened. When, naked after lovemaking (an activity increasingly rare in their age group, studies show, while other studies show also that both members of an aging couple like to pretend that their partners are movie stars during the business), he walked from bed to bathroom, Gail sometimes imagined that she was watching the retreat of a satiated woman. But when he returned after the scrubbing he considered necessary—Gail would have lain around in sweat and jism until morning—with his member shrunken and a smile stretching his bushy mustache, he looked male again. Her man.

A few ailments did afflict them. Gail's fibroids required a hysterectomy. Max had to have a hernia repaired. Various antidepressants gave Fox various side effects like constipation and patchy hair loss. But Sophia—she was never sick. And her gaunt attractiveness mutated into blinding beauty: the excellent bones and good teeth; the unlined skin that had never known a moisturizer; the pale hair, only slightly faded, bundled loosely at her nape. She still climbed, skied, went scuba diving. When she returned, frequently, to her Maine home, Hebe joined her. The Goddess of Youth had developed crow's-feet like everybody else, and her little teeth were yellowing. Sometimes the Chernoffs were invited for a weekend. They'd find Hebe chattering at Fox. They'd find Sophia atop an untrustworthy ladder, rewiring the porch lantern, or mounted on one of the gables as if it were a pony, shingling the roof. She had a boy's daring and a man's competence and a woman's grace. She seemed to be at the beginning of a very long life. Gail found herself jealous, or was it desirous?

Back home: "Sophia will bury the rest of us," Gail predicted to Max.

"Somebody has to be the last."

Sophia wouldn't be the last, she'd be the exception; but Gail kept this more precise insight to herself until she could share it with young Thea Whitelaw. One summer, Thea, working on her masters in teaching at Harvard, stayed with the Chernoffs between apartments. "Your mother may live for centuries," said Gail.

"Oh, she will," said Thea. "She's part cetacean. Cetus is Latin, from the Greek *kētos* . . ."

"Sea monster, yes. We grade-school teachers haul around a lot of facts. Pseudo-erudition." Gail spoke in a stern voice—pseudo-stern. She had grown close to this young woman, dark eyes like a rain cloud, brown hair in one thick braid.

SOMEONE IN THE SMALLER cohort has to die first, too.

One of those usually curable carcinomas sought out Fox. But in his case . . . not so curable. Still, several years went by: treatments, time off, new treatments, everyone knows the drill.

There had been no Whitelaw-Chernoff visits since the diagnosis. Fox's therapy took a lot of time. And the Chernoffs' son now lived in Savannah; his parents tended to travel south when they traveled at all. Max's weight hampered him a bit. Gail was frequently fatigued. Her eyelids had become pleated, but the rest of her face, she knew, was still lively, still pretty: the tilted chin, hers by right; the tilted nose, hers by rhinoplasty. She was glad they had sold their house and moved into a condo. Its kitchen had all the latest devices, and granite countertops, too. She didn't care if she never cooked another meal, but she liked laying palms and then cheek on the cool stone.

Thea was back in Maine, living in her father's house. Her mother was sometimes there; Hebe too. Thea was teaching fifth grade. She called one January morning.

"It's almost over, Gail."

"What do you mean? Max and your father talked just last week . . . well, last month . . . before Christmas. Is Fox in the hospital again?"

"No. He's limping around, can do just about everything but eat, takes stuff for the pain. I don't mean he's dying. I just mean he's dying."

The difference between the imminent and the soon: yes. There was also the inevitable, but they all belonged in that group, even cetacean Sophia.

"Come up, please," said Thea. "Bring music."

"Well . . . which music?"

"Beethoven?"

"Oh, too difficult. Max hardly plays now. Some kid stuff, that's all, for the neighbors' daughter." A brat, that little girl: or perhaps Gail hadn't yet made peace with her own no-grandchildren destiny. "The other morning he did do a marvelous riff on 'Oh, Mr. Sun,' " she admitted.

"What about the variations on the *Magic Flute* thing?"

"*Ein Mädchen—*"

"*—oder Weibchen*. Please don't tell me I'm pseudo-erudite."

"Okay," Gail said, complying with the request, and also agreeing to the program: Beethoven's Twelve Variations on Mozart's *A Maiden or Little Wife*.

III.

BANGOR. The plane banked over pines, over water. Thea's boyfriend was waiting for them at the airport. They got into his Piper,

Max taking the copilot's seat. This flight took just ten minutes. They landed on an oblong of earth with spruce trees at its margins. And then, in the boyfriend's Jeep, they drove along a rutted road from island to island, across meager bridges, until they reached the last island in the series, the familiar outcrop with its fifty-odd houses. The easternmost house, brown-shingled like the rest, belonged to Fox. A deep porch wrapped around the three sides of it that faced the fierce sea. Inside were angles, odd windows, nooks, all grown familiar through the years. The music room held a Steinway bought on the occasion of Fox's birth. In the attic stood a hard double bed. On it Gail and Max would make love as they always did here, as if it were a guestly obligation.

The big main rooms were farthest from the road. Their windows, and the front door, too, opened onto the porch and the sea beyond. The back of the house faced the road. Max and Thea's boyfriend carried the suitcases under a trellised arch, and disappeared. They'd climb the steps of the porch and enter the house. Gail wrenched herself out of the Jeep. She looked up at the rear of the house, where she saw, in a high window—the back-stairs landing, wasn't it?—a female form: Thea, carrying two pillows no doubt destined for their marital bed. Thea waved, continued upward. One story below, behind a window with purplish glass, stood Fox. He raised a hand. In the kitchen moved another female figure—Sophia. And in the now-open back doorway, which led into a kitchen of elderly appliances where the family took all its meals, stood little Hebe, hugging her own freckled arms in excitement. "Gail!" piped the Goddess of Youth, and ran down the wooden stairs and threw herself upon the unenthusiastic Gail.

And then, within the house, more greetings. Beauteous Sophia. Emaciated Fox. Thea, exhausted.

THEA AND GAIL had a long-established hideout. About two hours later—Fox asleep in his room, Max napping in his and Gail's, the boyfriend gone, Sophia and Hebe shopping for groceries, like mortals—the women found each other there. The room had been a pantry once and perhaps a meat larder before that. No heat reached it. Though the afternoon was not especially cold and a thin layer of snow was shrinking in the sun, their little place retained the iciness of the previous months. Gail wore her parka, Thea her grand-mother's patched sable.

"He looks awful, doesn't he," Thea said.

"Yes," Gail agreed. Fox's hair had turned the color of spume. His skin was nearly as transparent as the weak bulb hanging above their two sorrowful heads. He had joined them for lunch that after-noon without participating in it. He was kept alive on some canned medicinal nutrient to which he attributed his frequent vomiting. Treatments and their sequelae were what was killing him, he said; the disease itself had vanished, he claimed. "I'm cured and dead," he said, in helpless fury. The sound of his vomiting—Gail had heard it twice—was not the cascade of a drunk; it was a prolonged, unproductive gagging.

"I brought fancy chocolates. What was I thinking?" mourned Gail.

"Hebe has already swallowed the entire box. Pa likes high-tast-ing stuff like spiced crab cakes, runny cheese, and smoked meats. He adores bacon. So for a while Ma made bacon every morning and Pa ate it and pretty soon he chucked it up. Finally she wouldn't make it anymore and they started to have those fights they adore, shouting made-up footnotes at each other, Pa quoting from some-thing medical—"

"A digestive tract."

Thea managed a weak smile. "—and Ma invoking British novels, all those gentlemen gouty from port and pork. Also she quoted Deuteronomy—"

"Leviticus. 'And the swine, though he divide the hoof, and be clovenfooted, yet he cheweth not the cud; he is unclean to you.' "

"Whatever. Then Ma started making the bacon in the middle of the afternoon, while he's sleeping, like now. It's a drugged sleep, bacon won't wake him, the house burning to the ground wouldn't wake him. So he started getting up in the middle of the night to fry it himself."

"You could just not buy it."

"Oh dear, Gail, do *you* think swine is unclean?"

"Of course not. The pig is fastidious if given the opportunity."

"Oh good," said Thea. "Anyway, Pa yells that gout is one of the few conditions he doesn't have, and that Old Testament restrictions don't apply to Whitelaws. There's not a Yid in his lineage—sorry, Gail, it's the word he used."

"There's a Yid in everybody's lineage," Gail said, evenly.

" 'Ergo,' he goes on to say, bacon must be good for him. And Aunt Hebe is always his ally. She swears that bacon alone sustains her existence. What a useless existence it is . . . Oh, don't listen to me, I love her."

"Darling."

Gail was sitting on a high stool and Thea on a lower one, and it was an easy matter for Thea to lay her cheek against Gail's denimed thigh. They remained in this position for a while. Then Thea raised her head again. "Now I lock the bacon in the trunk of my car. So Pa goes without. But the fight isn't over. They won't stop fighting until he's dead." She swallowed. "He won't die while a fight is on."

"Then bacon is keeping him alive," said Gail.

DINNER, COOKED BY THEA and her mother, consisted of chicken, salad, and wine for everybody but Fox, who again ate nothing and drank only his thick green medicinal liquid. Thea's boyfriend returned. Hebe and Max gabbed about politics. Fox said nothing, focusing on the battle within. Sophia's lordly attention, too, was elsewhere. She insisted on cleaning up without assistance. Fox went upstairs to vomit, and didn't come down. The sea beat hard on the rocks. "I will take a walk in the perilous dark," Hebe announced. The boyfriend left. Gail and Max and Thea sat reading in the living room. Hebe came home and told them she was safe. "Surprising: I am so prone to mishap." The sea beat even harder on the rocks.

GAIL AWOKE in the middle of the night. She had forgotten to pack her Valium. Max was lightly snoring. It would be unkind to wake him, and for what purpose, anyway? She could tiptoe downstairs and into Fox's room, rummage around in his pharmacopoeia until she found something that induced sleep. So what if she laid her hands on a lethal medicament. To awaken a dying man would be worse than unkind.

She got up, and pulled somebody's oilcloth coat from a hook and put it on. (She'd forgotten to pack her robe, too. Sometimes it seemed that slippery places were forming in her brain.) She walked almost noiselessly down the back stairway and on the second floor switched to the main stairs, whose threadbare carpeting would muffle sound. But still every footfall produced a creak. She stopped, leaned over the banister.

Moonlight had entered the music room, brushing against disregarded heirlooms, dusting the Steinway with silver.

Fox and Sophia sat on chairs angled toward the broadest window. Their knees almost touched. Fox wore a striped hospital bathrobe, borrowed or stolen during one of his stays. Sophia was still in her corduroy pants and a ragged flannel shirt. But above their schmattes, what noble heads those aristocrats wore, even the one about to die. What enviable profiles. She tried to listen to the couple's soft, low conversation—she wasn't really a guest, after all; she'd been summoned to attend the dying, she had a schoolteacher's obligation to eavesdrop. But all she could hear were a few syllables that might have been, that should have been, that probably weren't "love" and "remember" and "afraid."

MAX TRIED THE PIANO in the morning. Fox lay on a ratty sofa. The weary Gail, hoping to remain unnoticed, hunched on a chair in the corner of the dim dining room where the family took none of its meals. She held the novel she'd brought, still unreadable. She could see the music room in one direction through an archway, the kitchen in another direction through a narrow door. The piano was in perfect tune. Fox's old cello case—the one he'd dragged from home to college and back again—stood in one corner.

Max left the piano and walked through the dining room. He didn't notice Gail. In the kitchen he poured some coffee and sugared it heavily. Fox now got up from the sofa. He unpacked the cello and inserted its post like a prosthesis. He sat on a stool with the instrument in front of him at an exaggerated slant. The post dug into the Aubusson. Fox was still wearing his sleeping garments and that robe whose stripes Gail had noticed last night. Now she saw that it bore yellow stains.

Sophia and Thea and Hebe sat on the porch. The weather was still unseasonably mild. Or perhaps seasonably—Gail knew that the Maine coast had experienced balmy winters two years in a row during the nineteenth century and also in 1929, another of the remembered factoids from her days of teaching. The boyfriend had not yet appeared. Gail could not remember his name. Did he remember hers? Was there anyone on earth who remembered 1929 and the daffodils that had perished by Valentine's Day? Fox drew the bow across the strings. He played a Bach suite, the stuff cellists warm up with. He ignored wife, daughter, and sister-in-law trooping in from the porch. They found Gail immediately. Sophia announced that the girls would skate while the boys practiced.

"I forgot my skates," Gail said.

"I have an extra pair," Thea said.

"They'll be too big."

"We'll stuff them."

"With what," Gail said, following the others to Thea's car. They drove from island to island until they reached the mainland. There they drove to their favorite pond, black, sprinkled with nubbles of ice like kosher salt. Thea's skates, with the addition of a pair of mismatched socks she'd snatched from the line, fit Gail as if made for her. Gail thought of the winter she'd taught her young son to skate; for a moment it was as if no time had passed since then, as if he were still that merry little boy and she his delighted mother.

She executed a few turns. Thea and Sophia were waltzing. But the Goddess of Youth was the star. In a long skirt salvaged from a Whitelaw trunk and a tight jacket and a top hat—Fox had worn it to somebody's inauguration—Hebe twirled, raised one leg and then the other, leaped, landed like a butterfly. Gail, quickly tired, watched her from the edge of the pond. How kind it would be of some real deity to shrink that scrap of a person, transform her into a piece of porcelain, and set her atop a music box to spin forever. "She rents a one-room cottage on a New Hampshire horse farm," Thea had said. "She comes up to prattle at Pa, takes buses to get here, about seventeen of them." But now Hebe's right blade seemed to catch on a protrusion of ice, or perhaps it was a root that had worked itself upward during the thaw, like a child throwing off its blankets. The top hat fell off and rolled in a wide arc toward the center of the pond. Hebe fell flat on her face.

Well, not really. "The body will do almost anything to protect its eyes and nose," Max had once said. "The hands shoot out—a lot of broken wrists happen that way. Only an unconscious person forgets his face. One night in the emergency room I saw . . ." and he'd gone on to tell her about a drunk whose tumble had resulted in total shattering; he mentioned the bones by name, like friends.

Max's capacious memory had stored everything he'd seen during his internship, before he abandoned the urgency of clinical work. Last night he'd told her that he thought Fox had at most a month to live.

Hebe lay still. But her face was turned to one side, so her nose probably wasn't broken. Sister and niece sped in her direction. She pushed herself into a crouch (her wrists weren't broken, either) and curled into a half-sitting position, legs (also unhurt) swept beneath her. Gail reached the threesome. Thea was kneeling beside her aunt. One side of Hebe's face had been severely scraped, but there wasn't much blood. "Okay?" Sophia inquired.

"We ought to attend to that skin," said Gail.

"I was all at once nauseated," said Hebe. She took Thea's hand and scrambled to her feet. Gail followed them to the shoreline. She turned her head once and saw Sophia gliding to the middle of the pond to retrieve the top hat, like a gentleman's gentleman.

THEY FOUND MAX ALONE at the kitchen table. "Fox is sleeping," he said. "What happened to you, Hebe? Let me see." Thea fished keys from her jeans and ran outside again. Gail saw her open the trunk of her car and lift out something wrapped in unyielding white paper. She came in again, threw the keys onto the counter, and opened the package, uncovering a slab of pink, glistening bacon. She sliced the meat and handed the slices to her mother, who was already standing at the old stove, already shifting a big black pan on the burner. The slices curled, puckered, bubbled. The aroma slowly filled the kitchen.

Gail set the table. Max advised Hebe to wash her face gently in lukewarm water. No emollient was required. Hebe went off to obey. Sophia served the first slices.

The fragrance grew stronger—the smell of defiance, of sumptuous caloric energy, of *treif*. Before the rage for standardization, Gail's fourth-grade class had done happy units on farm animals. Gail had of course prepared thoroughly. The sow is particularly motherly, she learned and then taught her charges; pigs of most breeds are prolific and also efficient at converting grain to flesh. Your pig has a small stomach within his ample frame. His fossil remains, the ur-peccary, were discovered first in China . . . This may explain the glory of Chinese food, she had silently speculated, though glory could not be explained, any more than life or death or sexual preference could. Once, when her son was about three, they had come across a toy pig in a store, a very small sow, scrupulously realistic. They counted the teats: twelve. "Here is where the milk comes out," she said. And they hugged each other in sweet remembrance of lactation . . .

"Trichinosis," Hebe said when she came back. "You get it from pigs, don't you?"

"*You* do," Max said. "Pigs get it from rats, though. But, yes, Hebe, if you eat raw pig meat you may ingest the encysted larvae of a roundworm and get very sick. So we cook bacon thoroughly, and it releases that tranquilizing scent."

"No wonder Fox craves it," Gail said, and suddenly she could no longer open her mouth.

Hebe said, with unaccustomed earnestness, "Maybe it really is bad for him." And Gail, lips pressed together, saw that Hebe loved her sister's husband in her arrested way—that those two sometime housemates must have a fairly good time together: one skating, one fiddling; one talking, one with his fingers in his ears; no need to bother with sex . . .

"Bacon's not bad for Fox," Max said. "Nothing is bad for him anymore." For all his lardy softness Max wasn't a man to cry. But the gentle voice broke and the narrow shoulders slumped and a pudgy hand covered the twitching mustache.

Sophia kept the slices coming for a while. Finally she stopped. Upstairs, Fox slept his assisted sleep. Thea stacked the dishes. Sophia handed bacon and keys to Gail, who went outside, locked the package in the car trunk, and then, bending, holding on to a stunted pine, threw up. Under her palm the bark felt like a tweed arm. She straightened and returned to the house.

NIGHT CAME AT LAST. They gathered in the music room after the dinner that everyone but Fox had eaten. To be festive he had poured his noxious nutrient into a champagne glass. He had inspected Hebe's face. "You will have a splendid bruise in the morning," he assured his fellow sufferer.

Beyond the dried eucalyptus situated in a tarnished pitcher on the piano, Max's face looked metallic—pewter mustache, pressed-tin skin. His eyes seemed like disks of aluminum under their sparse lashes. A stranger walking into the room would have fingered *him* as the dying man, not Fox, head bent, spindliness concealed by his cello.

They played. Two old men, their instruments older still but destined for a longer stay on earth. Perhaps the piece had rarely been played so faultily, perhaps never under such circumstances. The Twelve Variations on Papageno's tune had been written as a salon exercise for amateurs. Gail knew that. She knew that the opus was lesser Beethoven, unambitious Beethoven; she had learned much about music during the long decades of her marriage. Max messed up a passage. If she had been chosen by a man with an interest in modern art, in football, in cooking, she would have learned about those things. She herself had brought to the union a passion for teaching, and also a cigar box of pins and buckles and clips. She'd planned to add to the collection, to sell, to trade. A *dolce vibrato* by Fox went sour. Gail's hobby, neither encouraged nor demeaned, had failed to develop. The musicians got through all of the variations in a quarter of an hour.

The boyfriend clapped. Fox went upstairs to vomit. The boyfriend left. Max stood by the piano, his score under his arm. Hebe trotted up to him, her red face raised, wondering again about Vaseline. Thea and Sophia went around turning out the lights.

"Leave your face alone," said Max to Hebe. And to Gail, "You'll come upstairs soon?"

She nodded. In fact she followed on his heels. In fact, naked, she was in their hard bed before he was, and she wrapped him in her limbs with a spider's ardor. At the moment of irreversibility, the wave breaking, she thought not only of Michelle Pfeiffer, tonight's imagined partner, but of Michelle Pfeiffer wearing that bracelet of diamonds and silver and black enamel that Gail had denied herself. She blinked the trinket away, and its wearer too. Max returned from his ablutions. His naked pear-shaped body glowed in the moonlight; his eyes now looked like worthwhile coins. *Mein Mannchen*, she thought. My little man.

SHE SLEPT FOR A FEW HOURS. Then, awake as if she had been smacked, she got up and put on the oilcloth coat and went downstairs, not worrying about noise. The music room was empty. The door to the porch was ajar. Thea was alone out there. She sat on an aluminum chair, her arms resting on the porch's wooden railing, her head on her arms. With a light scrape Gail dragged another chair toward the young woman and sat down beside her. Thea raised her eyes. Their hands touched.

What was there to say? That the pair of oddly matched room-mates Foxcroft and Maurice had made a reasonable go of the lives they had been given to lead. That if anyone cares to inquire I have done the same. "Helping one man die—it is the work of many per-sons." She did say that.

From within the house they heard a groan—inanimate; the back door had opened. The footsteps of one person sounded on the wooden steps outside the kitchen. Then a little yawn: a car trunk opening—and a little clap: a car trunk closing. The pair of feet, seemingly stronger now, returned to the house, and the back door closed again.

Thea sat up straight.

"The car keys—I left them on the counter," Gail said. "He saw them, at dinner. Your mother saw him see them. I saw her see him see them."

There was a sizzle from the kitchen. Soon that heavenly fra-grance drifted in. The sizzle grew louder, like fingers snapping a joyous message: it's cooked, thoroughly. It's ready to be savored and swallowed and unresentfully disgorged, this sliced back portion of some magnificent pig.

CAPERS

PICKING UP LOOSE CHANGE—it was Henry's idea. An activity—not a crime, not even a misdemeanor. And these days any sport that aroused his enthusiasm was worth playing. It was so easy. The stuff lay all around them. It lurked under the mailboxes and in the corners of the elevator and on the sidewalk. It could be fished from chair cushions at the movies. Dorothy found oily coins in the gutter. She washed them and sometimes polished them. Once, in a diner, two quarters were lying on the counter near Henry and he picked them up. The counterman held out his hand. "Those are mine," he said. "My tip from the guy before you." Henry relinquished the money. On her stool Dorothy stared straight ahead. Henry would have kept those quarters—would have stolen them. Stealing *was* a crime. Yet it was the counterman who looked ashamed . . . ashamed for Henry, maybe.

The next morning she went downtown to do an errand. On a busy sidewalk she found herself plucking a purse from the gaping backpack of a careless young woman striding ahead of her. The young woman wore a red knit hat with a royal blue pom-pom. Dorothy—who had owned such a hat herself, a lifetime ago—drifted sideways to a window display. *Heavens*, she thought, counting the money in the purse. Forty dollars and change. *What are you doing. Run after her, run after her.* Ahead, the pom-pom bobbed above the crowd of shoppers. Dorothy stuffed the purse into her own handbag. *Take it to the police station, say you found it on the street.*

Instead she entered the subway and boarded the trolley that would trundle her home. Failing to hand the police a dropped purse was not a crime. She could keep the thing; it might even be legally hers. Or if she turned it in at the police station and that devil-may-care pompom didn't bother to report her loss, the purse might devolve to Dorothy, the honorable rescuer of a found object. Not until the trolley emerged into the light did she remember that she had not found the money. She had swiped it.

She confessed to Henry that night.

"How much?"

"Forty dollars, but even if it were forty cents—"

"Some spoiled college girl. Her daddy will make it up to her."

"Henry . . ."

"Let's try the horses."

The next day they took the train out to the race track and bet twenty dollars twice, and lost both times. "So now you've made retribution," said Henry in a merry voice. They rode back in warm silence, holding hands.

"Gambling is unreliable," Henry pronounced that night. "Picking pockets—that's the solution."

"To what problem?" He glared at her, but she went on. "Pocket picking takes training by a master, and Fagin's been hanged."

"I'll learn it on my own. Remember how I used to play Debussy? I can be light-fingered."

He'd made Debussy sound like Sousa, and he'd known that at the time. Now he reformulated the past—a habit of the elderly. Morality, too, got reshaped, and ethics. "Filching money from individuals is dangerous," she said in a knowledgeable voice. "Let's bypass cash."

"Bypass?" It was not a popular word.

"Cash is useful only to buy merchandise," she explained. "Let's go directly to the merchandise. Stores."

He grinned at her. "What a girl I married."

She grinned back, but her heart was wilting. This crumbling of old values must be a sign of dementia, mustn't it. Perhaps his was an encapsulated dementia, confined to mild misbehavior. Petty crimes would stave off worse senility. She knew some poor old fellows who tried to fondle waitresses.

Sometimes she still felt a craving. Early in the morning, say, when dawn turned their gray walls an intense lilac she liked to think of as whorish. Her hand would creep across the bedclothes like a blue-veined mouse. He'd be sleeping on his back, which he wasn't supposed to, because of the apnea. Snoring, stopping, snoring, stopping. She'd shake his shoulder just hard enough to make him turn over—away from her—onto his side. Usually he didn't wake up. That was okay. He needed what rest he could get. He slept so poorly, waking frequently, finally waking for good—for bad, really: waking cranky and staying cranky until the lunchtime beer, which turned him cheerful for a little while and occasionally even amorous. And so, sometimes, in the early afternoon . . . But he always needed the pill, and they had to wait an hour, and she was dry no matter how much of that old lady's gel she slathered on; she might as well just brush her teeth with it. And at that hour the light pouring into the bedroom showed them plainly to each other. The grooves on his face were often greasy. His scalp, underneath what hair was left, was pale as an oyster. Keratoses lay on her chest like pebbles. Her own hair had never achieved whiteness; sunlight cruelly revealed its similarity to straw. And if he were to kiss the hollow of her neck—which he had loved to do long ago, entering that silky purse above before the silkier purse down below, as he used to say—now he'd find the space above her clavicle filled with loose, shuddering skin, like crème fraîche. And it took him so long to come, pounding insistently as his younger self would never have done; and it would have taken her even longer, probably forever; but, spent, he rolled away, leaving her chafed and sad.

Long ago, during the first decade of their marriage, they'd had to snatch pleasure between jobs and child care and the sleep they were always short of. In the several decades afterward, sex was peaceful and considerate. Even ten years ago they were still warm with each other. But the best years were long ago, in college—parietal rules still in force then; immoral behavior still punished by expulsion. In college their problem was finding a site for immoral behavior. They had a few favorite places. The top floor of the university art museum, a storage space for paintings and sculptures waiting to be repaired, where they kept company with dark Annunciations and cracked nudes. The boathouse down by the river—they lay under overturned canoes. In early fall and late spring they visited the ocean, just a bus ride from school, its beach deserted by the end of the afternoon.

She liked to recall a particular October day. The water, too cold for more than a dip, rippled in shades of pewter and slate. They watched it for a while. Then he fell asleep. She grew chilly, and the one beach towel they'd brought lay on his chest. Carefully she slid it off, pausing to admire the auburn hair that curled there; then she wrapped her own body in the towel. "Dolly," he said, opening one morning-glory eye. "You thief. That towel is mine."

"Not anymore," and she was on her feet and running. It took him a few groggy minutes to get up and run, too. They ran across the length of the beach, half-naked boy chasing girl in bikini. Her long brown hair, thick then, flew behind her: the striped towel waved from her hand. She was headed toward a wall of low rocks that led from the road to the sea. He'd catch her when she started scrambling over them. Wisely she didn't try to run farther. Instead she turned abruptly and faced him, and he thudded against her as if shot by a cannon. She dropped the towel. They stood in a panting embrace. It wasn't foreplay, really: it was simple hugging, love throbbing from one heart to the other. When at last this exchange satisfied both, their thumbs entered each other's waistbands; in seconds the lovers were lying on the sand beside their apparel. Who cared if anybody walked by.

Soon afterward they married. They raised two calm daughters, now settled with their own families in Ohio. "Those investments certainly panned out," Henry would say with a smile, speaking of their progeny. The pleased grandparents visited their successful investments twice a year. They traveled elsewhere once in a while, bought new books at the bookshop, made charitable donations. As they aged they went on doing what everybody in their cohort did—paid the condominium fee, shopped for groceries, went to a movie and modest restaurant once a week. They joined a bird-watching group. They tended their ailments. But they'd become too weary for travel, and their tastes in reading had narrowed—thrillers, now, and old novels: all available free at the public library. They canceled their subscription to the symphony; they had an excellent stereo system at home, and the series cost so much. Tuesdays were free at the museum, so they dropped that membership, too. They dropped the *New York Review of Books*. Staying au courant could break their fragile budget. The pensions, the annuities, the long-term health insurance: all were sufficient. And yet—again like their cohort—they felt pinched.

"Merchandise—I'll try it first," Dorothy said. "I'm an experienced shopper."

At a convenience store she waited until she was the only customer. Then she slipped a quart of milk into her reusable shopping bag and pushed the little cart to the cash box behind which stood a melancholy Mexican woman—no, indigenous: she had an Aztec face; she was ready to be plundered. Dorothy turned her cart around and wheeled it to the refrigerated items and shoved the milk back into its case and removed it again and this time placed it in the cart. She pushed the cart to the woman and paid for everything that was in it.

She tried sneaking milk from the Russians, too. Again her nerve failed. A stout orange-haired woman stood behind a counter dishing takeout chicken and kasha, and her twin served up week-old salads. The whole place smelled of fish. Dorothy thought helplessly of the suffering of these people, generation after generation. At the cash register stood a younger sister of the other two. Dorothy took the quart of milk from her shopping bag and laid it on the counter with the rest of her groceries.

At the 7-Eleven the cashier looked slightly feebleminded. There was no way Dorothy would prey on him.

Each time she told Henry she'd stolen the milk.

His own effort had been a failure. At a men's store he'd put two pairs of socks into his jacket pocket and walked out. But when he got to the subway station, the socks were gone. Somebody had picked *his* pocket, he claimed.

"The socks probably fell . . .," she began.

A mighty scowl. "We've got to work as a team," Henry said. "One the distraction, the other the sleight-of-hand artist."

She was silent.

"Do want to run your own operation, Dolly?" he said, and chucked her under the chin. "Is that what you want?"

She wanted him—as he once was—but she didn't say that.

∽

DEPARTMENT STORES BECAME their theater of operations. They learned on the job. Some merchandise could be delicately edged off a counter by Dorothy while Henry and the salesperson discussed the similar items lying there for inspection. In this way they acquired a pair of suede gloves, an infant jumpsuit, a pen, a small picture frame, a jar of imported chutney. At the fine jewelry department she charmed a pair of men's cuff links into the right sleeve of her coat. Then, reviving the "tell me all about yourself" smile of her middle years, she rested her left elbow on the glass case and invited the jeweler to tell her all about semiprecious stones. Meanwhile she thrust her right hand into the coat's pocket and left it there until first one link and then the other dropped from the sleeve into her curled palm.

What to do with the booty? Well, they ate the chutney. The picture frame became a wedding gift. They gave the infantwear and the pen and the gloves to Goodwill. Poor people would put them to use, not guessing their market value, appreciating only their utility. Redistribution—that's what she and Henry were engaged in, Dorothy told herself. And although she worried about the immediate future of the duped salespeople, she wasted no pity on the big stores themselves, which could swallow their losses. Just to even things out, she sent generous gifts to the grandchildren from those very stores. But her sympathy centered on the agitated Henry. His spirits soared immediately after a snatch but plummeted a few days later. "We are not sufficiently exercising our talents," he grumbled one day. "We should start thinking about banks."

"Maybe stagecoaches," she said lightly. "What shall we do with these beautiful cuff links?"

He shrugged. "Goodwill."

"Somebody will spot their value and fence them. You should wear them, Henry. To a party."

"When were we last at a party? All we go to is funerals. When it's my turn—bury me in them."

"Okay," she said, sighing. "Banks, then."

"I'll read up on alarm systems." Then he giggled, and put his arm around her waist.

So off they went to the library, arm in arm. And there was the latest le Carré, with a waiting list six months long, traveling like an ordinary passenger in the returned-books cart. Henry picked it up.

He also found in the cart a book about installing your own alarm system, and motioned Dorothy to exit blamelessly through the theft-detecting turnstile, after which he carried the le Carré to the same stile and handed it across to her—"You forgot this, dear"—and returned to the desk to check out the alarm book. *Such darlings*, anyone who saw the pair might have thought.

They read the le Carré right away—Henry first—and then, early one morning, they slipped it into the library's return box. The book about alarms went in, too. "Too complicated," said Henry. "We need an expert."

"We need a vacation," she offered.

"Where?" sounding sulky.

"I mean . . . time off."

"To do what," sounding exhausted.

"The other day . . . I found our old birding glasses."

So they joined the birders again, and took some nice walks, and heard some lovely sounds, and made some new friends, and gradually went back to their old ways, thrifty but not stinting, careful but not stingy. Honorable.

THE REMISSION LASTED several months. Then one day they read of a luxury hotel opening downtown, and within it a number of high-end boutiques.

"Let's look it over," Henry said. "For old time's sake."

" 'That old gang of mine,' " she sang. "Henry, can we declare our criminal career a success?"

"Some of it was cruel."

"Crewel, also broidered," she said, employing the new tangential, illogical speech she had recently developed. " 'By the pricking of my thumbs,' " she continued. Quotations floated through her conversation as if dislodged from the walls of her brain. She often forgot where she'd put things.

"My pocketbook?" she'd cry.

And Henry would tell her he'd found it in the freezer.

On a Thursday afternoon they broke their date for a movie and early-bird special with the Halperins, and went downtown instead, offering as excuse a meeting with their financial advisor—an imaginary personage. They got dressed up for the expedition, and Henry wore his favorite vest, a fiery red. He had acquired it in a busy men's store simply by taking off his raincoat, putting on the vest, resuming his raincoat, and walking out. Dorothy's hair was in a loose bun these days. She wore a long flowered skirt and snug black jacket, both of which she had purchased some years ago.

"You could pass for a Renoir girl," Henry said. "Beautiful."

The large circular hotel lobby was beautiful too, in an austere way, all brown plush and rosewood. In the smoking room, a nickel rested in an ashtray. Smoking was not a crime here. "Come, darling," said Henry.

"O my darling, O my darling," she sang, and put the coin in her pocket.

A corridor of glassy stores led away from the lobby: window after window of tempting things—leather bags, jade elephants, a pyramid of face creams. "That substance promises the return of an eighteen-year-old complexion," Dorothy read aloud through the window. "Complete with blackheads," he promised. Antique books, men's accessories, luggage, timepieces. A tiny place called Silk. "There's a security guard," Henry remarked. "Oh, look at that chess set."

But Dorothy had dropped his arm. She was lingering at the doorway of Silk: scarves, shawls, handkerchiefs, even gloves, even belts. She floated in. "Are your worms kept in humane conditions?" she asked the saleswoman.

"Madame?"

"I'd like so much to see the scarf in the window, the one where blues shade into one another—yes, that one," and the saleswoman cupped the item in her hands as if it were a baby and then laid it on the glass case as if it were a baby's blanket. She from her side and Dorothy from hers marveled at the colors of the chiffon. The woman seemed sincere, but of course she could not feel the power of the blues, the way they called forth Dorothy's seemly life: the ink of the river at night seen from under a canoe, the ocean's mauve at sundown; the blue-green of shore reeds, the silver of spray. The brightness of Henry's young eyes and the cloudiness of his aged ones. The printed morphos on their granddaughters' pajamas. Her bridesmaids' gowns had been robin's egg blue; here was that shade repeated exactly in this fluid fabric. Here were the veins on her hands. Here was the sapphire of the Paris sky at evening. Here was the blue-purple shadow of one statue's head on another's paler back in that storage room at the top of the art museum. Here was the cobalt ring of the glaucoma probe. Here was the blue-gray ash that covered the nickel in her pocket. Last was the lilac of her bedroom at dawn.

"How much?" said Henry from the doorway.

"Five hundred dollars," said the saleswoman.

"Well, well," he stammered. "I've got some fine cuff links."

"They don't barter here, darling," Dorothy said, confidently. She walked toward him, throwing the scarf over her shoulder as if to demonstrate its versatility. She waggled her finger. As if he had received directions, he turned sideways and she nodded and slid past him and began to walk very fast toward the lobby.

"What?—Madame!—shit." The saleswoman came out from behind the case apparently hoping also to slide by Henry. But he had turned again within the doorway. His hands gripped its silvered glass jambs. His legs were apart on the silvered glass threshold. "Do not pass," he intoned. The saleswoman ran back to the case and pushed a button somewhere behind it and picked up a glass telephone receiver that had lain unseen on its glass cradle. Henry began to stroll. Dorothy was loping ahead, the scarf bunched over her shoulder, again like a baby. Henry sped up. Security tramped after him, though not too fast—an incident of thievery would be poor public relations. Dorothy reached the lobby. Henry had almost caught up with the graceful sprite, her bun loosening, the scarf now floating from her hand. She wheeled suddenly, and they collided, breast to breast and heart to heart. Mouth met mouth. The scarf fell to the floor.

Some people in the lobby looked up, as indifferent as aristocrats. The Silk saleswoman edged past security, dropped to her knees and crawled to the scarf and pressed it to her heart. Then she stood up and walked away. Security remembered something he had to do, and vanished. Henry and Dorothy unstuck themselves from each other and left the hotel hand in hand and hailed a cab.

The cab drove them to a dockside restaurant. There they looked at the harbor water shivering under the cold October sky. They looked at peaceful gulls and gulls in agitated flight. They looked at one another. They talked placidly and at length about things past, and not at all about things to come.

The Ministry
of Restraint

HAD HE EVER SEEN SUCH unappealing trams? Aquamarine, with azalea swirls. But: "Beauty is secondary," Alain reassured the mayor of Muñez. "My wife would find something to praise."

And so she would, the generous Isabella. Isabella was blond, and had been educated in the United States—she spoke English even better than he. For all that, she was unmistakably of their country, this coarse little Central American nation. The huge brown eyes told you that much, the curve of the calf, the noticeable clothes. "I am just this side of vulgar," she liked to tease.

"Beauty is secondary," Alain said again. Secondary to engineering—the trams were well constructed. Secondary to trade—they were part of an important deal with far-off Japan. Secondary to the governance of the country that he loved immoderately.

The mayor sighed with relief. "Your perspicacity—I gambled on it," risking a sort of wordplay, for Alain was minister of gaming. Through the years he had become confidante and advisor to almost everybody in government—his colleagues could rely on his discretion and good sense, and his lack of personal ambition let them take all the bows. Today he had come from the capital to inspect the trams on behalf of the minister of transportation.

Now he shook hands with the mayor, and, with grace surprising in a man his size, swung aboard a tram setting off down the broad central avenue. "Smooth," he called to the mayor from a window, and turned away perhaps a moment too soon. He hoped he'd never have to deal with this lout again, but of course he would: Dealing with louts was part of his caretaker's job . . .

Halfway to the train station, he got off and entered a café for a glass of wine and a slice of the local pâté, compounded of anchovies and hog liver. And another slice. During a conference he often thrust something into his mouth to avoid taking the last word. At home he raided the refrigerator. The family housekeeper knew which nights he woke up hungry, though Isabella slept through his absence from their bed. So perhaps he could be considered overweight . . . not if you asked his staff, who associated appetite with kindliness; and not if you asked the public, who didn't recognize his rarely photographed face so couldn't comment on his physique; and not if you asked his tailor, scrupulously silent as he enlarged another garment; but decidedly if you asked his daughter, who called him "Fatty." Isabella, though, appreciated the extra flesh around Alain's middle—she liked to finger it, even knead it, during lovemaking—just as she appreciated his bright blue eyes and thick hair. She might flirt with others, but always in the energetic, meaningless way of a woman true to her man. Alain was faithful, too.

The waiter stood ready to stuff another slice of pâté into his customer's arteries. "No, thanks," said Alain, smiling. He paid the bill and climbed a narrow staircase to a casino of the exact size—six tables—permitted everywhere except on the coast. There, big resorts flourished, drawing tourists from all over the world.

The draperies in the dim room were closed against the afternoon sun, giving the honest place the atmosphere of a thieves' den. The croupiers wore ill-fitting tuxedos and the manager's eyes glided every which way as if on the lookout for police. In fact he had strabismus. Alain bought an amount of chips equivalent to a week's salary. His companions at the roulette table had the peaceable look of habitués. He played black until he won a few times; then 13 through 24 until he was sitting behind two silos of chips. He ran his finger up them, down them . . . He bet again: on his wife's age at their marriage, 22; what a lighthearted loving girl Isabella had been then, still was, despite the decades, despite the death of their son at birth, not often mentioned between them, but sometimes. He did not bet on the boy's age, which was always zero; and anyway zeros belonged to the house. He bet on the age of their bold daughter, 16;

on the factors of his own age, 9 and 5. The darling ball ran, stopped, spun, popped out of its trough, grew still. When he had tripled his stake he quit.

And now he was eager to get home. He walked to the train station. He bought a ticket and boarded the late-afternoon express. The train was sleek and silvered. But Alain and the minister of transportation had persuaded the railroad to give passenger cars an old-fashioned design: a corridor down one side and compartments seating six on the other. Brass fixtures, mahogany panels, conductors wearing high-visored hats and double-breasted jackets—the whole first-class works, though there was just one class of ticket. He took a seat by the window—the train was only half full on this late-afternoon run. When it moved out of the station and turned slightly, revealing its gleaming curve, he leaned forward like a schoolboy and banged his forehead on the window.

The one other passenger in the compartment, seated opposite, made a sympathetic grimace. She was about thirty, and very tall. He calculated that if you added the length of her legs to the length of her torso to the extraordinary length of her neck to the length of her head she would reach six feet, his own height. Her forehead was narrow and her hair was pulled up into a sort of topknot, as if all that was needed to complete her beauty was a little extra height . . . He could hear his wife making that sort of wisecrack, though of course out of this woman's hearing; Isabella was rarely unkind. The woman's upper lip was constructed of two short peaks. She wore glasses: Their extreme convexity told him she was farsighted. She also wore an ur-dress, sleeveless, waistless, ankle-length, the same coconut color as her skin—perhaps she had dyed one to match the other . . .

She looked up from her book and awarded him a grave smile. "Minister."

"Ah . . . we know each other? Forgive me . . ."

"I am vice president of the Artisans' Union. You spoke to us a few years ago . . . about trust. Priests and doctors must be trustworthy. Gambling masters, too. 'When a country can trust its croupiers the polity is safe.' That's what you said."

The usual speech, no less sincere for being canned. "Forgive me, I remember you now," he lied. Perhaps she had been shorter then; perhaps she hadn't attained her full height until this afternoon. Though it was almost evening, wasn't it. The sun was already on the other side of the mountain. The fields there would be a melting gold, the hills beyond the fields rosy, and beyond them the capital's mellow buildings would still be drenched in light. But here the silver of the train reflected a darkening green.

"My name is Dea . . . ," she said helpfully. He didn't catch the surname. He was leaning forward again to watch the glistening locomotive penetrate the mountain—the locomotive, and the first passenger car, and the second. Then others, hidden from him as the train whipped itself straight, slid farther in. Their own car entered the tunnel now—there was a black moment. Then the lamps in the compartment began to glow.

He leaned back. She was reading again. Well, he too could read. He placed palm on briefcase; lists and tables lay within, a book of essays on agricultural reform. He read the book's lengthy introduction. He read the first essay . . .

There was a dull noise, heavy and prolonged.

There was a powerful shudder which shook both the strong vehicle and the passengers within.

The train stopped.

In an instant uniformed men were running along the corridors—a dozen Charles de Gaulles. Men in overalls and caps ran after them. Bringing up the rear flapped a frightened old woman dressed in black, one of those ancient widows the country harbored.

Dea took off her glasses. Her eyes were the dark indefinable metal of old coins. "What do you suppose?" she said.

A second black witch flew down the corridor—fleeing disaster, she probably thought, but running toward it in fact.

"I think there has been a cave-in," Alain said. He wondered how much stone and shale had fallen, and how much damage it had done, and whether anyone had been hurt.

Dea craned her long neck toward the window. The lamps within the train went out. The chalky sides of the tunnel turned a fitful lilac—the tunnel's own electrical system apparently only weakened, not destroyed.

"Someone will give us a report," Alain said.

"Yes, Minister. We need only make conversation. I was in Muñez buying materials for my work. I am a weaver."

"I was in Muñez vetting some trams as a favor to the minister of transportation. I am a dogsbody, by choice."

She nodded as if she understood, and perhaps she did. "Your first name is French."

"My mother," he said, packing into those words a transplanted Parisian yearning all her life for the boulevards. "Yours is . . . theological."

"Classical. My father was a schoolteacher. And a soccer coach."

"Ah . . . and do you follow our national sport?"

"My husband does."

They had seen the same recent movie, on which they disagreed. But they shared admiration for Borges, for Dufy. They smiled tolerantly at saint worship and all that. Dea was sure that death was soon followed by rebirth. "We travel through lifetime after lifetime," she told Alain.

A conductor appeared at their door, speaking not only to them but to the whole car, speaking as if through a megaphone. "A wall has crumbled," he shouted. A little girl ran up to him and pulled at his jacket. "The train—"

"Come back, Ella," called a man's voice.

"—stopped just in time," the conductor went on. "No one has been hurt, a few of our men bruised. But the train cannot proceed, and we must walk backwards through the tunnel."

"Walk backwards!" the child laughed. "Not me!"

"Well, walk forwards, but in the direction from which we came."

"I want to walk backwards," said the contrary child.

"Ella!" the man called again.

There was an orderly scramble from the train. A wheelchair and its feeble old occupant took some time to disembark. "My suitcase," fretted a woman. "Carry the thing yourself," snapped a man. "This way," called a voice from the rear.

Seventy-five passengers edged past the stalled train. They were beamed on by the workmen's battered torchlights. Only the figures were illuminated; the walls of the tunnel, the floor of the tunnel, even the air in the tunnel, was black. The little girl so eager to walk backward rode on her father's shoulders. A large fellow in a leather jacket carried the crippled old man in his arms; another carried the wheelchair, folded, above his head; a calm attendant in a flowered turban followed the threesome. Behind the last car the crowd reassembled, along with engineer and brakeman and conductors and firemen. The old man got resettled in his unfolded chair. Now they were addressed by the chief conductor, who wore epaulets.

"Ladies and gentlemen, we must return to Muñez. We will walk eastwards through the tunnel."

". . . an important appointment!" shouted a man.

"We regret the inconvenience. Tonight the transportation department will provide lodging in Muñez hotels. Tomorrow we will board buses to the capital."

"Buses go around the mountain, for God's sake," said the man with the important appointment. "They take eight hours."

"Alas . . . Railway personnel are ready to escort us now. Only a few miles. A small commuter train will be waiting at the mouth of the tunnel."

"The evening express will smash us to pieces . . . oh!" A trio of old women.

The chief conductor permitted himself a sigh. "All trains have been cancelled," he assured the crowd.

Alain planned the days ahead: no trains at all during the repairs, then one track opened, a small army of men deployed to direct operations first in one direction and then the other. There'd be television inaccuracies to correct, newspaper editorials to counter, extra buses to commandeer for that lengthy mountainside road. Private planes would rent themselves out to fly from the capital to Muñez and back again until one crashed into the mountain—no safe air route had yet been discovered.

The procession was led by the chief conductor. The other train workers distributed themselves among the passengers, their torchlights supplementing the tunnel's flicker.

Alain and Dea were near the end of the line. He carried his briefcase in his outer hand. In hers she carried a rattan sack containing samples of other rattan. Their inner hands were free. Occasionally their knuckles brushed. The man with the important appointment, who had broad but somewhat hunched shoulders, complained at length to a fellow traveler, apparently a stranger, who murmured with idle sympathy and occasionally turned his head as if searching for someone to take his place.

In half an hour the light from the torches melded with another light, a gray evening light. They breathed fresher air. The tunnel was behind them now; they stepped into knee-high grasses. An old wooden train waited. It had only three cars, and most passengers had to remain on their feet during the ride to Muñez. The man in the wheelchair and his attendant were stowed like baggage in one corner. The little girl Ella insisted on curling up in an overhead rack. Dea stood in the aisle, alongside the hunched man, who was still muttering. Alain stood beside Dea.

At the empty station—how many hours earlier had he boarded that fateful express train, right here?—the mayor was waiting under a grand nineteenth-century arch. He looked like the last soldier in a defeated army. He distributed hotel vouchers. Then he and Alain walked together to his office, past stone mansions with delicate balconies: mansions sacrificed to governmental need. Hibiscuses flourished everywhere: the national tree, beautiful but easily bruised. At the mayor's desk, from the mayor's chair, Alain spoke briefly on the telephone to the president, and briefly also to Isabella, who thanked God and cried a little, then at great length to the minister of transportation, and at medium length to his own second in command. By the end of the final conversation it was midnight.

"Minister—you are welcome to spend the night at my house."

"It's the oddest thing—I travel so much that now I can sleep only in hotels. But I thank you."

The mayor seemed relieved. Alain looked at his voucher, recognized the address, and set off along the main avenue. A late tram moved behind him like a bodyguard. Ahead the hotel was dimly lit. Alone, in its lobby, sat the woman. He had forgotten her name— Lea?—but he had not forgotten her. From the moment the train thudded to a halt, sharply braked by the quick-witted engineer—"I saw the side of the tunnel crack, half a mile ahead," the man would say on television. "I saw rocks appear in the crack; I knew what was happening; I prayed that the engine would stop clean and the cars behind not pile up, derail . . ."—from that moment of death averted, of survival ensured, Alain and the woman had been twisted together like cars in the wreck that hadn't happened. He approached her chair and held out his hand. She took it.

ALAIN REMAINED IN MUÑEZ another several days. There were officials to speak to before he returned to the capital to meet with another shaken bunch. For the next several months the unfortunate occurrence in the tunnel would call on his patience and his willingness to let somebody else end a conversation. By some miracle no plane crashed into the mountain.

The rest of the survivors rode to the capital the next day on the extra buses that had been pressed into service. Dea arrived home at five in the afternoon. Luc's pharmacy occupied the front of their house, and when she entered he was waiting on a customer, explaining the possible side effects of a medication. Seeing Dea, he interrupted his own speech, though without moving from behind the counter. He looked at his wife with his usual kindly upward stare—he was a short man—and his already pale skin paled further with relief renewed, gratitude renewed—they had spoken on the telephone the evening before, he knew she was safe, but still. From an expertly penned-in corner their two-year-old sent up a howl of welcome.

Dea did not work the next day. Instead she took her beloved son to the park, and they watched the puppet show, and listened to the band, and shared a giant dish of ice cream. But the following morning she returned to her trestle table in the back room of their house, a windowed studio looking out on a small garden fringed with hibiscus. The child played at her feet with tongue depressor soldiers and a castle made of empty pill vials.

Before she had left the capital for Muñez she had moistened sixty-seven strips of willow. She had inserted one end of each of them into the groove running around the circumference of an oaken disk: the base of a new basket. Now the construction rested upside down atop a mold of her own design. The willow staves, curving downward, had dried. The inverted, embryonic basket reminded her, as always, of a woman gone mad, a flat-headed woman with evenly spaced locks of hair revealing glimpses—sixty-seven of them, in this case—of a demented, featureless head.

She selected a long piece of flexible cane the color of an old man's teeth. She dampened it. She removed a single willow stave and slid the end of the cane into its place, at an angle, and returned the stave to the groove, fixing the new cane forever. She began to weave, removing and replacing every second stave as she worked. This first circumnavigation was always the most exacting, calling for the strictest control, and she could afford to concentrate on nothing else but the work of her hands, though she was alert to the child, and she knew that a light rain had begun outside, and she was aware too of a memory of another rhythm accompanied by a sighing, a more delicate music than she would have expected from a man so . . . robust. She rested a burning cheek against briefly idle knuckles.

IT WAS TEN YEARS before she saw him again. The capital is a big place, and people mingle freely, garments brushing garments in the squares and in the markets and in court. But Alain and Dea did not chance to meet in the public places. And Alain and Isabella did not go to crafts fairs; and Dea and Luc were not fans of the pageantry of government—the splendid inauguration of a new president during that decade, for all the attention they paid it, might have happened on another planet. The new president asked Alain to continue as minister of gaming.

Ten years. The concert hall was packed. The soprano, now an international star, had been raised in Dea's neighborhood; as girls they had been friends. Dea received a pair of tenth-row tickets. Luc chose to stay home with the children—there were three now—so Dea invited a fellow artisan, a young man whose abstract weldings were not yet famous.

Alain and Isabella were also in the orchestra section, a few rows behind and to the right of Dea and her companion. Alain had an excellent view of neck, ear, sometimes nose, a part of her brow. Her hair had been cropped. The soprano sang a program of familiar arias and love songs. She sang them to Dea—that's what he thought; she sang them on Alain's behalf.

Dea and her youthful escort stayed seated during the intermission. Alain and Isabella greeted friends in the lobby and drank champagne. Little sandwiches of smoked carp were particularly tasty. The second half of the program was Lieder. How varied she was, the soprano; how many strings she had to her larynx. He said that to Isabella—through her, really.

After the last "Brava," after the final encore, the members of the audience stood, slipped past each other, murmured . . . Dea turned. Ten years had added a single thrilling line to each of her cheeks. He sucked in his stomach. Their eyes met for several seconds.

My handsome companion is a friend only . . . That was all she wanted to say. She had much to boast of, though. She had become a master weaver. She taught at the crafts school. Her baskets, mostly handbags, were sought after by rich women, by tourists. She was working on an oval one at present—and the next day she returned to it, frowning, separating staves fiercely, choosing canes of conflicting colors, overlapping them, slewing and flitching. She made the lid of twined and strapped latticework, infiltrated with hexagonal weavings. It was a mad design. It would never catch on. It might not even sell, though her name smoked into the base was usually a guarantee.

That afternoon Alain took his daughter to the racetrack. She was twenty-six now, already divorced. He let her choose the horses. She chose according to the filly's name, or the name of the sire, or the name of the dam, or the color of the jockey's silks. Half-asleep, she watched the races on television in the clubhouse. Alain, leaning forward in his outdoor seat, followed each contest from start to finish. He panted, gasped, swore. They drove home with a small bundle of winnings.

AGAIN TEN YEARS PASSED. Another new president had just been elected. The inauguration took place in the Great Park, on a platform surrounded by flowers and facing a thousand folding gilded seats. On the platform sat the country's one Nobel laureate, several former presidents, the new president, and all the ministers, Alain included, though he would soon retire and receive the usual medals. There were four young cadets holding flags, one cadet from each branch of the military service. Dea's son, now serving in the air force, had been selected for this honor guard, perhaps because of his excellent school record, perhaps because of his unusual height. The families of everyone on the platform sat in the first, golden rows.

The oldest of the former presidents was very old indeed. He sat shrunken in his chair at the front of the platform, canes across his lap. Alain sat just behind him. Dea faced them from her aisle seat seven rows back. She shifted her body, and now she could see clearly the monkey face and diminished torso of the man whose current lifetime had lasted so long, and she could see, above his face, his face. Those remembered shoulders. Alain, for his part, could see the dark hair, the glasses, the long neck. Dea took off her glasses, hoping that their eyes might meet: But no, they were too far from each other. Nevertheless, they maintained a pseudo-gaze until the ex-president shuddered, and the long-sighted Dea guessed that he was foolishly about to rise. She rose. The president raised his rump and the canes rolled down his thighs and dropped to the dais and then to the ground. Dea strode forward. The old man stood and tottered and she saw that his crotch was wet. Alain slid out of his chair and caught the ancient figure beginning to fall and lifted him and held him in his arms like a dead child and watched Dea advancing and now their eyes did meet, but he was obliged to turn away in order to lay the ex-president across four chairs that had hastily been vacated. Alain bent down and opened the old man's shirt and loosened his belt. "I'm a doctor," said a fellow who had leaped onto the dais, and slipped his practiced hand underneath the shirt. The ex-president opened his eyes. Ambulance men appeared and policemen quieted the crowd (the four cadets stood without moving) and Alain, relieved of responsibility, straightened up in time to see Dea resume her seat. Luc raised his eyebrows at his wife. "CPR," she explained. The old man wasn't dead and thanks to Alain he wasn't hurt. "I faint sometimes," he insisted, "it's nothing." The ambulance took him to the hospital anyway. The inauguration went peaceably on. Afterward, Alain went to a grand dinner. During the meal he felt a roiling in his gut, ruining his appetite. Isabella shot him glances of easy compassion. She was still blond, still admired, still faithful.

Dea dined in a faux-rustic restaurant with Luc and their two younger children—the oldest, the cadet, had to continue holding his flag at the state dinner. Then parents and children went home. Everyone but Dea exhaustedly went to bed.

The complicated basket she had made on the day after the soprano's concert had become a splendid success. Now people begged for her creations. Fruit bowls, hods, wine totes, charming round overnight bags—she made them for film stars, television personalities, the wives of industrialists. She had woven a cradle for the granddaughter of the King of Sweden. She accepted as students only weavers already proficient. She was, according to the minister of culture, a national treasure. The house she lived in with Luc and the children had grown taller by a story, and the garden was improved, and the pharmacy had acquired granite counters, and the workroom was all glass now.

Tonight she did not turn to her current project—a woven jewelry case, seventeen little drawers moving as smoothly as if lubricated—but to a private matter, a sculpture slightly bigger than life-size. She had been working on it for years. That fibrous vegetable material, thickly woven, can be made to resemble naked flesh seems unlikely; but under Dea's hands this happened. Two standing figures melted into one. The slenderer of the two figures rested its head on the broader shoulders of the other figure, and atop the inclined head the hair was caught in a knot and sprayed outward.

Alain left the inaugural banquet early. A brief rain had slickened the streets. He walked atop his own reflection until he came to a warehouse. A car followed him, like the tram that night in Muñez. At the warehouse he gave a password, entered, sat down with some men—some roughly dressed, some finely, all smoking, all flush with cash. They played for a throbbing hour; cards were all the world. Alain won big twice—once on a straight, once on a bluff. A scarred player gave him a murderous stare. Then the men from the car came in with their guns raised and arrested everybody except Alain. He turned over his winnings to one of them. Oh, these necessary stings.

ANOTHER DECADE and then some—thirteen years. The glass workshop was now a playroom for grandchildren—the cadet had become a captain and a father. After the Museum of Modern Art bought the untitled sculpture, Dea withdrew from her students, finished current commissions but refused new ones, and enrolled in the Academy of Pharmacy. She had not forgotten the science she'd mastered as a schoolgirl. She needed only a year of training to qualify, to join her ailing husband as partner.

One day during the rainy season, Luc upstairs in bed with a worsening cough, a blind customer suggested that Dea turn on the lamps. "I can feel darkness, like flannel," he said as he tapped out with his cane. So she flipped three switches and then a fourth, and blew a fuse, and had to climb down to the basement where the fuse box lurked. While there she heard the two tones of the bell that meant the opening of the shop door. "One moment," she called, and climbed back up, grunting a little on her arthritic knee.

His hair was still abundant. Or, rather, it seemed abundant—but her clever eye saw that it was abundant anew, after a bout of baldness. Below this second growth his custard brow looked less like flesh than the statue now in the museum. His blue eyes had faded to mauve, the color of the tunnel's vault when the train's lights had gone out. His lips had thinned. Under the handsome suit his chest had caved in.

So he was dying, thirty years late.

"Alain," she said, breaking the long silence.

"Dea," he said, his voice cracking.

"Alain, my own . . . some other lifetime. I promise."

He nodded. She too inclined her head, and closed her eyes. She heard again the double tone of the bell.

At the Muñez hotel so long ago the room given to Alain was larger than Dea's. In silent agreement they had selected hers. It was square and white, and had a single narrow bed against the wall. The window looked out on the deserted avenue. He bathed first, then she; then, naked, they met in the middle of the room, and embraced as if they meant to weld themselves into one being. His strong arm around her back fixed her body to his. Her head rested on his shoulder. Standing that way, they told each other of their lives until then. They abandoned reticence, even courtesy: They kept interrupting each other.

"A game of chance—no thrill like it, not even . . .," he said. "Win or lose," he said.

"My parents wanted me to become a doctor," she said.

"I must go wherever it glows—casinos, track, lottery."

"I was willing to study medicine. But I changed my mind, like little Ella today. I found my vocation. My fingers, the cane, they were meant for each other."

"Cock fights in alleys, dice near dumps. Some fool knifed and left for—"

"The suitors who weren't terrified of my height, they were terrified of my passion. Only Luc, such a kindly man . . ."

"—dead." Dawn lightened the room. An early tram slid by outside their window. "I am responsible to my—"

"I am responsible to my—"

"—family," he whispered.

"—family," she moaned.

"—country."

"—hands."

He gave her that last word. He gave her his love. He would think of her almost every day for the rest of his life. Only his presence would he withhold.

They loosened their grip on each other then, and found their way to their only bed.

On Junius Bridge

I.

THE FIRST BRIDGE was made of stone. An ogre lived beneath it, the village people claimed—they were woodcutters and farmers, bred on fables. The stooped, bearded ogre, true to his kind, hungered for children. An eighteenth-century drawing of the bridge showed him crouched beneath the keystone with a sack. Miss Huk owned that drawing and displayed it near the entrance of her mountainside inn. She displayed, also, a photograph of the bridge, early twentieth century, grainy and unconvincing. It, too, through some trick of reeds and mist, seemed to reveal an ogre.

The stone bridge had arched over the narrow river separating the mountains from the farmlands around the town of Sklar. The Russians had planned to run a railway up into the mountains, the easier to deforest them. There had also been a plan to widen the road that wound from village to higher village. So Junius Bridge was torn down stone by stone. An iron structure—also called Junius— took its place. This Junius was flat, with side railings consisting of Z after Z: ZZZZ . . . The ogre went elsewhere during the construction of the iron bridge; at least that's what people told each other. Maybe he joined the Socialists. But he returned when the new Junius was completed, and he was said to live under it still, sleeping on one of the trestles, annoying youngsters making love on the riverbank with his high-pitched sorrowings.

The railway was never built and the road never widened.

MR. AND MRS. ALBRECHT and their son had crossed Junius Bridge five days ago. They'd spent those days among the mountains, driving from village to village. When they came downhill again and arrived at the inn, Miss Huk immediately suggested liquids in various forms—baths for them all, soup for them all, hot rum for the robust parents, hot milk for the elfin boy. She made these unasked-for recommendations from her seat at the registration desk in the large open space that served as reception area, common parlor, recital room whenever Andrei deigned to play: a place where the fire was always lit and pines stood guard on the other side of long windows. She knew that her authority would not be resented. It was the authority of the insignificant.

She was thin. Eyes, skin, hair, sweater, skirt, stockings, boots: all were the gray of leaf mold. A sharp nose poked out of a narrow face. She wore spectacles. Her voice was exceedingly soft.

"Thank you," Robertson Albrecht said now to Miss Huk's suggestions. "Though my wife prefers white wine."

"Yes," said Christine Albrecht. She had amber eyes and a wide rosy mouth, and there was a reddish tinge to her hair, as if the unmanageable stuff had been rouged.

"Chilled?" Miss Huk said to the American billionaire, to his ravishing woman.

"Chilled, oh, yes," Mrs. Albrecht said.

As if those light syllables were the command he was awaiting, the handyman bent toward the luggage. Despite narrow shoulders and womanly hips, he could lift the heaviest loads. With the child's satchel stowed under one arm and the father's briefcase under the other, he picked up the two suitcases and started upstairs. There were men who would not tolerate their briefcases being commandeered; Miss Huk had met several such tycoons. Robertson Albrecht didn't seem to care. Instead he turned to look at the room. Though thick-torsoed, he gave an impression of soldierly fitness. He took in (Miss Huk, attentive to his profile, noted shifts in the angle of the sparse lashes) the massive stone fireplace; the carpet whose complicated pattern could only be guessed, since its various greens were almost indistinguishable from one another; the carved benches flanking the fireplace in grim opposition; the upholstered chairs. The boy, on hands and knees, was behind one of the chairs, betrayed by a thin ankle in a rumpled sock, and a sneaker. The couple had now both turned their backs on Miss Huk to watch their child—to watch the chair which almost concealed him. Miss Huk glanced upward. The corner of a suitcase disappeared from the broad landing.

All was quiet. In the large bedroom upstairs and the small one connecting to it the handyman would place suitcases on folding racks, pull open the curtains, and push the windows outward. In the kitchen the cook, half of whose face was purple, was roasting a pig. The walleyed kitchen maid was stewing fruit. The rest of the small staff was busy, too, and the other guests were occupying themselves in their different manners; and Miss Huk sat at the register; and Mr. Albrecht stood beside Mrs. Albrecht, only the upper arms of their jackets touching, as if accidentally.

The boy was still on his knees. The foot wearing the sock and sneaker moved out of sight. The head appeared on the other side of the chair. Slowly he got to his feet.

Miss Huk turned her eyes on him. As she expected, he avoided her spectacled gaze. His own eyes were large and silvery. His hair was pale, too. His cheeks were gaunt and his chin pointed. He looked toward but not at his parents—toward Mr. Albrecht's rubbery features coated in dark skin, toward Mrs. Albrecht's beautiful face and unremarkable clothing. They both spoke excellent French, Miss Huk had noted. The boy walked forward with a mechanical grace. He stopped eighteen inches away from his mother and father. He was inserting a magnifying glass into its holder; he was dropping the device into the pocket of his khaki short pants: short pants worn, Miss Huk guessed, not in defiance of the snow outside but because he was attached to the garment. Maybe the color, maybe the pockets. "*Anthrenus scrophulariae*," Lars now said to the non-space between his parents, the line where their tweed arms just touched.

"Well, that's not surprising," Mr. Albrecht said to his son. Mrs. Albrecht said nothing.

Miss Huk also said nothing. *Those damned carpet beetles*, was what she thought.

When you run an inn in the foothills of the Mátra Mountains, an inn that boasts nothing in particular—a thermal spring of course, excellent food and wine of course, forest trails—you've got to attract people who have reason to be content with bathing, walking, eating, drinking, reading the books they've brought or the ones in the book room behind the stairs. If the inn is more than inn, or less, you are wise to offer something to offset that less or more. Miss Huk did offer something: Andrei.

"He's not our resident musician, not at all," she said a few hours later to the bathed, hydrated Albrechts. "He is a guest here like anybody else, semipermanent like many. He brought the harpsichord—it is his."

"By car?" Mrs. Albrecht asked, idly.

Miss Huk said yes, it is easy to enclose keyboard and strings in padding and of course the legs had been removed. Legs can be stowed in a sack. When Andrei plays for us, she informed the lovely, sorrowful face, he and the handyman carry the thing downstairs. And the kitchen maid carries the legs . . .

"In a sack," Mrs. Albrecht supplied, her eyes seeking the drawing of the bridge and its ogre.

Her husband said nothing. He was so still—like pudding.

"Yes, a sack. And then, in this room, near the windows there, the men and the girl reassemble the instrument, whirling the legs into place. They have all three become expert at the maneuver."

The kitchenmaid came in and suggested dinner. The gong sounded at the same time. Miss Huk rose, the Albrechts rose, Lars came out from behind his chair and moved slowly forward. "Will you join me at my table?" Miss Huk asked these newest guests. "It is the custom on the first night."

Lars paused. There was nothing wrong with his hearing. Reluctance rippled across his features, but he followed his parents into the dining room. Lit only by candles, the room held six tables. Four were quickly occupied. The Belgians took one. The topologist, beaming in his vacuous way, took another. S. and S. took the third table. S. and S. were women who preferred to be addressed by last initials only; too bad they bore the same initial, but the staff managed to oblige. One S. was Scottish, the other Norwegian. Miss Huk and the Albrechts seated themselves at Miss Huk's table, which stood on a low platform near the window. Beyond the window was the forest: dense, then denser.

"Like gods, those pines," Christine Albrecht said with an intake

of breath. "Druids—you've read about them, Rob, miraculous beings. In the isles, but maybe here in Hungary, too."

"Darling."

Miss Huk noted the wish to soothe. There was nothing wrong
with her hearing, either.

She cleared her throat with an effort. "*Pinaceae sylvestris*," she
said. "Any tales you have heard of their transformative properties
are only peasants' fancies. Winters here are hard. Magpies do foretell the coming of newcomers, and there is a circlet of twigs that
cures cramp. It's called *frázkarika*. But the pines are merely trees."
She coughed. What a long speech.

All the guests were now in place. The kitchen maid served soup,
and in a while she cleared the bowls; she brought the roast and the
stewed fruit and a salad of lightly steamed ferns. She took those
empty plates away when the time came. She brought cheese. The
room was filled with the almost-silence of feasting. A conversation
here, a hiss and a snapped remark there, false laughter from the
Belgians, one brief cry. The kitchen maid brought tarts. Lars ate a
single mouthful of soup, a single bite of meat, a single spoonful of
fruit, a single fern. He left cheese and tart untasted. "At midnight,"
said Robertson Albrecht to Miss Huk, "I would like to use your
telephone, to call my brother in New York."

"Of course. You are aware that we have no Internet access."

"I have no computer."

"No cell phone, no laptop, no wristwatch," his wife said with a
smile.

Lars raised his head. "*Albrecht fraternis*." He returned to not eating dessert.

Andrei didn't show up at dinner. He did come down to the parlor afterward, his big head like a burden on his skinny frame. Small
red blemishes chased each other along his jaw—he must have been
shaving with that straightedge. He nodded at the newcomers sitting side by side on the sofa but did not stop to introduce himself;
instead he joined the topologist at the chess table.

Christine Albrecht accepted cognac from Miss Huk. Miss Huk
then carried the tray of snifters to Andrei and the topologist, who
each took one. S. and S., occupied with needlepoint, were tee-
totallers. Miss Huk did not offer brandy to the three Belgians, still

lingering in the dining room, interfering with cleaning up. They were hikers who had not intended to be here, they claimed; but the storm two days ago had kept them from reaching Sklar. And then one thing led to another, as their leader said to Miss Huk— ringleader, in her opinion; if these men were hikers she was the Queen of the Night. "There's something about this place," he went on to say, shaking his hyena's head and smiling, an unconvincing routine. Some je ne sais quoi? But he didn't say that; only the British used that phrase. She wondered what the threesome was up to. Perhaps an infusion of pine needles was now thought to cure schizophrenia and these thugs were planning to buy up the forests, or rent them from the feckless government, or steal them from the ogre under the bridge.

Lars sat on a footstool in the window embrasure, looking out at the pine gods. Miss Huk laid the tray on a table, picked up a snifter, and wandered to the window herself. She kept a decent distance from the boy.

"In Buenos Aires people eat live beetles," she remarked. "A special kind of beetle. For their health."

Silence.

"The health of the Argentineans," she clarified.

Silence.

"Not of the beetles," she said to his reflection.

Silence. Then, "*Ulomoides dermestoides*," he said to hers.

II.

Two days later, when she was at the register, "Good morning," Mr. Albrecht said. He had come soundlessly down the stairs.

"Good morning," she echoed.

"Is your voice perhaps stronger in German?" he asked in German.

"No. In Hungarian only," she said in English. "And not much stronger."

He opened his hands to expose defeated palms.

"I don't intend to sell the inn," she said. "No, no," she answered his raised eyebrows, "you have said nothing about buying it; and yes, yes, you came here because you heard of the unusual properties of the place and you wanted to experience them for yourself."

One of the Belgians walked by, not looking at the businessman. The businessman didn't look at him, either. "But it is your nature to buy things," she continued.

"Habit, not nature," he murmured. "I don't want the inn, it is your empire." He carried his own empire in his head, and in his brother's head. She had read about it; it reached everywhere. "But I have observed you at work," he went on. "If you ever want a job . . ."

"Thank you," she said, meaning no. When she lay on her pallet awaiting death she wanted to remember a life that except for a few years in Budapest was contained here, her steps crossing and recrossing each other on this patch of mountain.

The telephone rang. The voice was hoarse, the language French, she recognized one of a pair of brothers. Bird-watchers. Sunday. "Yes," Miss Huk said into the volume enhancer.

LONG AGO, AFTER THE WAR, when the inn had been the property of her uncle and aunt, when she had been a little girl and then a bigger girl, reading stories to guests' young children in her already soft voice . . . Long ago, the guests had been proper burghers, spending with caution the money they had managed to hoard. There was no Andrei then. On Saturday nights fiddlers came up from Sklar to play old tunes, get paid, get drunk, stumble home across the bridge.

Her kind aunt and uncle sent her to university in Budapest. She studied science. But she could barely breathe in the city; she missed the holy forest air. Amid ordinary citizens she felt misplaced, even stolen. Her voice retreated into her larynx. She recognized solitaries like herself—the man who repaired her shoes, a woman in the park with a wondering look, a mathematics professor. But solitaries don't gather; someone must collect them.

She managed to stay long enough to earn her degree. Then she went home.

"I will live here," she told them.

"Oh, dearest, stay in the city, teach, marry. Why did we work except to spare you drudgery."

"This is my place."

"So much to do," they said, and sighed. "A lonely business, you have seen that," they said. "It is necessary to keep distant from guests, from staff . . ."

"Yes," she breathed.

She began as housemaid, at her own request. She scoured the stone floor of the kitchen; she learned the rudiments of the electrician's trade, the plumber's, the accountant's. Her uncle and aunt died, one after the other in the same month. She cried for the old man and she cried for the old lady. But her tears were without salt.

Gradually the inn's patronage changed. Unimaginative guests gave way to guests with secrets. Families yielded to isolates. Some people brought their own quilts; one old woman who came every summer carried a set of saucepans. Exhausted men drove up and deposited some relative for an unspecified amount of time. Word had gotten around as it always did, carried from village to village like legends brought by midwives—that place near the bridge: odd people could be themselves there.

The staff changed, too. One day the ancient handyman, often drunk anyway, dropped foaming to the ground. Two days later the new one arrived, thighs flapping against each other. Sitting with Miss Huk in the book room, his eyes blue lanterns, he offered the information that he had been accused of unhealthy practices.

"Peeping," she guessed.

"Yes. Because I like to sit alone in parks, within arcades, on riverbanks. I have no worse habits, no tendency. But the children . . . they tease me. Then they report me."

She hired him. She pensioned off the old cook. The new cook appeared, her face presented like a hatchet or the result of a hatcheting. The drifty-eyed kitchen maid appeared.

There was so much to do, so blessed much. Food, wine, towels; the register; windowpanes. Now she opened the ledger. Robertson Albrecht had withdrawn to a chair with a book, leaving her to her empire. There were bills to pay. There were new guests to get ready for—the bird-watchers, and a fat English couple with three kids. They came every year. The kids were foster children they had managed to adopt, the mother confided . . . confided to anybody who'd listen, in tones of urgent secrecy. "Only here do we feel like a family."

THREE O'CLOCK WAS A LOW TIME for everyone at the inn. Andrei stopped practicing and got into bed. The cook smoked outside. The handyman went somewhere. Guests retreated to their rooms or to the baths.

Often at three Miss Huk went into the kitchen. The kitchen maid was usually sitting beside the discolored samovar. She produced her shy smile. Miss Huk drew a chair up to the table, its top a thick slab for chopping. A cleaver hung from a loop strapped to its side.

Three drifted to three fifteen, to three thirty, to three forty-five. Things began to stir again. Andrei's afternoon sadness lessened, and he got out of bed. Sometimes the Sklar taxi brought a guest or retrieved one, and the driver came into the kitchen for a drop. The handyman reappeared, lugging a barrel. His form was not ungainly or unsatisfactory, Miss Huk thought: just another way for a man to be. Some nights, tuxedoed behind the bar, his beardless face slightly moist, his lips slightly red, he looked like a beautiful woman in drag.

Today, through the window, she saw him at the woodpile with his ax. A figure moved toward him. Robertson Albrecht. A polite exchange—she could imagine it. I need the exercise; may I? Certainly, sir. The American raised the ax, his muscles alive under their layer of unimportant fat, and he struck, and the wood split as if it were in his thrall.

At four the bell rang in the kitchen. The little kitchen maid carried tea and cake to the parlor. A few minutes later: "A royal banquet," Andrei exclaimed to Miss Huk, who had slipped into her place behind the register. He said the same thing almost every day. The Norwegian S. smiled at Andrei, exposing long gray teeth. "Oh, join us, Miss Huk," said the Scottish S.

"I've had tea, thank you." She had in fact had no tea, had communed with the kitchen maid without benefit of nourishment or words; but it would soon be time for a real drink. The little group warmed itself at the hearth. The handyman, now in his monkey suit, opened the bar. A Belgian came down the stairs. The topologist came down. Another Belgian came down. Lars crawled in from the book room—were there woodworms there? oh Lord. The third Belgian appeared. Everyone was assembled except the senior Albrechts—but, no, they were there, standing by the window, so solid, how could she not have seen them come in.

III.

ON FRIDAY, at that low hour of three, Miss Huk climbed to the handyman's room to deliver his linens. She laid the pile of sheets and towels on his cot . . . soft stuff, so that his sensitive skin would not pucker.

The turret had four windows, one on each side. Three of them looked out on glistening green boughs. From the fourth you could see Sklar in the distance. If you looked directly downward, you saw the kitchen garden and the little parking area. Only the inn's pick-up truck stood there now. The Albrechts' rented sedan was gone, she saw.

And she saw the stranger: thin black hair combed over a shining pate. She leaned forward for a better look and smacked her forehead on the handyman's window. She backed away and lifted his binoculars from the dresser.

Flat ears. A tan scarf. A bony face. A pointed black beard.

A scientist, you'd think.

He waited, this seeming scientist, his hands loose at his thighs, beside a birch tree. When Lars crawled into the parking lot the man pursed his thin lips. Lars did not raise his head at the whistle. But he got to his feet. He approached the stranger. He stopped at the usual distance of a foot and a half.

The man's lips moved in speech. Lars listened. They both squatted, and the man produced his own magnifying glass. More talk, more listening. When the man stood and walked toward the road, Lars followed.

Man walking, boy trailing; and both disappeared from Miss Huk's view.

She inhaled sharply, producing only a light whistle. She did nothing else. The inn allowed guests to do as they pleased. Children were the responsibility of their parents.

So she stood there, thinking of the stories she had read aloud. The merchant who traded his gold for a pair of wings. She had found that old book a few days ago. The brothers who mistakenly killed each other in darkness. She had offered to read to Lars. The peasants' sons who went out to seek their fortunes and had succeeded or failed. Lars had given her a hard look and scuttled away. The starling whose song shattered the mirror that was the world, and so the world had to begin again.

She was still at the window.

But the little figure: how brief his stay.

"You move like lightning," Uncle Huk had marveled.

She could still do that. In a minute she was on the second floor, then the first. The cook was not in the kitchen. The handyman was elsewhere. S. and S. sat in the parlor with their embroidery. The topologist amiably manned the registration desk. "The telephone rang," he said. "I took a reservation." Miss Huk, on her way upstairs again, bowed her gratitude. She knocked on Andrei's door. Oh, he'd hate this. But: "Yes," he called. She flew in, and there he was, and the kitchen maid was with him, her round face registering Miss Huk's entry without alarm.

"A man has taken Lars," Miss Huk rasped.

Buckling his trousers, Andrei sped out of the room. The kitchen maid grabbed his razor and scampered after him. Miss Huk brought up the rear.

On the first floor Andrei plunged into the kitchen, returned with the cleaver; and the three raced down the wooden steps of the inn and through the scrub to the road. They turned downhill. Patches of snow from the last storm still clung to the mud.

Miss Huk ran, and her thoughts ran, too. Perhaps the Americans had arranged to dispose of their child. They could not transform him. They could not cosset him forever. Her heart thudded. Lars would not love. He would not marry. He would not wonder, even; he would recognize and classify. He would learn more Latin names and remember each one. It was a kind of happiness—she could tell them that.

The three reached the shallow steps of Junius Bridge. Andrei raised the cleaver. The kitchen maid waved the razor. Miss Huk slowed to a walk.

The chief Belgian stepped into their path, both arms aloft. "The boy is safe," he said.

Lars was standing at the railing, near but not next to his father. The phony scientist was also standing on the bridge, his arms tied behind his back. The second Belgian was there, carrying a coil of rope. Beyond them, in the middle of the bridge, stood the Albrecht car, Mrs. Albrecht at the wheel, and next to it a strange green car, the third Belgian at its wheel. The cars would block traffic. When was there any traffic?

The Belgian with the rope marched the bound man forward and pushed him into the backseat of the green car and got in front beside his compatriot. Hikers indeed. The car backed off the bridge, turned, and headed toward Sklar.

Lars was examining something on the railing. She knew what it was. A speckled moth deposited her eggs here. The larva spun a cocoon around itself. The whole process was a biological curiosity—the moth should have chosen wood, not iron—but some ancestress had made the mistake long ago, when the Junius was reconstructed, and the error was replicated generation after insect generation; new moths kept emerging from the bridge.

Andrei and the kitchen maid, their weapons lowered, turned and began to walk up the road. The chief Belgian followed them. Christine Albrecht started her car and drove a few yards and picked up her husband. They sat side by side for a moment, not looking at each other, his hand covering hers on the wheel. Then they drove on toward the inn. Lars, after a final inspection of the cocoon, followed his parents' car.

When everyone was out of sight Miss Huk lowered herself down the bank. Her boots squelched on the mud. She peered under the bridge.

Blue eyes in a fat face stared at her.

"You know I would never . . .," he began. "I sit here of an afternoon, I like the design of the iron . . .," he began again.

"I do know," she reassured him. "Come home now."

She climbed the bank again. She was catching up with Lars . . . no, he had lagged behind. "The cocoon on the bridge," she said.

He turned his head toward her, though his gaze strayed elsewhere.

She kept him waiting. At last he looked at her.

"*Hepialus lemberti*," she rewarded him. His eyes locked themselves to hers for a moment, pupils penetrating pupils, like sex she supposed.

IV.

ANDREI DREW RIBBONS of sound from the painted instrument.

Lars sat like a stone on one of the carved benches. In a row of folded chairs sat the other guests and Miss Huk, all listening. The handyman, elbows on the bar, listened. The splotched cook, shoulder against the doorjamb, listened. Somewhere the kitchen maid listened, too.

Christine Albrecht seemed to be only half listening. She looked weary beyond repair. After the applause she slipped away. Robertson Albrecht watched her climb upward; Miss Huk, nearby, watched him. "May we go into the book room?" he said, his eyes still on his wife.

They sat side by side. "I am sorry about this afternoon," he said, with his tensile gravity. "We are used to kidnapping attempts, we are prepared for them. But I would have spared you."

She nodded.

"We will leave tomorrow, along with our offensive bodyguards." Silence lay between them like an animal. "Thank you for the comfort of your inn," he said. "Lars," he said, then paused. "Lars is not particularly precocious, doesn't read anything except entomology, doesn't even read very well."

She favored him with her expressionless gaze.

"My brother in New York, my partner, he too is . . . narrow."

She spoke at last, as loudly as she could. "It is possible that in a century or two the interpersonal will cease to be of value."

"Practiced by a few eccentric devotees," he agreed. "Like swordplay."

"I could keep the boy," she heard herself cry.

"No," he said, perhaps sparing her, perhaps turning the remainder of her life to ash.

Relic and Type

Jay's grandson—his only child's only child—married a young woman born in Kyoto. Mika had an enchanting chin, like a little teaspoon. She wore sweet pastel suits with bits of lace creeping out of their Vs. Who would believe that she spent her days making money from money? The young couple occupied an apartment in Tokyo where appliances folded up to fit inside other appliances. Woody, too, was an investment analyst.

"I think I'll take up Japanese," Jay told his daughter on the flight home from the wedding. She looked at him. At your age!—but she didn't say that. She was as tactful as his late wife, Jay thought, his eyes briefly stinging: Wellesley girls both. His daughter also didn't point out that there was no need for so heroic an effort—the young couple was fluently bilingual, and if they had children the hybrids would be brought up bilingual, too; and anyway, how often would Jay lay eyes on those children? She and her husband were hale enough to make the exhausting trip from Godolphin to Tokyo and back two or three times a year. Not Jay. Nor did his daughter mention that language study required an unimpaired memory. At seventy-five, Jay had difficulty recalling the names of traded Red Sox players, and it was a good thing that name tags had been provided to the members of his Class for their fiftieth reunion. At the Night at Pops the lyrics to "Fair Harvard" had also been handed out, another aid to recollection. The Class stood and sang:

> *O Relic and Type of our ancestors' worth,*
> *That hast long kept their memory warm,*

First flow'r of their wilderness! Star of their night!
Calm rising thro' change and thro' storm.

Jay still had a respectable baritone. Sonny Fessel, his old room-mate, who had made a fortune in rhinoplasty, could barely manage a croak. But Jay, despite his strong voice, wasn't altogether well. He suffered from a blood disorder. The disease was indolent now, but who knew what it had in mind. And his pressure was high.

The ivory hands of the stewardess removed his tray. "I'm looking for something to do," he explained to his daughter. He was retired from a career as an actuary that had ended with an honorable stint as state insurance commissioner (Woody had inherited Jay's skill with numbers; "numeracy," they called it these days). He'd given up his weekly squash game when the club adopted the new, soft ball and enlarged the old courts. His town, Godolphin, a leafy wedge of Boston, was governed by a town meeting —a glorious circus—but its week-long sessions occurred only twice a year. The rituals of Judaism left him cold. His immigrant grandfather wrapped in a tal-lith was a sentimental memory, not a model. His father's religious involvement had begun and ended with Brotherhood breakfasts, and Jay himself had quit Sunday school the day after his bar mitz-vah. But now . . . he was dawdling through his days, his appetite flat, his blood thin. The study of anything might be a tonic.

Once back home he investigated workshops for elders at Godol-phin High School. Bookbinding? Stained glass? He considered the nonsectarian courses given at the temple: Is Zionism Dead? maybe, or Great Jewish Women, taught by the rabbi herself, a blonde with an old-fashioned pageboy haircut. But Japanese I, offered at the Godolphin Language Center, trumped Theodor Herzl and Rosa Luxemburg. When Jay read the course description he breathed again the scent and heard the sounds of his recent week in Japan—blossoming, rustling trees; glowing incense sticks at noisy city shrines; a soupy smell at a particular noodle shop where "The Girl From Impanema" had been playing on a radio next to the register. He remembered fabrics, too. On the Philosopher's Walk, in Kyoto, he had encountered a group of uniformed children who did not separate to let him pass but instead surrounded him, engulfed him in their soft navy serge. His new granddaughter's grandmother, a handsome woman with hair dyed deep brown, had come to the wedding in a traditional garment—crimson silk, with a cream sash. He almost hadn't recognized her when the family met in a restaurant a few days later—she was wearing her everyday pants and turtleneck then. Her English was serviceable. "Hoody is gentle and kind," she said to Jay. *We are so pleased*, she implied.

"Mika is a *shaineh maideleh*," he said, dredging up two of his fifty Yiddish words. He grinned—an air of mischief had always endeared him to women. "A lovely girl," he said, though he failed to tell her he was translating. She would think her hard-won English defective; oh well.

THE AUSTERE BEAUTY of the teacher of Japanese I eclipsed Mika's prettiness as the sun the moon. Nakabuta-sensei remained standing for the entire ninety minutes of the first weekly class. Twelve pupils around a table stared up at her. The classroom in this converted hilltop mansion looked out across the river at Cambridge, at the brick Houses of Harvard, with their bell towers. The leftmost House had sheltered Jay and Sonny Fessel.

"Japanese grammar," Nakabuta told them in her rich, unaccented English, "will seem at first incomprehensible. Please forget your attachment to plurals. Please divorce yourself from pronouns. Try to float like a lotus on our pond of suggestion and indirectness."

A few cowed pupils dropped out early in the semester. Those who hung on were businessmen or scientists or programmers whose work took them frequently to Japan, or they were young people who had lived for a while in the country and could conduct a slangy conversation. Jay was a category unto himself: the tall old man with a few streaks of red in his white hair, stains refusing to fade; the codger who hoped to converse with descendants as yet unconceived.

In July the young couple came to Godolphin to visit Jay's daughter and son-in-law. And Jay, too, of course. Jay told Mika, in Japanese, that warm weather had arrived early in Massachusetts next spring; no, last spring; no, *this* spring. The tomatoes were delicious, weren't they. He inquired after her father and mother and grandmother, *chichi* and *haha* and *baba*, remembering too late that these appellations were overfamiliar. She replied that her family's health was good, thanks, and she was sorry to see he was using a cane. She spoke in considerately slow Japanese. Ah, just his arthritis attacking, he explained; *flaring up* was the phrase he would have preferred, but you said the words you knew, which were not always the ones you meant.

THE SECOND YEAR, Sugiyama-sensei, small and plain, introduced the class to the passive mood, which sometimes implied reluctance and sometimes even exploitation. She gave vocabulary quizzes every week, and taught the students to count strokes when they were learning to write kanji—like slaves counting lashes, Jay thought. She counseled them to practice the ideograms without paper and pencil, to limn the things with their fingertips on any convenient surface.

During that summer's visit Jay took the pregnant Mika for several walks around Godolphin. His arthritis was better and he didn't need the cane. He showed her the apartment building he'd grown up in, the park he'd played ball in, the high school he'd graduated from—all outwardly unchanged through the years. The deli even is still doing business, he reported, his syntax correct in Japanese and faithful to Yiddish, too. The population was not so diverse when I was a boy, he managed to say, though the adjective he used really meant "various." We were then only Jews and Irish and . . . he didn't know how to say *Protestants*, so he killed them off. Now we are Russian, and also Vietnamese, and also South American, and many others there is no necessity to mention, the entire final phrase contained in a one-syllable word that he unfortunately mispositioned. Mika nodded anyway, and Jay felt proud of himself, proud of all he'd learned from Sugiyama-sensei. Sugiyama's devotion to teaching Japanese had made up for her own rather awkward English: *burn*, *barn*, and *bun*, on her tongue, were all the same word.

YAMAMOTO-SENSEI, the third-year teacher, pronounced English very well. His delivery, though, was alarming. His speech was interrupted by giggles, snorts, and the *n-n* of agreement, less extended than the *n-n-n* of disagreement. Jay recoiled from this gasping, spittled fellow. In Yamamoto-san's sallowness, in the rosy wetness of his lips, in the short fatness of his nose with its exposed nostrils, in the black rims of his spectacles, he was a painful reminder of Feivel Ostroff, who had invaded Jay's eighth-grade class more than six decades earlier. Feivel and his siblings exuded an old-world whiff that most Jewish families had vigorously sprayed away. Under ordinary circumstances the Ostroffs would not have achieved Godolphin—the father kept a little grocery in a deteriorating section of Boston, and the brood lived over the store. But the feckless father died, and the mother's brother, made prosperous by the war, moved widow and orphans into a big apartment on Jefferson Avenue whose rent he undertook to pay. He bought them necessaries and even bikes.

If the Orloffs had been Chasidic they would have become part of a tribe wearing queer puppet costumes; they'd have attended the Chasidic day school. Or if the Orloffs had been Orthodox they'd have worn yarmulkes and attended the Orthodox school. But they were not Chasidic, not Orthodox, not even particularly observant; they were merely dark, scrawny, and embarrassing. Their lunch boxes were crammed with hard-boiled eggs and pickles. Feivel laughed at his own jokes. Some students made friends with him—he could be helpful with Latin homework, and in those days Harvard still required proficiency in an ancient tongue. Jay, all A's anyway, ignored him.

But he couldn't ignore Yamamoto. Jay meant to conquer the Japanese language; Yamamoto's territory was in his battle plan. And there was a similar determination in Jay's classmates—there were only four others now. It was as if they were attending not the decorous language center but the night school to which his grandfather had dragged himself a century earlier, even after ten hours of work, because on English his whole future depended.

Three of the others had been with Jay since the beginning—two businessmen and a programmer—and the fourth was a new pupil, a young woman who'd begun her Japanese studies in college. She was now living with a doctor from Kobe. Jay wondered what their offspring would look like—the young woman was pale and freckled, with parched hair and transparent eyelashes. Jay's new great-grandchild, according to the pictures on the Web, was an untroubled blend of both families: he had, in charming miniature, his mother's chin and hair and eyes, his father's curly mouth, and Jay's own father's noble schnozz. In one of the pictures Mika's grandmother held the baby on her lap. She was wearing glasses, her expression unreadable.

Yamamoto was an expert drillmaster. He made the class repeat verb conjugations and honorific forms and onomatopoeic words until Jay became *mukamuka, kurakura, gennari* . . . nauseated, dizzy, and exhausted. But Yamamoto was not entirely to blame; Jay's disease was at last on the offensive. Well, it was his fate, wasn't it; his *unmei*. Yamamoto stood during the drills, breathing noisily, waving his arms, almost shouting through his noxious giggles. He was like a soldier . . . like a Japanese soldier . . . like a Japanese soldier in the war films of Jay's boyhood. He was dressed in salaryman's clothing—utterly black suit, utterly white shirt, dark red tie—but he might as well have been wearing green tanker coveralls with drawstrings at waist and ankles. His mouth was always slightly open; his short white teeth grazed his plump lower lip. He liked to slice the air with his hand. Chop. Chop.

Drills were only part of the weekly class. There was also the humbling return of corrected homework, and kanji tests, and videotapes in which overwrought actors enacted workplace dramas—someone has to make an emergency presentation, someone else almost doesn't land a contract. What a perilous life Woody must be leading. The students conducted general conversations initiated by Yamamoto.

Sheila-san, what did you do last weekend?

Cooked shabu-shabu, did tennnis, worked in the garden, did Japanese study.

Did you, now. Ralph-san?

Grilled beef, did golf, saw a movie, did Japanese study.

Sensei, what did *you* do? somebody usually inquired. There followed a sentence didactically employing modifiers, idioms, and contractions. Yamamoto hopefully attended a Red Sox game, but the pitiable Sox surrendered six runs. At a concert a skillful quartet performed a composition written just for them. A dog was struck on the street and ended up in trouble: dead. During these narrations the incisor-notable mouth, framed at the corners with saliva, was open in its customary smirk, a replica of Feivel Ostroff's anxious smile.

In high school Feivel had put on enough weight to become merely thin. He had learned to giggle less. By the time he and Jay were freshmen together across the river (Feivel's uncle paid for room and board as well as tuition) he was calling himself Phil. He majored in classics; he wrote his senior thesis on Ovid. In Jay's eyes, Feivel-Phil retained the feverish eagerness of a greenhorn, but now he was one man among ten thousand, less odd than many—less bizarre than a couple of Inuits, less exotic than the Ismaili prince, less greasy than the Brooklyn smart alecks shuttling between class and lab, preparing themselves for distinguished scientific careers and, it turned out, a couple of Nobels.

Phil Ostroff paid court to a dowdy Radcliffe girl named Dorothea, also a classicist, whose parents were professors in some college on the prairie. Phil and Dorothea, both summa cum laude, were married right after graduation by a justice of the peace. They went off to graduate school in Chicago, where the university paid them handsome stipends for the honor of their presence.

DURING THE SPRING semester of Japanese III, Passover began on the Saturday night before Easter. This weekend I will attend a religious banquet, Jay said. Bread may not be eaten. Using my dear wife's recipe, my dear daughter will make soup. We will eat chicken, sweet potatoes, fruit, crackers, special fish.

Matzoh, amplified Yamamoto. As for *gefilte*, there is no Japanese equivalent.

Sheila would prepare the traditional Easter meal: ham, sweet potatoes, fruit. One businessman was going to the game and the other would be visiting family in New York and the programmer planned to organize his collection of compact discs. He would arrange them by century first, he said; within century by composer; within composer by . . .

Yamamoto's lower lip stretched under his awning of teeth. Next week we will enjoy hearing about your system. Tonight's class is over.

As for this weekend, Jay insisted. Sensei wa?

The teeth flared at him. I will attend a seder.

A guest at the feast, Jay thought: the stranger in your midst . . . But the teacher went on. My wife will prepare the meal. I will conduct the service.

"In Hebrew?" the startled Jay inquired, in English.

Yamamoto turned his head away from this impertinence. "Hebrew is a difficult tongue," Jay should have said—that would have been a respectful way not to ask the question. But respect be damned—the question and its companions begged for answers.

～

IF YOU HAVE LIVED in Godolphin all of your seventy-seven years except the four in Cambridge, you can find out anything; you know who to ask.

"He's married to a dentist from Worcester," Carol Glickman told Jay. It was June; Jay had lain in wait for her at the library; he knew she went to the senior movies there. "One of those young women who can do it all."

Jay thought of Mika, pregnant again, continuing her career from her home computer, which no doubt converted itself into a changing table after the market closed. "Mrs. Yamamoto . . . Dr. Yamamoto . . . she's Jewish?"

"Yes, whatever we mean by that these days. Some of her family have baal-teshuvaed, become sort-o-dox." Carol laughed. Jay would have laughed in return, but he knew his breath stank from the noxious pills he was now obliged to swallow. Carol paused, went on. "Some of them are probably Quakers or Zennists or whatever. Did you know that Feivel Ostroff's daughter is an Episcopal priest?"

"Feivel wasn't at my reunion," Jay belatedly remembered.

"He died last year. Best-loved teacher at Dartmouth, or was it Williams. Made Latin popular, and Greek too." She paused again. Was he supposed to express condolences?

"How are you, Jay?" she said at last, in a light voice. Her husband, a judge, had served on the Anti-Defamation League with Jay. She was widowed now, like Mika's grandmother. Her hair was dyed, again like Mika's grandmother: the same shade of bark . . . How was he? She could see how he was: yellow and shrunken. She could probably figure the likelihood of his living another year. Jay the actuary had already figured it: zero.

"I'm not long for this world," he said, unmischievously, turning his head to exhale. She opened her mouth, ready to give comfort. "Another time," he begged, and fled.

IN SEPTEMBER HE WENT to High Holy Day services for the first time in years. His grandfather's tallith lent a semblance of flesh to his frame. He sat at the end of the pew, contemplating a quick getaway. The rabbi wore dramatic white robes. She carried the Torah down the aisle, followed by some shuffling elders: his contemporaries, he supposed. She paused at Jay's row, and he managed one of his old playful smiles. His teeth were still good. She waited with her burden, half smiling herself, and he remembered to touch the scroll with his prayer book and bring the book back to his lips, though it grew heavy on the return journey, as if it had acquired the weight of Numbers.

In October he went across the river to a boring lecture on the Japanese economy. In November he went to the Game in the rain, and left at the half. The following week he visited Widener Library on his alumnus pass, fifty dollars a year. The library stacks had recently been strengthened but not reconfigured. Between steel shelves the aisles were as narrow as ever. Standing on Level 3, his feet on the old stone floor, his body brushed by books as gentle as Kyoto schoolchildren, he felt like a boy again. But there was not one volume he cared to read.

He hadn't cared to enroll in Japanese IV, either. He was too weary. But what he'd accomplished gladdened him. He could make his way through children's picture books. He could speak to the *shaineh maideleh* at the Japanese tchotchke shop. He could recognize several hundred kanji; and at night, floating in his bath, he could still draw a few of them on his wasted thigh. At his favorite sushi bar he listened to words flying from one sashimi master to another. Occasionally he fearlessly asked the meaning of an expression. His hematologist, a tiny Indian, urged him to eat and drink anything that agreed with him. Not much agreed with him, but Japanese beer and raw salmon were no worse than oatmeal and applesauce.

Chicken soup did lie lightly on his stomach—Jews were right about that. Wulf's, the only kosher market left in town (there had been half a dozen during his childhood), cooked up a batch every few days and put it in jars. Jay bought a jar on Sunday, ate what he could during the week, threw out the rest. Sunday after Sunday the bearded man at the cash register looked at Jay without recognition. His mind was on higher things, maybe his inventory.

Jay's clothes had grown roomy. On one of his rare good days he bought two pairs of chinos, apparently back in style, at the local Gap. And a navy blazer, size what?—small, God help him. His daughter dropped in every day to say hello and straighten the apartment. They were both silently waiting for the doctor to mention hospice. Meanwhile he could still make his weekly trek to Wulf's.

And it was at Wulf's, on a Sunday morning, that he saw Yamamoto again, and the Yamamoto family, four children in total. Jay stepped behind a rack of spices. From this hiding place he inspected the dentist-wife. She was surprisingly pretty, and slender despite many pregnancies. She was wearing a felt hat with an upturned brim. Fetching. He recognized it as the substitution made by modern Orthodox for the matron's wig. Rich brown hair curled below the hat. She was pushing a cart in which a two-year-old lorded over groceries. Yamamoto walked behind her, wearing an infant in a sling. Two little boys marched in the space between their mother and father, and talked in light voices—English, he noted. The children, even the infant, had the straight black hair of Woody's little son; they had similar dark eyes, too, angled more gently than if their blood were pure. The boys wore yarmulkes. Likewise Yamamoto-san, their Yiddische chichi.

So this was the current trajectory of an immigrant's career—this leap from one ill-favored group into another. What had happened to those necessary decades—generations, even—spent dissembling among the Yankees? Jay the commissioner, Glickman the judge, Fessel the surgeon—how delicately they'd mingled with the favored. And bold Feivel Ostroff, applying himself to pagan texts, had managed a complete metamorphosis. Somewhere a bishopric was no doubt waiting for his daughter the priest . . . And here, where shelves of canned mackerel faced shelves of boxed kasha, the Yamamoto children, crossbred progeny of two outcast clans, confidently trotted. Assimilation had become as passé as the jitterbug.

Forgetting to conceal himself behind the spices, Jay stood up as straight as his pain allowed. He was still what he was born to be—an Anti-Defamation Jew; a citizen of Godolphin, Mass; a loyal Harvard man. Papa Yamamoto was perhaps immune to the lure of the Houses across the river. But in this new world of interchangeable gods, and of females dressed up in priestly robes like drag queens . . . in this world where nations who'd tried to obliterate each other ended up in the same bed, and where your offspring hurled themselves across the planet and forgot to return . . . in such a world the enduring things, really, were bricks and bell towers, a library and a stadium. They remained, they steadied you until the end—flow'rs in your wilderness, stars in your night. He'd reveal this truth to the rabbi when she made her dutiful visit to the almost dead.

A nearby church bell chimed. With his jacket floating around what was left of him, Jay moved from spice rack to register. "Chicken soup," he said, in a voice just audible above the call to the faithful. He received the jar and put money into the impassive hand. "I'll see you next week," Jay promised, or maybe pleaded. It was all the same to the man with the beard.

LINEAGE

"GOOD MORNING, Mrs. Lubin."

Silence.

"Professor Lubin," the doctor corrected, consulting his clipboard.

Silence.

"How are you feeling?"

Contemptuous silence.

"Do you know why you are here?"

Strenuous silence.

"You have suffered a neurological event, a transient ischemic attack . . ."

"Stroke," she said at last. She was lying on a hospital bed whose aluminum side bars were half raised. An unused IV pole stood in a corner of the room. The second bed was unoccupied. A fuzzy Cézanne print hung on the mustard wall.

"Stroke? Well, not yet, we hope not at all. I'm pleased that your voice is so strong. I am Dr. Mortimer Lilyveck and this is Dr. Natalie White and this is Dr. Eric Hauser. Dr. Hauser will ask you a few questions."

Silence.

Dr. Hauser cleared his throat. "What month are we in?"

Her eyes strayed to the window, to the snowy Chicago sky. They returned to Dr. Hauser with a glare.

"Who is the president?"

The glare intensified.

"What is your age? Where were you—"

"Ninety-two," she said. "It should be on your records. I was born in 1914. In Brooklyn." Young Dr. Hauser produced a grimace probably meant to be heartening. It might have earned him the firing squad years ago, far away. "My father was born in Russia," she said, more slowly. "He was the . . . He was . . . He was the . . ." and the voice, suddenly aged, quavering, slipped into a different language. There it regained its strength.

He was the tsar. Little Father.

She spoke rapidly now, in this other tongue.

"*He dressed simply and bathed in cold water. He carried a metal pocket case containing a portrait of his wife, the empress Alexandra. He loved the forceful empress. My mother was not forceful. He did not love my mother.*

You don't wish to hear this history, you indifferent Americans. But there will soon be another ischemic attack . . ."

"Ischemic attack . . ." Dr. Hauser, with a second ghastly smile, seized the familiar words.

"*. . . and so I wish to . . . tell. I am not the last of the Romanovs— there are collateral descendants here and there, one operates a cleaning establishment—and I am not even a legitimate Romanov, and I am not even legitimate; but I am the sole surviving offspring of Nicholas II and Vera Derevenko. I could, if I were so inclined, claim the treasure supposedly residing in a French Bank. I could claim the crown now under glass in Moscow. I could claim all those eggs Fabergé made for my family.*

My mother, Vera Derevenko, was the daughter of a doctor in the royal household. She had trained as a nurse. She and Nicholas copulated in the woods surrounding Nicholas's favorite residence, Tsarskoye Selo, in June 1913, when the world was at peace. And then Vera went back to her St. Petersburg hospital and discovered she was pregnant. She fled to America. There I was born. My father knew nothing of me, he was the tsar."

"Professor Lubin, it would help if you spoke English," said Dr. Lilyveck.

"Whom?"

". . .?"

"Whom would it help?"

"Us."

She made a weary gesture. "The empress Alexandra *and the children, my half siblings, destined to die in a basement, were away at the time, on holiday, in the Crimea. The doctors and tutors, too. Rasputin was drinking and fornicating in another province. Nicholas, head of state, remained in Tsarskoye Selo to examine documents and sign them, to read letters and answer them. Ministers visited him continually. The duma was a joke.*

My mother, too, had stayed behind to arrange some matters for her father the doctor.

The tsar walked alone every day in the woods. She also. Theirs was not an assignation but an accident. I happened by chance.

Have you seen our land in the spring? I myself have not, nor in any other season; but my mother described it to me during her final illness fifty years ago. Mud; well, the mud is famous. A sweet confusion in the woods, young leaves furring the birches, immense red pines, willows. You can hear the new blackbirds. They will be shot . . ."

She aimed two fingers at Dr. White, who did not flinch, did not even lower her eyes.

". . . *in autumn. There was a ravine where crystal water bubbled. On a branch hung a funnel-shaped ladle made of birch. They drank the cold fresh water. They walked along a winding path to an unused hunting lodge. They spoke of Dickens, of Dürer . . . favorite topics of well-bred Russians. In the late-afternoon sun the air was full of amber droplets, and everything was as if bathed in warm tea—the trees, the wet lane, even the faces of the two people who had not yet touched one another. This is the* Russian spring."

Dr. Lilyveck touched his balding head. "There is a translator. She is not in the hospital today."

"My mother's eyes *were hazel and her teeth were widely spaced. Her skin was freckled, her curly hair light brown. As a member of the household, she had seen that Nicholas was prodded and worried by the adored empress and the detested monk. She pitied the Little Father. She was not raped that afternoon, not seduced; seigneurial right was not exercised. She collaborated in her own deflowering. His hands were gentle. His eyes were the brown of a thrush, and his beard too. There was only a little pain. There was extreme sweetness.*

And then came an extraordinary moment. She looked up, into his brown gaze, and she saw his murder, the murder that would take place five years later, in July, Dr. Hauser."

"It's January," he said in a low voice.

"Eight, she saw *eight corpses—man, wife, five children, serving-maid—and a crushed spaniel, dying. The corpses, first shot, were then chopped, drenched in acid, burned, and buried. These meager remains were identified later by the metal photograph case and the skeleton of the spaniel, whose body had been tossed into the grave.*

My mother saw other future things, disconnected images. She saw an open-eyed little girl, dead of typhus, or was it starvation, or was it the bayonet. One of the millions of the Little Father's children to die during the coming civil war. She saw Trotsky in his greatcoat. She saw Zinovyev the apparatchik getting out of a limousine whose seats were covered with bearskin. She saw members of the cheka, blood dripping from their fangs. She saw Lenin dead from stroke or perhaps poison.

When news of these happenings reached her ears in far-off Brooklyn she merely nodded.

Good doctors, there is a figure in Russian legend: a domesticated bear, I cannot remember the name given him, call him Transient Ischemik . . ."

"Transient ischemic, yes," Dr. Hauser encouraged.

". . . *who has the power to foresee the future but not the language to reveal it. He can only gaze at his masters from the hearth—sorrowfully, for the future is always grievous. So it was with my mother—she spoke little, she spoke less, she spoke hardly at all, she might have been an animal. In Brooklyn, despite her nurse's training, she worked as a lowly attendant in an institution for the feebleminded. We lived with an impoverished female cousin. The few sentences my mother did say she said in* Russian."

"The translator will come tomorrow."

"Afterwards they stood and straightened their clothing. He *picked up the framed picture of his wife, which had fallen out of his pocket. He raised my mother's fingers to his lips. Separately they returned to the palace. She never saw him again.*

She would hear many times that he had been autocratic, weak, extravagant, indifferent to his subjects, deserving of the epithet 'Bloody.' She did not contradict.

All this she told me in a spate of verbosity the night she died."

Dr. Lilyveck said, "You need not think of death."

She closed her eyes, banishing him, banishing his two subordinates. She recalled and then chose not to recall her pinched girlhood apartment on Avenue J and the two gloomy women who had raised her; her long and indifferent marriage; her unimportant contributions to topology; her only son, victim of cancer at thirty-five. Another dead Romanov. And she, propped up in a bed under three watchful pairs of eyes . . . might she at this late hour be invested with that old bear's power to envision the future? Plagues, civil disruptions, babies born monstrous—any wag could foretell those catastrophes. No. Her gift was to witness not what was to come but what had been. She thought of the Little Father, Nicholas, abandoned before his death and disregarded afterward, remembered now only by a stroked-out mathematician who had not known him but could nevertheless see khaki garments. Beard. Kindly eyes. Mouth smiling at the freckled nurse who on a warm afternoon had soothed his troubled spirit. A solitary incident, one moment of singular ease, its issue one life of singular unremarkableness: hers. And with her passing would die not the memory of the incident—that memory had perished with Nicholas, with Vera—but the memory of its deathbed telling. The reputation of the tragic tsar . . . no further stain . . .

She opened her eyes. The doctors were still there, writing on their clipboards, exchanging glances, as thorough as the cheka. "My mother was mad," she said hurriedly in English. "Her story was merely an invention," she recanted, "to console me for my shameful birth. The season is winter, Dr. Hauser. The president is . . . a boob."

Dr. White touched her hand. *Little Mother*, she said in the old woman's tongue. *If a lie, a generous one. And if the truth, safe with you and me. Rest now.*

A few minutes later, in the hall, "Natalie," snapped Dr. Lilyveck. "Your command of Russian—an unexpected talent. The patient's prattle: what was it?"

"Mortimer," Dr. White said sweetly. "A folktale, more or less."

Girl in Blue with Brown Bag

THEY HAD MANY THINGS IN COMMON, the man of sixty-seven and the girl of seventeen. They were both undersized. Their eyes were a similar light blue, though Francis's vision was excellent, requiring reading glasses only for very small print, and Louanne's was poor—she glared at the world through spectacles so thick they seemed opaque. They lived in mirror-image apartments on the second floor of a double brownstone. (Such solid burghers' buildings were the mainstay of housing in Boston and its nearer suburbs, Francis said often, probably too often.) Louanne lived in her apartment with her uncle and aunt. Francis lived in his alone. Both preferred ice cream to pastry. Both favored backpacks.

Francis's worn pack was almost empty nowadays. It held a book or two, the morning *Globe*, the neglected reading glasses, the betaine powder he had to mix with water and drink every four hours. But the pack was, he liked to think, his sartorial trademark. During the forty years he'd served in the Great and General Court of Massachusetts—first in the house, then in the senate—he'd disdained a briefcase. His pack had been full then.

Louanne's was full now. It bulged with high school textbooks. She was studying chemistry, calculus, English, French, and Constitutional law. Constitutional law was a new and experimental course for gifted seniors. She had some trouble with it because it presumed a knowledge of American history. She'd come to this streetcar suburb from Russia only two years earlier, as a sophomore; American history was offered in the freshman year.

"American history is finished," she'd muttered to him on a memorable afternoon the previous September. They'd met on the staircase. She was coming home from school, he was going out for a stroll.

"What do you mean, Ms. Zerubin?"

"I mean that I've never learned it and I can't take it now," and she explained further. "Please call me Louanne, Mr. Morrison," she wound up.

Her name was no more Louanne than his was Édouard Vuillard. She'd snatched it from some country singer she'd seen on TV the morning she arrived from Moscow. "All right, Louanne. Please call me . . ." He hesitated. Senator?

"I'll call you Mr. Francis, Mr. Morrison. Mr. Francis, aren't you sort of American history in your own person. You're an embodiment." She was two steps below him. Her raised face was flushed. He saw dandruff in the parting of her dull hair, weasel-brown. "I mean, serving as a lawmaker all those years—you've only just retired, my uncle told me. And your ancestors were Pilgrims. Didn't they sail on one of those ships?"

"The *Pinta*."

"I thought it had another name. Mr. Francis, could I come to you for instruction? I would consider it a weighty favor," she added in an imperious tone.

He backed up a stair. "Oh, my dear, you see, my hobby, looking at paintings, it takes up much of my now freed time. I am a museum trustee, too; I serve on the Acquisitions Committee—"

"Once a week, I could come once a week."

How long had she been planning this attack?

"We get out at noon on Wednesdays," she said. "It's the afternoon the teachers go to meetings." She moved up a stair and threw her backpack beside her feet. He wouldn't be able to descend without leaping over the pack. "You may assign texts," she continued. "I will read them. I am thorough."

He knew she was thorough. She was a thorough housekeeper. On Saturday mornings her aunt left the apartment door open, as did Francis, honoring the unbuttoned quality of the day. He had seen Louanne vacuuming on her knees, reaching her wand far underneath the sofa. She was thoroughly plain—ungroomed, unadorned, her wardrobe limited to jeans and denim jackets—as if she'd made it her mission to complete what nature had begun.

"You may give quizzes," she offered.

He had never seen her with a schoolmate. She was thoroughly friendless . . . And did his retirement really promise to be thoroughly fulfilling? Did *he* have so many friends?

"Instruction?" he said. "Wednesday afternoons? I will consider it a privilege."

And so had begun their modest tutorial, six months earlier, conducted mostly in Francis's living room—they were sitting there today, a cloudy March Wednesday—and sometimes at the museum and sometimes at a nearby pond. They didn't adhere strictly to the original curriculum—the Constitution, the colonial period—but drifted into art and nature and even pedagogy.

"I disapprove of yes-or-no questions. Your essay answer is very good," he said one day, handing her back a test she'd shown him. She'd earned a B-plus.

"What wrong with yes-or-no? Either you remember something or you don't, and if you don't you've got a 50 percent chance . . ."

"A test is a teaching device. It should encourage the student to consider the uncategorical, the ambiguous."

She grumbled a little at that. "I never give my clients tests. They'd throw them back at me." Her clients, three lawyers who'd answered an ad she'd placed in the paper, were perfecting their conversational Russian, which was already excellent.

Sometimes Francis and Louanne strayed into the area of personal history. "You have never married," she remarked one afternoon, with comradely spurning of tact. "Perhaps you prefer men."

"I like women and I like men, both at arm's length." He even liked homely outspoken schoolgirls with an odd attachment to a motherland in ruins.

On a different occasion, pausing near the pond, she'd told him she planned to go back to Russia after high school. "And would not you also return to the country of your birthing?" she demanded of his raised eyebrows.

"Birth," he said; she'd asked him to correct her errors. "I was born here," he said, unable to keep pride out of his voice.

"Then exile is unknown to you."

"Terra incognita," he admitted, but she had no Latin, and he was obliged to explain the phrase.

Today, while a sudden sun turned Francis's pale green room paler, they were worrying the subject of representative government.

"Didn't you ever lose an election?" she asked. "In those whole four decades?" She took off her glasses to clean them, revealing the ice blue eyes, the colorless lashes. She put her glasses back on.

"No, I never lost. But sometimes my opponents were obviously unfit," he said. "The Republicans liked to put up somebody, even if the somebody had no experience, no convictions, no sense of the principles of government."

"But people voted for you also when your opponent was not an asshole. People wanted you. Why?"

"I identify with the commonwealth," he ventured. Then, recognizing eagerness in the almost-imperceptible ripple of her stiff face and the shifting angle of her glasses, he continued. "I see the commonwealth as an extension of myself—its public gardens my flower patch, its public libraries my bookshelves, its police my bodyguard, its ball team my . . ." He glanced at the seventeenth-century map of Massachusetts over the sofa: a retirement gift from his colleagues.

"Please don't stop."

". . . its ball team my sandlot, its state hospitals my mad aunt." He was quoting himself, the curse of old age. But she didn't know that. "I believe that the family, variously defined, defined sometimes as one solitary celibate, is both the paradigm and the ward of the state. I believe that . . ." Now he did stop. "Louanne . . . I think that's enough for now."

"No, please! Tell me about your first senate running."

"Race. We'll take that up another day."

"All right. And another day, we'll go again to the museum."

"Yes."

"Which day?"

Francis looked at his watch. "This day."

THEY GAZED AT THE VUILLARD FIRST, as always. The artist's mother sits in profile at a table, cutting out fabric—the fabric a kind of plaid, her dress a kind of check, the wallpaper dotted with pears. A cupboard is rough country wood. The lamps are unlit and there is no window, but light from an unseen source catches Mme Vuillard's nape, her bun, her ear, the side of her jaw, her spectacles; it catches, too, a brass bowl, and half of a covered dish. The light comes from behind the painter, or from the painter, or from the man and girl now standing in front of the work. "How natural it all looks," he said; he'd said it before. "But a painting is an artificial work"—this was a new topic. " 'It calls for as much cunning as the commission of a crime.' "

She was silent.

"Those are not my words," he admitted.

"The words of Monsieur Vuillard?"

"The words of Monsieur Degas."

"Also a bachelor who lived with his mother?"

"No, he had a more . . . active life."

They moved away. The girl did not care for paintings of bourgeois characters in their parlors any more than she cared for workers' posters—he knew that because he knew what she did care for: frontal Holy Families, coy Annunciations. Someday, an angel might appear to her, too, announcing not love, nothing so ambitious, but perhaps, at last, friendship.

They strolled and looked; then, in the museum's café, they drank tea. Francis ordered ice cream, Louanne a napoleon. "I need its strength," she explained. She was off to meet her clients, now demanding to be taught slang.

"They are up to no good," Francis predicted. "Profiteers."

"I think so, too," she said with indifference. "Though they are rich already." She usually conducted the class at their office, but sometimes at the home of one of the clients, an Italianate villa in a western suburb. She had to take two buses to get there, but she always got sent home in a taxi.

"They want to be richer," Francis told her.

"Doesn't every citizen?"

They said good-bye under an elm tree. Their small figures were probably distorted by the hunch of their backpacks, Francis thought: they could be mistaken for garden sculptures. Louanne headed downtown to the office of her dubious clients. Francis crossed a city park, ghostly purple in the early twilight. "My backyard," he exulted.

Yet there were many things they did not have in common, the retired legislator and the sojourner. Language facility, for instance—Louanne spoke Russian, German, English, and rudimentary French; Francis, despite his schoolboy Latin and Greek, was monolingual. Health, for another example—his shortness was merely hereditary, and his heart condition, discovered by lab tests, gave him little discomfort; she, on the other hand, was stunted, and her eyes would need corrective lenses for the rest of her life, and her aunt knew nothing about nutrition. And politics—the elder Zerubins distrusted all forms of socialism, even the mild redistributive tendency of the Democratic Party. They had voted Republican since naturalizing. As for Louanne, she sneered at the presumption of equality. "So everyone has been given the right to higher education by some deity," she sneered. "And so teachers in slum schools give out A's for rap lyrics, and two-year colleges teach how to sell advertising on television. Democracy!" She would have welcomed the return of the Romanovs.

Still, how comfortable he had become at their Saturday dinners. The beef and barley stew, discs of fat decorating the surface. The salad—potatoes in sour cream, a chopped scallion the meal's one green vegetable. A figgy dessert that you ate with a spoon. The dyed aunt, her sequined sweater one size too small. The bald, jowly uncle. The niece. The overhead chandelier casting a rancid light. A wheezing, arthritic dog. The paintings: offerings of magical events in primary colors, all by the hand of a single untalented émigré. A religious reminder: the Giotto Madonna and Child, its gilt frame matching the halos. Francis thought of his beloved Vuillard; and he moved this worthy family from its beige apartment hung with faux Chagalls and one terrible reproduction of a masterpiece into a room of patterns, sunlit through blinds. Everything would be tactile: the mustache of the man, the over-lipsticked mouth of the woman, the spot of gravy on the denim cuff of the girl who was teaching herself to use her left hand. "For what purpose?" she said, echoing Francis's question. "I want to be ambiguous."

He didn't correct her, partly because others were present, partly because she had perhaps said exactly what she meant. In her left hand the fork waved, wavered, and sometimes overturned.

Afterward uncle and niece played chess, and Mrs. Zerubin did needlework, and Francis and the dog watched the fire. How satisfying domestic life was when you could shut the door on it at the end of the evening and cross the hall and then shut a second door, your own.

ANOTHER WEDNESDAY: April now. They discussed love of money. "De Tocqueville noted it almost two centuries ago," he said.

"You do not love money, Mr. Francis."

"Well, you see, I have never felt poor. And I don't care about . . . oh, fine clothes, or travel, or haute cuisine. And who needs an automobile in this intimate city?"

"So what do you care about? What are your transcendent values?"

She was proud of the phrase; her smirk told him so. Well, if he had to name something: the relative importance of honesty, the primary importance of loyalty . . . "Truth," he heard himself lying.

She sighed. "What besides truth?"

"Beauty," he helplessly admitted.

"Personal beauty?"

He nodded: it was a yes-or-no question.

Her jaw hardened.

"And the beauty of a sycamore," he said, "and of a receding city street, and of a work of art, of course you know that." And the beauty of solitude, he silently added.

"And the beauty of a diamond? I could get you a diamond," she said. "My aunt's cousin Kolya, the rascals he knows . . ."

"Jewels don't interest me." How had he allowed this interrogation to begin? "Civility, that's another of my transcendent values, and also—"

"Beauty," she repeated. "I could get you that."

"What do you mean, Louanne? You have already brought beauty into my life." He withstood her glare. "The beauty of . . . your extraordinary young mind, and of our conversations."

"Yah," she spat.

THREE WEDNESDAYS LATER she came in carrying, by its strong handles, a big brown bag. Her expression was portentous, as if in imitation of an announcing angel. She lowered the bag with officious care and pulled out something surrounded by a narrow frame. She set it on the floor so that it leaned against the grasscloth wall.

It was perhaps twelve by eighteen inches. It was Vuillard's mother again, seen full face—an older face, shadowed: a face that might bend over a grandchild's cradle, say, or the sickbed of an invalid. Broad brow, kindly eyes, and an upper lip that resembled a gentle awning. What she was bending over was a glass vase filled with flowers, mostly daisies, but also anemones and irises. The background was only a suggestion of wallpaper.

The painting was signed.

"I saw it weeks ago," Louanne said, shrugging out of her navy peacoat. "In that house. It was in some sort of guest bedroom just to the side of the bathroom. I went to pee and I opened that door—it's always closed—and I put on the light and I saw it."

"Louanne," in a whisper.

"I wasn't surprised—the house is full of stuff like this. They're loaded, those thugs. They buy stuff to wash money, you know that, Mr. Francis. In Russia they get more loaded, like you said."

". . . *as* you said."

"As. So I took it. Yesterday. Because the guy's wife has left him, and he's going to Moscow tomorrow, and no one will know it's missing for weeks, and then he'll think she—"

"Louanne," he said, still breathless.

"It wasn't just hanging there for anyone to grab, don't think that," she said. "There was this security clasp I had to figure out. And getting the bag—that was no picnicking, either. I had to buy a scarf at Bloomie's, and ask for the bag from the bitch saleswoman, and then return the scarf the next day and keep the bag."

"Louanne." It seemed to be all he could say. His chest hurt.

She stood before him, sturdy as a guard, not quite his height. "What?"

Personal property, it's a right, he thought. *Thieving, it's a crime*, he thought. *There's a social compact*, he thought.

But she knew all that. She had memorized ethical principles the way she might have memorized the rules for rolling out pastry—stuff she would recite but never practice. And he would not rebuke her. Loyalty was what counted most; he'd told her that, or meant to.

"Aren't you going to say anything?" she said, hands on hips.

"Thank you," he managed.

HE HUNG THE PAINTING, the following Tuesday—it had taken him that long to decide where. He'd thought first of hanging it in the bedroom—no one else went in there except the cleaning woman. He thought of his small study: roses on the carpet, lilies on the wallpaper, books, a flame-stitch armchair, and cockatooed draperies almost concealing the single narrow window. He considered the kitchen and the bathroom and the communal hall between his apartment and hers; he considered the back stairway, whose steps wore rubber treads. He considered his clothes closet.

In the end he hung it in the living room, over the fireplace. The portrait of his great-grandfather (attorney general of the commonwealth, 1875–1880) was relegated to the bedroom, replacing the mirror, which itself went into the back of the clothes closet, appearing to double his thrifty wardrobe.

His great-grandfather, bearded, one hand resting on the laws of the commonwealth, had thrown his noble gaze across the room at the early map of Massachusetts. Portrait and map had provided an axis of honor. The Vuillard corrupted the room.

"Attractive," said a former colleague who'd come over for some advice. "New?"

"Relocated," Francis said, holding his breath. The conversation turned to the present governor, such a dimwit.

"Oooh, Mr. Morrison," said the cleaning woman.

"Nice," said the man who came to fix a leak in the bathtub, but he seemed to be referring to the apartment in general.

Louanne's glasses glinted at the painting on her first few visits after the bestowal; then they didn't. She was writing a paper on the Electoral College. Discussions of that valuable, antiquated procedure occupied their sessions. At the Zerubins' they talked about dogs and baseball.

Nowhere could he find news of the theft. The painting had probably been stolen to begin with. He could not identify it in the catalogue raisonné; even under the heading "Privately Held" he could not find *Mme Vuillard with Flowers* or anything like it. Still, its most recent possessor must have noted its absence by now. Perhaps the Russian mafia was making confident plans to kill him.

Louanne was still teaching those dirty lawyers. "And the one in the grand house, if he should mention that he's been robbed?" asked Francis.

"He hasn't mentioned."

"If he does?"

"In which language?"

"Oh . . . English."

"I'll say: 'Speak Russian.' "

"In Russian, then."

"I'll look sympathetic." To demonstrate, she slanted her head and pursed the corners of her mouth, an executioner checking the knot on a noose.

He loved the gift she had given him. As time passed he did not love it less. Nor did he get used to it: the woman's head so close that her voice could almost be heard; the economy of line and the limited palette; the slight distortion of the angle of the head; the lack of a grand idea. The humble daisies. A humble artist: secondary even in his heyday.

"Our constitution is more specific than yours, because we do not rely on the judiciary," she was saying one Wednesday. "Judges were considered an extension of the Little Father, and—"

"Yes," Francis said, though he was not certain of the accuracy of her statement. "Louanne, my dear, we must relinquish the painting."

Her glasses stared at him.

"I cherish it," he went on. "But it is too much for me. I will die of it."

"You will die of a heart attack. Isn't that why you take that powdered stuff?"

"The betaine is to *prevent* my dying."

"To delay it. Anyway, no one ever died from beauty."

"Then I will be the first."

Silence while she surveyed him. It occurred to him, not for the first time, that her spectacles probably reduced what was before them. "I've still got the big brown bag," she admitted. "But I've been teaching those crooks at their office lately. I don't know when I'll be at the house again."

"We cannot return it to them, Louanne. It demands a public place. A shared arena, a location where any person, moneyed or penniless, cultured or gross, passionate or indifferent, can benefit from its—"

"Mr. Francis?"

He halted. With effortful simplicity he said: "It belongs at the museum."

"Oh. So donate it."

"Well, no, not with its murky provenance." He did not want her deported. "We must slip it in."

"Like a bomb?"

"Like a bomb."

"My great-great-uncle threw a bomb. They shot him for it. Asshole."

She was referring to her relative, he hoped.

"Good morning, Nick."

"Mr. Morrison, good morning," the guard said. "Good to see you. Ah . . . the young lady will have to check her parcel."

He had hoped for exactly this: that the Big Brown Bag would prove a distraction, that his familiar backpack, rarely challenged, would not be challenged now, though it wasn't the familiar one after all. It was new, considerably bigger, still fairly flat though.

"The young lady is well known to me; she's carrying her art supplies," Francis said. "Show him, Louanne." And Louanne, feigning resentment, pulled out one by one a sketch pad, a sketch board, and pencils bound in their middle by a rubber band, fanning in both directions just as Vuillard's daisies fanned upward from the mouth of the vase and their stalks downward into the expertly rendered water. Louanne then turned the bag upside down. A paper clip fell onto the floor.

"She's going to copy a Rembrandt," Francis confided. "Drawing a painting, it trains the hand." The guard had to turn his attention to the visitor behind them. Louanne scraped up her tools.

They trotted upstairs to the Rembrandts. Louanne put some lines on paper. Then they trotted downstairs again, to the members' lounge. From there they went to the trustees' rooms and from there slipped down an out-of-the-way staircase to the basement and then farther, to the basement of the basement. There stood a dozen lockers, a few closed and padlocked, the rest ajar.

She helped him off with his backpack as if it were an overcoat and she a maid, a maid in a blue denim shirtwaist. He'd never before seen her in a dress. Francis unzipped the pack. Louanne withdrew the item without removing its bubble wrap. Francis slid it gently into a locker and closed the door.

Louanne took a padlock from her pocket, slipped it through matched metal loops, snapped it shut. She offered him the key on her palm. He shook his head. Her fingers closed over it.

Later, he figured, she'd swallow the key. She'd probably been practicing the maneuver. No matter: the painting would escape from captivity, in ten years or maybe fifteen—whenever a committee of janitors determined that the locker was abandoned. The padlock would be forced open, the locker's secret brought to the director. A mild excitement would flutter the art world. Somebody would judge the painting authentic; somebody else would declare it an anonymous donation; the curious manner of its donation would be remarked. It would be hung on the wall of a numbered room. But first it would be displayed in an exhibition of recent acquisitions. He'd mail her an invitation and a round-trip plane ticket.

Following the girl up one stairway and the next, stopping for breath on each skimpy landing, he acknowledged to himself that Louanne might by then have vanished into a dark corner of Moscow, he into the blinding fluorescence of a nursing home. "*Ars longa*," he muttered.

She turned her head. "Just a few more steps," she assured him.

Jan Term

February 5

Dear Ms. Jenkins,

    Josephine Salter has informed me that Caldicott Academy will not grant an extension for her Jan Term paper until you receive a request from me. Consider this that request. Of course Josephine could not meet the deadline; there was an upheaval in her family due to her stepmother's unexpected return on January 31 after a two-month absence. You probably know, too, as does most of the town, that her father greeted his wife's homecoming by throwing crockery at the wall and pouring Scotch into the family's aged computer. Josie and young Oliver, whom the family calls Tollie, were more welcoming.

    Let me say, for whatever it's worth, that Josie was an asset to Forget Me Not during January—the customers miss her respectful presence and I miss her height. Standing on only a telephone book she could reach bibelots from my highest shelf. She seems to have learned something about antiques, too. Nevertheless, I continue to think that Jan Term is Caldicott Academy's devious method of giving teachers an extra month's paid vacation and in the process driving parents frantic with worry. The fifteen-year-old girls who volunteer at shelters, veterinary establishments, ethnic restaurants, and Central American villages are at risk for TB, psittacosis, salmonella, seduction, kidnapping, and deep boredom. Josie, working at my store, at least avoided the first five.

    How are you, Eleanor? I've got an Edwardian inkwell you might want to take a look at.

                                                          Rennie

February 15

Dear Ms. Jenkins,

Thank you for granting me an extension for my Jan Term paper. I didn't need as much time as I first thought. Per your suggestion, I had kept daily notes on three-by-five cards, and as you predicted, it was not onerous to, after reading over the cards several times and arranging and rearranging them as if playing FreeCell* and thinking about them deeply, make an outline. (The preceding sentence demonstrates why you should not split an infinitive, so I left it in rather than correct it in case you need a reality example for the tenth-grade grammar unit.) My outline followed the helpful schema you provided: Why I Chose, What I Did, Some Things I Learned. After constructing the outline, writing the essay was pretty straightforward. I made the required three drafts on three successive days, starting on the morning my father gave me a typewriter (our computer had met with an accident). I found footnotes useful and deployed them according to <u>The Chicago Manual of Style</u>, numbering sequentially.

And so here is my paper, which I dedicate to my late mother. As you may know, though it was before your time, she too attended Caldicott Academy. She often shared with me her school-day memories, though she called them flashbacks. LOL.

Josie

* Similar to Solitaire

My original plan for a Jan Term project was to read to the blind. I'm told that I have a pleasing voice. Before she died of a tumor[1] my mother lost her vision, and so I read to her every afternoon just as she had read to me when I was little, mostly <u>Grimm's Fairy Tales</u>, our favorite book. But readers to the blind are sent all over the Boston area, hither and yon, and I needed a workplace close to my stepbrother Tollie's day care center, since his own mother was not at home at the time and therefore I was in charge of him and also of our household, which numbered three. So I applied to Forget Me Not, a nearby antique shop, because you can learn a lot of history from the artifacts of the past. Ms. Renata McLintock, owner and proprietor, warned me that what I would learn mostly was cleaning and a steady hand in pouring liquids, and she hoped that my progressive, prolapsed[2] school had taught me how to compute the 5 percent Massachusetts sales tax and that I would remember to do so.[3]

In this paper I will refer to Ms. McLintock as "Rennie," since she asked me to call her that. She doesn't know where her mother dug up Renata.[4] Rennie was right about what I would mainly do. I vacuumed the floor and the furniture (I did that at home in January, too) and I scrubbed the little bathroom in back and then dumped

---

1 Glioblastoma

2 <u>Sic</u>

3 I think she was joking but maybe not—some people have forgotten elementary arithmetic. Tina, my stepmother, cannot even balance a checkbook, though she is an excellent guitarist and knows all about hemidemisemiquavers and can follow directions as to rhythm and speed and can also ignore them when interpretation demands. I can compute 5 percent of anything in my head and I can also do elementary calculus. So can Tollie, who is four.

4 My mother got Josephine from <u>Little Women</u> and Dorothy from <u>The Wizard of Oz</u>.

the contents of the pail into the window boxes, for which I was responsible.[5] I climbed a ladder and polished the brass chandelier which dates from 1775 or thereabouts. It has been wired and fitted with 60-watt bulbs.

Those were my computational and cleaning duties. Some were daily and some were weekly. Also I assisted Rennie at hostessing tasks. Forget Me Not is like the village well of colonial times, a period we studied last year. At the village well, news and gossip and advice were exchanged. Women went away from it with water and also with strength and self-esteem, though some did find pleasure in making others feel wrong or stupid. But of this unpleasant type there were only a few at Forget Me Not. I will mention a particular person later. Also we have many customers who come in just to chat and don't buy anything. Some want a smattering of comfort, like the one whose daughter had gotten rolled over by Princeton,[6] and others want a lot of solace, like the woman whose son had just died.[7] I became able to tell the difference between the two and to make tea for the first type and for the second type to pour sherry without spilling any.

This takes me to the main part of my paper: What I Learned at Forget Me Not in addition to techniques of polishing metal and how to wheedle the credit card machine into working. I learned the distinguishing features of various jewelry styles: Victorian, art nouveau, art deco, and post–World War II until about 1950 (Rennie doesn't carry anything later than 1950). Victorian is delicate and elaborate. Art nouveau is inspired by natural and mythological themes like dragonflies or enchanted women, set in sinuous designs. Art deco is geometric and employs motifs like ziggurats and lozenges. World War II introduced synthetic materials, and Rennie has some Bakelite slave bracelets that look like butterscotch silk. All

---

5   I learned this gardening technique from Tina, a conservationist. Scummy water is good for houseplants and outdoor plants alike, though Mrs. Bluestein, Caldicott's science teacher as you know, says she's from Missouri, a remark which apparently indicates disbelief.

6   Not admitted in the first batch

7   AIDS

this jewelry and estate silver and Chinese ceramics are the store's bread and butter. Rennie's particular specialties are pottery made by the Saturday Evening Girls and Victorian mourning jewelry.

The Saturday Evening Girls grew out of the arts and crafts movement in England of the 1870s, based on the reformist ideals of John Ruskin and William Morris. Those two important men advocated a return to hand craftsmanship, not just for aesthetic quality but also for the purpose of furthering social and educational goals.[8] At the turn of the nineteenth century, in Boston's crowded North End, just a few miles from Forget Me Not, a group of young Italian and Jewish immigrant women gathered on Saturday nights to make ceramics, guided by an altruistic socialite.[9] She wanted the Girls to earn money and also work in a healthy and uplifting environment. But people didn't buy the pottery, because its prices were higher than mass-produced wares. Now the dishes are prized and collectors pay a lot of money for them, often to Rennie. The pottery is simple and colorful and sometimes decorated with barnyard motifs; if you didn't know it was urban, you might call it rustic. Either way it is pretty—Rennie and I both think so.

Victorian mourning jewelry is a horse from a different glue factory.[10] Rennie and I don't much care for it but it is all the rage today, and a few Goth girls of my acquaintance (not Caldicott students) wear gutta-percha hair ornaments decorated with death's heads. Mourning jewelry was meant to be a souvenir to remember a loved one and also a reminder of the inevitability of death. Mourning rings reached the height of popularity in England after the death

---

8 I would note that this is in keeping with Caldicott Academy's own high ideals.

9 The North End is still mostly Italian. Tina is of Italian descent and has acquaintances there. She stayed with a particular Friend all the time she wasn't with us, experiencing her own Jan Term as she said to me. She came every weekday to visit Tollie at his day care center. I am putting this down because I know there is a rumor that she is an indifferent mother. She is a very good mother. Some people confuse mothering with housekeeping.

10 Rennie's phrase

of Prince Albert, in December 1869.[11] In England, rings were often inscribed with the name, age, and date of death of the lost person. Early rings were made of black enamel. Later ones were jet.

Since this is a research and observation paper, I have mostly kept anecdotes and speculations and digressions out of it or tucked them into footnotes that a reader can skip. Anyway, I am taking Journal Writing next semester. I did observe the operational details of a small retail business, so I will report on that. Rennie let me look at her ledger, which is of the pen-and-ink variety. Her accountant urged her to get a computer but finally said "Oh hell."[12] In Rennie's handwriting, each letter and number slants at a 60-degree angle to the line. It's more legible than many fonts.[13] Rennie also took me with her on a few house calls. I saw how shrewd you have to be at sizing up the worth of individual items and also entire roomfuls of stuff. In one huge mansion the owner had just died[14] and there was wonderful silver, as you would expect. But in a couple of awful apartments, Rennie found some unusual objets d'art. She always paid what they were worth, though of course not as much as she hoped to sell them for.

I also observed and attempted to emulate her various ways of dealing with customers beyond serving tea and/or sherry to the obviously unhappy ones. She shows patience to people who can't make up their minds and also to those who need to think it over, which really means ask their husbands. She is firm with dealers who want a deep discount. She allows returns always. She puts up with a lot but doesn't put up with everything. For instance, that unlikable woman referred to earlier came in frequently just to gab. The woman usually didn't pay attention to me, but one day when Rennie was finishing up with somebody else she asked me to show her a jet mourning ring. I did, and told her that the finest jet was

---

11 Typhoid fever

12 <u>Sic</u>

13 Rennie's penmanship is called Copperplate. It was developed in England in the eighteenth century. Early American copybooks continued the use of this plain script. Caldicott is considering returning to cursive instruction in the early grades, an excellent idea but too late for me.

14 Myocardial infarction

mined in Whitby, England. Whitby got used too much, and today it is illegal to mine there because the only jet left is in seams in the cliffs over the town. To remove it from the cliffs would cause them to tumble down. In this case, overmining led to undermining. In the middle of my mini-lecture, which I had practiced on other customers with good results (i.e., sales), she said, too sincerely, You have a beautiful voice. Then she said, Who are you? and I told her my name, first, middle, last. She said Salter I know your family your mother was a saint your stepmother is a slattern your father is a tyrant. Like that, with no punctuation. I'm surprised she didn't say your brother is on the spectrum. Rennie hustled her out in thirty seconds, maybe less, mentioning untruthfully that we were going on a house call, and she actually turned on the alarm and locked the door with the three of us outside it for verisimilitude. We watched the woman go away.[15] Then we went next door to the deli and had lunch, which Rennie paid for (usually I bring a Tupperware container of last night's meat loaf, or macaroni with a little lettuce from the night before that, or creamed chipped beef from even earlier if it hasn't gone bad). Over lunch Rennie gave me a recipe for All-Week-Long minestrone, a vegetable soup that lasts from Sunday through Saturday. I would have made it on the weekend but Tina came home and we went back to takeout, which Tollie prefers anyway. It was that lunchtime that I told Rennie that Tollie's breakfast

---

15 This is perhaps the place to correct the woman's mistakes. My mother was not a saint. She didn't do anything to end wars or cool the globe or rescue the homeless. When a pie crust crumbled she told it to fuck itself [sic]. She was very nearsighted and didn't sew, and even wearing her eyeglasses, she blinked a lot, which because she was so tall made her look like a confused giraffe, but not a saint. Tina is not a slattern, just disorganized. She's twenty-three. She was eighteen when she met my father and got pregnant with Tollie. While she was staying in the North End with her Friend, she thought about her life here and came to the conclusion that its pluses outweighed its minuses. My father is not a tyrant. He's absentminded and preoccupied with biostatistical research and sometimes gets quite irritable, but he's turning over a new leaf. My brother is on the spectrum. I love him very much even when he stares silently into his thoughts, maybe especially then.

every day is a scoop of vanilla ice cream and half a cup of coffee. He won't eat anything else. Very few people would have refrained from comment, but Rennie just nodded. Very few people have the discreetness to run a village well. I hope I can attain that quality, as I am thinking of the antique business as a career.

I will conclude with a discussion of old spectacles. Rennie acquired a small collection of them from a gentleman who was selling some clocks she really wanted. She asked me to make the glasses my project, so I numbered them and arranged them in large box which I lined with velvet, and I did some research and wrote its results on a placard in an elegant font (we still had a computer) as follows:

A BRIEF HISTORY OF SPECTACLES

The ancients used reading stones—single pieces of glass which magnified what was before them. The Franciscan friar Roger Bacon (1220–1292) determined that a convex (converging) lens could assist people with weak or aged eyes (presbyopia). In Florence, nineteenth-century glassmakers produced concave (diverging) lenses for nearsighted (myopic) persons. But all these aids were single lenses only. The earliest pictorial record of eyeglasses is <u>Saint Jerome in His Study</u>, by Ghirlandajo. This shows that eyeglasses were made not necessarily during the time of Saint Jerome (347–420) but definitely during the time of Ghirlandajo (1449–1494). They have been in use ever since, with frames of gold, copper, leather, bone, baleen, and tortoiseshell. Benjamin Franklin invented bifocals.

In this display you see nineteenth-century spectacles showing Victorian tendencies—filigreed gold, ivory ornaments, and, in one pair (#4), a setting for jewels on the temple pieces. The jewels themselves have been lost. Very few of these spectacles have any refraction (prescription) in their lenses, which indicates that they were used mainly for adornment, but the pair without temple pieces (#2, pince-nez) does magnify greatly, and the steel-framed eyeglasses (#7) were made for a very nearsighted person.

I sold three spectacles, each for $50, making a net profit of $150—Rennie pointed out that the spectacles had cost her nothing because they were baksheesh[16] from the gentleman unloading clocks. She showed me that the entry in the ledger mentioned only the clocks. She wanted me to take the $150, but I reminded her that Jan Term is supposed to be a volunteer activity. Then take a pair of glasses, she said, sort of snappishly. So I chose a pair with no refraction, because my eyes are twenty-twenty, like my father's. My glasses have plain silver frames in an oblong shape. I wore them one night while I was making dinner and my father and Tollie were playing their preprandial chess game. While I was sautéing tofu, I felt my father looking at me, and finally he said, You have restored your mother to our household. This shows how wearing spectacles can alter a person's appearance and even influence the vision of a bystander! Then Tollie said "Checkmate," for the first time ever, which shows how even an adept adult can be bested by a child if he (the adult) is not paying full attention. I include these instances to demonstrate that during Jan Term I acquired unexpected information. The most important off-label thing I learned was that non-inquisitiveness like Renata McLintock's, along with just plain Being There, beats all the good intentions of friends and neighbors, even the ones who left casseroles on the back porch.

Establishments like Forget Me Not help preserve things of the past, and this adds to our general knowledge of history. Antique stores have been criticized for pandering to what's low in human nature—acquisitiveness and narcissism. But the acquisition of items gives aesthetic pleasure to those who acquisition them as well as to those who will view them in their eventual resting places, museums. As for narcissism, I do believe it is here to stay. The art of personal adornment has been practiced ever since Eve found out she was naked. Also, people like to buy other people beautiful things to show their love. My father bought Tina a welcome-home present of demantoid garnet earrings dating from late in the Belle Époque.[17] He gave her one earring and left the other in Rennie's safe, to be reclaimed in the future, a kind of good-behavior reward. That's his way, and Tina says she can live with it now.

---

16 Baksheesh means free but for the purpose of sweetening the deal.

17 1871–1914

Elder Jinks

Grace and Gustave were married in August, in Gustave's home—a squat, brown-shingled house whose deep front porch darkened the downstairs rooms. The house lot had ample space for a side garden. But there were only rhododendrons and azaleas, hugging the building, and a single apple tree stranded in the middle of the lawn. Every May, Gustave dragged lawn chairs from the garage to the apple tree and placed them side by side by side. When Grace had first seen this array, in July, she was reminded of a nursing home, though she wouldn't say anything so hurtful to Gustave—a man easily bruised, which you could tell from the way he flushed when he took a wrong turn, say, or forgot a proper name. So she simply crossed the grass and moved one of the chaises so that it angled against another, and then adjusted the angle. "They're snuggling now." The third chair she overturned. Gustave later righted it.

They had met in June in front of a pair of foxes who made their own reluctant home at Bosky's Wild Animal Preserve, on Cape Cod. Gustave was visiting his sister in her rented cottage. Grace had driven in from western Massachusetts with her pal Henrietta. The two women were camping in the state park.

"You're living in a tent?" Gustave inquired on that fateful afternoon. "You look as fresh as a flower."

"Which flower?" Grace was a passionate amateur gardener as well as a passionate amateur actress and cook and hostess. Had she ever practiced a profession? Yes, long ago; she'd been a second-grade teacher until her own children came along to claim her attention.

"Which flower? A hydrangea," Gustave answered, surprised at his own exhilaration. "Your eyes," he explained, further surprised, this time at his rising desire.

Her tilted eyes were indeed a violet blue. Her skin was only slightly lined. Her gray hair was clasped by a hinged comb that didn't completely contain its abundance. Her figure was not firm, but what could you expect.

"I'm Grace," she said.

"I'm Gustave," he said. He took an impulsive breath. "I'd like to get to know you."

She smiled. "And I you."

GRACE WAS EMPLOYING a rhetorical locution popular in her Northampton crowd—eclipsis: the omission of words easily supplied. Gustave, after a pause, silently supplied them. Then he bowed. (His late mother was Paris-born; he honored her Gallic manners even though—except for five years teaching in a Rouen lycée—he had lived his entire life in the wedge of Boston called Godolphin.)

Grace hoped that this small man bending like a headwaiter would now brush her fingers with his mustache—but no. Instead he informed her that he was a professor. His subject was the history of science. Her eyes widened—a practiced maneuver, though also sincere. Back in Northampton, her friends (there were scores of them) included weavers, therapists, advocates of holistic medicine, singers. And of course professors. But the history of science, the fact that science even had a history—somehow it had escaped her notice. Copernicus? Oh, Newton, and Einstein, yes, and Watson and what's his name. "Crick," she triumphantly produced, cocking her head in the flirtatious way . . .

"Is your neck bothering you?"

. . . that Hal Karsh had hinted was no longer becoming. She straightened her head and shook hands like a lady.

GUSTAVE HAD WRITTEN a biography of Michael Faraday, a famous scientist in the nineteenth century, though unknown to Grace. When he talked about this uneducated bookbinder inspired by his own intuition, Gustave's slight pomposity melted into affection. When he mentioned his dead wife he displayed a thinner affection, but he had apparently been a widower a long time.

In Northampton, Grace volunteered at a shelter, tending children who only irregularly went to school. "Neglected kids, all but abandoned by their mothers," she said, "mothers themselves abandoned by the kids' fathers." Gustave winced. When she went on to describe the necessity of getting onto the floor with these youngsters, instructor and pupils both cross-legged on scabby linoleum, Gustave watched her playfulness deepen into sympathy. She'd constructed an indoor window box high up in the makeshift basement schoolroom; she taught the life cycle of the daffodil, "its biography, so to speak," including some falsities that Gustave gently pointed out. Grace nodded in gratitude. "I never actually studied botany in my university," she confessed. The University of Wichita, she specified; later she would mention the University of Wyoming, but perhaps he had misheard one or the other—he'd always been vague about the West.

A LAWYER FRIEND of Gustave's performed the wedding ceremony in the dark living room. Afterward Grace sipped champagne under the apple tree with Gustave's sister. "Oh, Grace, how peaceable you look. You'll glide above his little tantrums."

"What?" Grace said, trying to turn toward her new sister-in-law but unable to move her head on her shoulders. A Godolphin hairdresser had advised the severe French twist that was pulling cruelly at her nape; Henrietta had urged the white tulle sombrero; Grace herself had selected the dress, hydrangea blue and only one size too small. Her grandchildren, who with their parents had taken the red-eye from San Francisco, marveled at the transformation of their tatterdemalion Gammy—but where had her hair gone to? "What?" said the stiffened Grace again; but Gustave's sister forbore to elaborate, just as she had failed to mention that Gustave's first wife, who had died last January in Rouen, had divorced him decades ago, influenced by a French pharmacist she'd fallen in love with.

Gustave and Grace honeymooned in Paris, indulging themselves mightily—a hotel with a courtyard, starred restaurants, a day in Giverny, another in Versailles. They even attended a lecture on the new uses of benzene—Gustave interested in the subject; Grace, with little French and less science, interested in the somber crowd assembled at the Pasteur Institute. They both loved the new promenade and the new *musée*, and they sat in Sainte-Chapelle for two hours listening to a concert performed on old instruments—two recorders and a lute and a viola da gamba. That was the most blissful afternoon. Gustave put the disarray of their hotel room out of his mind, and also the sometimes fatiguing jubilation with which Grace greeted each new venture. Grace dismissed her own irritation at Gustave's habit of worrying about every dish on the menu—did it matter how much cream, how much butter, we all had to die of something. Light streamed through the radiant window, turning into gold his trim mustache, her untidy chignon.

AND NOW IT WAS SEPTEMBER, and classes had begun. Gustave taught Physics for Poets on Mondays, Wednesdays, and Fridays at nine, The Uses of Chemistry those same days at ten. He taught a graduate seminar in the philosophy of science on Thursday evenings. The first two weeks the seminar met in the usual drafty classroom. But then Grace suggested . . . Gustave demurred . . . she persisted . . . he surrendered. And so on the third week the seminar met in the brown-shingled house. Grace baked two apple tarts and served them with warm currant jelly. The students relived last Saturday's football game. Gustave—who, like Grace, professed a hatred of football—quietly allowed the conversation to continue until everyone had finished the treat, then turned the talk to Archimedes. Grace sat in a corner of the living room, knitting. The next day marked their first separation since the wedding. Gustave had a conference in Chicago. He'd take a cab to the airport right after The Uses of Chemistry. Early that morning he'd packed necessary clothing in one half of his briefcase. While he was reading the newspaper she slipped in a wedge of apple tart, wrapped in tinfoil. After they kissed at the doorway his eye wandered to the corner she had occupied on the previous evening. The chair was still strewn with knitting books and balls of yarn and the garment she was working on, no doubt a sweater for him. She'd already made him a gray one. This wool was rose. His gaze returned to his smiling wife. "See you on Sunday," he said.

"Oh, I'll miss you."

She did miss him, immediately. She would have continued to miss him if she had not been invaded, half an hour later, by two old Northampton friends bearing Hal Karsh. Hal was visiting from his current perch in Barcelona. He would return to Spain on Sunday. Hal—master of the broken villanelle, inventor of the thirteen-line sonnet; and oh, that poetic hair brushing his eyebrows, hair still mostly brown though he was only eight years younger than Grace. Those long fingers, adept at pen and piano but not at keyboard—the word processor was death to composition, he'd tell you, and tell you why, too, at length, anywhere, even in bed.

Gustave's upright piano could have used a tuning. Grace had meant to call someone, but she had been too busy putting in chrysanthemums and ordering bulbs and trying to revive her high school French. The foursome made music anyway. Lee and Lee, the couple who brought Hal, had brought their fiddles, too. Grace rummaged in a box of stuff not yet unpacked and found her recorder. Later she brewed chili. They raided Gustave's *cave*. They finally fell into bed—Lee and Lee in the spare room, Hal on the floor in Gustave's study, Grace, still dressed, on the marital bed. Then on Saturday they drove to Walden Pond and to the North Shore, and on Saturday night Cambridge friends came across the river. This time Grace made minestrone, in a different pan—the crock encrusted with chili still rested on the counter.

Hal wondered what Grace was doing in a gloomy house in a town that allowed no overnight parking. Such a regulation indicated a punitive atmosphere. And this husband so abruptly acquired—who was he, anyway? "She picked him up in a zoo, in front of a lynx," Lee and Lee told him. He hoped they were exercising their artistic habit of distortion. Hal loved Grace, with the love of an indulged younger brother, or a ragtag colleague—years ago he and she had taught at the same experimental grade school, the one that demanded dedication from its faculty but didn't care about degrees. (Hal did have a master's, but Grace had neglected to go to college.) Hal thought Grace was looking beautiful but unsettled. Did her new spouse share her taste for illicit substances, did he know of her occasional need to decamp without warning? She always came back . . . When Hal had mentioned that the Cambridge folks would bring grass, Grace's eyes danced. Well, nowadays it was less easy to get here. In Barcelona you could pick it up at your to-bacconist, though sometimes the stuff was filthy . . .

This batch was fine. They all talked as they smoked; and recited poetry; and after a while played Charades. It was like the old times, he thought. He wished Henrietta had come along, too. "I have no use for that fussbudget she married," Henrietta had snapped. But the fussbudget was in Chicago.

It was like the old times, Grace, too, was thinking. And how clever they all were at the game; how particularly clever in this round, Lee and Lee standing naked back to back while she, fully clothed, traversed the living room floor on her belly. Odd that no one had yet guessed "New Deal." Odd, too, that no one was talk-ing, though a few moments earlier there had been such merry laughter; and Hal, that man of parts, had put two of his fingers into his mouth and whistled. At Lee? Or at Lee? In silence Grace slithered toward the hall and saw, at eye level, a pair of polished shoes. Pressed trousers rose above the shoes. She raised her head, as an eel never could—perhaps she now resembled a worm, ruin-ing the tableau. The belt around the trousers was Gustave's—yes, she had given it to him; it had a copper buckle resembling a sun-burst within which bulged an oval turquoise. When it was hanging from his belt rack among lengths of black and brown leather with discreet matching buckles, the thing looked like a deity, Lord of the closet. Now, above dark pants, below striped shirt, it looked like a sartorial error, a *misalliance* . . .

Scrambling to her feet, she found herself staring at Gustave's shirt. Where was his jacket? Oh, the night was warm, he must have taken it off before silently entering the house fifteen hours before he was expected. Her gaze slid sideways. Yes, he had placed—not thrown—his jacket on the hall chair; he had placed—not dropped—his briefcase next to that chair. She looked again at her husband. His exposed shirt bore a large stain in a rough triangular shape—the shape, she divined, of a wedge of tart. She touched it with a trembling forefinger.

"That tender little gift of yours—it leaked," he said.

He surveyed his living room. That naked couple had attended his wedding, had drunk his champagne. A pair of know-it-alls.

Their names rhymed. The other creatures he had never seen before. A skinny fellow with graying bangs advanced toward him.

"Gustave, I want you to meet—," Grace began.

"Ask these people to leave," he said in a growl she had never before heard.

They seeped away like spilled pudding . . . Lee and Lee, first, dressed in each other's clothing, clutching their overnight cases and instruments, kissing Hal on the rush toward their car and its overnight parking tickets. They didn't kiss Grace. The Cambridge crowd didn't kiss anybody. But Hal—he stood his ground. He was a head taller than Gustave. He extended a hand. "I'm—"

"Good-bye."

"Listen here—"

"Get out!"

He got out, with his satchel in his left hand and, in the curve of his right arm, Grace. At the last minute she turned as if to look at Gustave, to plead with him, maybe—but it was only to snatch up her pocketbook from the hall table. Next to the pocketbook she saw a cone of flowers. Sweet peas, baby's breath, a single gerbera. An unimaginative bouquet; he must have picked it up ready-made at the airport stall.

GUSTAVE CLIMBED THE STAIRS. The guests had apparently cavorted mostly on the first floor; except for the two unmade beds in the spare room, the only sign of their occupation were towels like puddles on the bathroom tiles. He went into his study and his eye flew to the bookcase where, in manuscript, between thick bindings, stood his biography of Faraday, still in search of a publisher. No one had stolen it. On the carpet lay a book—open, facedown. He leaned over and identified it as a Spanish grammar. He kicked it.

Downstairs again, he heated some minestrone—he had not eaten anything since his abrupt decision to abandon that boring conference and come home early. The soup was tasty. He looked for a joint—how sweet the house still smelled—but the crowd had apparently sucked their whole stash. He did find, in one corner, a recorder, but he couldn't smoke that. He put all the plates and glasses into the dishwasher. He tried to scrub the remains of chili from a pot, then left it to soak. He vacuumed. Then he went upstairs again and undressed, and, leaving his clothes on the floor—these gypsy ways were catching—slipped into Grace's side of the bed. With a sigh he recognized as an old man's, he flopped onto his back. His thoughts—which were uncharitable—did not keep him from falling asleep.

But a few hours later he found himself awake. He got up and went through the house again. He threw the Spanish grammar into the trash bag he had stuffed earlier and lugged the thing out to the garage, knowing that anyone who saw him in his striped pajamas under the floodlight at three o'clock in the morning would take him for a madman. So what. Their neighbors considered them a cute couple; he had overheard that demeaning epithet at the fish market. He'd rather be crazy than cute. He relocked the garage and returned to the house. And surely he had been deranged to marry a woman because of her alluring eyes. He'd mistaken a frolicsome manner for lasting charm. She was merely frivolous, and the minute she was left unsupervised . . . He stomped into the living room. That rose-colored garment in progress now shared its chair with a wine bottle, good vineyard, good year . . . empty. He'd like to rip the knitting out. The yarn would remain whorled; he'd wind it loosely into a one big whorl. When she came back she'd find a replica of Faraday's induction coil, pink. Come back? She could come back to collect her clothing and her paella pan and the bulbs she kept meaning to plant. He picked up the sweater. It would fit a ten-year-old. Insulting color, insulting size . . . he went back to bed and lay there.

GRACE, TOO, WAS AWAKE. The hotel room was dark and malodorous. Hal slept at her side without stirring, without snoring. He had always been a devoted sleeper. He was devoted to whatever brought him pleasure. Under no circumstances would she accompany him to Barcelona, as he had idly suggested last night. (He had also suggested that she buy the drinks at the hotel bar downstairs; she supposed she'd have to pay for the room, too.) Anyway, she had left her passport next to Gustave's in his top drawer. She hoped he'd send it back to her in Northampton—she had not yet sold her house there, thank goodness, thank Providence, thank Whoever was in charge. She hoped he'd send all her things, without obsessive comment. She wanted no more of him. She wanted no more of Hal, either: it was enough that she had shared his toothbrush last night, and then his bed, and was now sleeping—well, failing to sleep—in one of his unlaundered shirts.

How hideous to have only yesterday's lingerie. Unshaved underarms were one thing: grotty underpants quite another. What time did stores open on Sundays? She'd slip out and shop, get a new sweater, maybe—that would pick up her spirits. She remembered the half-finished vest for her granddaughter she'd left on the chair; she hoped Gustave would send that back, too . . .

"Amelie . . .," muttered Hal.

"Grace," she corrected.

If only she were back in Northampton already, where everyone was needy and she was needed. She wished she had never visited that wild-animal preserve at the Cape, had never paused to look at those foxes. She wished she had not married a man because he was learned and polite, especially since he had turned out to be pedantic and sanctimonious.

FROM TIME TO TIME that Sunday, Gustave thought of calling the lawyer who'd married them—she happened to specialize in divorce. Instead he read the papers, and watched the football game. What a sport: force directed by intelligence. He prepared for tomorrow's class, the one in which he and the students would reproduce one of Faraday's earliest experiments in electrification. They'd all come carrying foil-wrapped water-filled film canisters with a protruding nail. These were primitive Leyden jars in which to store electricity. The electricity would be produced by a Styrofoam dinner plate nested in an aluminum pie pan—the kids would bring these friction makers, too. He went to bed early. He could see a low autumnal moon above the mansard across the street—well, only the upper half of the sphere was visible, but he could supply the rest.

GRACE BOUGHT, among other things, a yellow sweater. She took her time getting back to the hotel. She found Hal showered and smiling. During a long walk by the river she listened to his opinions on magic realism and antonomasia—she'd forgotten what that was, she admitted. "The use of an epithet instead of a proper name," Hal said. " 'The Fussbudget,' say." He told her of the Spanish medieval farsa, which was related to farce. And just when she thought her aching head would explode, it was time to put him into a cab to the airport. He seemed to have enough cash for the taxi. He thrust his head out of the open window as the vehicle left the curb. "My apartment is near Las Ramblas, best location in Barcelona," he called. She waved. The cab disappeared, and her headache with it.

She went back to their room, now hers, and read the papers and enjoyed a solitary supper in front of the TV, watching a replay of that afternoon's football game. Nice intercept! Such brave boys there on the screen. But Gustave had been brave, too, hadn't he, scorning savoir faire as he cleansed his house of unwelcome revelers. How red his face had become when Hal theatrically held out his hand . . . he'd felt wronged, hadn't he, or perhaps *in* the wrong; maybe he thought she'd summoned her friends, maybe he thought he'd failed her. If she ever saw him again she'd tell him about Hal's lonely rootlessness. She'd tell him about poor Lee and Lee's barn of unsalable paintings, if she ever saw him again . . . She put on her new nightgown and went to bed. She could see a curve of the dome of the Massachusetts statehouse, just enough to suggest the whole.

THE LECTURE ROOM was shaped like a triangle. The platform, holding lectern and lab bench, was at the apex, the lowest part of the room; concentric rows of slightly curved tables radiated upward toward the back. Three students sat at each table. The professor stood at the lectern when he talked, moved to his lab bench for demonstrating. He and the students employed their identical homemade equipment. As he talked and demonstrated—creating the electric charge, storing it—the students imitated. There was expectant laughter and an occasional excited remark and a general air of satisfaction. Only a few of these poets might change course and become physicists, but not one of them would hold science in contempt. "Faraday made this experiment with equally crude apparatus," he reminded them. "And with faith that it would work. Faith—so unfashionable now—was his mainstay."

The woman in the back row, alone at a table, without pie plate or film can, wished that she, too, had the implements, that she could obey the instructions of the measured, kindly voice; but mostly she marveled again at the story that voice was telling of the humble young Faraday setting himself upon his life's journey. "He considered that God's presence was revealed in nature's design," wound up the little man. He looked radiant.

When he at last noticed the figure in the yellow sweater, he was cast back to an afternoon in Paris when that same glowing color had been produced by sun refracted through stained glass, and the lips of his companion had parted as she listened to winds and strings send music aloft. She had thrilled, she had become elevated, she had generously carried him with her . . .

The lecture concluded to applause; the teenagers dispersed; the professor materialized in the chair next to the visitor's.

They looked at each other for a while.

"I'm Grace," she said at last.

"I'm Gustave"—and how his heart leaped. "I'd like to . . . get to know you."

Another long pause while he belatedly considered the dangers in so ambitious an enterprise, for he too would have to be known, and his shabby secrets revealed, and his out-of-date convictions as well. They'd endure necessary disappointments, and they'd practice necessary forgivenesses, careful to note which subjects left the other fraught. Grace's mind moved along the same lines. Each elected to take the risk. Gustave showed his willingness by touching the lovely face, Grace hers by disdaining eclipsis. "Me too," was all she said.

VALLIES

DESMOND CHAPIN OPENED HIS DOOR to a spare, plainly dressed woman of about forty, nose tilted, reddish hair in a strict bun. "Miss . . ."

"Valerie Gordon," she said.

"The new nanny."

"Well . . . If we all suit each other." She had a faint Canadian accent.

"You remind me of somebody," Desmond said, escorting her into the living room. When Val did not respond, he plunged on anyway. "Mary Poppins?"

She shook her head. "I'm not like Mary Poppins. I'm sometimes fanciful, but I don't work magic. I like courtesy, but I don't care about manners."

This was Val's first interview in the nanny line and she considered it a rehearsal. She had no references other than clerical. After shaking hands with Deborah Chapin, she said hello to the four-year-old twin boys. They grinned and giggled.

"I have a special rapport with twins," she dared to say to the boys. "You see, I am . . ."

But they were already running out to play in the fenced-in backyard.

Desmond asked why she was leaving office work. Too repetitive, after twenty-odd years, she told him—too penitential. Yes, she could manage simple housekeeping; yes, prepare simple dinners on occasion; yes, mending. "Simple mending," she clarified.

Deborah wrote down the names of Val's references, office managers all.

Desmond said: "I am puzzling the difference between courtesy and manners."

"Oh . . . one is innate, the other learned."

Val left the rehearsal. She guessed that Deborah had been writing with invisible ink. But the next day a telephone offer came— "though we would be even happier," Deborah said, "if you'd live with us, and the salary would be the same. Would you reconsider?"

"I won't live in, sorry."

Sigh. "We want you anyway."

Val's new career began.

The Chapins gave her a car with two child boosters and told her she should consider it hers. She used it sometimes, though most of her outings with the boys were by bus, trolley, or subway, or on foot. And since her flat didn't have a parking space she kept the car at the Chapins' and walked back and forth to work. If the Chapins asked her to babysit at night, she left without escort at the end of the evening, ignoring Desmond's doomsaying. "I know this is safe old Godolphin, the most dangerous things here are the oak-leaf skeletonizers, still, Val . . . it would take just a minute to drive you." But each time she said no, strode down the path, turned her head at the gate, and gave him an impish smile perfected long ago. He probably couldn't see it. She tramped home without mishap.

SHE STAYED WITH THE CHAPINS for five years, until they went bankrupt. She would have stayed longer—the twins loved her, she always knew which was which, she had a nest egg and could go without pay for a while—but no, it would add to his humiliation, Desmond said; and anyway they were going to move out of town.

The Chapins introduced Val to the Greens and their three little girls. The Greens hired her instantly, although they were disappointed that she wouldn't occupy their attic retreat. But Val still wouldn't leave her basement flat. In winter she appreciated the warmth of the nearby furnace, in summer the cool of the half-submerged rooms. Meager sunlight slipped like an envelope into one after another of her high windows and then lay on the floor as if waiting to be picked up. Solitude, silence . . . living in would subject her to constant voices and movements, bothersome even in a courteous family, worse still among the irrepressible kin she'd grown up with.

She spent several contented years as the Greens' nanny. But then their work took them to Washington.

Sitting with Val at the kitchen table, Bunny Green said: "Think about coming with us. The capital . . ."

"No, but thank you."

Bunny sighed. "You are a gem. I wish you had a twin."

Val looked at her lap.

"One of my friends is pregnant again," Bunny said, "and that scattered family around the corner needs a nanny, though they don't know it yet. Your telephone will be ringing off the hook."

Not quite. She did get some offers as she met one family after another. But no situation would do. One house was located on the edge of Godolphin where it met a western suburb—she'd have to take two buses to get there. Another family had piled lessons and activities on their four children—Val would become a chauffeur. A third had an ill child who needed constant attention. The burdened mother's eyes silently pleaded. But Val said firmly, "I'm sorry, but I've found I am unsuited to such work."

So she took a temporary job—a couple with a three-year-old was staying in Godolphin for the summer. She'd start searching again in the fall, though without confidence. The Chapin and Green references counted in her favor, but her manner probably worked against her—that hint of the governess that Desmond Chapin had spotted was out of fashion. And by now either her color or her age made her a misfit on the playgrounds. Beautiful women from Uganda and Burkina Faso, thin and smooth enough to be teenagers, tried to include her as they watched their charges from benches, but they soon lapsed into their dialect, or French, and their kids didn't approach Val's shy three-year-old. British au pairs avoided her as if she were a headmistress. Scandinavians smiled at her as if she were a pet. The mommies—there were some of those, too, unmannerly—ignored her entirely: they were too busy boasting about their children as if someday they meant to sell them.

She missed the Greens. By the time they had decamped, their girls did not need supervision at the park or anywhere else—they needed only dinners when their parents were out and occasional reminders about homework. But they craved her company, especially at bedtime. They wanted to hear the tales that Val had concocted with them when they were younger. Case Histories of Ethical Dilemmas, Val called her stories. The girls called them Vallies. They took place in vaguely medieval cities. Royalty lived at a distance, and there was no romantic love and no hidden treasure; but there was sometimes casual enchantment and once in a while a quest. In one Vallie a girl's ailing mother was partial to caterpillar sandwiches: Was the daughter obliged to prepare the meal? And then share it? In another, a six-year-old boy wanted to watch a beheading—the penalty in Vallieland for sanctimony. Was he too young to see gore or would he become enlightened, and someday join the campaign against capital punishment? After a greedy squire was transformed into an ox, should he be put to the plow, or was change of identity punishment enough?

Yes, she missed the Greens. She wondered what they were doing this Monday morning . . . had they made friends in Washington? She still missed the Chapin twins, who must be almost in high school. She missed the three-year-old now back in California. But mooning over losses, regretting a child no longer in sight . . . that never got her anywhere. It was nine o'clock and she'd better hurry. She had an interview at ten.

The entire family was present at the interviewing—the parents and their two daughters and their son. Nine, seven, five. The father taught at the local university—a form of mathematics, he grudgingly revealed. "Topology." He had a strawberry mark on his left cheek, no more disfiguring than a stripe on a shirt. The mother was petite, almost child-sized herself, with colorless messy hair and a long elfin nose. "I don't work," she said. "I don't work yet," she corrected. "I'm looking for a craft." The children were quiet and appeared healthy, though the boy—the youngest—was too thin, and did not meet her eyes. "Your references," Professor Duprey said tonelessly, "are impeccable." Their shabby townhouse was located on the Boston end of Godolphin, a short walk from Val's apartment.

But with the Dupreys it was a condition of employment that she live in.

How flexible her principles had become. This family had no gaiety and she guessed they hadn't much small talk, either. Silence and solitude might still be hers. And Godolphin had become less safe at night, at least for a woman walking alone. A developer had recently bought her apartment house and might turn it into condominiums.

She followed Professor Duprey down a perilous staircase. The others trooped after them. They entered a group of rooms which resembled her own, even to the tiny high windows. Light would slot itself downward in the same impersonal way.

"Yes," said Val. "But I have a lease," she remembered.

"There'll be a penalty for breaking it. We'll pay," said the professor. "You'll have Thursdays and Sundays off, twenty-four hours each."

A civilized form of servitude, then. But she had never indulged in much of a social life since leaving home—an occasional afternoon movie with one of her few friends.

"It isn't that we go out much, Miss Gordon," said the wife. First names would probably not be the rule here.

"They don't go out at all," said Win, the nine-year-old.

"But the household requires another adult," said the professor.

"If God had wanted people to have three children—," began Mrs. Duprey.

"—he would have created a third parent," finished young Liam, and this time he did look at Val.

AND IF VAL HAD WANTED to live in a houseful of adults and kids and bugs (the Dupreys' screens needed patching) she might never have left her own noisy family in their ramshackle Toronto house, where no one had a room to herself; she could have watched the generations replace themselves; she could have made up Vallies for whatever children were around. What she wanted, she had discovered at twenty, was a life alone, with a family at fingertip distance. And she'd gotten that for a while, hadn't she, with the Chapins and the Greens and that little girl this summer . . . She swatted a mosquito. Besides insects flying in through the screens, there were beetles making free with her kitchen as well as with the one above it—Theirs. First names were to be avoided, so she thought of her employers as pronouns. He, She, They. The pair of Them.

He was tall and ill-kempt. She was a child herself. She burned the meals or left them half cooked, sewed buttons on the wrong garments ("You'll start a new style," Val comforted Fay, the second daughter, who was dismayed at a cardigan adorned with toggles).

And She started projects and then abandoned them, didn't care that insects ruled the household. She was at ease only with the children and, gradually, with Val.

There was no heat between the pair of Them. No anger, no resentment, no merriment. They might have been brother and sister forced to live in reduced circumstances in order to bring up younger siblings. As for the three siblings, undemanding and obedient, they quickly attached themselves to Val, but shared her as scrupulously as if they'd made a compact.

The girls walked themselves to school. Val escorted Liam, who spent his mornings at a different school. She stood quietly when he stopped to stare at things. At an irregular stone wall held together not by mortar but by the stone layer's skilled placement of rocks. At the buds, half-opened petals, full blooms, and spent ovals of a hibiscus. He remarked on the progress of one form to another day by day. He squatted to examine deposits of dogs. "This dog's owner is not doing his share," Val remarked. "He should follow his pet with a pooper-scooper."

"Then we would not get to see the dog's shit," said the child, "and imagine the circumstances of his insides." His utterances were few and precise. She supposed he was some sort of genius. They were all precocious—even the incompetent Mrs. Duprey seemed like an overbright twelve-year-old.

The nearby playground had whimsical sculpture. Liam often clumsily climbed a stone turtle and occupied himself in counting something, molecules of air, probably. Val sat on a bench, ignored by the usual collection of adults. They went there many times that fall. For lunch he ate a single carrot stick and half a cheese sandwich. She wondered how he'd take to caterpillars.

At home Val encouraged the children to make their beds in the morning; she encouraged Mrs. Duprey to straighten the marital bed and to dust and sweep once in a while. Val herself ran the vacuum cleaner over carpets whose pattern had been lost decades ago. And eventually it was Val who shopped for groceries, cooked the meals, called the exterminator, had the back stairs repaired, remembered to leave the money on the oversize dining table for the weekly cleaning woman (cash was kept loose in a kitchen drawer, available to everyone; Val paid herself out of it). That giant dining table had probably come with the house. The wicker living room furniture, no cushions matching—it had probably come from Goodwill.

One Saturday in December she suggested a trip to a large discount shop to buy new school clothes. Val drove the family car. She saw to it that the children were properly outfitted. Liam liked a shirt of madras plaid, and Val bought three of them, each a variation on the others. Mrs. Duprey wandered among the clothes for teens and found some navy blue dresses suitable for French orphans. Val bought her half a dozen.

It was a while before she resumed the Vallies. The children, talented readers all, still liked to be read aloud to at bedtime—at least the girls did, curled up on either side of Val on the wicker couch in the living room. On a footstool Liam would stare at the blackened fireplace. The children liked the unbowdlerized Brothers Grimm; they liked Robin McKinley's fantasies, with their complicated psychologies.

Then one Wednesday night: "*Tell* us a story, please," said Win. "You do tell stories; your résumé said so."

"Well . . . mine aren't exactly stories."

"What, then?"

"Interactive dilemmas. Together we invent situations that require resolution. Then we invent some resolutions. Then we choose among them, or don't."

"Please," said Win.

"Once upon a time," said Val, "in a peaceful house in a peaceful village, a lodger came to the inn. He was a dark, quiet man: a woodworker. He carved beautiful spoons and ladles and spindles, and he charged fair prices. After a while he was able to buy his own cottage and build a studio next door—a big, open barnlike thing, only three sides to it. The children in the village gathered where a wall might have been, to watch him work.

"One day an official from the prince of the district stopped at the village to speak to the mayor about something financial, or maybe agricultural. On his way out of town he passed the woodworker's cottage, slowly, for the house was pretty and the horse thought so, too. In the studio the woodworker was carving a puppet, and several children were watching. The official reined in his horse. The woodworker looked up. The men's eyes met. The official turned his horse around and went back towards the mayor's house at a lei-surely trot.

"It turned out that the woodworker had spent time in the prince's dungeon being punished for a crime. Not an ordinary crime, though. A crime against a child." A figure crept close to the couch: She. "And the official's dilemma was this: was he bound to tell the mayor that there was a person with such tendencies in their midst?

"He thought and thought. His horse drew to a halt. They both pondered."

"He was bound to tell only if the tendencies hadn't . . . hadn't gone away," said Fay.

"Such tendencies rarely go away entirely," said Mrs. Duprey.

"The carver had done his penance," said Win.

"What happens if the official tells the mayor?" said Fay.

"Then the dilemma flies off his shoulders onto the back of the mayor," said Val. "Should the mayor let the woodworker's past be known to the village?"

"The woodworker would be shunned," said Win. "He'd leave."

"Three walls—everyone can see what he does," said Liam.

"Let him alone unless he builds a fourth wall," said Win.

"Until," corrected Mrs. Duprey.

That was that. There were no tuckings-in for this gang. The chil-dren just wandered off. Their little mother, too.

THE NEXT DAY, Thursday, was Val's day off. She went to the mov-ies with a friend. And Friday the Dupreys had one of their rare evenings of guests—another family and its children. Val cooked two meat loaves and let the kids mix the salad. Though she was invited to join the table—as she had been invited at the Chapins', the Greens'—she declined as always. She stood at the kitchen win-dow and looked through screens she'd installed at the transformed garden, now shades of gray under the winter moon: but she knew where the tulips she'd planted would come up, and the allium later.

Saturday night: "Please, another dilemma!" cried Fay. And Sun-day, too, this time joined by Him as well as Her. He sat in a chair by the fireplace, stern as any mayor. And She on the floor beside the couch, and Liam on the footstool, and the girls next to Val, Fay stroking her arm.

They took these positions several nights a week while Val re-cycled the old Vallies, some of them inventions, some embellish-ments on real or half-real incidents. Finally she couldn't remember any more. Well then, invent some more, embellish . . .

"There was a large town that climbed up the side of a mountain," she began, "a bustling town, prosperous, most people happy, some miserable of course. People had big families in those days . . ."

"They expected to lose some children," said Mrs. Duprey.

"They practiced redundancy," said the professor.

"One household was particularly numerous—nine offspring, assorted uncles and aunts, a grandfather. They didn't have much money, for none of them liked to work, but they were generous with what they had. There were three cows and some hens. Usually someone remembered to feed them. Mum did the cooking for the family and Dad did the repairs on the house.

"Right in the middle of the lively crowd were twin girls, not identical. One was spirited. She had light curly hair that went its own willful way. People couldn't seem to help loving this tousled girl. The other one, who was pretty, too, hovered between a sense of duty and a wish for fun. She was organized; the family trusted her to manage their skimpy finances. Her hair was black and reliably straight, like licorice.

"Perhaps the lighthearted girl was also scatterbrained. At any rate, when she was nineteen, she found she was with child. The child's father had scampered. This had happened to one or two of her sisters. Such an event was accepted, was even applauded. The new child, like the others, would be everyone's. Everyone would care for it. There would be only an increase of the family's easy happiness . . .

"But the child was born—"

"Defective," said Mrs. Duprey.

Val swallowed. "Yes, the infant, a girl, was born deformed and also defective, the kind of child who cries all the time and is un-rewarding to care for. Her red ringlets"—Val's hand fluttered to her own hair—"seemed like a curse. The town witches would have done away with her. The priests offered to take her to their House of Compassion on the far side of the mountain and bring her up with others of her kind. A magician wanted to transform her into an amphibian. But the family wouldn't listen to those ideas. 'Hope,' they said—Hope was the poor infant's misbegotten name—'Hope will be brought up in our midst.' 'She will have the best life that can be given to her,' said the oldest and laziest sister.

"There was only one silent voice—one person whose vision of the family had been darkened by the event, who inwardly damned its members as feckless and forgetful."

"A twin sister," said Liam.

"Who knew she'd do all the caring," said Win.

"*She* would have accepted the magician's offer. A nice frog," said Fay.

"Or the priests," said Mrs. Duprey.

"Or even the witches'. Euthanasia," said the professor.

"But she would not have been listened to," said his wife. "Even though she was—"

"So what should she do?" Val quickly interrupted.

"Run away," came all five voices at once.

A FEW WEEKS LATER, on a rainy Sunday, Val was having a cup of tea near the movie theater, waiting to see a new Afghan film. A man dressed in clothes that had once been good sat down opposite her. His teeth, too, had deteriorated, but his smile remained charming nonetheless, and of course she recognized him.

They had recently returned to town. Val asked for news of the twins, and Deborah. Desmond asked for news of Val.

"I'm nanny in a professor's family now," she said. "I'm also dogs-body and housekeeper. I find I rather like it."

"Do you live in?"

". . . yes."

"I've thought of you off and on through the years," said Desmond. "I remember that first day, when you reminded me of Mary Poppins. But it wasn't Mary Poppins, really—it was the actress who played her in that movie, who played in so many movies, remember, Julie Andrews. She was once an adorable English ingenue, and she was still adorable years later. You weren't a governess type, and neither was she. You were a party girl in disguise."

Val said nothing to this discourteous unmasking.

"You've cut your hair at last and let it curl the way it wants to. More youthful . . . you're only fifty, yes?"

"Forty-nine." Sallie was forty-nine, too, if she hadn't already died of self-sacrifice. And Hope . . . Hope would be thirty. Val remembered the painful birth, the big head with its red fuzz finally emerging from between her thighs, the instant realization that this misshapen infant would not be like other children except maybe in her attachment to her mother.

Desmond said: "With that flighty coiffure I'll bet you remind yourself of the girl you were."

"The girl I left behind," said Val in a low, flat voice.

AUNT TELEPHONE

I GOT MY FIRST TASTE OF RAW FLESH when I was nine years old. I had been taken to an adult party. My father was out of town at an investors' conference and my brother was spending the night at a friend's; and my babysitter got sick at the last minute, or said she did. What was my mother to do—stay home? So she brought me along. The affair was cocktails and a buffet featuring beef tartare on pumpernickel rounds and a bowl of icy seviche— this was thirty years ago, before such delicacies had been declared lethal. The party was given by the Plunkets, family therapists: two fatties who dressed in similar sloppy clothing as if to demonstrate that glamour was not a prerequisite for rambunctious sex.

My mother and I and Milo walked over to the party in the glowing September afternoon. Our house and Milo's and the Plunkets' all lay within a mile of each other in Godolphin, a leafy wedge of Boston, as did the homes of most of the other guests—the psychiatrists and clinical psychologists and social workers who made up this crowd. They were all friends, they referred patients to one another, they distributed themselves into peer-supervision subsets—a collegial, talkative crew, their envy vigorously tamped down. Their kids were friends, too—some as close as cousins. I already hated groups, but I was willy-nilly part of the bunch.

Among the adults, Milo was first among peers. He produced paper after acclaimed paper: case histories of children with symptoms like elective mutism and terror of automobiles and willful constipation lasting ten days. I longed to become one of his fascinating patients, but I knew to my sadness that therapists rarely treated their friends' children no matter how sick and I knew, also, that I wasn't sick anyway, just ornery and self-centered. In his published work Milo gave the young sufferers false first names and surname initials. "What would you call *me*?" I asked him once, still hoping for immortality.

"Well, Susan, what would you like to be called?"

"Catamarina M."

He warmed me with his brown gaze. ("The eyes," Dr. Lenore once remarked to my mother, "thoroughly compensate for the absence of chin.")

Milo said: "Catamarina is your name forever."

So I had an appellation if not symptoms. All I had to do was stop talking or moving my bowels. Alas, nature proved too strong for me.

Milo's colleagues respected his peaceable bachelordom: they recognized asexuality as an unpathological human preference, also as a boon to society. He had been born in cosmopolitan Budapest, which gave him further cachet. His liberal parents, who were in the bibelot business, had gotten out just before World War II. So Milo was brought up in New York by a pair of Hungarians, penniless at first, soon rich again. He inherited a notable collection of ancient Chinese figurines.

On the day of that party Milo was wearing his standard costume: flannel slacks, turtleneck sweater, tweed jacket. He was then almost fifty, a bit older than my parents and their friends. His hair, prematurely gray, rose high and thick from a narrow forehead. It swung at his nape like a soft broom. He was very tall and very thin.

Dr. Will Plunket gave me beef tartare in a hamburger bun. But the Plunket boys wouldn't let me join their game of Dungeons and Dragons. So, munching my feral sandwich, I wandered in the fall garden still brightened by a glossy sun. On a chaise on the flagstone terrace sat a woman I didn't know. She looked sulky and bored. Dr. Judah joined me for a while and wondered aloud if fairies nested under the chrysanthemums. I frowned at him, but when he went inside I knelt and peered under the mums. Nothing. After a while Milo found me. In his soft voice he talked about the greenery near the stone wall—basil was rumored to cure melancholy, marjoram headaches, ground ivy conjunctivitis. He bent, picked up a handful of the ivy, stood, and crushed a few leaves into my palm. "Not to be taken internally." Then he, too, went in.

I drifted toward the terrace. "How lucky you are," drawled the woman on the chaise, and she drank some of her cocktail.

"Yes. Why?"

"To have such an attentive aunt," she said, and drank some more.

"My aunt lives in Michigan."

"She's here on a visit?"

"She's in Europe this month."

"I mean the aunt you were just talking to."

"Milo?"

"Her name is Milo?"

I raced into the house. I found my mother standing with Dr. Margaret and Dr. Judah. "You'll never believe it, that patient on the terrace, she thought Milo was my aunt!" My mother gave me a ferocious stare. "My *aunt*," I heedlessly repeated to Dr. Margaret, and then turned to Dr. Judah. "My—" but I couldn't finish because my mother was yanking me out of the room.

"Stop talking, Susan, stop right now, do not say that again. It would hurt Milo's feelings dreadfully." She let go of me and folded her arms. "There's dirt on your knees," she said, though dirt was not usually denigrated in this circle. "Filth."

"Garden soil," I corrected.

My mother sighed. "The woman on the terrace is Dr. Will's sister."

"I wish Milo *was* my aunt."

"Were."

"Were? Why?"

"Condition contrary to fact." As our conversation slid into the safe area of grammar, we returned to the party. Milo was now listening to Dr. Will. It didn't seem to me that Milo's longish hair was more feminine than Dr. Will's black smock. But this once I would obey my mother—I would not again relate the error of the woman on the terrace. I hoped that Milo hadn't heard my earlier exclamation. Not for the world would I hurt his feelings; or so I thought.

MILO CELEBRATED THANKSGIVING here, Passover there, Christmas twice in one day, first at the Collinses and then at the Shapiros.

He smoked his after-dinner cigar in everybody's backyard. He came to our annual New Year's Day open house, which I was required to attend for fifteen minutes. I spent that quarter hour behind a lamp. My parents, shoulder to shoulder, greeted their guests. Sometimes my mother slipped her hand into my father's pocket, like a horse nuzzling for sugar.

Milo went to piano recitals and bar mitzvahs and graduations. In August he visited four different families, one each week. He *was* an aunt, my aunt, aunt to many children born into our therapeutic set, if an aunt is someone always ready to talk on the telephone to worried parents—especially to mothers, who do most of the worrying. Those mothers of ours, full of understanding for their patients, were helpless when their own offspring gave them trouble. Then they became frantic kid sisters, reaching for the phone. Bad report cards, primitive behavior on the playground, sass, lying, staying out all night, playing hooky—for all such troubles Milo was ready with advice and consolation. He knew, also, when a child needed outside help—strangling the cat was a sure indication. Usually, though, it was the parent who required an interpretation and also a recommendation to back off. "No, a joint today is not a crack pipe tomorrow," he memorably assured Dr. Lenore. Dr. Lenore's daughter was, of course, listening on the extension. We were all masters of domestic wiretapping—slipping a forefinger between receiver and the button on which it rested, lifting the receiver to our ear, releasing the button with the caution of a surgeon until a connection was soundlessly established.

THE JULY I WAS TWELVE I ran away from overnight camp. The day after I arrived home, surly and triumphant, I eavesdropped on Milo and my mother. Milo was suggesting that my mother praise me for taking the bus rather than hitchhiking on the highway.

"She stole the bus money from her counselor," my mother said.

"Borrowed, I think. Encourage her to return the money by mail."

"Shouldn't she be encouraged to return herself to camp?"

Milo said: "To the hated place?" There was a talcum pause as he drew on his cigar. "To the place she had the resourcefulness to escape from?"

"It's difficult to have her home," my mother said, with a little sob.

"Yes, Ann, I can imagine," said Milo. And then: "It is her home, too."

There was a silence—Milo's the silence of someone who has delivered a truth and my mother's the silence of someone who has received it. And a third silence, a silence within a silence: mine. "It is her home, too," I heard. The gentle living room. The kitchen whose window looked out on birds and squirrels and sometimes a pheasant that had strayed from the more suburban part of Godolphin. The attached office where my mother saw patients during the day. The bedroom where in the evenings she received those patients' panicky calls and where she herself called Milo. My brother's room with his construction projects in various stages of completion—though a year younger than I, he was already an adept mechanic. My own room: posters, books, toys outgrown but not discarded, clothing pooled on the floor and draped on lamps. A long window led from my room onto a little balcony. My mother had once planted impatiens in boxes on the balcony but I let the flowers die. Without recrimination she had watched me neglect—desecrate, even—a generous space in the house. The house that was hers, too.

For the remainder of July I babysat for the kids next door, treating them with a pretend affection I ended up feeling. ("Hypocrisy is the first step toward sincerity," Milo had written.) I made a small effort to straighten my room. ("A token is a cheap coin, but it is not counterfeit"—same source.) In August we went to Cape Cod.

Our determinedly modest bungalow faced the sea; there was no sandy beach, but we had become used to lying on our strip of shingle. The house had four small bedrooms. The walls were thin, providing perfect acoustics. There was a grille and an outdoor shower. Sometimes my father grilled fish; sometimes he and my mother prepared meals together in the inconvenient kitchen, where they bumped into each other and laughed.

As always Milo came for the third week. I could hear him, too, turning over in bed or splashing in the bathroom, just as I could hear my parents' soft conversations, my brother's indiscriminate farting. The small family—still too large a group for me. "I want to work in a private office," I said one morning.

"You could be a psychiatrist," said my unimaginative brother.

"Private! By myself! Nobody comes in."

"Ah. You could be a bank president," Milo said. "They are rarely interrupted."

"Or a hotel housekeeper," my mother said. "Just you and piles of linen."

"Or an astronomer, alone with her telescope," my father said. That was the best offer. "The work requires a bit of math," he added, mildly.

Later that day Milo took my brother and me to Bosky's Wild Animal Preserve. We visited Bosky's once or twice each summer. The wildest animals there were a pair of foxes. Foxes are devoted parents while their offspring require care. Then they separate, and next season they find new partners. But Bosky's two downcast specimens were stuck with each other year after year. The male peacock didn't seem to have much fun, either. His occasional half-hearted display revealed gaps in his feathers. A pichi, a female rock snake, a few monkeys chattering nonsense—these were our wild animals. But beyond the pathetic cages was a large working farm, with chickens and turkeys and an apple orchard and a field of corn. A pony in a straw hat dragged a cart around the cornfield. Two other chapeaued ponies could be ridden around a ring, though not independently: you had to endure, walking beside you, one of the local teenagers who worked at Bosky's. These louts did not hide their contempt for nag and rider.

The rock snake was fed a live white mouse every two weeks. This public meal was unadvertised but word got around. When we got to Bosky's that day with Milo, there were a dozen small children already gathered in front of the snake's cage. Their parents, wearing doubtful expressions, milled at a distance. My brother went off to the ponies. Milo and I were tall enough to see over the children's heads, so we two and the kids viewed the entire performance—the lowering of the mouse into the cage by Mr. Bosky, the terrified paralysis of the rodent, the expert constriction by the snake, and then the mouse's slow incorporation into the snake's hinged mouth. She fed herself the mouse, whose bones were all broken but who still presumably breathed. In it went, farther in, still farther, until all we could see was its tiny rump and then only its thin white tail.

The little kids, bored once the tail had disappeared, drifted toward their pained parents. One skinny mother vomited into a beach bag. Milo looked at her with sympathy. Not I, though.

"A recovering bulimic," I told him as we moved away.

"Giving herself a thrill?" he wondered. "Could be," he said, generously admitting me into the company of interpreters.

I love you, Milo, I might have said if we said that sort of thing.

IN THE FALL I BEGAN to attend school regularly, forcing myself to tolerate groups at least for a classroom hour. I had to choose a sport so I went out for track, the least interpersonal of activities. I did my homework in most subjects. I made up the math I had flunked the year before.

My mother needed to call Milo less often.

I even achieved a kind of intimacy. My best friend—almost my only one, really, unless you counted Dr. Judah's daughter and Dr. Lenore's daughter and the younger Plunket boy, who were all in my grade—was an extra-tall girl with an extra-long neck. Her parents had been born in India. They both practiced radiology. Their daughter planned a career in medicine, too, as casually as a child of other parents might look forward to taking over the family store. Anjali—such a beautiful name—was plain and dark, with drooping lids and wide nostrils. Her last name was Nezhukumatathil— "Where my father comes from, the equivalent of Smith."

She lived a few blocks from us. She and I walked home along the same streets every day, rarely bothering to talk. Our route took us past the stretch of row houses that included Milo's, past his small, low-maintenance garden: a dogwood tree, a cast iron white love seat below it, pachysandra around it. Milo's front door had two bells, one for the living quarters, one for the office and playroom. He was always working in the late afternoon, and so I didn't tell Anjali that I knew the owner of that particular narrow house.

But one May at five o'clock there he was on the lacy bench, he and his cigar. A patient had canceled, I immediately understood. There was an exchange of hellos and an introduction; and then— after Milo had poked the cigar into a tin of sand beside the love seat—we were inside; and Milo was telling Anjali the provenance of some of his figurines and showing her his needlepoint utensils. How had he guessed that this mute camel liked small things and delicate handiwork? If I'd been walking with Sarah—another girl I sometimes made myself pal around with, a very good runner— he'd have known to put "Hair" on the stereo and discuss stretching exercises. Ah, it was his business. I sipped a can of Coke. You might guess that it tasted like wormwood, that I was full of jealousy—but no: I was full of admiration for Milo, performing his familial role for this schoolgirl, comfortably limited by the imminent arrival of the next patient; within ten minutes he'd give us the gate. And he did, first looking with a rueful expression at his watch. "Good-bye, Anjali," he said at the door. "See you soon, Susan. Thank you for bringing your friend," as if I had done it on purpose to display my hard-won sociability.

A block or so later Anjali made a rare disclosure—she'd like to live like Milo.

"In what way?" I asked, expecting mention of the figurines, the needlepoint, even the dogwood.

"Alone."

Me, too! I wanted to confide. But the confidence would have been false. I already guessed that someday I would marry and produce annoying children. I was not as bold as Milo, as Anjali. Nature would again prove too strong for me.

August: just before senior year. I ran every morning; it was no longer an obligation but a pleasure. The third week Anjali came to the Cape to visit me, and one of my brother's friends came to visit him, and Milo came to visit the family. He swam and baked blueberry pies and treated us to impromptu lectures on this and that— the nature of hurricanes; stars, though I had already dismissed astronomy as a career; the town of Scheveningen, where, at the age of four, he had spent the summer. He liked to recall an ancient Dutch waiter who had brought him lemonade every afternoon and talked about his years as a circus acrobat. "Lies, beautiful lies, essential to amour propre."

"To the waiter's amour propre?" I asked.

"And to mine. Taking lies seriously, it's a necessary skill."

In bathing briefs, muscular and tanned, Milo could not be mistaken for a woman. But my brother's friend, whose schoolteacher parents were not part of our exalted circle, told my brother that Milo was so fucking helpful he was probably some cast-off queen. My brother didn't hesitate to repeat the evaluation to me. "A queen!"

"There's filth on your knees," I snapped, but of course he didn't get the reference. I was furious with all three of them: the unappreciative guest, my unfeeling brother, and Milo, who had brought the accusation on himself with his pies and his reminiscences. He'd encouraged the taciturn Anjali to talk about ancient artifacts, too. Apparently they were her prime interest nowadays. Apparently Anjali and Milo had run into each other at the museum during the spring—some dumb exhibition, pre-Columbian telephones, maybe. Afterward he had treated her to tea.

On Thursday of that week Milo and I drove Anjali through a light rain to the bus station—she had to get back to town for a family party. She jumped out of the backseat and threw her traveling sack, studded with tiny mirrors, over her bony shoulder. "Thanks," she said in her toneless voice. (She had properly thanked my mother back in the bungalow.) She slammed the door and strode toward the bus.

Milo opened his window and stuck his head into the drizzle. "There's a netsuke exhibition in October," he called.

She stopped and turned, and smiled at him, a smile that lasted several seconds too long. Then she boarded the bus.

We watched the vehicle pull out.

"Shall we take a run to Bosky's?" Milo said.

"The place is swarming with ants," I said. "Bosky's formicates," I showed off. Milo was silent. "Sure," I relented. It was his vacation, too.

On that damp day Milo paid his usual serious attention to the wild animals: the foxes forced into monogamy, the impotent peacock, the dislocated monkeys. He glanced at the languid snake, still digesting last week's meal. He stopped for an irritatingly long while at the cage of an animal new to the preserve, an agouti from Belize that was (an ill-painted sign mentioned) a species of rodent. "Among Belizeans he's considered a tasty meal," Milo told me; he knew more than the sign painter. "The agouti himself is herbivorous. A sociable little fellow. He shares a common burrow system with others of his kind."

"Does he. Like you."

He gave me his interested stare. "I eat meat—"

"I shouldn't have said that," I muttered.

"—though it's true that I have lost my taste for beef tartare. It wasn't a terrible thing to say, Catamarina M. We all do live, your parents and I and our friends, in a kind of mutual burrow, and the telephone makes it even more intimate, especially when one of you children sneaks onto the line—it's like a hiccup, I listen for it. In what way did you insult me?"

"I suggested you were a rat," I said, confessing to the lesser sin. What I had suggested, as I feared he knew, was that he was an inquisitive dependent animal, exchanging advice for friendship; that for all his intuition and clinical wisdom he did not know firsthand the rage that flared between individuals, the urge to eat each other up. Strong emotions were not part of his repertoire. But they had become part of mine during Anjali's visit as I watched her unfold under his radiant friendship—envy, hatred, fury . . . *Once I saved you from ridicule, you ridiculous man.*

"A rat," he echoed. "Nevertheless, you are my favorite . . . niece."

"I'm supposed to take that lie seriously? Up your goulash, Milo."

"Susan—"

"Go home." I took several steps away from him and his friend the agouti. Then I whirled and began to run. I ran past the pichi and the monkeys and into the farm area, scattering hens and chickens and little kids. "Hey!" yelled Mr. Bosky. I vaulted the railing of the ponies' riding ring and ran around it and vaulted back. "She's crazy," remarked one of the local boys, in surprised admiration. Perhaps I could sneak out one night and meet him in a haystack. I ran straight into the corn, between stag lines of stalks.

Past the corn was another field where lettuce grew close to the ground. I skirted it—I had no wish to do damage to Bosky's. I ran, faster still, enjoying one of those spurts our track coach taught us to take advantage of—a coach who, without concern for feelings or individuality, made us into athletes. I slowed down when I reached the woods, and padded through it like a fox free of her partner; I slithered, like a snake who has to catch her own mouse. On the other side of the woods was the highway. I crossed it carefully—I had no wish to grieve my parents, either. Another narrow road led to the rocky beach, a couple of miles from our house. I walked the rest of the way. My brother and his friend were sitting on the porch, amiably talking with Milo—Aunt Milo, Queen Milo, Dr. Milo, who so evenly distributed his favors. He and I waved to each other, and I went around to the outside shower and turned it on and stood under it, with all my clothes on.

~

As I had noticed, my mother was calling Milo less frequently. By that last year in high school, it seemed, she didn't call him at all except to remind him of the New Year's party.

And later, talking with children of the other therapists when we were home from college, or, still later, when we ran into each other in New York or San Francisco, I learned that all of our mothers eventually stopped consulting Milo. Partly, I think, they had less need for his advice. We kids were at last growing up. And our parents had incorporated and so no longer needed to hear Milo's primary rule about offspring—"They owe you and society a minimal courtesy. Everything else is their business"—just as they had incorporated his earlier observation about physical punishment: "It's addictive. Rather than strike your child, light up a cigar."

And perhaps, too, they had to flee their older sibling, the one who had seen their wounds.

A few of them may have even believed the rumor about Milo: that he was paying so much attention to Anjali N., a high school girl, that her parents had to warn him off. That fable had been astonishingly easy to launch. I merely related it to Dr. Margaret's daughter—two years younger than I, grateful for my attention. Then I swore her to secrecy.

At any rate, we grown offspring discovered from each other that Milo himself began to initiate the telephone calls, eager to know the progress of the patients, the anecdotes from the latest trips, the news of the children—especially the news of the children.

"Nosy," said Dr. Lenore's daughter.

"Avaricious," said Benjy Plunket, who had practically lived at Milo's house during his parents' divorce. "When I was in college he wanted to study everything I was studying—he even bought himself a copy of my molecular biology textbook, stuff new since his time."

"He managed to tag along on the Apfels' Las Vegas trip," said Dr. Lenore's daughter.

"People outlive their usefulness," Dr. Judah's daughter summed up.

"It's sad," we all agreed, with offhand malice.

My mother still answered when Milo called (machines allowed other old friends to screen him out) and she tolerated his increasingly discursive monologues. And she kept inviting him to our

Cape Cod house, and when he joined our family on a cruise to Scandinavia it was because she and my father enthusiastically insisted. Others were less generous. The Apfels, who had lost heavily in Las Vegas, broke with him entirely.

WE ARE ADULTS NOW. We prefer e-mail to the telephone. Many of us still live in Godolphin. None of us has entered the mental-health professions. Even Anjali failed to follow her parents into medicine. She teaches art history in Chicago, and has three daughters. Nature proved too strong for her, too.

Some of our children have problems. But though the aged Milo is still working—is esteemed adviser to an inner-city child-guidance center, has done pioneering work with juvenile offenders—we don't consult him. He reminds us too much of our collective childhood in that all-knowing burrow; and of our anxious mothers; and of the unnerving power of empathy. We're a different generation: the tough love crowd. And there's always Ritalin.

I do keep in touch with Milo. It's not a burden: my husband and I are both linguists, and Milo is interested in language. "There is a striving for design in the utterances even of the schizophrenic," he has written.

I inherited the Cape Cod house, and Milo comes to visit every summer. He and I and my two sons always pay a visit to Bosky's. The wild-animal preserve has dwindled to one desperate moose, one raccoon, and those poor foxes, or some other pair. The snake has retired and the agouti is gone, too. But the farm in back continues to flourish, and the ponies get new straw hats every season. My kids have outgrown the place but they understand that old Milo is to be indulged.

A white mustache coats Milo's upper lip. His hair, also white, is still long. His hairline has receded considerably, and he's subject to squamous carcinomas on the exposed brow. Advised by his dermatologist, he covers his head. In the winter he sports a beret, in the summer a cloth hat with a soft brim.

Today, wearing the summer hat and a pair of oversize cargo pants that look like a split skirt, he is riding one of the ponies. That saddle must be punishing his elderly bones. Maybe he's trying to amuse my sons. Certainly they are entertained. When he reaches the far side of the ring they release unseemly snickers.

"Granny Wild West," snorts one. "Madame Cowpoke," returns the other. Meanwhile Milo is bending toward the kid who's leading his pony—eliciting a wretched story, no doubt; offering a suggestion that may change the boy's life or at least make his afternoon a little better.

I'd like to smack both my sons and *also* smoke a cigar. Instead I inform them that Milo represents an evolved form of human life that they might someday emulate or even adopt. That sobers them. So I don't mention that he was once valued and then exploited and then betrayed and finally discarded; that, like his displaced parents, he adjusted gracefully to new circumstances.

We stand there, elbows on the railing, as Milo on his pony plods toward us. We smile at him. Within the rim of his bonnet, his face creases; below the soapy mustache his lips part to reveal brown teeth. He is grinning back at us as if he shared our mild mockery of his performance: as if it were his joke, too.

SELF-RELIANCE

WHEN CORNELIA FITCH RETIRED from the practice
of gastroenterology, she purchased—on impulse, her daughter
thought—a house beside a spring-fed pond in New Hampshire.
She did not relinquish the small apartment of her widowhood,
though—three judicious rooms with framed drawings on the gray
walls. This apartment, in the Boston suburb of Godolphin, was a
twenty-minute walk from the hospital where Cornelia had worked;
and her daughter lived nearby, as did both of her friends; and at
Godolphin Corner she could visit a good secondhand bookstore
and an excellent seamstress. One of Cornelia's legs was slightly longer than the other, a fault concealed by the clever *tailleur*. "Do you
think there's anybody what's perfect," her aunt Shelley had snorted
when, at fifteen, Cornelia's defect became apparent. Aunt Shelley had lived with the family; where else could she live? "You're a
knucklehead," added that gracious dependent.

The place by the water—Cornelia had had her eye on it for years.
It reminded her of the cottage of a gnome. "Guhnome," Aunt Shelley used to miscorrect. The other houses in the loose settlement by
the pond were darkly weathered wood, but Cornelia's was made of
the local pale gray granite, sparkling here and there with tiny golden
specks. It had green shutters. There was one room downstairs and
one up, an outdoor toilet, a small generator. Aquatic vines climbed
the stones. Frogs and newts inhabited the moist garden.

She spent more and more time there. At the bottom of the pond,
turtles inched their way to wherever they were going. Minnows

traveled together, the whole congregation turning this way and then that, an underwater flag flapping in an underwater wind. Birches, lightly clothed in leaves, leaned toward the pond.

There was no beach. Most people had a rowboat or a canoe or a Sunfish. They were retirees like Cornelia, who passed their days as she did—reading, watching the mild wildlife, sometimes visiting each other. Their dirt road met the main road a mile away, where a Korean family kept a general store. Thompson the geezer—Cornelia thought of him as a geezer, though he was, like her, in his early seventies—sat on his porch all day, sketching the pond. Two middle-aged sisters played Scrabble at night, and Cornelia joined them once in a while.

"I worry about you in the middle of nowhere," her daughter, Julie, said. But the glinting stones of the house, its whitewashed interior, summer's greenness and winter's pale blueness seen through its deep windows, the mysterious endless brown of the peaked space above her bed . . . and pond and trees and loons and chipmunks . . . not nowhere. Somewhere. Herewhere.

"CORNELIA, GOOD SENSE demands that we treat this," the oncologist said. "A course of chemo, some radia—" He paused. "We can beat it back."

She stretched her legs—the long one, the longer. She liked her doctor's old-fashioned office with its collection of worn books in a glass-fronted case. The glass now reflected her own handsome personage: short hair dyed bark, a beige linen pantsuit, cream shirt. A large sapphire ring was her one extravagance. And only a seeming extravagance, since the stone, though convincing, was glass. The ring had been Aunt Shelley's, probably picked up at a pawnshop. But the woman who now wore this fake article was a woman to trust. People *had* trusted her. They'd trusted her with their knotty abdomens, their swollen small bowels, their bleeding ceca, their tortuous lower bowels. Meekly they presented their anuses so she could insert the scope and guide it in, past the rectum, the sigmoid, the descending colon . . .

"Cornelia?" He too was reliable—ten years younger than she, a slight man, a bit of a fop, but no fool. Yes, together they could beat back this recurrence, and wait for the next one.

"Well, what else can we do?" she said in a reasonable tone. "Will you ask your nurse to schedule me?"

He gave her a steady look. "I will. Next week, then."

She nodded. "Write a new pain-med scrip, please. And the sleeping stuff, too."

ON THE WAY NORTH she stopped at Julie's house. The children were home from day camp—two enchanting little girls. Julie hugged her. "How nice it's summer, I'm not teaching, I can be with you for the infusions."

"Bring a book." She hated chatter.

"Of course. Some lunch now, what do you say?"

"No thanks." She touched her hair.

"And there's that lovely wig, from the last time," Julie said, shyly.

They waved good-bye: younger woman and children in the doorway, older woman in the car. It was a lovely wig. A bumptious genius of an artisan had exactly reproduced Cornelia's style and color, meanwhile recommending platinum curls—hey, Doc, try something new! But she wanted the old, and she'd gotten it. There wasn't much she'd wanted that she hadn't gotten: increasing professional competence, wifehood, motherhood, papers published; even an affair years ago, when she was chief resident—she could hardly remember what he'd looked like. Well, if Henry had been less preoccupied . . . She had failed to master French and had lost her one-time facility with the flute. She was unlikely to correct those defects even with a remission. She had once perforated a colon, early in her career—it was repaired right away, no complications, and the forgiving woman remained her patient. She'd had a few miscarriages after Julie, then given up. Her opinions had been frequently requested. She'd supported Aunt Shelley in that rooming house, so messy; but the old lady, who liked bottle and weed, refused to go into a home. At retirement Cornelia had been given a plaque and an eighteenth-century engraving. Novels were okay, but she preferred biographies. If she hadn't studied medicine, she might have become an interior designer, though it would have been difficult to accommodate to some people's awful taste.

She stopped at the general store and bought heirloom tomatoes, white grape juice, a jug of water. "The corn is good," advised the proprietor, his smile revealing his gold tooth.

"I'll bet it is. I'll be in again tomorrow."

Now the tomatoes nestled in the striped bowl on her kitchen counter. For a moment she regretted having to leave them behind, their rough scars, their bulges. Then, eyes wide open, the knowledgeable Cornelia endured a vision: emaciation, murky awakenings, children obediently keeping still. She squinted at a bedside visitor, she sat dejectedly on the commode, she pushed a walker to the corner mailbox and demanded a medal for the accomplishment, she looked at a book upside down. The mantle of responsible dependency . . . it would not fit. With one eye still open, she winked the other at the tomatoes.

She changed into her bathing suit and took a quick swim, waving to the Sisters Scrabble and the geezer. Back in her house she put on jeans and a T-shirt, tossed the wet suit onto the crotch of a chokecherry tree. What should a person take for a predinner paddle? Binoculars, sun hat against insidious sidelong rays, towel, and the thermos she'd already filled with its careful cocktail. Pharmacology had been a continuing interest. "I'll swallow three pills a day and not a gobbet more," Aunt Shelley had declared. "You choose them, rascal."

Cornelia pushed off vigorously, then used a sweep stroke to turn the canoe and look at the slate roof and stone walls of her house. Just a little granite place, she realized; not fantastical after all. She had merely exchanged one austerity for another. She thought of the tomatoes, and turned again and stroked, right side, left, right . . . Then, as if she were her own passenger, she opened a backrest and settled herself against it and slid the paddle under the seat. She drank her concoction slowly, forestalling nausea.

Sipping, not thinking, she drifted on a cobalt disk under an aquamarine dome. Birches bent to honor her, tall pines guarded the birches. She looked down the length of her body. She had not worn rubber boat shoes, only sandals, and her ten toenails winked flamingo.

The spring was in the middle of the roughly circular pond. Usually a boat given its freedom headed in that direction. Today, however, the canoe was obeying some private instructions. It had turned eastward; the lowering sun at her back further brightened her toenails. Her craft was headed toward the densely wooded stretch of shore where there were no houses. It was picking up speed. Cornelia considered shaking herself out of her lethargy, lifting the paddle, resuming control; but instead she watched the prow make its confident way toward trees and moist earth. It would never attain the shore, though, because there seemed to be a gulf between pond and land. No one had ever remarked on this cleavage. Perhaps it had only recently appeared, a fault developing in the last week or two; perhaps the land had receded from the pond or the pond recoiled from the land; at any rate, there it was: fissure, cleft . . . falls.

Falls! And she was headed directly toward them. All at once a sound met her ears . . . plashing not roaring, inviting not menacing, but still. As the canoe rode the lip of the new waterfall she stood up, never easy to do in a boat, more difficult now with substances swirling in her veins. She grabbed an overhanging bough, and watched in moderate dismay as her vessel tipped and then fell from her, carrying its cargo of towel, paddle, binoculars, sun hat, and almost-empty thermos.

What now? She hung there, hands, arms, shoulders, torso, uneven legs, darling little toenails. She looked down. The rent in the fabric of the water was not, after all, between water and shore: it was between water and water. It was a deep, dark rift, like a mail slot. She dropped into it.

Into the slot she dropped. She fell smoothly and painlessly, her hair streaming above her head. She landed well below the water's surface on a mossy floor. Toenails still there? Yes, and the handkerchief in the pocket of her jeans. A small crowd advanced, some in evening clothes, some in costume.

"Cornailia," whispered her Dublin-born medical-school lab partner. How beautifully he hadn't aged. "Dr. Flitch," said her cleaning woman, resplendent in sequins. "Granny?" said a child. "Cornelia," said a deer, or perhaps it was an antelope or a gazelle. She leaned back; her feet rose. She was horizontal now. She was borne forward on an animal along a corridor toward a turning; the rounded walls of this corridor were sticky and pink. "Rest, rest," said the unseen animal whose back was below her back—an ox, maybe, some sort of husband. They turned a corner with difficulty—she was too long, the ox was too big—but they managed; and now they entered a light-filled room of welcome or deportation, trestle tables laden with papers. She was on her feet. "Friends," she began. "Sssh," said a voice. Some people were humbly hooked up to IVs hanging from pine branches. They ate tomatoes and sweet corn and played Scrabble. Some were walking around. I'm chief here, she tried to say. She lay with a feathered man. "Don't you recognize me, Connie?" He presented his right profile and then his left. That boiled eye . . . well, yes, but now she couldn't remember his name. She was on her back again, her knees raised and separated; ah, the final expulsion of delivery. Julie . . . She was up, dancing with a rake, holding it erect with lightly curled fists. Its teeth smiled down at her. She saw her thermos rolling away; she picked it up and drank the last mouthful. She kissed a determined creature whose breath was hot and unpleasant. "I'm a wayward cell," it confided. The talons of a desperate patient scratched her chest. Then the breathable lukewarm water enveloped her, and she felt an agreeable loosening.

A sudden rush of colder fluid, and the room was purged of people, apparatuses, creatures, animals. Everyone gone but Dr. Fitch. Her tongue grew thick with fear. And then Aunt Shelley shuffled forward, wearing that old housedress, her stockings rolled below her puffy knees, a cigarette hanging from her liver-colored mouth. How Cornelia and her sisters had loved climbing onto Shelley's fat thighs, how merrily they had buried their noses in her pendant flesh. "Scamp," she'd say with a chuckle. "Good-for-nothing." No endearment was equal to her insults, no kiss as soothing as the accidental brush of her lips, no enterprise as gratifying as the attainment of her lap.

A scramble now, a rapturous snuggle. One of Cornelia's sandals fell off. Her forehead burrowed into the familiar softness between jaw and neck.

"Stay with me," she whispered. Something was pawing at her . . . Regret? Reproval? Oh, get lost. This was bliss, this sloppy and forgiving hug. Bliss, again, after six dry decades. "Stay."

It could not last. And now there was no one, no relative, no friend, no person, no animal, no plant, no water, no air. Cornelia was not alone, though; she was in the company of a hard semi-transparent sapphire substance, and as she watched, it flashed and then shattered, and shattered again, and again, all the while retaining its polyhedrality, seven sides exactly—she examined a piece on her palm to make sure, and it shattered there on her lifeline. Smaller and smaller, more and more numerous grew the components. Expanding in volume, they became a tumulus of stones, a mound of pebbles, a mountain of sand, a universe of dust, always retaining the blue color that itself was made up of royal and turquoise and white like first teeth. The stuff, finer still, churned, lifted her, tossed her, caressed her, entered her orifices, twirled and turned her, polished her with its grains. It rose into a spray that threw her aloft; it thickened into a spiral that caught her as she fell. She lay quiet in its coil. Not tranquil, no; she was not subject to poetic calm. She was spent. She was elsewhere.

SOMETIME LATER the geezer rowed out to the middle of the pond. He had been watching the drifting canoe for the last hour. A person's business was a person's business. He saw that his neighbor was dead. He tied the prow of the canoe to the stern of his rowboat and towed her ashore.

These stories originally appeared, sometimes in different form, in the following publications: "On Junius Bridge" in *Agni*; "Day of Awe" (as "To Reach This Season"), "Home Schooling," "The Noncombatant," and "The Story" in *Alaska Quarterly Review*; "Aunt Telephone," "Chance," "Elder Jinks," and "Granski" in *Antioch Review*; "Allog," "Capers," and "ToyFolk" in *Ascent*; "Binocular Vision" and "Inbound" in *Boston Globe Magazine*; "Settlers" in *Commentary*; "The Ministry of Restraint" and "Vallies" in *Ecotone*; "The Coat," "How to Fall," "Jan Term," and "Lineage" in *Idaho Review*; "Self-Reliance" in *Lake Effect*; "Hanging Fire" in *Massachusetts Review*; "The Little Wife" in *Ontario Review*; "Relic and Type" in *Pakn Treger*; "Mates" and "Unravished Bride" in *Pleiades*; "If Love Were All" in *turnrow*; "Girl in Blue with Brown Bag" in *West Branch*; and "Purim Night" and "Rules" in *Witness*.

"Inbound," "Day of Awe" (as "To Reach This Season"), "Settlers," "The Noncombatant," and "Vaquita" were published in *Vaquita* (University of Pittsburgh, 1996). "Allog," "Chance," "ToyFolk," "Tess" (as "Tess's Team"), and "Fidelity" were published in *Love Among the Greats* (Eastern Washington University, 2002). "If Love Were All," "Purim Night," "The Coat," "Mates," "How to Fall," "The Story," "Rules," and "Home Schooling" from *How to Fall: Stories*. Copyright © 2005 by Edith Pearlman. Reprinted with the permission of Sarabande Books, www.sarabandebooks.org.

"Chance," "Allog," and "Self-Reliance" were selected for *Best American Short Stories* in 1998, 2000, and 2006, respectively. "Mates" and "Elder Jinks" were included in the *Pushcart Prize* volume in 2001 and 2008, respectively. "Hanging Fire" and "The Story" each won the O. Henry Prize and were included in that annual in 1978 and 2003, respectively. "Vaquita" was reprinted in *20: The Best of the Drue Heinz Literature Prize*.

DATE OF FIRST PUBLICATION

Hanging Fire, 1977
Settlers, 1986
The Noncombatant, 1992
Binocular Vision, 1993
Day of Awe, 1994
Inbound, 1995
Rules, 1995
Vaquita, 1996
Chance, 1997
Home Schooling, 1998
Allog, 1999
ToyFolk, 1999
Mates, 2000
Unravished Bride, 2001
Fidelity, 2002
If Love Were All, 2002
The Story, 2002
Tess, 2002
How to Fall, 2003
The Coat, 2004
Purim Night, 2004
Girl in Blue with Brown Bag, 2005
Granski, 2005
On Junius Bridge, 2005
Self-Reliance, 2005
Aunt Telephone, 2006
Lineage, 2006
Elder Jinks, 2007
Relic and Type, 2007
The Little Wife, 2008
The Ministry of Restraint, 2008
Capers, 2009
Jan Term, 2009
Vallies, 2010

Pushkin Press

Pushkin Press was founded in 1997. Having first rediscovered European classics of the twentieth century, Pushkin now publishes novels, essays, memoirs, children's books, and everything from timeless classics to the urgent and contemporary.

Pushkin books represent exciting, high-quality writing from around the world. Pushkin publishes widely acclaimed, brilliant authors such as Stefan Zweig, Antoine de Saint-Exupéry, Antal Szerb, Paul Morand and Hermann Hesse, as well as some of the most exciting contemporary and often prize-winning writers, including Pietro Grossi, Héctor Abad, Filippo Bologna and Andrés Neuman.

Pushkin Press publishes the world's best stories, to be read and read again.

*